| AUTHOR | CLASS |
|---|---|
| ALFRED Hitchcock's | SC |

| TITLE |  |
|---|---|
| a choice of evils | X |

# alfred HITCHCOCK'S
# A CHOICE OF EVILS

Edited by Elana Lore

SEVERN SH HOUSE

Most of the stories in this book were first published in *Alfred Hitchcock's Mystery Magazine*. (The only exceptions are the stories by Stanley Cohen, Robert L. Fish, Joe L. Hensley, and Clark Howard.) Grateful acknowledgment is hereby made for permission to include the following:

*The Battered Mailbox* by Stanley Cohen; copyright © 1983 by Stanley Cohen; used by permission of the author. *Center of Attention* by Dan J. Marlowe; copyright © H.S.D. Publications, Inc., 1968; reprinted by permission of the author. *Lesson for a Pro* by Stephen Wasylyk; copyright © H.S.D. Publications, Inc., 1973; reprinted by permission of the author. *Aftermath of Death* by Talmage Powell; copyright © 1963 by H.S.D. Publications, Inc.; reprinted by permission of the author. *Enough Rope for Two* by Clark Howard; copyright © 1957 by Clark Howard; reprinted by permission of the author. *A Change for the Better* by Arthur Porges; copyright © 1963 by H.S.D. Publications, Inc.; reprinted by permission of Scott Meredith Literary Agency, Inc. *A Killing in the Market* by Robert Bloch; copyright © 1958 by H.S.D. Publications, Inc.; reprinted by permission of Scott Meredith Literary Agency, Inc. *Do It Yourself* by Charles Mergendahl; copyright © 1958 by H.S.D. Publications, Inc.; reprinted by permission of Harold Matson Company, Inc. *Lost and Found* by James Michael Ullman; copyright © H.S.D. Publications, Inc., 1973; reprinted by permission of the author. *Passport in Order* by Lawrence Block; copyright © 1966 by H.S.D. Publications, Inc.; reprinted by permission of the author. *Moonlight Gardener* by Robert L. Fish; copyright © 1971 by Robert L. Fish; first published in *Argosy;* reprinted by permission of Robert P. Mills, Ltd. *Courtesy Call* by Sonora Morrow; copyright © H.S.D. Publications, Inc., 1967; reprinted by permission of the author. *Restored Evidence* by Patrick O'Keeffe; copyright © H.S.D. Publications, Inc., 1972; reprinted by permission of Cathleen O'Keeffe. *The Standoff* by Frank Sisk; copyright © H.S.D. Publications, Inc., 1967; reprinted by permission of Scott Meredith Literary Agency, Inc. *A Fine and Private Place* by Virginia Long; copyright © H.S.D. Publications, Inc., 1973; reprinted by permission of the author. *Dead, You Know* by John Lutz; copyright © H.S.D. Publications, Inc., 1967; reprinted by permission of the author. *A Certain Power* by Edward D. Hoch; copyright © H.S.D. Publications, Inc., 1968; reprinted by permission of the author. *Hunters* by Borden Deal; copyright © 1958 by H.S.D. Publications, Inc.; reprinted by permission of the author. *The Driver* by William Brittain; copyright © H.S.D. Publications, Inc., 1971; reprinted by permission of the author. *Class Reunion* by Charles Boeckman; copyright © H.S.D. Publications, Inc., 1973; reprinted by permission of the author. *Mean Cop* by W. Sherwood Hartman; copyright © H.S.D. Publications, Inc., 1968; reprinted by permission of Alex Jackinson, Agent. *Kill, If You Want Me!* by Richard Deming; copyright © 1956 by H.S.D. Publications, Inc.; reprinted by permission of the author. *Welcome to My Prison* by Jack Ritchie; copyright © 1957 by H.S.D. Publications, Inc.; reprinted by permission of Larry Sternig Literary Agency, Inc. *Come Into My Parlor* by Gloria Amoury; copyright © H.S.D. Publications, Inc., 1967; reprinted by permission of the author. *Lend Me Your Ears* by Edward Wellen; copyright © H.S.D. Publications, Inc., 1973; reprinted by permission of the author. *Killer Scent* by Joe L. Hensley; copyright © 1981 by Joe L. Hensley; reprinted by permission of the author and the author's agent, Virginia Kidd. *Dear Corpus Delicti* by William Link and Richard Levinson; copyright © 1960 by H.S.D. Publications, Inc.; reprinted by permission of the authors. *Knight of the Road* by Thomasina Weber; copyright © 1963 by H.S.D. Publications, Inc.; reprinted by permission of

2

3

This title first published in Great Britain 1987 by
SEVERN HOUSE PUBLISHERS LTD of
40–42 William IV Street, London WC2N 4DF

British Library Cataloguing in Publication Data
Alfred Hitchcock's A choice of evils.
1. Detective and mystery stories,
American
I. Lore, Elana
813'.0872 [FS]   PS648.D4
ISBN 0–7278–1452–4

026382964 5

Printed and bound in Great Britain

# INTRODUCTION

Which would you choose? Nooses, poisons, guns, or knives? A murderer has all these options, and more. Even an otherwise innocuous bar of soap has lethal possibilities in the right hands.

Perhaps something less messy would be more to your liking—a spot of forgery, a bit of blackmail, or, for the adventurous insomniac, a dram of cat burglary.

The possibilities are endless in the choice of evils, and the odds are stacked in favor of the resourceful criminal.

This collection is filled with a variety of ingenious and suspenseful choices of evil, written by the leading perpetrators of good mystery fiction.

**Elana Lore**

# CONTENTS

# The Battered Mailbox

## by Stanley Cohen

The first Sunday Harry Warner found his mailbox lying on the ground, he thought little about it. The mail was still in it. He knew he'd only done a so-so job of mounting it on the rough-hewn cedar post, and he assumed the mail carrier must have knocked it loose. He braced it with light wood strips when he set it back in place.

A few Sundays later, he found the mailbox back on the ground, splintered braces and all. But this time it could not have been the mail carrier. He'd already brought in Saturday's mail. He called the town's police station.

"We're aware of the problem," the officer stated. "We get quite a few calls but we've never been able to catch them at it."

"These kids need to be caught and locked up," Warner snapped. "A town such as ours should be free of this kind of thing."

"We're doing what we can," the officer said patiently. "If we pick them up, we'll be in touch with you."

"Don't these kids know that tampering with a mailbox is a federal offense?"

"I really couldn't say," the officer replied.

Dissatisfied with the policeman's answers, he called the federal postal authorities from his office the next day.

"You're quite right, Mr. Warner. It is a federal offense. But we can't investigate these or that's all we'd ever do. I'm afraid we leave them to the local authorities. Have you called the police in your town?"

On the way to the lumber yard later that day, Warner noticed quite a few other mailboxes on the ground. He also noted that those still in place were well fastened to their posts. His would soon be also. He bought heavy lumber and long wood screws and when he'd finished remounting the box, he was certain it would never be removed from the cedar post again.

His apprehension about the mailbox eased after two or three weeks. He was pleased with the new installation, which was not only sturdy, but also rather appealing in design. Its lines were clean

9

and trim, yet suggestive of strength, and the box was prominent among the others on the quiet suburban road, jutting out defiantly, provoking the Saturday night raiders to just try and knock it from its perch.

Two months later, as he walked out his driveway to get his *Sunday Times*, something about the mailbox looked strange. When he reached it, he found it had been crushed by a large rock which lay on the ground next to the post. One side of the sheet-metal box was completely caved in. He clenched his fists and stared helplessly at it for several minutes. Then he looked at the rock and fantasized about crashing it into the skull of the rotten, teenage misfit who was terrorizing him.

He wondered what man's son could have done it, what child in that pleasant, affluent community had grown up so totally without a sense of restraint that he found pleasure in that kind of destructive behavior. The child needed to be caught and his face slapped from one side to the other until he completely understood the sanctity of other people's property.

He calmed himself and spent a half-hour pounding out the collapsed side, reshaping it so the door would still close. The box was a mess, but it was functional. As he worked on it, he wondered if any of the passing cars contained the kid who'd done it. He finished and decided he was not going to willingly let it be attacked again. If federal and local authorities couldn't be counted on, he'd catch the animals himself.

Much to his wife's annoyance, he began maintaining a vigil every Saturday night from midnight till daybreak. All social commitments were adjusted to meet this condition. He sat in total darkness in the breezeway of their house, staring through the glass louvres at the mailbox by the road. At dawn, he went to bed and slept till noon.

The break came sooner than he expected, on the sixth Saturday night of his campaign. He was dozing when he heard the rhythmic sound of a handsaw. It was almost 3 A.M. A shiny car stood near the mailbox. He tiptoed from the breezeway and grabbed the six-foot length of steel pipe he'd kept by the door. Then he ran toward the street, holding the pipe in front of him.

One boy was sawing at the cedar post and another stood and watched. They did not hear him until he was almost upon them. When they finally looked up and saw him approaching, they jumped into the car, but before they could pull away, he brought the pipe down across the hood with all his strength.

"What the hell are you trying to do?" shouted the boy driving. He had been the one with the saw. The other one seemed totally frightened.

"When you get home," Warner shouted back, "just tell your parents that the hood of their nice new car was wrecked by the man whose mailbox you were cutting down. Tell them to feel free to call me."

"Why, you son of a bitch," snarled the boy. "I'm tempted to run over you."

Warner drew the pipe back and held it poised. "You want this through your windshield?"

The boy gestured with his fist. Then he started the car and roared away, his tires screaming. Warner walked calmly into the house, phoned the police, and gave them the license number of the car.

Warner relished the call he received from the town's police station the next day. Yes, he would certainly be more than glad to come to the station and make the necessary identification and sign the required papers to press charges.

The confrontation was quiet. The boy's name was Ronnie Gerardo and he was just eighteen. His father was present, and Warner was struck by the family resemblance. The boy's clothes were flashy and he stared at Warner as if he were being done an injustice. But a mistaken identity was impossible, since the car with the crushed hood was parked in front of the station. The father was indifferent toward Warner and the complaint. He was clearly protective of his son. The Gerardos lived in another, equally affluent part of the town, a mile or so away.

The boy's accomplice had not been identified but Warner didn't care about him, in view of the difference in behavior of the two the night before.

The police sergeant examined all legal aspects of the proceedings, including the federal offense overtones. And although he didn't say as much, it became clear during his comments that any action taken against the boy would hinge almost entirely on Warner's testimony, because they had no other case against him. Gerardo asked Warner if he would drop charges if the mailbox were replaced to his complete satisfaction and he was assured the incident would never happen again.

Warner looked at young Gerardo. "Are you ready to apologize? Do you understand the significance of what you've done?" When it was obvious the boy was not going to give him any satisfaction, Warner said to his father, "I feel you need to be thinking about why a child of yours has been driving around nights pulling stunts like this."

Both father and son scowled at Warner.

The sergeant explained that the boy would be held until bail could be set and paid. After a moment of silence in which all present looked around at one another, the sergeant motioned to young Gerardo to follow him down the hall to one of the spotlessly clean, seldom used cells. Warner and Gerardo were still seated when they heard the cell door clang shut.

When the sergeant returned, Warner stood up and asked, as if he'd just thought of something, "Sergeant, may I speak to Ronnie alone?"

The sergeant turned to Gerardo who looked mildly surprised, but after considering it for a few seconds, shrugged indifferently. The sergeant led Warner down to young Gerardo's cell and let him into it, leaving it unlocked. The youth was sitting on the edge of the cot.

After the sergeant had disappeared, Warner said, "I would have considered going along with your father's offer but I don't even think you're sorry you did it. Are you?"

The youth remained silent.

"You're not," Warner said. "It's obvious. Why do you have to go around destroying other people's property? Would you mind telling me what pleasure it gives you? Or what need it fills?"

The boy studied him but didn't respond. He appeared to be paying little attention to the questions.

"Well?" Warner said. "Aren't you going to answer? Let me ask you this. Have you ever thought about having the shoe on the other foot, maybe? Would you want someone to come and destroy your property? What if they wrecked something that meant a great deal to you?"

The boy maintained his silent, penetrating stare.

"Have you thought about the fact that what you're doing is sick? That's what unprovoked vandalism is. It's sick. You're not committing a crime out of need. Because you don't need anything. What you need is help. Do you know that?"

The youth's eyes glowed with hate.

"Well?" Warner said impatiently.

"Are you going to drop the charges like my father wanted or not?" young Gerardo asked. His expression was free of any emotion.

"You've got to be made to understand that what you did was wrong," Warner answered.

"Because, if you don't," the boy said quietly, "I'm going to burn your house down." Then he added, "And I won't get caught doing it."

Warner's knees sagged with fear. It could easily happen. The statistics on unsolved arson cases were staggering. He thought about the well-kept home he'd shared with his wife all those years, a house which showed the fruits of many hours of painstaking labor. He visualized it being consumed by uncontrolled flames. He saw himself standing before it, helpless, feeling the heat.

He focused his thoughts back on the boy's deepset eyes, which were still boring into him. Warner was frightened. He was deathly afraid the youth was capable of carrying out his threat. But he couldn't let him know it. Besides, the history of the world was an endless parade of events which proved that appeasement never worked. Never. He had to respond in kind to the threat. He had to try to frighten the boy or at least deter him. "Do you fully understand the significance of what you just said?" he asked, finally.

"I just hope you heard me," the boy answered.

"Then let me ask you one more question." Warner mustered all his strength and concentration in trying to appear as cool and assured as the boy seemed to be. "You care anything about your parents?"

A glaze of confusion moved across young Gerardo's eyes. "What's that got to do with anything?"

"Just this," Warner said, almost whispering. "If something like that happens to my house, I'm going to know you did it. Understand? And then I'm going to kill both your parents. And I won't get caught, either. So think about that before you start playing with matches."

The youth's eyes widened slightly but he didn't speak.

Warner turned and walked out of the cell. As he moved down the hall, he thought about what he'd said and began to shake. He'd wanted something big enough to stagger the boy, to totally and dramatically counteract any trace of serious thought the boy might have had about putting a match to his house. But from another standpoint, Warner had made a threat on someone else's life. He'd actually verbalized it. In apparent seriousness. Prior to that moment, he would have considered himself totally incapable of saying anything like that, even in jest.

He was trembling when he reached the room where the sergeant and Mr. Gerardo waited. "Do you know what your son just told me?" he said to Gerardo. "Can you guess? Your son threatened to burn my house down if I didn't drop charges." Then he looked at the sergeant. "Did you hear that? I want you to make a note of it. Now, while his father is present. Make a note of it. Just in case."

"What did you say to him?" the sergeant asked.

"I told him he was sick and needed help."

Warner chose not to tell his wife about the boy's threat. He knew what effect it would have. She was easily frightened and would probably want to move completely away from the community. He called the police sergeant the next day and was advised that young Gerardo had been released on a small bail to his parents' custody. Warner had difficulty sleeping that night.

He called his insurance agent the following day and insisted on a complete reappraisal of his house and contents with the premium adjusted as necessary. He wanted maximum possible coverage in the event of fire.

"Okay, Harry, if you insist," the agent said. Then in a lighter tone, "You sure you're not planning to burn the place down yourself?"

"Don't even say it as a joke," Warner answered.

Several restless weeks passed for Warner. When he had almost succeeded in getting the incident out of his mind, a tiny news item appeared in his local paper. Among recent court cases, Ronnie Gerardo had been found guilty of vandalism, given a suspended sentence, and released on a short period of probation to the custody of his parents.

Warner read the article several more times. The boy had spent a total of one night at the local police station. Some might feel that one night was more than reasonable for one mailbox. Except that the size of the crime was not the issue. Young Gerardo was disturbed and needed to be locked up and treated accordingly.

A short time later, Warner came abruptly face to face with the Gerardo boy in a local supermarket. After recovering from the momentary shock, Warner managed a slight smile and said, "Hello, Ronnie, how's it going?"

Young Gerardo regarded him for a few seconds and then said, "How's your furnace working? Getting plenty of heat?"

Warner felt weak and was unable to respond. The boy continued staring at him and walked past him down the aisle. Warner turned his cart and hurried after the boy. "You did wreck our mailbox. Right? And God knows how many others. For God's sake, Ronnie, stop and think about what you were doing."

The boy ignored him.

As soon as Warner arrived home, he called the police station. He wanted to tell the sergeant about the incident in the supermarket. But the Sergeant Rubano who had been on duty on the Sunday young Gerardo was brought in was no longer on the town's force. He had recently moved to Pennsylvania and gone into some kind of business.

Warner tried to explain the background of the case and the significance of the supermarket incident to the new officer. The new man was polite enough, but Warner could sense that the story wasn't getting through to him. "Look it up in the file on the case," Warner said. "If you'll just look it up, I'm sure Sergeant Rubano made a note at the time."

"We'll check it out, Mr. Warner."

"I can assure you I'm not making this story up."

"Of course not, Mr. Warner. And we'll keep an eye on things."

Warner got off the phone. It had become obvious that the more he tried to explain the matter to the new sergeant, the more his own credibility skidded.

As the date approached for his company's annual expense-paid week in Florida, Warner found himself in a deep quandary. Although he had trouble sleeping *in* the house, he was even more apprehensive about leaving it unoccupied. When the date arrived, he chose to go. The last few months had left his wife very distraught and she needed the vacation. Before leaving, he called the police, as he had always done routinely when they planned to be away. He asked them to keep an eye on the house until he returned.

The chartered plane left on Saturday and they received the call at their hotel early Sunday morning. . . . A fire of unknown origin. . . . An investigation was under way. . . . They repacked and took the next plane back. The flight seemed interminable, the longest they could ever remember.

His wife stood and wept as Warner paced back and forth on the lawn in front of the wet, charred remains of the house, tears streaming down his own face. His neighbor spotted them and came over. The town's volunteer fire department had responded promptly but the house just seemed to have been enveloped in flames so quickly that the firefighters had been able to do little more than keep it from spreading to other houses.

Warner strode into the police stationhouse and demanded that the chief of police be called in. "You know who did this, don't you?" he shouted, after the chief arrived.

No, the chief replied, they didn't know who did it, or for that matter, if anyone had maliciously done it, although there were distinct indications that it might have been arson. They were presently investigating.

"Ronnie Gerardo set fire to our house," Warner screamed. "He told me he planned to do it."

The chief studied Warner for a few moments and then stated that Warner's accusation was a rather strong one. He asked if there was any basis for it.

Warner calmed himself enough to relate the details of the mailbox incident and the conversation he'd had with the boy afterward. "Look it up in the file on the case. I'm sure you'll find it."

The chief had the new sergeant pull the file and they went over it but found no reference to the boy's threat.

"Then contact the man who was the sergeant at that time. He'll confirm it. I don't know why he didn't write it down. I told him he should." Warner was quieter, almost plaintive.

The chief asked the sergeant to try and reach Rubano in Pennsylvania. When they got Rubano on the line, the chief turned on a phone speaker so all present could hear. He briefed Rubano on the fire and asked about the previous incident.

"I recall it quite well," Rubano replied. "Warner pressed charges and then asked to speak to the Gerardo boy alone. He definitely claimed at the time that the boy threatened arson."

"Wouldn't you say he's carried out his threat?" Warner shouted at the little speaker.

"I'm afraid I can't be of much more help than to repeat what I remember," Rubano replied.

The chief ended the conversation with Rubano and then turned to Warner. "We'll certainly interrogate the Gerardo boy as part of our investigation," he said.

Warner and his wife checked into a motel. Their insurance coverage, which was rather complete, included living expenses for the emergency period.

Since both of their cars had been in their garage and consequently had been lost in the fire, they went out the next day and bought two new ones. Warner then began calling local contractors to discuss rebuilding his home. His wife felt strongly that they should sell the lot and move to another town, but Warner adamantly refused to consider it.

That evening Warner received two phone calls. The first was from the chief of police. He had sent two investigators out to talk to Ronnie Gerardo the previous evening. Young Gerardo denied ever making the threat on the house. As for his whereabouts on Saturday night at the time of the fire, he claimed he was with three of his friends. These three boys had also been interrogated and all three confirmed young Gerardo's story.

"Three friends!" Warner shouted. "Are you going to settle for that?"

"I'm sorry, Mr. Warner, but there's not much more we can do until we have a little more to go on. We're continuing the investigation."

Warner's second call was from his insurance agent. "Harry," he said, "I called because I wanted to let you know the insurance company that has your homeowner's policy is questioning why you wanted your coverage increased so completely just weeks before the fire."

"Well, didn't you tell them?"

"You mean, about the Gerardo kid and his threat?"

"Of course."

"Well, yes, Harry, I mentioned that. Then they called me back and said they checked with the police and apparently the boy denies making the threat."

"Then what are you trying to say?" Warner asked. "That they think *I* burned it down? Of course the little animal denies everything. What would you expect him to do? Look, I was in Florida when. . . ."

"Now, take it easy, Harry. Everything's going to be all right. I just said they were asking a few questions. That's all." He paused. "One of their questions, Harry, did you have to buy *two* new cars the first day?"

"But we need two cars."

After Warner had gotten himself reasonable assurance that the company would stand behind the policy, he got off the phone.

His wife, who'd listened to his end of both conversations, said, "Can't we please move away from here? Let's move to one of the towns on the other side of the plant."

"No." Warner snapped. "Absolutely not."

Harry Warner spent the last two days of his week's vacation standing in his yard, watching the workmen clean away the charred rubble that had once been his home and all of the treasures and possessions he had accumulated in it. Occasionally the workers turned up something salvageable, a glass paperweight or the like. He thought of these objects painfully as "artifacts," found among ruins.

Despite his wife's continued protestations, he'd made a deal with a contractor to rebuild the house exactly as it had been, as quickly as possible. He'd sent his wife shopping for a new wardrobe to keep her distracted. His fellow employees were still in Florida.

Earlier in the week, he'd watched the police officers, two uniformed and two in plain clothes, go over the property for the third or fourth time, taking pictures and looking for leads of any kind. They'd been able to find nothing. They'd brought in a cop from the city nearby, an arson expert, and he'd stated that it looked like it might have been arson, done skillfully with gasoline, but he couldn't be sure. They'd interrogated everyone in the neighborhood, but the fire had started very late on Saturday night. They'd questioned the Gerardos and the parents of all the boys who supported young Gerardo's alibi. The boys had apparently been together, in one of their basement recreation rooms, shooting pool.

Warner went by the stationhouse to see the chief again. "You've got to find some way to link that kid to the fire," he protested. "You know as well as I do that he did it."

"Mr. Warner, our entire department has been working on little else all week. I think you know that. But so far, I'm afraid we don't have much."

"That kid is a public menace!" Warner said in a raised voice. "You've got to get him off the streets. God knows what he'll do next. Everybody in this town knows about him."

"We're doing all we can, Mr. Warner. We can't make arrests without some kind of case."

Several weeks passed. The new house was framed and topped out. Warner made his weekly visit to the stationhouse.

"I'm sorry, Mr. Warner, but once again we have nothing new to report. We consider the case still active and we keep hoping we'll come on to a new lead, but until we've something to go on there's really not much we can do."

"That's not good enough," Warner said quickly.

The chief looked up. "What do you mean?"

"Nothing. Nothing at all," Warner said. He ended the conversation.

He left the stationhouse and drove to a nearby sporting goods store where he asked to see handguns. "Something for recreational target practice," he said. "Something that doesn't require a license."

The proprietor sold him a twenty-two semi-automatic with ammunition and then answered Warner's questions about loading and firing the gun. Warner was clearly inexperienced with firearms. When Warner presented a credit card to pay for his purchase, the proprietor noted the name on it and looked up momentarily. Their eyes met. Without comment, the proprietor made the call to check Warner's credit and then completed the sale. Warner took the gun to his room and hid it in a drawer.

That evening Warner received a call from the chief of police. "I understand you've bought a handgun."

"It's only a target pistol. I'm joining the pistol club at the plant."

"Don't they furnish guns?"

"I prefer to use my own."

"Mr. Warner, I must tell you that this has me very concerned."

"Chief, this gun does not require a license and I really don't feel I have to answer any further questions about it."

The next night Warner received another phone call, this time from young Gerardo's father. "I hope you're not planning to try something stupid," he said.

"I don't know what you're talking about."

"Look, my kid told me what you said to him that day."

"Mr. Gerardo, if he told you what I said, then he must have told you what he said that prompted me to say it. Right?"

"He's a kid. He just happened to say the first thing that popped into his head. Look, it's bad enough you made him spend a night in jail and have a record because of that little bit of mischief involving your mailbox. You didn't have to do that. I offered to replace it and see that it never happened again. I'm sorry about your unfortunate fire but quit trying to blame it on my son. The police have already established that he had nothing to do with it."

"Mr. Gerardo, I don't believe for one minute that you think your son had nothing to do with it. The boy is sick. Don't you see that?"

"I'll say it once more, Mr. Warner. I hope you're not planning to try something very foolish."

"You needn't worry, Mr. Gerardo. I don't do foolish things."

As Warner hung up the phone, his wife looked across the motel room and asked about the call in a somewhat disturbed tone.

"It was the boy's father," Warner said.

"I gathered that much."

"The man is an idiot," Warner snapped and would discuss it no further.

When Warner arrived in the room from work the next day, he found his wife getting her things together to leave. She'd found the gun.

"I'm planning to join the pistol club at work."

She looked at him in disbelief. "That's something new."

"It's true," he said.

"You've always talked about how strongly you feel that no guns should ever be kept at home. Am I right?"

"Times have changed," he said.

"You should have let the boy's father fix the mailbox," she said as she continued packing. "I'm going to stay with my sister Ruth for a while."

"But that's ridiculous."

"We can be in touch by phone," she said with a note of finality.

Warner's life fell into a routine. He lived alone at the motel and went to work each day exactly on time. Often during his lunch hour he went to check on the progress of the house. He ate his meals by himself and spent evenings watching TV in the room or going to an occasional movie. And every Tuesday and Thursday after work, he went to his company's clubhouse and spent an hour at the pistol range, becoming proficient at the use of his new gun.

He frequently called his wife, insisting that she come back. She stated that she would not return unless he got rid of the gun and gave up his intention of moving back into the house when it was completed. He refused to yield on either matter.

One Saturday night at around midnight Warner left his motel room and drove across the town. As he approached the Gerardo home, he turned off his lights, driving the last block in darkness. He pulled up and stopped across from the Gerardo home. He sat quietly in the unlit car, watching the house. When occasional cars drove past, he ducked out of sight.

Several hours went by. A car approached at greater than usual speed, braked, and cut recklessly into the Gerardo driveway. It stopped with a shudder just inches away from the rear wall of the spacious double carport.

Warner watched young Gerardo hesitate before going inside. The youth stood in the driveway and squinted at Warner's car across the street. He walked down the driveway, crossed the street and approached it uncertainly.

When he came face to face with Warner, he gasped and dropped to the pavement where he lunged toward the back of the car. He ran a few zig-zagging yards on hands and knees and dove into the shrubbery on the opposite side of the street. He crept along the ground behind the shrubs until he approached his house and then dashed behind the cars parked there. A few seconds later, he slipped into the house.

Warner watched and smiled as he saw lights come on behind draped windows.

Within minutes one of the town's radio cars pulled up behind Warner, its revolving lights ablaze. The two cops got out and stood behind the opened doors of their car, their service revolvers drawn. They inched forward, watching Warner in the beams of their headlights.

When one of them reached Warner's open window, Warner asked, "What are you trying to do?"

"I think we're supposed to ask you that," the officer said. "Get out of the car."

"There is no law which requires me to do that under the circumstances. Therefore, I will not do it."

The cop looked across the top of the car at his partner. Then he looked back at Warner. "May I see your license? There is a law which requires you to show me that."

"Glad to," Warner said pleasantly. He took out his wallet and handed the cop his license.

The cop holstered his gun and examined the license with his flashlight. "Mr. Warner, would you mind getting out of the car while we search it?"

"Have you a warrant?"

"Under the circumstances, we don't need a warrant."

"What are the circumstances?"

The cop hesitated. "Suspicion of carrying dangerous weapons."

"You won't find it. I didn't bring it."

"Mr. Warner, would you mind telling us what you're doing here?"

"I like it here."

"You can't stay here. You're going to have to move along."

"There is no law which forbids my parking here and sitting in my car. And I don't intend to move."

The cop looked across the car at his partner who motioned to him. They walked to the rear of Warner's car and exchanged a few words. Then they got back into the cruiser. They left their revolving lights in operation.

Warner watched them in his rear view mirror for ten or fifteen minutes, irritated by the pulsating illumination that flooded in and out of his car. He finally started his engine and drove away. They followed him back to his motel and, as he climbed the staircase to his room, he saw them pull into the motel's parking area and cut their lights and engines.

Warner received a call from the chief of police the next morning. "Would you mind telling me what that business was all about last night?" the chief asked.

"I was keeping an eye on things." Warner paused and then added, "I wanted to see what time the kid got home."

"What business is it of yours? Leave police work to the professionals."

"That kid burned my house down. What did you do about it? Tell me that."

"We've been over that, Warner. We can't point any fingers at anyone without evidence. Meanwhile, you're getting a new house. Are we going to have to assign a man to follow you around?"

Shortly after receiving the chief's call, he got a call from his wife. She was going to Florida for a week or so with Ruth and her husband.

"When are you going to come back to me?" he asked plaintively.

"I think I've already answered that question."

He hesitated. "Have a good time," he said with a soft voice.

* * *

Toward the middle of the following week, a small item in the society section of the newspaper caught Warner's eye. Mr. and Mrs. Gerardo were leaving with several other couples on a cruise. That meant the boy would be staying home alone. There had to be a way. He sat in his room in the big leatherette chair, jotting notes on a pad of paper, scribbling, tearing off sheets, starting fresh. After a couple of hours, he began to smile. He flipped to a fresh page in the pad and composed a detailed list.

On the following Saturday he left the motel in the morning with his new pistol in his pocket and took a bus to the center of the nearby city, leaving his own new car parked in its usual place near his entrance to the motel. He went to his sister-in-law's house and, using his own set of keys, took his wife's car. He drove to a bustling discount store and bought a five-gallon gasoline can, a hammer, a package of large nails, and a length of plastic tubing. Before returning to his own town, he used the tubing to siphon gasoline out of the car and fill the can.

The rest of the day was tedious. Nothing more to do until late that night. He couldn't risk going back to the motel.

Well after midnight, he drove to the vicinity of his new home under construction. Taking care not to be seen by his neighbors, he parked his wife's car in an unobtrusive spot, took his gasoline can, hammer, and nails and walked to the new house. The night sky was clear enough; he'd need no extra light.

He found a plank of wood and drove a large nail into it. He placed the plank by the side of the driveway where he could easily find it later. He removed the top from the gasoline can and walked around the house, sloshing a ring of gas on the unpainted shingles that formed the lower perimeter of the house. He set the empty can near the board with the nail and put the nails and hammer inside the garage. Then he set out on foot for the Gerardo house, ducking out of sight to avoid being seen by the occasional car that drove by.

Young Gerardo didn't finally pull his car into the driveway until nearly dawn. As the boy got out of the car, Warner materialized from the shadows of the carport. "Hello, Ronnie."

The boy froze when he saw the gun. "What are you doing here?"

"How would you like to burn my house down again?"

"What are you talking about?"

"Come on. Let's go over in your car. Get in."

"What are you gonna do?"

"Just get in the car, Ronnie."

Warner kept the muzzle of the gun close to the youth's side as he had him drive slowly back to the house under construction. They pulled into the driveway and Warner directed him to get out of the car, keeping the gun aimed at point-blank range. Then Warner held out some matches. "Here, Ronnie. Go ahead. Light it. Have yourself some more fun."

"What's the matter with you? You sick or something? Wasn't once enough?"

"I thought you'd like doing it again. But if you wouldn't, listen, you don't have to. Go ahead home. I just wanted to have a little fun with you."

"If you're smart, you *will* let me go," the boy said.

"I said you could go."

Without further comment, young Gerardo got back in the car and started the engine. Warner grabbed the plank with the nail and jammed it, nail upright, behind a rear tire. When the youth started the car rolling backward, a hissing sound emanated from the tire and it went quickly flat, stopping the car. The youth jumped out to see what had happened.

"You came to burn it down again and you ran over a nail," Warner said. "Too bad."

"What are you talking about?"

"Watch." Warner struck a match and touched it to the gasoline on the shingles. The fire quickly caught and began to move along the base of the house.

"You must be crazy. I'm gonna tell the cops you did it. I'm gonna tell 'em this whole thing."

"Think they'll believe you?"

Without warning, the boy shoved Warner, knocking him down, then dashed across the yard and broke into a dead run toward his home.

Warner got up and set the empty gas can on the floor in the rear of the youth's car. Then he hurried off to the other car and drove away as the line of flame continued traveling around the perimeter of the house.

Dawn was just beginning to break when he reached the motel and there were no signs of life anywhere as he pulled his wife's car into a corner of the parking lot. He tiptoed up to his room and entered quietly. Nothing left to do but wait for the phone to ring.

# Center of Attention

## by Dan J. Marlowe

**B**rent Wilson smoothed the lapels of his dinner jacket before stepping in front of his eight-by-ten-foot window, more to be expected in a department store than in a ground floor cooperative apartment. He enjoyed the stares of passersby negotiating the wide sidewalk outside. Seen from the street, the 30-inch color TV, the hi-fi with its numerous shiny dials and knobs, the highly polished Danish modern furniture, the well-stocked bar, and the tasteful prints contributed to a projection of Wilson's image of himself as a sophisticated clubman taking his ease before going out to dine.

Wilson delighted in showcasing himself each evening for the plebeian hordes although he never acknowledged the existence of the people outside the window. He was careful at all times to act as though brick separated him from the street instead of glass, yet moved about the handsome room in the peculiar sidling gait of an actor unwilling to turn his back upon his audience. The hint of the slightest notice by anyone passing by—especially a woman—gave him the most intense pleasure.

The telephone rang, and he crossed the room leisurely to answer it.

"Is this Mr. Wilson?" a husky feminine voice inquired.

"Yes, it is." Conscious of the carefully centered telephone table, Wilson raised his chin slightly to keep the flesh of his neck smooth and firm, erasing the suggestion of the double chin forming in his thirty-fifth year.

"My name is Gilda."

"Gilda?" Wilson touched the fingers of his free hand to his brow in the theatrical gesture of a man thinking. "I don't——"

"We've never met. I just wanted to talk."

He kept his expression amiable, but his voice hardened. "Whatever you're selling, I don't want it."

"Oh, no!" the husky voice protested. "I see you night after night standing in your living room, and it's almost as though I know you.

I got your name from the directory in the building lobby and your number from the phone book. I'd just like to talk."

He wondered which of the regular passersby she was. A nut, of course, but it was flattering. "Tell me about yourself, Gilda."

"My looks, you mean? Well, I'm five six, a hundred twenty-five pounds, naturally blonde and quite attractive, I'm told, and I was graduated from college with a degree in psychology."

"Beauty *and* brains," he remarked, arranging his features in a whimsically amused pattern. The self-description was far from revolting. "Would you care to stop in for a drink?"

"Oh, no! We can never meet. I'm just looking forward to our having long, honest talks together."

A real nut, he decided. "If you stopped in, we wouldn't have to waste time talking, would we?"

She giggled. "You're forceful, aren't you? We—I've got to hang up," she interrupted herself. "I'll call tomorrow night. Eight o'clock."

The following evening he stood beside the bookcase near the telephone, waiting for her call. It didn't come until ten after eight. "Bet you thought I wouldn't call," she said cheerfully.

He was annoyed with her for having made him wait and himself for having waited. "It hardly mattered," he said stiffly.

"You don't sound very comfortable. I fixed myself a highball before dialing you. Listen!" He heard the tinkle of ice cubes against crystal. "Why don't you fix yourself a drink at that cute little bar of yours? Then we can talk in comfort."

"A good idea," he said, mollified, and set down the phone. The bar was on the other side of the room, the furniture not having been arranged for his convenience but to display it most attractively from the audience's viewpoint. He poured two inches of a rich, golden bourbon from a cut-glass decanter and added a splash of soda from a matching siphon. "That's better," he said into the phone.

"Good!" she exclaimed vigorously. "Did I say last night that I'm very intelligent? I was on the dean's list all through college. My grades were fan*tas*tic."

"How long have you been out of school?" he asked, having a sudden vision of a forty-five-year-old square-rigged barkentine.

"Three years."

"You're sure you don't want to stop in one of these evenings?" He seated himself in a leather armchair facing the window, took a sip from his drink, and crossed his legs carefully.

"Oh, no! My husband would have a fit if he knew I even *talked* to you!"

Another restless housewife, he thought cynically. "I didn't know you were married."

"Ever since my freshman year in college. The washing machine in the sorority house broke down, and Steve came to fix it." There was a slight pause. "He's the stupidest man in the world."

There was a woman standing outside the big window, her nose almost pressed to the glass. Wilson stretched his left arm and glanced at his ultra-thin wristwatch. The woman looked embarrassed suddenly and hurried away. Wilson smiled. "If that's the way you feel about him, Gilda, why did you marry him?"

"At first there was sex, silly. He *is* a handsome animal. A hunter—outdoorsman. You know. But now I can't talk to him."

"There's always divorce," he suggested, uncrossing his legs deliberately and re-crossing them the other way.

"That's impossible."

"Impossible? Why?"

"He's too possessive. I know him. I'm a psychology major, remember?"

Wilson took a long, slow pull at his drink for the benefit of a middle-aged man who had paused in front of the window. The man lingered an instant before moving on. "Then what will you do?"

"I told you I was smart. I've arranged—he's at the door. Good night."

"Tomorrow?" he said quickly.

"Mmmmmmmmmm." The telephone clicked in his ear.

The next evening Wilson put on his maroon smoking jacket and mixed himself a drink while he waited for her call. She was right on time. "Hi!" she announced herself. "It's Gilda."

"You sound—excited. Have you been drinking?"

"No. I'm just happy. My problem is solved."

"Steve agreed to give you a divorce?"

"Better than that. A divorce can be so messy. No, I told him all about you and our phone calls, and I said we were in love and wanted to get married."

"You're not under the impression that any part of that statement is true?" he demanded, coldly furious.

"Of course it's not true. I'd never marry *you*! You're almost as bad as muscle-minded Steve, with your posing in your window the way you do. I think you're the most narcissistic, self-centered individual—" her voice went on and on.

He jerked himself upright from his armchair, for once forgetful of how the ungraceful movement must appear to anyone outside "Listen to me, you—you female," he began.

Her husky laugh interrupted him. "Steve is very possessive, very primitive, and very angry. Goodbye, Mr. Wilson."

"Goodbye? What do you—"

A blue sedan squealed to a stop at the curb in front of the big window, and a man sprang from it quickly, dragging a long-barreled rifle after him.

Sweat popped out on Brent Wilson's brow, and he cried frantically "Gilda!"

"I'll call the police now so there'll be no chance of his getting away," she said calmly.

Brent Wilson stood transfixed as the rifle barrel swung in his direction and yellow-red flame spurted from it, crazing the eight-by-ten window in a spider-web pattern. A heavy weight smashed into his chest, and he slid slowly to the floor, sprawled awkwardly upon the Oriental rug, while the front of the maroon smoking jacket gradually turned a darker shade.

# Lesson for a Pro

## by Stephen Wasylyk

**M**y drive off the ninth tee climbed toward the dark, low-hanging clouds, hooked suddenly into a stand of trees, and ended in a discouraging rattle as it ricocheted from trunk to trunk. I swore.

Virgo Fletcher chuckled. Virgo always enjoyed another man's misfortune. Small and wiry, with the beginnings of a sagging potbelly, he wore a golf cap pulled low over his narrow face. Even though we spent almost every afternoon together on the course, the outdoor hours and the sun didn't do much to tighten the sagging jowls and the puffy eyes. Virgo destroyed whatever good the exercise did with a little too much drinking and too many women.

I picked up my tee. "See if you can do better," I said.

Virgo planted himself firmly, waggled his driver and swung. The result was a straight-as-a-string drive down the fairway, at least two hundred and fifty yards. He chuckled again, increasing my dislike for him that had been growing for weeks. I hoped that I could stop playing with him soon. Virgo would do anything to win, even to shaving a stroke whenever he thought he could get away with it.

I forced myself to get into the golf cart alongside him and he headed down the fairway.

He was president of the local bank, a position he used to advantage with the young women the bank hired, another facet of his personality I found abhorrent. He was a pincher and a patter, and many of the young women who weren't flattered by his attention quit after a few days. Some stayed, because there was no understanding women and particularly Virgo's wife, who knew of his escapades yet still clung to him as if he were something valuable.

I had been playing with Virgo for months now, not because I enjoyed his company but because of his position. I had come to this Midwestern town to lie low after pulling a bank job in another state, and had met him on the course. When I found out just what he did for a living, I couldn't resist cultivating him. The money from my last job wouldn't last forever, and it seemed to me that playing golf with Virgo would give me an insight into the bank's operations.

It did, but not quite enough as yet. I was still probing for an angle.

Virgo cleared his throat. "There's a new girl at the bank. Her name is Olivia and she seems quite receptive. I am doing quite well with her."

"Why tell me?" Virgo thought I was a footloose swinger who had settled in town to recuperate from an operation and he was always trying to impress me.

"I'm looking for advice. My wife has seen her and suspects I am interested. I am. In fact, I would consider marrying Olivia if I were free. I finally asked my wife for a divorce. She said no, not under any circumstances." Being free was a constant theme of Virgo's conversation.

"All right, then," I said. "You're stuck."

He sighed. "I would certainly like to get rid of her."

Irritated, I snapped, "There are many ways."

"You mean kill her?"

"It's done every day."

"I wouldn't be capable of something like that."

"Then hire someone."

He stopped the cart in the middle of the fairway. "Can that be done?"

"There are people around who make it their business."

"I wouldn't know where to begin."

An idea flickered in the back of my mind. I'd been looking for a way to take Virgo's bank. Perhaps he was handing me the combination to the vault.

"Would you know where to find someone? You don't talk about your past, but I get the impression . . . " His voice trailed off.

I stepped to the ground and grabbed a couple of irons. "I'll think about it. Right now I'm going to play my second shot," I said.

I left him sitting there while I searched for my ball. Virgo wanted his wife dead and was willing to pay for it. I could give him the names of several men, but what was in it for me? There should be a way I could convert that wish of his into profit.

I found my ball. There was no choice but to chip out to the fairway and waste a stroke. I swung halfheartedly, more important things on my mind.

Also no longer thinking of golf, Virgo had driven over to his ball, his thin face turned to me.

I took a five iron and hit a sweet shot that clung to the green as

f it had been coated with glue, waved off Virgo and the cart and
tarted walking.

Virgo drove his next shot over the green into a sand trap, some-
hing that he never did. It was clear that Virgo was hooked. All I
eeded to do was to reel him in. By the time I reached the green,
had worked it out.

Virgo looked at me, wanting to talk, but I waved him off. "Play
our shot," I said.

He nervously blasted out of the trap onto the green just as a light
ain began to fall. We both putted out and headed the cart toward
he refreshment stand.

"Beer," I said to the attendant. When we were served, we moved
way from him and the other golfers. I looked out over the rolling
reen hills and smiled slightly. I intended to find out just how serious
Virgo was, and this was a good place to discuss it. No one could
verhear or suspect any collusion between two men out for an after-
1oon of golf.

The other golfers headed back toward the clubhouse, leaving us
alone except for the attendant, who picked up a paperback and began
:o read. The rain came down harder, pattering against the shingled
roof of the shelter.

Virgo cleared his throat. I looked away from the pleading in his
eyes, wanting him to stew a little more, to beg a little. There was
no one I would rather fleece more than this jittery Virgo.

"We were talking," he said.

"We were talking about killing your wife," I said brutally.

He seemed to shrink a little.

"Doesn't sound pleasant when you come right out with it," I said.

"No, it doesn't sound pleasant," he admitted. "You said I could
hire someone."

"The money could be traced and you would be the first suspect."

"Then what—"

"I have a plan," I said. "I'll take care of everything. There would
be no way to suspect you."

His face lightened. "You're sure?"

"Positive. Don't you want to know the price?"

"I guess so. How much?"

"All the cash in your vault."

He looked as if I had hit him. "I don't understand."

"All right. Listen carefully," I said slowly. "We will handle it
exactly as though the main purpose was to rob the bank, not to kill

your wife; therefore, no one will suspect the real reason. But to mak
it come off so that there are no questions, I will actually rob th
bank. I will use the money to pay the man I hire, and keep the res
as my payment. It will not cost you a cent personally and insuranc
will cover the bank loss. You don't have to do a thing except wha
I tell you to."

His voice sank to a whisper. "What is your plan?"

"I will hire a man to do the actual job. Don't ask me who he is o
how I know where to find him. He and I will come to your hous
early in the morning. He will hold your wife as hostage while I tak
you to the bank. You will open the bank and the vault for me
supposedly to protect your wife. I'll take the money, leave and pic
up my man. By that time, your wife will be dead and you will neve
see either of us again. When you report it, it will look like anothe
bank robbery where something went wrong. No matter how muc
you are questioned, your story will sound real. The only thing yo
will have to do, which I am sure you will handle admirably, is to ac
properly shocked and grief-stricken after your wife is found. Now
you can back out and we will forget the whole thing, or you can no
and I'll go ahead. Think it over. Once you commit yourself, you don'
turn back."

Virgo's conversation had indicated that he had wanted for a lon
time to be free, but I was asking him to commit himself to murder
It was one thing to talk about it, another actually to do it. I wondere
if Virgo had the nerve.

He lowered his chin, then raised it slowly.

"You agree?" I asked.

He nodded firmly. "When will it be?"

I leaned back and finished my beer. The rain was coming dow
hard now, mist masking the landscape. I had the feeling that
should move fast, to pin Virgo down before he had time to chang
his mind.

Today was Tuesday. I would have to do some driving and some
telephoning, and it would take a couple of days to import the mar
I needed. "Friday morning," I said.

I could see him relax and I knew why. Playing with him ever
day, I had learned it wasn't the kind of town that dealt a great dea
in checks and charge accounts. Cash flowed pretty freely and mos
of it ended inevitably in the bank. Every Tuesday and Thursday
afternoon, an armored car picked up any excess cash on hand and
traded new bills for old, to maintain an even balance in the bank

That meant the money in the vault on Friday morning would be at its lowest ebb. Virgo liked that. He would lose less money that way.

"How much will be in the vault?" I asked.

He thought for a moment. "Perhaps fifty thousand."

It sounded low to me but it was a small town with no big Friday payrolls to consider. "Make sure it isn't less than that," I told him. "The man will probably want ten and I see no reason for me to go through with this for less than forty."

He nodded. "Fifty thousand will be there."

"Fine," I said. "We won't be playing golf anymore. Just go about your business for the next few days and forget this conversation. Don't try to get in touch with me." I looked at the rain, debating a dash to the clubhouse. "Would you like another beer?" I asked.

"No," he said. "I don't think I could stomach it."

I sat there, sipping my beer and wondering if Virgo would back out. It was a possibility to be considered and something that had to be forestalled. I would move immediately. If he had no way to get in touch with me, he would have no way to jam the wheels I intended to start rolling.

I checked out of my hotel as soon as I got back and drove to a motel on the outskirts of another town about twenty miles away. That evening, armed with a handful of change, I began making phone calls from the pay booth on the corner.

I located Snick Gator in Chicago, only a short overnight hop away. He listened and declared himself in. I gave him directions to a local motel, hung up and continued dialing.

Virgo was under the impression I was going to hire one man because that was the plan I had explained to him, but I hadn't told him everything. I needed one more specialist and it took some time to find Pete Matso in a bar in St. Louis. He agreed to drive up and meet me at noon the following day.

I went to bed that night content. Things had started to move.

Wednesday morning, using a false name and address, I picked up a battered, nondescript, used sedan with a good engine. If it ran for two hours it was good enough for me, since I intended to use it only for the robbery. I buried it in an obscure corner of the motel parking lot and went to meet Pete.

He was in the bar when I got there, a tall, thin, long-haired type with a face that seemed to bear a perpetual grin, probably because to Pete life was one big lark, especially if he were behind the wheel of a reliable fast car.

He nodded. "You said you had something big, Griff."

I slipped into the booth opposite him, ordered a beer and waited until the slim waitress left, Pete's eyes following her swinging hips. "It's big," I said.

"You want me to be a wheel man?"

"Nothing that simple. The job I have for you can be dangerous and you can turn it down with no hard feelings. If you take it on, I'll pay you five thou, half now and half afterward."

The waitress dropped off the beer and moved away after giving Pete a big smile.

"Lay it on me, man," Pete said.

"I want you to stage a collision with an armored car."

His grin grew wider. "You want to heist it?"

"Nothing like that. I just want it out of commission for a few hours."

"What's the pitch?"

"It picks up money at a bank I intend to take Friday morning. If it doesn't make the pickup, chances are that all that money will be waiting for me."

"Maybe I should get more than five thou."

"Take it or leave it," I said. "I will also go for the cost of a used car you can use."

"No point to wasting money. I'm a little tired of the wheels I'm using now. My insurance will cover something new. Rather have my own anyway because I know how it handles. You have a spot picked out or do I set it up?"

I took him about ten miles outside of town to a straight stretch of road the armored car followed on the way to pick up the cash at Virgo's bank. I knew it always took the same route and always passed at the same hour every Tuesday and Thursday afternoon, because I had scouted it thoroughly for weeks while looking for an angle to take Virgo's bank. Intersecting the straight stretch, another road came out from behind a grove of trees. From a car parked there, you could see the truck coming, but the trees would hide the car from the truck. The car could pull out suddenly, so suddenly an accident would be unavoidable. The truck could swerve but there was really no place to go. I explained it to Pete.

"It can be done, man," he said, "but it's a little hairy. A guy could get hurt."

"I pay all hospital expenses," I said. "It's part of the deal."

He thought for a moment before his grin became wider. "You're on, man. I don't get too many chances to mess up an armored car. I'll stop it for you. How will you know if it works?"

"I'll swing in behind it a few miles down the road, holding far enough back so I don't get into trouble." I pulled out my roll and dealt out his twenty-five hundred dollars in big bills.

Pete grunted. "Don't you have anything smaller?"

I grinned. "Not until Friday. You want to wait?"

He folded the money and slipped it into his pocket. "Not likely, but if I don't pull this off right, money isn't going to mean a thing. I'll look for you tomorrow."

I took him back to town and dropped him off. I wouldn't be seeing Pete again until the accident.

My other man was due in that night, which would give us time for a dry run in the morning. After dinner, I waited for his call in my motel room, sitting in a soft chair, my feet propped on the low cooling unit before the window, watching the passing traffic and thinking of Virgo Fletcher.

I didn't trust him. He hadn't asked enough questions about me or my past for an operation as important as this. He had simply accepted me and my plan. I wondered if Virgo had been doing a little investigating and planning on his own.

If I were caught, I'd be locked in all by myself. No one would believe that Virgo had been part of it.

The phone rang harshly and I looked at my watch. Snick was in town.

A half hour later, I was in his motel room.

Snick was a big man, broad through the shoulders and thickening through the middle, the battered face and puffy ears leaving no doubt as to how he had once earned a living. I had known many ex-fighters, most of them no longer with it. Not Snick. He looked cold and vicious and mean, still alert and sharp, and his one big asset was that he would follow orders faithfully as long as the pay was right.

I paced the small room while I explained it all to him.

"It sounds simple," he said.

"We'll use two cars," I said. "We'll meet at the house. I'll take the man to the bank while you take care of his wife. When you're through, you'll leave and meet me later. If they tag me and I don't show, you'll be able to get clear. Tomorrow morning, I'll pick you up and we will go over the layout so that you'll know exactly what you're doing. It leaves just one question. How much do you want?"

"Five G's," he said promptly. "All in advance. If they finger you, I don't want to be stuck. My end will be done."

"Fair enough," I said. "You could have asked for more. But I'll pay you half now and half Friday morning."

"I could lose on a deal like that."

"If anything happens to me, I'll see that you get your money." Again I peeled twenty-five hundred from my roll. "You can't spend this in two days even if you hit the bottle real hard. Stay out of sight. You're the kind of man people remember."

I left him then. There was a movie down the street from my motel, so I parked my car and decided to kill a few hours. The movie wasn't good. X-rated flicks were still a novelty in this town so the place was crowded. I left halfway through the film. If I wanted to see a nude doll parading around, I preferred her in the flesh in my motel room rather than bigger than life-size on the screen in full color, but the way I was situated at the moment, women were out—until Friday.

The next morning I picked up Snick and took him out to Virgo's house, which was a stone-rancher surrounded by trees, and outside of town so there were no close neighbors to become curious or to hear anything strange. From there, I took him to a small dirt road about five miles away, where I intended to pay him off.

When I was certain he knew the layout and wouldn't get lost, I dropped him and headed for Pete Matso's motel. I had no real qualms about Pete doing his job, but a man has been known to change his mind if something that seemed a little more important appeared. In Pete's case, it would be a woman. He had money in his pocket and I had noted him eyeing the waitress in the bar, but what made me a little nervous was the way she had traded looks with him.

I needn't have worried. It was well into the afternoon when Pete came out, the waitress on his arm. He gave her a friendly pat and climbed into a bright yellow fast-back parked in front of his room. I followed as he drove off.

He had allowed himself plenty of time. I made sure he was headed in the right direction, then turned off and went directly to the next town to see if the armored car were on schedule. It was. I picked it up on the outskirts and settled back a good distance away to tail it. The last thing I wanted was for the driver to look into his rear view mirror once too often and see the same car, but the Thursday afternoon traffic gave me a hand, weaving in and out, passing both of us so that the pattern of cars behind the armored car was constantly changing. As we approached the road where Pete was waiting, I closed the distance a little.

We were indicating close to fifty when I saw the flash of bright yellow scream out of the side road and knife into the front of the armored car. The big steel box swerved and rocked, narrowly missing oncoming traffic, while the yellow car spun, tires screeching.

I pulled over and stopped, joining the other drivers who were pouring out of their cars. I sprinted to the armored car. If it weren't disabled, Pete had wasted his time.

He had done well. The right front wheel was smashed in at an awkward angle, the tire flat, and the coolant poured steadily from the radiator. I went back to Pete's car.

He had said he needed new wheels. He would get them. The yellow fastback was totaled, the left front mashed flat, the whole front of the car out of line with the body. Several men were lifting Pete out of the car. He had a gash on his forehead, was clutching his ribs, and his left leg was bent where there should be no bend. They laid him on the roadside grass.

I pushed close. He looked up and saw me and in spite of the pain, one eye closed in an elaborate wink.

Pete was a good man.

I got out of there before someone decided I would make a good witness, and drove back to my motel. Locating Pete to give him the rest of his money and something extra for his medical bills would be no problem. There was only one hospital to which they could take him, and before I left the next day I would go there as a visiting friend. I grinned as I drove off. Pete would have one faithful visitor. The waitress would be around. I was sure of it.

There was nothing to do, then, but wait until Friday morning.

I treated myself to a big steak dinner, picked up a half dozen bottles of beer, and spent the evening before the TV, watching some sort of detective story that I couldn't quite follow, much less understand how the guy solved it just before the final commercial. I fell asleep during the late news, the feature story of which was the armored-car accident, complete with a film clip of Pete being wheeled into the hospital.

I woke at six on Friday morning to a dull, overcast day that hinted at rain, slipped the silencer on my pistol and dropped it, together with two stocking masks, into my attaché case among several rolls of wide adhesive tape.

I was to meet Snick in front of Virgo's house at seven. He was there when I arrived. I handed him a mask. Snick was too easily recognized to take any chances. My description, on the other hand, could fit dozens of men. We walked up to the front door and rang the bell.

Virgo's wife swung the door open. Before she had a chance to realize what was going on, Snick had clamped a hand over her mouth and hustled her into the house. I followed, my gun in my hand. It was just possible that Virgo might have had a change of heart and I would have to straighten him out.

He was at the breakfast table. He looked up with a strange expression on his face as if he couldn't believe I was there, but he made no move.

I leveled the gun at Mrs. Fletcher's head. "Don't say a word," I told her.

Her face was white and her blue eyes wide. She didn't understand, but she obeyed. It was the first time we had met and I could understand Virgo's desire to get rid of her. She was a prim-looking woman, with a harshly-boned face that was emphasized by an expensive hairdo that might have looked good on a younger woman. I had no doubt she made life miserable for Virgo.

I tossed Snick a roll of tape. "Hands and feet, and one strip across the mouth."

I waited until he was finished. "Now you," I said to Virgo. "Let's go." I nodded to Snick. "You know what to do."

His mouth twisted in what passed for a smile.

I hustled Virgo out of the front door and behind the wheel of my car.

Virgo's voice was low. "That's the man who will do it?"

"He's the only one I brought," I said.

"Now that it is happening, I find it hard to believe."

"Believe it," I said. "We just teed off on the eighteenth in the most important game of your life and taking a bogey can kill you. From here on, we play par or we're in trouble. Be prepared to do some Academy Award acting. The people at the bank will be around to act as witnesses."

"I'm not sure—"

"It's too late for you not to be sure of anything." I held the gun to his head. "From now on, you have nothing to say. Drive, and do it carefully."

The bank had a side door on a parking lot that the employees used before opening time. While Virgo fumbled for the key, I slipped the stocking mask over my head and followed him inside. Two women were already there and their vocal cords became paralyzed at the sight of me and the gun. I had Virgo tape their ankles and wrists together, hands behind their backs, and slap a strip of adhesive across their mouths. I dragged them out of sight behind the counter.

"The vault," I said to Virgo.

"The time lock—" he began.

"It had better be open."

"It has a minute to go."

"You'd better hope no one else walks in here during that minute."

I held my wrist out, eyes fixed on my watch. So far, things had gone smoothly, but I still didn't trust Virgo. Maybe he had fixed the time lock on the vault so that it wouldn't open and I'd be stuck here with no way to get at the money.

The clock clicked very nicely at the end of the minute.

"Open it," I said to Virgo.

His hands trembled and there was a sheen of perspiration on his pudgy face as he worked the combination. I heard the tumblers click as he hit the last number. If he were acting for the benefit of the two women, he was doing an excellent job.

"Open it," I said again, waving the gun under his nose.

Virgo was no longer pale. His face had acquired a light tinge of green, and he was really beginning to worry me. He opened the vault as if he were an old man with palsy.

I yanked the door wide.

The vault was big and square, cabinets along one wall evidently containing the bank's valuable papers. The other wall held shelves—empty shelves. Where there should have been money, there was none.

Virgo didn't have to tell me what had happened to it. Now I knew why he was green, why he was so frightened. *He had taken it himself.*

It was beautiful. With the money gone, only I could be accused of taking it. Why else had I come to the bank and forced Virgo to open the vault? No one would suspect him. He would not only have his wife dead but he would also have all that money to help him enjoy himself with Olivia.

He hadn't been acting at all. Virgo had been frightened and for a very good reason, I knew now.

He had taken the money from the vault before I got there. I had no time to look for it, no time to force the hiding place from him. About all I could do at this point was to kill him.

I grasped him by the collar and slammed him into the vault, backing him up against the shelves and jamming the gun hard under his chin. "Where is it?"

"Gone," he gasped. "Where you can't find it."

I could feel the perspiration trickling down my neck. I had to do something. The other employees would be arriving, the bank was due to open soon.

I thought of Pete smashing that armored car and ending in the hospital. I had been proud of that idea, but all it had done was give Virgo more money. He had been way ahead of me, his brain working much faster than mine.

I backed off and lifted the gun. Virgo started to shake, sure I was going to kill him, but I had to give the little man credit for having a great deal of nerve. I knew it hadn't been only the money, or getting his wife killed at no cost. It was simply that Virgo *had* to win, had to beat me. I should have realized that after playing golf with him.

Still, I owed Virgo something that would make him remember me.

I squeezed the trigger, the silenced gun louder than usual in the small vault. Virgo spun and fell to the floor, whimpering in surprise when he found he was still alive.

I had put a bullet into his thigh. It would be some time before he played golf again. I moved fast then, out the door, stripping my mask off as I went, hopping into my car and hightailing it out of town.

Snick was waiting for me. He held out his hand.

I handed him the money. "You did what I told you to?"

"No problem at all. She'll be in good shape as soon as they take off the tape."

I grinned. Score one for my side. Virgo would be very surprised to find his wife still alive. From the beginning, I had no intention of killing his wife for him. Why should I do Virgo a favor?

"You clean out the bank?" asked Snick.

"There isn't a dollar left in the vault," I said truthfully.

"Next time you need some help, call me," he said.

"I'll do that," I promised.

His wheels threw gravel as he took off. I abandoned the used car within walking distance of my motel and picked up my own. I still had to pay Pete.

No one at the hospital stopped me even though it was too early for visiting hours. I stepped into Pete's room.

He had a bandage around his head and his leg was in a cast.

"I knew you'd show, Griff," he said. "How did you make out?"

"No problem," I lied. I peeled off the money I owed him and added five hundred. "Here's your cash."

"Listen," he said. "I think maybe you did me a favor."

"Getting you smashed up? You look like a disaster."

"That's the idea. Some lawyer was in here this morning. He says I can sue that armored-car company and collect."

"How much?"

"He figures a hundred thousand."

"He'll take half."

Pete shrugged and winced. "So I'll be fifty thousand ahead. Anytime you have something like this going, call me."

"You'll be the first," I promised.

I walked out of the hospital, thinking that Pete would probably end up making more out of this deal than anyone.

I checked out of my motel, slung my bags into the trunk and headed out of town, pulling up at a service station and diner on the outskirts.

"Fill it up," I said to the attendant in the station, watching the woman crossing the macadam from the diner.

She was tall and well-built and dressed for traveling in pink hip-hugger slacks, light blue pullover jersey and a white scarf around her head. She wasn't what you would call beautiful but she had a nice, lean body, a wide mouth and long-lashed eyes that could speak a language all their own.

I knew Virgo liked the type. That's why I had imported her to try to get an angle on breaking open Virgo's bank. I hadn't expected him to want to marry her.

"Hello, Olivia," I said.

"No problems?" she asked as she handed me her suitcase.

I sighed. "Plenty. Virgo turned out to be a very sneaky little guy." I placed her suitcase with mine.

"I knew that the first time he propositioned me," she said. "What happened?"

I told her about it as we drove. It had started to rain and the windshield wipers clicked monotonously.

She let quite a few miles speed by before she started to laugh.

"What's so funny?" I asked.

"You and Virgo," she said. "Each trying to double-cross the other. I think he came out slightly ahead."

"Not really," I said. "He may have the money but when he gets over the shock of finding his wife is still alive, he will realize he can't use it. If he turns up with a great deal of cash, she will be very suspicious. Besides, when he finds you gone, he will suspect that you left with me. That will bother him for a long time."

"You make it sound simple," she said, "but you are forgetting you are out more than ten thousand dollars."

I grinned. "It was worth it. Even an old pro like me can learn something from a potbellied, small-town banker."

"What's that?"

"A man who will cheat at golf will cheat at anything," I said.

# Aftermath of Death

## by Talmage Powell

The disease has a jawbreaking technical name," Dr. Mallory Ames said. "But in layman's language, Nicky Colgren died of breakdown and malfunction of the liver. Liver failure, you might say."

Ames sighed heavily as he gave the news to Ronald Clary and Hadley Lawrence. Lawrence, an attorney, had summoned his two friends to his office. It was early evening and the large office building had an air of desertion and desolation.

Managing editor of the city's leading newspaper, Clary stirred quietly as he lighted a cigar. A powerfully built, balding man, Clary's eyes were normally diamond-hard windows on a personality not easily shocked or dismayed. "I suppose," he mused, "I owe it to good old Nicky to write the obituary myself."

"It's difficult to think of him being gone," Lawrence said.

"There was little I could do," Dr. Ames said. "We can repair the heart, replace the kidney. But when the lowly liver quits, we might as well close up shop."

"You were with him until the end?" Lawrence asked.

"Of course," Ames nodded. "From the first symptom until the moment when I had to put my signature on the death certificate, I was in constant attendance. It was the least I could do for Nicky."

Lawrence moved slowly behind his desk and sat down. He was a dark, thin man, with the look of temperament in the fine lines of his face. The desk was massive, hand-rubbed walnut in keeping with the rest of the large imposing office.

"Old Nicky," he murmured, "no more bumbling for him, dubbing them off the tee or slicing his irons in the rough."

"He hadn't a bad life," Clary said. "Over fifty years of it. Ineffectual and slightly ridiculous at times, true. But with all that inherited wealth, he had a good, solid shield."

"He wasn't the same Nicky at the end," Ames said. "With the pudgy grin and little-boyishness gone, he was just a tired old man with a thin, graying mustache and pouches under his eyes."

43

"Liquor and women," Clary said, "and the parties he was always bustling around preparing for."

"His most serious interests," Lawrence agreed. "You know, when you get right down to it, he had nothing in common with us three. I wonder why he clung to us as friends?"

"We were his points of contact with a world that had more substance than his own," Clary said. "And I suppose it bolstered our own egos to have him around."

Ames nodded acceptance of the point Clary had made; then the doctor turned to the attorney. "Hadley, why'd you call us down here?"

"I have a letter from Nicky." Lawrence opened a drawer in his desk. "It was written night before last and delivered to me by special messenger. Attached to it were instructions for the three of us to read it jointly in the event of Nicky's death."

Clary and Ames glanced at each other and drew involuntarily closer to the desk. Lawrence sat holding the white, sealed envelope for a moment. Then he picked up a thin, golden letter opener. The ripping of the envelope was inordinately loud and jarring in the silence that had come to the office.

Lawrence went pale as he skimmed over the letter.

"Come on, Hadley!" Clary snapped his fingers. "It was meant for all three of us."

"I'm not sure you want to hear it."

"I'm certain we do," Ames said. A robust, rather florid, stuffy-looking man, the doctor glared briefly at his friend.

"Sure," Clary said. "Read it aloud, Hadley."

With another moment's hesitation, the attorney took a breath and began reading in a voice that faltered every now and then:

"Dear Pals,

"I suspect, from Mal's demeanor, that this mysterious liver ailment is going to knock me off. I should at least like to die from a man-sized cause. Instead—wouldn't you know it—the bumbling nitwit will expire from a fouled-up liver, of all things.

"Don't protest, friends. I didn't use the word nitwit lightly. I have known, since I was a kid smothered by governesses and nurses, that the word described me well. I know further that you have always secretly thought of me in presicely such terms.

"However, the ineffectual clown must have his say. If I impressed you none whatever in life, I shall do so in death.

"You believe you are married to respectable, moral women of great character. But the fact is I've been loved by the wife of one of you. I discovered a kind and degree of passion in her you never dreamed existed. On many occasions—at my whim and desire—she has come to me.

"So, friends, while there was an element of condescension in your friendship for me, I must assure you it was ill-founded. I cannot depart permanently as nothing more than the buffoon who was tolerated around the clubhouse and at the cocktail gathering.

"Instead, I prefer to die knowing I have assumed an importance in your lives and an image in your minds it was never my privilege to enjoy during a lifetime that, I must confess, was most lonely, though not altogether frustrating.

"Most Sincerely,
"Nicky"

Hadley Lawrence dropped the letter to his desktop. An absolute silence held the three men as they stared at the letter.

Clary's face grew redder with each passing second. His upper and lower teeth made contact through his cigar. Ames lost all appearance of being the medical harbinger of hope.

Lawrence began trembling. "I know one thing—it couldn't have been Lucille he was talking about!"

Ames jerked his eyes up to glare at the lawyer. "Are you implying that Doris . . ."

"Or Maureen?" Clary demanded. He reached across the desk and grabbed Lawrence by the lapel. With an angry sound, Lawrence pulled away.

Lawrence stood at bay before the two men a moment. Nineteenth-hole jocularity might never have transpired between the three men. They stood with hackles up, memory of friendship growing dim.

"I'm not implying a thing," Lawrence said finally, straightening his jacket. "He referred to someone other than Lucille, that's all."

"I won't stand here and listen . . . " Clary began.

Ames reached and stopped Clary's fresh movement toward Lawrence.

"I suggest we be as objective about this as we can," Ames said.

"You're a doctor," Clary said. "You know how to be clinical. But I . . .

"A man who runs an important newspaper should have the same sort of self control," Ames said. "So should a prominent attorney. Now—let's not play right into his hands."

A faint relaxation came to Lawrence's narrow shoulders. "Of course, you're right, Mal. Nicky hoped we'd react in just this way."

"Certainly. No doubt he visualized the scene and got some satisfaction from it."

"A shoddy way to die, if you ask me," Clary said.

Lawrence reseated himself. "Shoddy, yes. But I suppose you can't go through an entire lifetime, carrying the things Nicholas Colgren had inside of him, without it affecting you."

"The point is," Ames said, "what are we going to do about it?"

"Destroy the letter," Lawrence said.

"You can burn the paper," Clary said, "but you'll never destroy the content of the letter. It'll be with us forever; we can't escape this."

Lawrence put his head in his hands and groaned. Clary lit a fresh cigar and went over and dropped into a chair. Ames stood disconsolate in the middle of the room, looking from one to the other of them.

He leaned across the desk, grasped Lawrence's shoulder, and shook it.

"Hadley . . . get a grip on yourself, man! And you too, Ronald. Get on your feet. On your feet, I said!"

When he had their full attention, Ames said, "We must face and accept this thing squarely, you know. We have no other choice. And then . . . then we must never speak of it again. What has happened in this office tonight must never go beyond it."

"You mean we let Nicky get away with it?" Clary demanded.

"What would you suggest doing to him?" Ames said.

"The rotten coward!" Lawrence's voice shuddered. "Knowing he would be out of our reach, beyond harm . . . "

"Mal," Clary said, "are you suggesting I look at my wife for the rest of my life without ever really knowing the truth?"

"It isn't what Nicky anticipated," Ames said. "It's the only way we can cross him."

Ames let his words sink in. Then he went on: "We all know the women in question, and we know that Nicky did have a certain boyish appeal, a unique charm. We can assume that he deliberately used every means at his disposal to cultivate the affair. And he had many years in which to do it. It made for a situation which in all probability will never recur. It's more than possible that the woman in question will never step out of line again, with Nicky gone."

"I've got to know!" Clary said. "I can't stand . . . "

He broke off. He stared at the other two men. His face colored. "Don't get me wrong! I know damn well my wife isn't the woman!"

"Then you just hang onto that belief," Ames said. "Nicky has given each of us the power to destroy himself. You remember it. It was what Nicky wanted."

Clary and Lawrence breathed heavily in the silence.

"You're right, of course," Clary said grudgingly.

"But it's going to be hard," Lawrence said, "looking at her across the breakfast table, seeing her before her mirror combing her hair out . . ."

"Regard it," Ames advised, "as the penance we must make for the faulty friendship we gave Nicky."

His words seemed to bring a feeling of finality into the office. The three became stiff and awkward as they regarded one another.

Ames turned abruptly and started toward the door. He paused, looked over his shoulder. "Meet you at the club usual time Sunday?"

Clary busied himself relighting his cigar. "As a matter of fact, I won't be able to play golf this weekend. My wife . . . There's an antique show she mentioned wanting to see."

Lawrence's hands moved about rapidly, doing nothing with the items on his desktop. "Been neglecting the roses," he murmured. "Guess I'd better do some cutting and spraying Sunday, and water the lawn."

Ames nodded, more to himself than to them. There was a brief glint of regret and loss in his eyes. Then he went quickly from the office.

His footsteps echoed as he left the deserted building.

As he got into his car, he thought that it was too bad Clary and Lawrence had been involved. It had all been between him and Nicky, really, from the evening he'd returned early from the medical convention and followed Doris secretly to a certain motel.

# Enough Rope for Two

## by Clark Howard

The Greyhound bus pulled into the Los Angeles main terminal at noon. Joe Kedzie got off and walked out into the sunlight of a city he had not seen in ten years. Instinctively, he headed for Main Street. He walked slowly, recalling how the stores and clothes and cars had all changed. No more double-breasted suits. Very few black cars—mostly red and yellow and pink and chartreuse now. The stores were all modern, larger, with a lot of glass. And the skirts—a little longer maybe, but tight in the right places. He pushed the thought of women from his mind. There would be time for them later. After he had his hundred grand.

At Main he turned the corner and began to pass the cheap bars and honky tonks he had known so well. He remembered the shooting gallery, the penny arcade, the strip joints, the cafe where the pushers made—and probably still make—their headquarters. This part of the world will never change, he thought. If I was sent up for another ten years, it would still be the same when I got back again.

Between a bar and a Chinese hand laundry was the entrance to the Main Line Hotel. Kedzie opened the door and walked up the six steps to the lobby. A young, pimply-faced man was behind the desk. He held a racing form and studied it sleepily. Kedzie stood at the desk until it became apparent that the youth was ignoring him; he then reached across the counter and yanked the racing form out of his hand. The clerk jumped up, his face flushing.

"What's the idea!" he demanded.

"Just want a little service," said Kedzie calmly, laying the paper on the desk. "Does Madge Griffin still live here?"

The desk clerk tried to act tough. "Who wants to know?"

"Don't play games with me, punk," said Kedzie harshly, "or I'll break your arm! Does Madge Griffin live here or doesn't she?"

"She lives here," said the clerk, scared now. "Room two-twelve."

Kedzie nodded. He left the desk and walked across the lobby and up a flight of stairs. Two-twelve was the last room at the end of the dingy hallway. He stood before the door and lighted a cigarette, then rapped softly. Madge's voice came through the door.

48

"Who is it?"

"Errol Flynn. Open up."

He heard her walk across the room; then the door opened. She stood framed in the doorway, her eyes widening, plainly startled.

"Joe!"

"Hello, Madge."

She moved aside, as he moved forward, to let him enter. The room was small, not as crummy as he had expected, but still crummy enough. He walked to a chair and sat down. She watched him curiously for a moment, then closed the door and leaned back against it.

"How've you been, Madge?" he asked in his matter-of-fact tone, as if he had seen her a month ago instead of ten years ago.

"I've been getting along, Joe. How have you been?"

He grunted, but did not answer. He looked her over, taking his time. Ten years older, but she still had it, and just enough of it wherever it belonged. He decided that she was just a little heavier in the hips than when she had been his girl. Still—and this thought amused him—she wasn't then, and still wasn't now, the kind you would want if you had a hundred grand.

"How'd you know where to find me, Joe?" she asked suddenly.

"Just a guess. I figured you'd come back here. It's just about your speed."

"What's that supposed to mean?" she demanded, her eyes flashing angrily.

"Forget it, baby," he said easily, and to change the subject added, "have you got a drink?"

She walked over to the closet and took a nearly full bottle of gin from the shelf. "There's nothing to mix it with," she said. "Want it straight?"

He shook his head. "It would probably knock me out. Forget it."

She put the bottle back on the shelf. Kedzie crushed out his cigarette and lighted a fresh one. It figured, he thought. A bottle of gin in the closet. Madge never could stand the stuff. But gin was always Maxie's drink. He's not far away. Just wait and be patient. He'll show up.

Madge walked over to the bed and sat down. They began to talk, idly, pleasantly. Two people have a lot to talk about after ten years. Kedzie waited for her to mention Maxie, but she did not. That convinced him that she knew where he was. And the minute she left the room and got to a telephone, Maxie would know that he, Kedzie, was back in town.

They talked until five o'clock. Finally she asked, "What are you going to do now, Joe?"

He decided to play it straight. "What do you mean?"

"I mean, have you got a place to stay tonight?"

"No, not yet. I'm so used to having my bunk waiting for me, I guess I forgot that I have to take care of those things myself now." The bait had been dropped. He waited for her to snap at it. After a moment's hesitation, she did.

"Why don't you let me get you a room here, Joe? Then you won't have to bother looking for a place."

"Well, I don't know, Madge. I don't—"

"Look, I'll tell you what—I'll go down to the desk and get you a room, and then go down the street to Jasi's and get a pizza and some cold beer. You can lie down and rest while I'm gone; then when I get back, we can eat right here in the room. You looked tired, Joe. Why don't you take off your coat and lie down for a while."

"Well, I am pretty tired. First bus ride in ten years, you know."

"You just rest, Joe." She picked up her purse quickly. "I'll only be a couple minutes."

When she was gone, he took off his coat and stretched out on the bed. It won't be long now, he thought. Five minutes from now she'll be in a phone booth. Maxie should be here by eight o'clock.

Madge returned an hour later with the food. Kedzie pulled a small writing desk up to the bed and put the pizza on it. He sat down on the side of the bed and began to eat. Madge opened two cans of beer and brought them to the table. She drew up a chair opposite him and sat down.

Kedzie ate sparingly and left half the beer in the can. He was not accustomed to highly seasoned food, much less alcohol. Later, when he had his money, he would eat only the best.

It was nearly seven when they finished eating. Kedzie lighted a cigarette and walked over to the open window and the lights of Main Street.

Madge walked over and stood beside him. "What are you thinking about, Joe?" she asked.

"Just the lights, down there—how many times I dreamed about them while I was in the joint."

"Was it really bad, Joe—all those years?" Her voice was gentle, sincere. It was a tone that Joe Kedzie did not accept coming from her.

"No," he said sarcastically, "it was a hell of a lot of fun. I wanted to stay, but they wouldn't let me. Said you had to leave when your time was up."

Once again he saw the anger flash in her eyes. He didn't care. She had served her purpose as far as he was concerned, for she had told Maxie where to find him.

"You always were like that, Joe!" she said hotly. "Always crawling into your shell, always keeping everything to yourself, never trusting anybody. You haven't changed a bit in ten years!"

He looked at her coldly, feeling the urge to slam his fist into her face. He wanted to tell her he hadn't grown stupid in ten years, that he wasn't so blind he hadn't figured out she and Maxie had caused him to fall after the payroll job. He wanted to scream out to her that he had thought about that possibility even before the job. He wanted to let her know the reason they hadn't pulled off their little double-cross completely was because he had figured out another hiding place for the money beforehand, had put it in a place only he knew about.

Kedzie was at the point of cursing her, when a knock sounded at the door. A moment's hesitation, apprehension, and Madge walked over to the door, opening it.

For the second time that day, Joe Kedzie looked upon a face he had not seen in ten years. Maxie had not changed much. He still looked like what he was—a sharpie. You can spot a guy like him anywhere, thought Kedzie. Handsome, always smiling, shifty-eyed, overdressed. The kind that's always on the make for a fast buck.

"Hello, Joe-boy," said Maxie, with a false air of friendliness.

"Hello, Maxie." You son of a bitch, thought Kedzie, you took ten years away from me!

Maxie stepped in and closed the door. He walked casually to the bed and sat down. Madge moved to a chair in the corner, away from both men. Kedzie dropped his cigarette out the window and sat back against the sill.

"Heard you were out, Joe-boy," said Maxie. "Thought I better look you up before you left town."

"What makes you think I'm leaving town?" asked Kedzie calmly.

Maxie flashed the wide smile that was his trademark. He leaned back on his elbows. "Just thought you might be heading back toward

El Paso. Thought maybe you might have left something around there someplace."

"The only thing I left in El Paso was a day of glory for the local cops."

"Nothing else?"

"Nothing that you've got any interest in, buddy."

Maxie sat up quickly. His jaw tightened and both hands closed into fists. "Look, Joe," he said harshly, "I've waited for that dough as long as you have! I've got a right to my share!"

Kedzie remained calm. He casually lighted another cigarette. "The only difference is, Maxie," he said easily, "is that you waited outside while I waited inside."

"That's the breaks, Joe." Maxie stood up. His face was serious, challenging. "The money's still only half yours."

Kedzie looked down at the floor. There was a hundred thousand dollars riding on this play. There was no sense in risking it all with Maxie at this late date. He thought of the tail that had followed him from prison, that had expected to be taken right to the dough; the trouble he'd had throwing the tail clear off the track. After all that, it made sense to play it easy for a while longer.

"I'll lay it on the line for you, Maxie," he said. "I figure I'm entitled to that dough more than you. I figure I've earned it by taking the rap for the job. So I don't intend to split that package with you or anybody else."

Anger showed plainly on Maxie's face. Got to make it good, thought Kedzie. If this doesn't work I'll have to kill him right now, right here. He continued talking.

"The only thing that's holding me back is that I need a stake to get to the dough. I need some cash—a couple of hundred at least—and a car. I want some clothes, so I can get out of this burlap I'm wearing."

Maxie's anger had clearly changed from anger to curiosity. It's working, thought Kedzie.

"I'll make a deal with you," Kedzie went on. "You get me a car, a couple of hundred bucks, and some decent clothes, and I'll cut you in for a quarter of the dough. You'll get twenty-five grand, no strings attached. How about it?"

Maxie looked thoughtfully at Kedzie, thinking that it wouldn't be easy to force Kedzie to tell him where the money was hidden.

"I'll go along with that, Joe-boy," he said, and added quickly, "—but only on one condition."

"Name it," said Kedzie.

"I stay with you every minute from here on out, and we go for the money together."

"How about the car," asked Kedzie, "and the other things?"

"I'll fix it so Madge can get everything you want. You and me will stay right here in this room until we're ready to go for the money."

"It's a deal," said Kedzie. "And if you can get what I need tonight, we'll leave in the morning."

"The sooner the better," grinned Maxie eagerly. "Madge can go out and rent a car tonight. On the way back she can stop at my place and pick up clothes for you."

"How about the two hundred?"

Maxie smiled. "I've got three bills in my pocket right now. A long shot came in at Hollywood Park today. So we're all set, Joe-boy. Two days from now we can be in El Paso."

It was Joe Kedzie's turn to smile. "We're not going to El Paso, partner," he said slyly. "Surprised?"

Maxie's grin vanished and suspicion shadowed his face. "What do you mean?" he asked quickly.

"The dough isn't in El Paso. It's in New Mexico—right out in the middle of nowhere."

Suddenly Maxie began to laugh, somewhat hysterically. He laughed long and loud. He was thinking of all the hours and days he had spent asking questions in El Paso, trying to follow every move Joe Kedzie had made, trying to trace where Kedzie had hidden the money.

Joe Kedzie also began to laugh, but he was not thinking about the past, only the future.

At ten minutes before eight the next morning, Joe Kedzie and Maxie walked out of the Main Line Hotel onto Main Street. Kedzie had shed the rough grey suit the prison had discharged him in, and now wore slacks and a short-sleeved sport shirt. On his arm he held one of Maxie's sport coats. Maxie, following him, carried a small tan suitcase with their extra clothes.

They walked down the block to a green Ford sedan Madge had rented for them. Maxie unlocked the car and tossed the suitcase on the back seat.

"You drive," said Kedzie. "I don't have a license." Maxie nodded and slid behind the wheel. He turned the ignition on and started the motor. Before he could shift into gear Kedzie spoke again. "How about the two hundred, Maxie?"

Maxie looked at him oddly. "I've got it," he said flatly.

"Give it to me," said Kedzie.

Maxie shook his head in anger and disgust, but he drew a wallet from his inside coat pocket and counted out two hundred dollars in tens and twenties. He tossed the bills, with a display of anger, on the seat between them. Kedzie gathered them up, folded them neatly in half, and put them in his shirt pocket.

They drove out to Sunset Boulevard, then swung onto the Ramona Freeway. Kedzie sat back and relaxed, feeling fresh and invigorated on his first free morning in ten years. He ignored Maxie completely and interested himself in looking out the window at the stores and the cars and the girls.

The car sped along, through Monterey Park, Covina, past Pomona, and on into San Bernardino. By eleven o'clock they had reached Indio. They stopped for gas and Kedzie got out and picked up a roadmap. They left Indio on Route 99, heading south.

At one o'clock they pulled into El Centro. Maxie stopped at the first highway restaurant outside town and they went in and ordered lunch. Kedzie borrowed a pencil from the waitress and spread the roadmap out on the table. He began to figure their mileage. When he was finished, he said, "It's a little over three hundred to Tucson. If we drive straight through, we should make it by nine tonight."

"How far do we have to go past Tucson?" asked Maxie irritably.

"Not far," said Kedzie.

"Getting anxious, Maxie?" Joe Kedzie asked, smiling.

Maxie cursed as he got up from the table. He went over to a pinball machine and dropped a coin into it. Kedzie watched him, thinking, If you'd spent the last ten years where I did, rat, you'd have more patience.

They pulled into Tucson, tired and dirty, at nine-fifteen that night. All along the highway they saw NO VACANCY signs lighting their path. Finally, five miles past the eastern city limits, they found a motel room.

Maxie registered at the office and they dropped the suitcase off at the room. Then they drove back into Tucson for something to eat. It was nearly midnight when they returned to the motel and went to bed.

By eight o'clock the next morning, they were on the road again. Kedzie decided he'd take a chance and drive; he was tired of just sitting. Fifty miles southeast of Tucson they turned off onto Route 666 and headed north. The highway made a wide, sweeping arc around the Dos Cabezas mountain range, then swung south again. Shortly before eleven o'clock they crossed the State Line into New Mexico. The first roadsign they saw said: Lordsburg 20 Miles.

"We're about there," said Kedzie casually. "It's about an hour's drive after we pass Lordsburg." Maxie grunted. "We'll have to stop in Lordsburg," continued Kedzie. "There's some things I have to buy."

Maxie glanced at him suspiciously. "Like what, for instance?" he asked irritably.

"Like a long piece of rope, for instance."

"What the hell do we need a rope for?" demanded Maxie.

"You want the money, don't you? Well, we'll need a rope to get it. The package is at the bottom of a forty-foot well that must've gone dry a long time ago."

Maxie's mouth dropped open. "Well, I'll be damned!"

"We'll need some other things, too—a flashlight, maybe a small shovel in case we have to do some digging. I guess a couple of feet of sand could have blown down that well in all this time."

In Lordsburg they stopped at the first large General Store they came to. Inside, Kedzie asked the clerk for sixty feet of strong rope. The clerk led him into the storeroom and showed him several large bolts of rope. Kedzie picked out the sturdiest he could find and the clerk began to measure off sixty feet. Kedzie walked back out into the store and picked up a small hand shovel from a display rack. He handed it to Maxie. When the clerk brought the heavy roll of rope out, Kedzie took this, too, and handed it to Maxie.

"Put this stuff in the car," he said easily. "I'll get a flashlight and be right out."

Maxie turned and carried the things out of the store. After Kedzie had picked out a flashlight and batteries, he walked across the room to a glass showcase. He appeared casual as he looked over the merchandise. When the clerk approached him, he said, "Let's see one of those target pistols."

The clerk opened the case and took out a medium-sized, black automatic pistol. "This is the Sports Standard," he said, going into his sales pitch. "One of the best made. Only weighs half a pound. Shoots .22 shorts or longs. A real accurate piece for targets or small game."

"How much for this one?" asked Kedzie.

"That's the six-and-three-quarter barrel. It'll run you forty-four fifty plus tax."

"Okay," said Kedzie quickly, glancing toward the front door. "Give me a box of shells too, and then figure up the whole bill."

Outside, Maxie closed the door of the car and walked back to the store to see what was keeping Kedzie. When he looked through the window, he saw Kedzie forcing bullets into a magazine. A new target pistol lay on the counter before him. Maxie's face turned white and his hands began to tremble. He watched Kedzie shove the loaded magazine into the grip of the weapon and tuck the gun in his belt, and under his shirt.

Maxie turned and walked back to the car, feeling sick. He opened the door and slid under the wheel. He looked at the dashboard. Kedzie had done all the driving that morning; he had the car keys. He knows, thought Maxie helplessly. He knows I fingered him after the payroll job and now he's going to kill me for it. He never meant to give me a split of the dough. The whole deal was a trick to get me out here so he could kill me!

Suddenly a thought occurred to Maxie, a possible way out.

He turned in the seat and looked back at the rope and shovel lying on the floorboard. Quickly he reached back and opened the suitcase. He fumbled through the soiled clothing and drew out his shaving kit. His hands shook as he unzipped the case.

When Kedzie got back to the car, he found Maxie sitting calmly behind the wheel. He got in and handed Maxie the car keys. "Take Route 80," he said, "south out of town and keep going until I tell you where to turn."

The highway ran in an almost straight line past Lordsburg. It was a thin grey streak surrounded on either side by dry, flat land. The brilliant sun overhead moved up to a point directly in the center of the sky as the noon hour approached. It cast its heat down onto the sands of the Hidalgo country and made all living creatures look for shade. By twelve o'clock the temperature had risen to a hundred and one.

Inside the car, Joe Kedzie sat sideways with one hand inside his shirt and against the cold metal of the gun. Maxie kept his eyes straight ahead, squinting against the sun. They moved along in silence, passing no other traffic. Kedzie had also taken this into account in his plan. It was common in the desert for people to avoid being out in the noonday heat. Kedzie had counted on having the desert all to themselves.

A half-hour later, they passed a wide place in the road called Separ. Kedzie had remembered that name for ten years—had kept it in his mind by spelling it backwards; what it spelled backwards made it easier to remember.

"You'll come to a turn in the road up ahead," he said. "About three miles past that is where we turn off. First road on the right."

Maxie didn't answer. He had not spoken a word since Lordsburg. When they came to the road Kedzie had indicated, he turned off the highway. The blacktop was pitted, rough. Maxie looked at Kedzie for instructions. "Just keep going," said Kedzie. "It's not far now."

They bumped along for eight miles. The terrain around them began to rise slightly in places, forming low knolls and finally small hills. Kedzie watched the mileage dial intently, glancing ahead from time to time for familiar landmarks. Finally he saw the old dirt road cutting off at an angle from the black top. "Turn there," he said, pointing ahead.

Maxie turned off. The dirt road was smoother than the blacktop had been and the car settled down to a level ride again. The road curved down into a washed-out gulley that had once been excavated for mining. Kedzie watched through the rear window until the blacktop passed from sight. Then he turned to Maxie and said, "Pull over, partner."

When the car stopped, Kedzie got out quickly. Maxie stepped out on the driver's side. The two men faced each other across the hood of the car.

"You know, don't you, Joe?" said Maxie simply.

"Yeah, Maxie, I know." Kedzie drew the automatic from beneath his shirt and held it loosely.

"I don't know what made me do it, Joe," began Maxie. "I just—"

"I'll tell you why you did it, rat," interrupted Kedzie harshly. "Two things—Madge and a hundred grand!"

"I don't know what came over me, Joe," continued Maxie desperately. "I just didn't realize—"

"Never mind!" snapped Kedzie. He waved the gun toward the car. "Get that rope and shovel out."

Maxie dragged the heavy rope out, threw it over his shoulder, and picked up the shovel. Kedzie directed him down a narrow path, following a few feet behind. The path ended at the entrance to a mine shaft which was near the gulley bottom. Twenty feet off to one side was the dry well. It had once been surrounded by a three-foot brick and clay wall, but most of the wall had deteriorated and fallen. Only one beam remained of a pair that once had held a small roof over the then precious supply of water. The wheel that had raised and lowered a bucket now lay broken and rotted in the dust.

"There it is, Judas," said Kedzie sardonically. "That's Joe Kedzie's private bank."

Maxie stopped and half turned when Kedzie spoke. "Keep walking," warned Kedzie, raising the gun. Maxie resumed his pace. Kedzie lowered the gun again.

When Maxie got to the edge of the well, he dropped the rope to the ground. For a moment he stood staring down into the deep hole; his right hand gripped the small shovel tightly. Suddenly he whirled and hurled the shovel at Joe Kedzie's face.

Kedzie stepped easily aside and the shovel slammed into the wall of the mine shaft. He laughed and said, "Nice try, rat." Then he leveled the target pistol and pulled the trigger.

The bullet struck Maxie in his stomach. He stumbled back, grasping the wound with both hands, but did not fall. Kedzie fired a second time, and a third. Both bullets smashed into Maxie's chest. He fell backwards, dropping head first into the well.

Kedzie stuck the gun in his belt and walked slowly to the edge of the well. He calmly lighted a cigarette, then took out the flashlight and directed its beam into the dark pit. The well was so deep that the beam failed to reach the bottom.

When he had finished his cigarette, Kedzie bent down and picked up the rope. He dragged one end to a large boulder, around which he wrapped it securely, tying it. Then he walked back to the well and dropped the rest of the rope into the blackness. He heard a thud as it struck bottom.

Carefully, he sat down on the well's edge and began to lower himself into the hole. He braced his feet flat against the wall, arching his body, descending one cautious step at a time. Soon the darkness of the well surrounded him. He edged farther and farther below the surface.

The rope snapped just before his feet reached the halfway mark. Kedzie screamed; the darkness rushed up past him for a fleeting second; then he slammed into the hard ground at the bottom.

He rolled over, dazed, his head spinning. He reached out in the darkness and felt the wall. His body ached all over and his head was beating wildly. The rope had fallen on top of him and was tangled around him. He pulled it away from his body and forced himself up into a sitting position. As he leaned back against the wall of the well, he felt very sick. For a moment he thought he was going to faint. He sat very still and sucked in deep breaths of air to calm himself.

It's all right, he thought over and over again, it's all right. I can get back up without the rope. The well isn't too wide. I can brace my feet against one side and my back against the other and I can work my way back up. It'll be hard and it'll take a while, but I can do it. I can make it back up without a rope. I can make it.

He rested for a moment until the nausea passed, then fumbled in his pocket for the flashlight. He felt pain, too, but the excitement of his fall and of his predicament did not allow him to dwell on it. He was relieved when he switched on the flashlight and saw that the fall had not damaged it. He found the piece of rope that had fallen with him, gathered it up until he had the broken end. He was puzzled that such a strong rope would break under so little weight. He examined the end carefully under the light. Only a few strands, he saw, had been torn apart. The rest had been neatly and evenly cut—and on an angle so that it could not be easily noticed.

Maxie was the only other person who had handled the rope. He must have cut it while he had been in the car alone!

Kedzie flashed the light around until it shined on Maxie's face. He cursed the dead man aloud. Then he laughed. It won't work, Maxie, he thought. I can still make it. I can still get out—rope or no rope!

Kedzie pushed himself to his feet. Excruciating pain shot up through his right leg and he fell back to the ground moaning. He tried again, staggered, and fell a second time. He groaned in agony. The pain in his leg was unbearable. Desperately he twisted into a sitting position again and drew up his trouser leg. He shined the light on his leg and saw that the flesh between his knee and ankle was split apart and that a jagged bone protruded through the opening.

He leaned back against the wall, feeling fear well up in his body and overshadow the pain. His hand dropped to the ground beside him and he felt a hard, square object. He shined the flashlight down on it and saw the plastic-wrapped package he had dreamed of for ten years. Tears ran down his face and he began to tremble. Suddenly he grabbed up the package, swore. To hell with his broken leg. Maxie

hadn't beat him yet out of that hundred grand. He had one good leg;
he'd make it out of there.

Clutching the package, Kedzie worked his back up the wall in an
attempt to get upright. He made it, panting hard, sweating. Now
he had to shift his weight onto his broken leg. He waited a moment
before trying, waiting for his breathing to still.

Terrific pain knifed through him, the instant he tried to place a
little bit of his weight on his broken leg. He fell to the ground in
pain and despair. He still held to the package, but the flashlight had
fallen from his hand, its beam of light unextinguished and directed
straight along the ground to Maxie's face.

The way it looked to Kedzie, the dead man was smiling at him.

# A Change for the Better

## by Arthur Porges

There is something peculiarly frustrating about a blackmailer, as compared with other criminals. Unlike a thief, a swindler, or a sex fiend, he is just as dangerous behind bars as when free. He sells something a dozen times, but still retains a clear title to it. If the victim buys a negative, he may be sure copies have been made, so that the transaction settles exactly nothing. And when information is peddled, the situation is even less satisfactory, since such a commodity can pass to a hundred people without leaving the blackmailer's possession at all. It is still his to sell again—for life.

For life—only in that phrase lies the criminal's vulnerability. Dead men tell no tales. Not in person, but no blackmailer worth his salt ever puts his own life on the line. Always there is a letter, left in a safety deposit box, or with a friend, and marked: To be opened in case of my death. It is made quite plain to the victim that by killing his tormentor, he gains nothing whatever. At worst, exposure; at best, a new leech to deal with.

Gene Sinclair was a blackmailer, and one of the best. He paid well, himself, for secrets, and then put on the squeeze. He bought from people too timid or inexperienced to use the knowledge themselves: maids, cooks, hairdressers, and the like. He picked his victims with great care. They had to have money, above all. A wealthy man or woman with a place in society to protect—that was always good. Better still, if they had children to shield from some terrible truth. Occasionally, but not often, you could even find a child willing to be blackmailed in order to protect his parents, especially if they were old and sick, and still thought of a forty-year-old man as their baby.

Sinclair was not just an ordinary blackmailer, that is to say, a grubby, small-souled person capable only of this most cowardly crime. He was intelligent, witty, personable, well-read, and even lovable to those who didn't probe very deeply. In fact, he had no soul at all, and nerves of brass. He lived well, tipped generously, and subsidized young blondes who liked convertibles, furs, and gambling at Las Vegas. It was nothing but the best for Gene Sinclair. And, contrary to all the homilies ever written, he slept ten dreamless hours each night.

At this moment he was making a collection at one of his best sources. The young woman who sat facing him in the living room of the big house had a pinched look about her nostrils. He had always admired her eyes, which were large and the blue of wood-smoke. The rest of her wasn't bad, either, Sinclair reflected, not for the first time. A slim figure, but rounded in the best places; long legs that didn't sprawl, as they often seemed to on the Las Vegas blondes; and a look of well-scrubbed elegance that came from generations of money.

"You told me last time I'd not be bothered again for a month," she said bitterly.

"And I meant it," he assured her, showing white teeth in a killing smile. "But roulette just isn't my game, and yet I always succumb."

"So I must finance your gambling."

"I'm afraid so. Right now you're my only client with sufficient cash."

"You're quite wrong. I have no money left. Maybe next month—"

"Let's not waste time. Your father is the best neurosurgeon in the country. Why, that operation on Prince Fuad must have netted him at least five thousand dollars, and probably more."

"I can't ask him for any more. I just can't."

"Would you rather I went to your fiancé? I'm sure he'd like to know that his bride-to-be had an illegitimate child at the age of fifteen. His parents would be even more interested; I understand they think of the Cabots and Lodges as upstarts."

The blue eyes flashed.

"If George knew about you, he'd beat you to death."

"Oh, he could do it, easily enough. A top athlete," Sinclair said thoughtfully. "Not that I'm a weakling; but he's in fine condition, no doubt, while I've been dissipating. Blondes and gambling are not exactly muscle-builders. But dear George would never be so foolish, would he? You know my ground rules. Give me any trouble, and my charges go up in proportion."

"He'd kill you!"

"That would be twice as silly. I've left a letter with a friend, telling him just where to find my secret files. It's to be opened in case of my death, a very obvious precaution.

Her shoulders slumped in defeat. It was inevitable, yet always gave him pleasure. The worm twisted and writhed, but invariably found itself under the boot-heel.

"Unless you get me some cash in a hurry, Lisa, honey, I'll have to charge for overtime."

"All right; you win. I don't know how I'll explain it to my father . . ." Her voice trailed off in a sob.

"That won't be necessary."

She turned with a cry, and Sinclair stiffened.

"Dad! I thought you were at the hospital."

The tall man, slightly stooped, gave her a reassuring smile, but his eyes, a much colder blue than hers, remained fixed on the blackmailer.

"I've always known about my daughter's mistake," he said evenly. "She was only a child at the time. Possibly George's parents would understand, too, but I can't risk it."

She stared at him in amazement.

"But all these years—you never said—"

"Why should I? I knew your visit to Marilyn was not just a vacation; remember, I'm a doctor. It seemed best to let you think the secret was your own. Why do you suppose the adoption went through so smoothly and without publicity?"

"Still," Sinclair drawled, "you let her pay me. Very sensible. Now why not save the heart-to-heart talk until I've left. Just pay up, and I'll intrude no longer."

"I think not," the doctor said, his eyes glacial in their stare. "I didn't put in this rather melodramatic appearance just to act as paymaster. You are finished, Sinclair."

The blackmailer's lips narrowed, and he gave a grimace of distaste that was almost comical in its emphasis.

"Do I have to spell it out again? How can people be so stupid? I don't just carry information here"—he tapped his head—"but always leave a letter with somebody. So if you're thinking of killing me, just forget it. The moment my death is known, no matter what the cause, my friend will open that letter. And then he'll either spill the beans, or take over where I left off."

"I've no intention of killing you," the surgeon said calmly. "As you've pointed out, that's no solution."

His daughter was watching him in bewilderment.

"But, Dad. I don't see how—"

"Leave it to me, Lisa."

He pulled a gun from his pocket. The muzzle pointed squarely at Sinclair. The blackmailer shook his head in disbelief.

"I really ought to print a little booklet," he said irritably. "Didn't I just explain the situation? You can't kill me, and I don't want to hurt you; I never carry a gun. So put that thing away; it makes me nervous."

"I wouldn't take your word for anything," the doctor said. "Go over to the wall, and assume the position. I'm sure you know what it is; they use it on all the TV programs. Move!" he added sharply, waving the gun. "Hands against the wall, feet away from it; you know what I mean."

Sinclair looked at the grim face again; the eyes seemed filmed with ice. It was almost certain the old boy didn't mean to shoot, but if pushed, who could tell? The blackmailer knew character, and this surgeon could be dangerous. Maybe he had some idea of killing him and hiding the body. Conrad wouldn't open the letter if Sinclair merely vanished. But the doctor wouldn't know that; besides, not even he could dispose of a body that easily. Assuming an expression of bored tolerance, the blackmailer went to the wall.

Cautiously, the old man searched him, finding no weapon.

"Just stay put," he ordered, and went to a large secretary. He unlocked a door, and as Lisa watched wide-eyed, took out two pairs of handcuffs. Deftly, with his surgeon's fingers, he cuffed Sinclair's hands behind him. "Feet together, now," he directed, and when the command was obeyed, used the other pair of cuffs on the man's ankles.

"This is all very silly," Sinclair said angrily, conscious now that no matter what happened, Dollie would have left the Eagle Bar in a huff. Pity; she was a tasty dish. "It's just going to cost you extra."

"There are other ways of shutting a man up besides killing him," the surgeon said.

"What d'you mean? Gonna cut my tongue out? I can write, you know!"

"I assumed as much. And even if completely paralyzed, you could work out a code with your eyelids, or something. You see, I've given quite a bit of thought to you."

Sinclair felt his neck-hairs tingle, and his back was suddenly cold.

"You mean you thought of deliberately paralyzing me! That would be inhuman!"

Even as he said it, and before the doctor's ironic chuckle, he realized the fatuity of the remark.

"A ruthless animal like you," the surgeon said, "never understands that some day, some place, he'll meet an even more ruthless animal—and one with greater ingenuity. As for being inhuman, let me tell you something, Sinclair. This morning I had to blind a four-year-old girl. She had a glioma, a brain tumor, and if it stayed in, she would die. It was her optic nerve or her life. Do you know what that poor child said when she came out of the anesthetic? She cried: 'Mommy! Mommy! I can't wake up!' She doesn't even know what blindness is. Now what do you think your life means in comparison with hers? Damn little, believe me; damn little."

"What are you talking about? Blinding me won't solve anything, you old fool!"

"You missed the point. Who said anything about blinding you? I was commenting on the relative value of life; no matter what people say, it's not an absolute. No, I'm not going to hurt your sight. A blackmailer lives by his memory."

"Dad!" Lisa exclaimed, her face chalk white. "You can't!"

"Oh, but I can; I must; and I will. Why, it might even make a decent fellow out of him!"

Thoroughly alarmed, Sinclair attempted to get to the door, but the hobbles made him take a crashing fall. He lay there half-stunned, and the old doctor, moving like a panther, closed in, hype in hand. Before the blackmailer could resist, the needle jabbed relentlessly home into his arm.

"Just relax now," he said in an ironic tone. "You won't feel a thing. But when you come to, your memory will be gone."

"No, don't!" Sinclair begged. "I'll go away! I'll never bother you again!"

"Of course, your word is good enough for me," was the quietly savage reply.

"They'll find out what you did! You'll go to prison."

"Not likely. Assuming a thorough investigation, a good man might spot the brain damage, but it'll never be traced to me. I'll keep you in my private surgery here until the very small wound is healed. It takes only a long needle through a corner of the eye-socket to do the business, you know. And if I slip a little, you may have some other minor disabilities—say a dragging leg, a few tics, a touch of muscular dystrophy, but it won't be malicious—just an unfortunate accident."

"The letter!" Sinclair gasped, fighting to remain conscious.

"Ah, yes, the letter giving the location of your secret files. I wonder where they might be? A small office in some quiet business neighborhood; or maybe you prefer a big and busy building, where nobody can meddle. No matter; you'll tell me where they are."

"Look, let's make a deal. I'll take you to the files. You can destroy the birth certificate, all the papers."

"Sorry," the doctor said. "Not when your real files are in your head."

"Sooner or later my friend will open that letter. You can't win against me."

"You're wrong. I'm going to put enough scopalomine into you to make the sphinx talk. You picked the wrong man to keep secrets from, Sinclair. Truth serum and a spot of hypnosis will do the job nicely. Sweet dreams! He's gone under, Lisa."

"Dad," the girl said shakily. "Are you really going to operate?"

"You can't beat a blackmailer by using kid gloves. Remember Mike Garrity, the one they say is the cleverest thief alive?"

"Yes. He had that simply beautiful child. Janie, wasn't it?"

"Right. When I saved her life, I made a friend. After Sinclair talks—and he will—I can depend on Garrity to get to those files and clean 'em out. And he'd die before telling anybody about it."

A chilly smile touched his lips.

"In a way, we're helping Sinclair, too; giving him needed therapy. After all, was anybody more in need of a massive personality change?"

# A Killing in the Market

## by Robert Bloch

I may not have much time to set this down.

To make things worse, the pen leaks, and there isn't very much paper. You'd think that for forty dollars a day, the hotel would furnish a decent pen. At least they could replace the supply of stationery once in a while. Of course, I suppose I could call room service and ask for more, but I don't dare to have anyone nosing around.

It's just that I want to write this out while I still have the chance. Maybe it will help explain a few things. At least it might be of interest to a few eager beavers—the kind of people who've always dreamed of a chance to make a big killing in the stock market.

That was my idea. I wanted to make a killing. And now I have, only—

I suppose I ought to begin at the beginning. And say that my name is Albert Kessler, and up until a little over three months ago I worked in Wall Street. I was a clerk in a brokerage house. Maybe I'd better not mention the name of the firm. It isn't important, anyway.

Up until then, nothing was important. Including myself. I was just another guy, holding down just another job. My idea of a big deal was to get out fifteen minutes early and catch a seat in the subway, instead of having to stand up all the way home. That's another laugh—home. One furnished room, in the Bronx. A small order of nothing. But that's all I had. That, and the big dream.

I guess everybody who ever worked in the Street has had the same dream. It's one of those things you think about when you bounce around in the subway, or on the mattress in your crummy room. You can't help but think about it, and hope that tomorrow it's going to come true.

Tomorrow, that's always when you're going to get the break—when you'll just happen to run into this character with the golden touch. He's a plunger, and every time he plunges he comes up smelling like a rose. Somehow you manage to make friends with him, and

pretty soon he's giving you the word on a good thing, and before you
know it you're a character yourself. A real big operator.

Sure, I know what it sounds like. But after you spend a little time
working in the Street, you can't help but think that way. Because
you occasionally see the dream come true. Bernard Baruch isn't the
only one who ever made a killing. You hear stories about guys who
started out as runners and ended up buying their own seats on the
Exchange. Sometimes they made all their money on the Big Board,
and sometimes they branched off into investing in their own firms.
The oil men, those Greek shipping magnates, people like that; they
prove it happens.

But it doesn't happen to everyone; not to guys who just moon
around and wish. You've got to do more than dream. You've got to
keep your eyes open and figure the angles. And you've got to wait.

That's what I did. For over two years I waited. And I planned. I
saved my dough, too. Not much—a pitiful three thousand. But at
least I held onto it. A lot of the other dreamers aren't willing to save
and wait. They're suckers for every crazy rumor on the Street, and
they use the Dow-Jones like a scratch-sheet. It's five bucks on Steel
to win, or ten bucks on Industrials to place or Utilities to show. The
*Journal* is their racing-form, and they make graphs and charts and
follow stock performance records back for years. They play systems
or they play hunches—but all of them go for broke.

That two-dollar window stuff wasn't for me. I didn't believe in tips
or theories. Sure, the Market is a gamble, but gamblers aren't always
winners. The winner, in the long run, is the man who has a sure
thing from the start.

I kept my eyes open trying to spot that winner. Instead of studying
the market, I studied the customers.

And that's how I found Lon Mariner.

There's no sense going into all the details of how I made up my
mind. Half a dozen times beforehand, I thought I'd located my
man—a big investor, who consistently moved in at the right time,
then moved out again after a quick profit. But each time, sooner or
later, the customer I had my eye on pulled a goof, or started hedging
with gilt-edge stuff at a small profit. Over the years I kept track of
several investors; in New York, or in our branch offices.

But it wasn't until three months ago that I made my discovery.
Lon Mariner, who always pulled a sure thing out of the hat. He put
fifteen thousand into a small aircraft company, three days before
they landed a big Navy contract. He pulled out with fifty thousand

and bought into some electronics outfit I never heard of—until they declared a split, then a dividend, and bounced up eighteen points. He took his profits and went into oil, dumping his stock the morning before a nose-dive. Next there was a flier in a Texas railroad that was gobbled up by a bigger combine within a week. By this time I was really following his orders, which came in through our Frisco office. And I was surprised to find that after a month or so he was operating out of Cleveland. But the pattern continued. What he bought didn't make sense; the important thing was that everything he touched turned to gold. Copper, radar, TV in Cleveland; then a big utilities deal out of Boston. He never missed on timing. In eleven weeks he was in on every spectacular rise, every major split across the Board. I figured he'd run his fifteen thousand up to several million. Then he placed his next whopping order out of our Chicago office.

That's when I quit my job and went to Chicago.

All I had was three thousand dollars and this wild idea of mine. At least I thought it was a wild idea, after I actually got on the plane. Here I was, chasing halfway across the country to locate a perfect stranger—or maybe a stranger who wasn't so perfect—in hopes that I'd get him to cut me in on his big deal.

I did some sweating on that flight when I really took stock of the situation. After all, what did I know about this Lon Mariner, anyway? He wasn't in *Who's Who*. And he didn't have a D&B rating, either. I hadn't dared to make any direct inquiries through any of our branch offices. All I really knew about him was that he was the guy I was looking for—the guy with the golden touch. From now on, I'd have to play it by ear.

The minute I got off the airport limousine at the Palmer House, I took a cab over to our Chicago office on LaSalle Street. I still had my company I.D. card—so I forgot to turn it in, is that a crime?—and I flashed it. I said I'd been sent out here to contact one of our clients, and had Mr. Mariner been in today?

Well, it turned out Mr. Mariner hadn't been in—today or any day. His orders came by phone and his bank drafts by mail. I went clear up to the Vice President In Charge Of, but nobody could tell me anything more about the man.

But I did find out he was staying at a hotel on the Gold Coast. *This* hotel.

I hotfooted it over, yesterday afternoon, and plunked down my forty bucks for this room—complete with air-conditioning, television, and a lousy pen.

Forty bucks was only the start of my investment. Ten bucks more made sure that the room clerk put me on the same floor—he even showed me Mariner's name on the register, and his suite number. It was 701, right down the corridor from my room. He didn't remember much about Mariner's appearance, because he hadn't seen him since. Said he'd come in alone, without very much luggage, and that he was "average-looking." Medium height, brown hair, middle-aged.

I spent another ten bucks on the bellboy. All he could tell me was that Mariner ordered all his meals sent up to him, and that he didn't go out much except in the mornings when the maid service cleaned up.

By this time it was almost seven o'clock, and the maids were off duty. I had to settle for a talk with the waiter who served him his meals, a guy named Joe Franscetti.

For the usual ten, Franscetti said yes, he'd come down from Mr. Mariner's room after clearing away the supper dishes. Apparently, Mariner hadn't made any impression on him at all; I got the same vague description of an "average-looking" guy. The waiter couldn't remember anything he'd ever said to him, or even how he usually dressed.

"But I can tell you what he had for dinner," he said. "Shrimp cocktail, the prime ribs—medium rare, I think it was—baked potato, Waldorf salad, coffee, apple pie. And you know what he tipped? A lousy half a buck!"

I thanked him and went away. It was a little discouraging. I hadn't come all this way to find out that Lon Mariner liked his meat medium rare. And even the fact that a guy on a five million dollar winning streak is a poor tipper didn't mean very much to me.

There didn't seem to be anything I could do at the moment. No sense going to the house dick. It had been risky enough asking the questions I'd asked, because the last thing I wanted was to call attention to myself. I suppose everyone figured I was a private eye, and that was bad enough, but at least it was some kind of an excuse.

Anyway, I'd learned nothing useful, and from now on I was on my own. So about seven-thirty I ended up back in my room, with the door open. If I sat in a chair at a certain angle I could keep my eye on 701. Just in case Mariner *did* go out.

Of course, there was nothing to prevent me from just marching down the hall and knocking on his door. Except that I wasn't ready for that yet. Before talking to Mariner, I had to make up my mind about him. When I did speak to him, my conversation was going to be mighty important. I couldn't afford to muff the deal, and I had to decide what I intended to say. And that would depend on sizing up my man, first.

There was just one thing running through my mind right now. Mariner must be some kind of a nut.

On the face of it, there wasn't anything particularly screwy about what I'd heard concerning him; lots of quiet, middle-aged guys are a little on the timid side, and prefer to keep to themselves if they live alone. But under the circumstances, the pattern didn't make sense. If *I'd* cleaned up millions in the market in three months, *I* wouldn't be hiding out by myself in a hotel room, and that's for darn sure.

So he was probably a psycho, like all those eccentric recluses you hear about who end up dying in a basement with a fortune in cash stuck under the mattress.

I sat there for a long time, thinking about it. And the more I thought, the worse I felt. Because it's pretty hard to get close to that kind of a nut. They're the suspicious type, delusions of persecution and everything. They don't trust strangers, and nobody's their friend.

On the other hand, there was something wrong with the picture. I was paying forty bucks a day. And Mariner, even if he was a stingy tipper, must be shelling out close to a hundred for his suite. Besides, during the last few months, he'd moved from Frisco to Cleveland to Boston to Chicago—and trips like that cost dough. Even if he was making millions, he wouldn't be inclined to spend an extra dime if he was just another eccentric. Those guys hole up in the slums and stay put, and they eat stale crackers instead of shrimp cocktails.

So there must be some other reason why Mariner was keeping himself under wraps. I got a sudden hunch.

Could it be that he was the stooge or front-man for some syndicate? *That* made a little better sense to me. Sure, it could explain a lot of things. Including why he stuck to his room. Probably he got his information or his orders by phone. It was a cinch one or the other came from someplace, unless he just got tips on the market out of dreams.

I was beginning to get a terrible yen to visit his room and see if I could spy on him while he was under the influence of H, or operating his ouija-board, or whatever he did. Maybe he kept a collection of shrunken heads, and they talked to him.

On the other hand, it might be a lot smarter to check the switchboard girl tomorrow and see if she'd just keep track of any phone calls coming in or going out of his suite, and slip me the word.

I looked at my watch. Almost ten o'clock, and nothing had happened. I was tired. Better turn in and sleep on it. In the morning I'd decide what to do.

So I got up and and went over to the door to close it.

Just as *his* door opened, and he came out.

I knew it was Mariner the mintue I saw him. Middle-aged, middle-sized, brown-haired; he wore a plain blue suit and a white shirt, and the face above the collar was the kind you could forget even while you were looking at it.

I guess I've seen ten thousand such faces in my time—crowded into elevators, jammed into subways, bobbing along the street. Looking at them had never made me sweat, but I was sweating now. Because this face was worth five million bucks. Lon Mariner, the man with the golden touch.

Now I got a look at his back. He was trying his door, making sure it was locked. Maybe he kept a lot of cash inside. Maybe I could stick around and pick the lock. No, that was too dangerous. What I had to do was follow him and pick his brains.

I put on my coat while he walked over to the elevator. I figured I could dash out and make it just in time, but I figured wrong. Because the car stopped before I reached my door, and he got in.

Then I was swearing, and running down the stairs. I hit the lobby in one minute flat, but he wasn't there and the elevator was already going up again. I could see the lights flickering on the numerals—two, then three, then four.

I shook my head. Should I wait for the car to come down again and talk to the elevator boy, hoping he'd remember which way the man in the blue suit had gone? Or should I dash outside and try to find him?

I decided to get going. I started across the lobby, trying not to break into a run, and scooted past the entrance to the cocktail lounge. Something caught my eye as I went by. The back of a blue suit.

I stopped.

Mariner was sitting at the bar, all alone, way down at the end.

The sweat rolled down my sides as I walked into the place. I chose a stool about twenty feet away from him; there wasn't anybody between us. In fact, outside of a couple off over in a booth, we had the whole joint to ourselves.

The bartender, a fat guy with a mustache, was pouring Mariner a drink. Cognac, from the looks of the glass. He saw me and came down to my end of the bar.

I ordered a beer and swivelled around on the stool so that I could get a good look at my man.

The waiter had certainly been right; Lon Mariner was "average-looking." I didn't get a clue from his ready-made clothes, and there wasn't a hint of anything unusual in his ready-made face, either. He was just another guy.

The more I studied him, the worse I felt. I'd been sure that after I had a chance to get a close look at him, I could size him up and figure out the best way to approach him. But he just sat there, a bump in a blue suit on an overstuffed log. He didn't seem to be enjoying his drink, he wasn't listening to the radio, and he never looked around at the bartender or at me. He had about as much life as a window-dummy, and he wasn't nearly as handsome.

All at once he signaled for another drink. And when the bartender brought the bottle and poured, he slugged down the shot and told him to refill. Then, after he paid, he mumbled something and the bartender left the bottle standing there on the bar.

*That* told me something, at last. That, and the way he sat there, all stiff and frozen, all right, because he was afraid. I recognized the symptoms, now. He was scared to death about something and even more scared that he'd show it. So he sat and drank.

I had my cue, now. I waited until he'd poured and downed his fourth drink. Then I glanced around, checking to see that the place was still almost empty, and slid off my stool. I walked down along the bar and stood next to him. He could see me in the bar mirror, and I noticed the way his fingers tightened around his empty glass.

"Mr. Mariner," I said. "I've been looking for you."

If he'd turned around and thrown the glass at me, that would have been one thing. If he'd turned pale, gasped, or slumped to the floor in a dead faint, that would have been another. But what he *didn't* do was still more effective.

He didn't move.

He'd been frozen before; now he was dead. He tightened up, all over, as if *rigor mortis* was setting in. I had the feeling he'd stopped breathing, just stopped completely.

"I want to talk to you, Mr. Mariner," I murmured.

He didn't turn his head and his lips never moved. But a sound came out of him, and then faint words.

"You must be mistaken. My name's not Mariner."

I shrugged. "Of course it isn't. But that's the name you signed on the hotel register. That's the name you've been using on all your business deals. I know."

He reached out and spilled himself another drink. Not poured—spilled. I watched him do it, waited while he wavered the glass up to his lips and gulped. Then he whispered again.

"How did you find me?"

"That isn't important," I answered. "I've been keeping an eye on you for quite a while."

"Then I was wrong all along, wasn't I? I thought I could get away with it. But they knew all the time, didn't they?"

"I'm all alone, Mr. Mariner."

"Yes. But they sent you."

I hesitated, then decided how to play it. "Nobody sent me. This was my own idea. I've been studying your stock market operations for months. You see, I work for the firm you've been doing business with. And I wanted to talk to you about your methods."

"My—methods?"

For the first time there was a recognizable expression on his face. You could almost call it a smile. He turned his head just a trifle and stared at me. "Then I was wrong. You're just an—an ordinary citizen?"

"Very ordinary, I assure you. But I have an extraordinary curiosity about you. Or about any man who can do what you've been doing in the investment field. I thought we might discuss your methods."

He was really smiling, now. He poured another drink, and his hand was perfectly steady.

"Well, I don't know—"

He was confident once more, ready to brush me off. I knew how to handle that.

"Listen, Mr. Mariner. I'm not the nosey type, but you've already told me enough so that I know you're in some kind of trouble. You don't exactly welcome publicity, do you? I mean, you wouldn't want any stories in the papers about mysterious millionaires, or men travelling under assumed names who have secret methods of beating the stock market. I could go to the phone right now and call the reporters—"

"You wouldn't!"

"Of course I wouldn't. Because you're going to talk to me, instead. Just me. And if you can tell me what I think you can, I'll have every reason to keep my own mouth shut in the future, just the way you do. There it is, Mr. Mariner—my cards are on the table. I want in."

"All right. We'll talk."

"Good."

"But not here. Not like this. In my room."

"Fine. Let's go up." I waited for a moment, then repeated it louder. "Let's go up."

But he wasn't listening to me.

He wasn't looking at me, either. He was staring into the bar mirror. I followed his glance.

Behind us, in the doorway of the cocktail lounge, stood a tall blonde. She had, among other things, the biggest pair of eyes I'd ever seen. She was worth looking at for a number of reasons, but her eyes were what held me.

The eyes held Mariner, too. He looked at her and his mouth opened and closed, and he froze up again. Really froze.

She didn't smile, and she didn't say anything, and she didn't even come closer. She just gave him that long look and then she beckoned.

Mariner stood up. "Excuse me," he muttered. "I must go now. I have an engagement."

"What about our talk?" I said.

"Oh, yes. Suppose we say ten o'clock tomorrow morning, in my room?"

I grabbed his arm. "You wouldn't try to pull a sneak, now would you? Remember what I said about the reporters."

"I remember."

"All right, see you at ten, then. But no funny business. I mean it, Mr. Mariner."

"I promise."

And then he was walking over to her, following her out of the place. I watched them go, saw them head across the lobby in the direction of the elevators. He couldn't find an exit that way, and I was pretty sure he wasn't looking for one—not with that tall blonde on his arm. In a way I didn't blame him for cancelling his appointment and putting me off until tomorrow. If a blond like that ever beckoned to me, I'd cancel my appointments, too. I doubt if I'd be ready to see anyone even at ten the next morning.

But I'm still the suspicious type. I waited a few minutes, then got up and went out to the desk. The Room Clerk on duty was my ten buck boy.

I leaned across the counter and flipped a bill his way, very quietly. He palmed it, just as quietly. "Yes, sir?"

"About Mr. Mariner," I said. "He didn't check out, did he?"

"No party by that name checked out, no sir."

"Well, in case he does, any time between now and tomorrow morning, I want you to call me. And right away, before he gets past the desk here."

"Certainly, but—"

"But what?"

The clerk was frowning. "I don't believe we *have* a party by that name here at the hotel."

I knew how to frown, too. "What do you mean, you don't have such a party? Lon Mariner, in Suite 701. You're the guy who tipped me off about him in the first place.

"I am? You must be mistaken, sir."

"Now, look—"

"You look, sir." The clerk flipped through the registration list. "Here's our guest-entries for the past week. No Mariner, is there? Are you sure you have the right name?"

"Am I sure? You showed me, yesterday. Give me that!" I grabbed and squinted. I saw my own name, and ran my eyes along the signatures above it. Paige, Stein, Tenn, Klass, Phillips, Graham—no Mariner.

"What kind of a business is this?" I was getting a funny feeling in my stomach. "Who's in Suite 701?"

"Let's look at the card-file. Over here, sir." He stepped to the next cage, where the billing entries were kept. He pulled out a yellow card. "Suite 701 has been vacant all week," he told me. "Just rented it tonight. Party named Fairborn. Here, see for yourself."

The funny feeling spread from my stomach upwards. My heart was pounding.

"But that's Mariner's suite," I said. "Little middle-aged guy, with a blue suit. You must have seen him going through the lobby just now, with a big blonde—"

The clerk shook his head. "No, sir, I didn't."

"But he was just in the bar; I talked to him."

"I'm sorry, sir—"

I turned my back and ran for the elevator. By the time I got to the seventh floor, my heart was in my mouth; and it wasn't from the fast ride, either.

I went down the corridor, right to 701, and banged on the door. My heart was in my mouth, but I could still talk. And when the door opened, I did.

"Mr. Mariner," I said. Then my voice trailed off. I was looking at the blonde with the big eyes. And she was looking at me.

"You have the wrong room, I believe."

"I don't. Where's Mariner?"

"Who?"

"The guy in the blue suit. You came up here with him less than half an hour ago. This is his room."

She shook her head. "Sorry, but you're mistaken. This is my room. I'm Miss Fairborn."

"But I saw you two together—"

The big eyes narrowed. "Now, wait a minute. I've been in this room ever since I arrived this evening. I don't know what you're talking about. If you doubt my word, you can check with the desk downstairs."

"I already did. But I know you and Mariner were together, I saw him leaving the bar with you."

"Ah. The bar. You were drinking there."

"Never mind that stuff. I'm not drunk! What'd you do with Mariner?"

The door opened a trifle more. A man put his head out behind Miss Fairborn. He was a big man, with steel-gray hair, and he didn't look like Mariner at all. He looked like trouble.

"What goes on here?" he demanded.

Miss Fairborn shrugged. "I don't know. Some drunk, looking for a friend. You'd better handle him, Harry."

"Glad to."

But I wasn't being handled. I backed away. "All right," I said. "So I made a mistake. I'm sorry."

Harry started to say something, and then stepped aside. I recognized the waiter, Joe Franscetti. He was coming out, wheeling a service table.

I waved at the three of them. "Excuse it, please," I muttered. "I'll go quietly."

And I went, around the corner, hearing the door close behind me. I stood there, waiting until Joe Franscetti caught up with me. He wheeled his table along, head down. I stepped out and grabbed his elbow.

"What gives?" I asked. "Where's Mariner?"

"Who? What's that again, mister?"

"I asked where's Mariner? The guy in 701?"

"But I just come from there. You saw me. There's this dame and her boyfriend, they just had dinner."

"I know. Only that's Mr. Mariner's room. You served him all last week, you said so. Remember?"

"Mister, are you all right?"

"Of course I am. But everybody else has gone crazy. Now look here, you told me about Mariner yourself. The brown-haired guy in the blue suit, the one who only tipped fifty cents. Prime ribs medium rare, Waldorf salad."

"Mister, that room's been vacant all week. I never saw anyone like you say, and I never saw you before, either. You better lie down, you don't look so good."

I knew how I looked, but there was no sense wasting time. There was still the bell-captain; he'd know if a certain bellboy was on duty.

Downstairs I went. I found the bell-captain. My boy was on, to-night, and I caught him over in a corner of the lobby. This time I decided to make another investment.

"Here," I said, waving the bill under his nose. "This is a hundred bucks, see it?"

"Yes, sir."

"Now I've no idea what they might have paid you to clam up, but I've got a hunch they didn't go higher than twenty. So you might as well sell out to the highest bidder."

"I don't follow you, sir."

"It's very simple. Yesterday you and I had a little talk together. I was asking you questions about a man named Lon Mariner. In Suite 701. You described him to me, said he never went out except while the maids were cleaning up. Right?"

His eyes watched the hundred-dollar bill as it waved under his nose. Then he shook his head.

"Sorry, sir. I don't remember anything like that. I mean, I couldn't have told you such a thing, because 701 was vacant until this eve-ning. I know for a fact—I took the party up myself just a few hours ago. A big blonde."

The hundred went back into my pocket and I headed back into the bar. It was still deserted, and the fat bartender came right over.

"Yes?"

"Remember me?" I asked. "I was in here earlier this evening."

"That's right."

Well, at least he admitted *I* had been here. Now I was ready to try for double or nothing.

"Remember the guy I was talking to?"

Silence.

"He left before I did, with a blonde."

"A big blonde?" The bartender brightened. "Sure, she was in here just a couple minutes ago. I served her a—I forget just what."

"She was in here before then, looking for this guy in the blue suit. He sat down at the end of the bar, drinking cognac. I spoke to him. Then she came along and they left together. Now do you recall him?"

The bartender shook his head. "I didn't see them. I didn't see you talking to anyone, either. You were all alone." He wiped the bar. "What's the matter, sir? You don't look so good."

"I don't feel so good," I told him. "Go away."

He went away and I sat there. No use talking any more. He wouldn't remember. None of them remembered. But I did.

I remembered an old English movie they keep reviving on television. *The Lady Vanishes.* This dame sees another dame and talks to her, and later everybody swears she doesn't exist. Of course she does; she's been kidnapped by spies.

Then there's the yarn that pops up every now and then about the woman in the hotel room; she disappears, too. I guess it started way back in the 1890s—it was supposed to have happened in Paris, during some kind of International Exposition. Turned out the woman had cholera and they hushed everything up in order to avoid a panic when she died. They even repapered her room overnight.

Come to think of it, I'd read a lot of detective novels with the same idea. And usually there was a dame involved, and a spy or murder plot.

Somehow I couldn't swallow it in connection with Mariner. Spies don't play the market. And I didn't think he had cholera, either, or even Asiatic flu.

But he *was* scared.

That I remembered. He'd been scared when I talked to him, wondering if *they* had sent me. So who were *they*? The Syndicate, maybe? He'd recognized the blonde, and gone along quietly. Gone along up to the suite, where the gray-haired man named Harry was waiting. He'd gone along, even though he was scared to death.

*Scared to death.* Was that it? Had they killed him?

It didn't seem logical, from any angle. You don't kill the goose that lays five million golden eggs. You can't get away with it, even in Chicago, in a swank hotel.

But they had gotten away with *something.* And that was the screwiest part of it. They'd made everybody forget Lon Mariner had even existed, including people who'd seen him just a little while before he vanished. They'd removed his name from the registry, and even from the billing cards. Was it just bribery? I doubted it, somehow. You can't take such chances. Sooner or later somebody would come looking for Mariner and put on the pressure. Clerks, waiters, bellboys couldn't be trusted to keep their mouths shut when the heat was on. Somebody would come, and someone would sing. Bribery wasn't good enough.

How about threats? That might work. But the people I'd just talked to didn't seem frightened. They were just puzzled. It was as if they actually believed that Lon Mariner had never existed.

That was the point I kept coming back to.

Why was it so important to make sure nobody believed there had ever been such a man?

And *how* had they managed the trick? If the deal involved murder, then certainly the killers would be more interested in concealing their presence than the presence of the victim. Yet the blonde had registered openly, showed herself around. She'd even come back here to the bar, probably while I was out in the lobby, and talked to the bartender. He said she ordered a drink from him, he couldn't remember what.

He couldn't remember—

I got a flash. A flash of those enormous eyes, and the two of them in here, all alone. The blonde leaning over the bar and telling him he couldn't remember. Not bribing him, not threatening him, but *telling* him. Hypnotizing him into forgetting.

Wild?

Perhaps, but I was wild now, too. When plain facts don't make sense, you've got to look for something fancy. And hypnotism works. It works fast, under the right conditions, with the right operators. That blonde would be the right operator. She could get close to the clerk or the bellboy; they'd look—being men—and they'd listen. And the waiter, Joe Franscetti, had been right up there in the room with her, serving a meal. That left the bartender to deal with. So she slipped down here and slipped him a mental Mickey.

I felt a little better, but not much. Because Mariner was still missing, and I didn't know why. And *they* knew that *I* knew.

What I needed now was an ace in the hole. But I didn't have one. The best I could do was a gun in the suitcase. At the time, I'd worried a lot about packing one along. It seemed risky, and I really didn't expect to use threats on Mariner. Now I was glad I had it.

Because there was only one thing left for me to do. I'd have to go up to my room, get the gun, and knock on the door of Suite 701 again.

I got up and went out into the lobby. I took the elevator. I got off at the seventh floor. I tiptoed down the hall, past 701, to my own room. I took out the key and opened my door very quietly. I stepped in.

And then I stumbled, reaching for the light. I started to swear, under my breath, but I should have prayed instead. Because my having stumbled is what must have saved me.

The blow came out of the darkness behind the door, and if it had landed on my head, I'd have been a goner. As it was, my shoulder almost broke. But I ducked, and turned, and was just coming up with a right when two things happened simultaneously.

The light clicked on, and the man named Harry stuck a gun in my ribs.

"Now, march," he suggested.

We marched. There was nobody in the corridor to watch the parade go by. Nobody cheered when we halted before the door to 701.

He knocked. The door opened and Miss Fairborn looked out at Harry. "Did you get him?" she whispered.

"Yes," Harry murmured. "I got him." He pushed me into the room and closed the door.

"Then why didn't you knock him out?" she asked.

"Changed my mind," Harry said. "I think we might have other plans." He winked. "Understand?"

Miss Fairborn nodded, then turned. Those great big beautiful eyes stared at me.

"Cut it out," I said. "I don't hypnotize easy."

She sighed. "I know. That's why I didn't try. It wouldn't work on you because you wouldn't cooperate. You were too suspicious."

"Sorry. That's my nature."

"I'm sorry, too. If only you hadn't come, if only you'd go away now—but of course it's too late."

I looked across the room at the bed. "Where's the money?" I asked. "I thought it might be piled up here, ready for shipping."

Harry rubbed his chin with his free hand. I knew where the other one was, of course—it was holding the gun. And I knew where the gun was, too—still in my ribs.

"You had to guess, didn't you?" he said.

"Yes. I guessed. So where is it, might I ask?"

"You're in no position to ask anything, but I'll tell you. The money has already been shipped."

"And Mr. Mariner?"

"He's been shipped, too. Or will be, soon."

"Then it's like I thought. Murder."

"You did a lot of thinking, didn't you?"

"Why not?" I shrugged. "I knew Mariner was afraid for his life. That's why he kept running from city to city; that's why he holed up here. He practically turned blue when I spoke to him and he admitted *they* were after him. I didn't know what he was talking about until Miss Fairborn showed up. He was twice as frightened then, but he went along with her. So it all adds up, doesn't it? We were after the same thing—the secret of how he managed to make all that dough in such a hurry.

"The only difference is, I was working alone, and I intended to go about it in a nice way. You teamed up and put on the pressure. You were ready to threaten him, ready to kill him. And you did. I still can't understand how you figured you'd get away with it, but you did."

I paused as another thought struck me. "How did you manage to erase his name from our company records? Was it hypnosis again—the way you operated here in the hotel?"

Miss Fairborn nodded. "We have teams operating in every major city."

"That must cost dough. Of course, with five million involved—"

"Multiply it by ten," Harry said. "Mariner just made a little extra on the side, after he thought he'd sneaked away from us."

"From you?"

"You got your story a bit twisted. You see, we all work for the same outfit?"

"Syndicate?"

"Not the one you mean. It's a group of investment people. Their names don't matter. Let's just say they are wealthy and influential people who want to become still more wealthy and influential. They are in a position to get advance tips on a lot of inside deals—but there are laws governing the right to speculate independently in the affairs of your own company. So they conceived this idea of pooling their resources, setting up a private organization to make investments. As long as secrecy is maintained, they can make many millions in profits each year. All they needed was a front man."

"Mariner?"

"Exactly. A nobody from nowhere. Someone who followed orders; and a few trained people like us to keep an eye on him, check up to make sure he didn't get out of line. And it worked well, for the past few years. He must have brought in well over fifty million in stocks and bonds alone."

"But no one man could make that much money without making headlines as well. And I never heard of him until I stumbled across his trail three months ago, as a small investor."

"Exactly. Up until three months ago, his name wasn't Mariner. He used half-a-dozen other names over the years. That was part of the plan, to keep switching identities. And that was part of our job—to go around, when he changed his name, and erase memories of his previous existence. As I told you, we have similar operatives all over the country.

"Then, about three months ago, he decided to change his name on his own. He'd been armed with advance information, told what to invest and where to invest it. So he decided to skip out on us and work for himself. He took the Mariner name, started to dodge around the country. In ninety days he managed to pile up close to five million in cash profits. Then we caught up with him." Harry rubbed his chin again.

"Why are you telling me all this?" I asked.

He grinned. "Because I like your face."

"You're not going to try to kill me, too," I said. "You couldn't get away with that."

"Certainly not." He took the gun out of my ribs. "Here, you might as well have this, too." And he held the weapon out to me.

"But—"

"Go ahead, take it. It isn't loaded, anyway. Besides, it's your gun. I found it in your suitcase."

I blinked. "Why—"

Miss Fairborn smiled at me. "I think I know what Harry has in mind," she said. "He's asking you to join us. Aren't you, dear?"

"That's right," Harry said.

"You see," she said, "now we need someone to take Mr. Mariner's place. And since you seem to be alone in the world—"

"Exactly." Harry nodded pleasantly. "An ideal candidate."

"What if I don't like the idea?" I asked.

"Nonsense! That's why you followed Mr. Mariner, wasn't it?" Miss Fairborn said. "Because you wanted to make millions. That's been your big dream for a long time, hasn't it? Well, this is an opportunity to make your dream come true. From now on you'll be doing just that. You'll go from city to city—under a variety of names, of course—and you'll invest a fortune in securities. By the time the first year is ended you'll probably take in more cash than anyone else in the market today. What more could you ask from life?"

"But I won't be allowed to keep it. And I'll have to live under cover, in hotels, with people like you spying on me night and day, watching every move I make."

"The penalty of wealth," Miss Fairborn said.

"I won't have anything, not even a name. Nobody will know me, or even remember me after you've erased their memories."

"But think of the romance of being a man of mystery."

"I am thinking of it," I said. "And I don't like it. I don't like your proposition, and I don't like you. What's there to prevent me from just walking out of here, going to the police, and telling them your whole story? For that matter, I can probably get them to find Mariner's body."

"Probably," said Harry. "Suit yourself. But if you change your mind within the next hour, come on back. We'll be waiting right here for you."

"I won't be back," I told him, opening the door.

"Yes you will," Miss Fairborn called after me. "This is what you've always wanted. I'm sure you'll see it our way."

But, as I walked down the hall to my room, I didn't see it their way. I didn't understand it at all. They admitted murdering Mariner and they could have murdered me, too, just to be on the safe side. If their story was true, it would be worth the extra risk. Instead, they offered me this fantastic proposition—this living death. Why?

I didn't see it. Not until I was actually back in my room, not until I walked into the bathroom and saw him lying there in the tub, with a bullet in his forehead. The pillow through which it had been fired lay on the floor next to the tub. They'd thought of everything. The pillow had muffled the sound of the shot. And that's why Harry had come to my room. He'd murdered Mariner with *my* gun. No wonder he'd given it back to me!

Yes, I saw it now. The corpse was in my room, the fingerprints were on my gun. I'd been looking for Mariner, told everyone about him. Running away wouldn't help. If I wanted to get out of this, I'd have to rely on them. And that meant taking Mariner's place.

Only knowing what I did about the Syndicate, I'd never be able to try what Mariner had tried. I'd never get up enough nerve to run away and attempt to make money on my own. I'd just go on stooging forever—or until they decided they'd had enough.

I thought about it for the full hour. But long before the hour was up, I'd made my decision.

Finally, I walked back to their room and knocked on the door.

Miss Fairborn opened it. Her big eyes wide and luminous in welcome.

"All right," I said. "You win. But get me out of here, fast. I can't stand that body in there—"

She smiled. "Certainly. We've contacted our superiors and all arrangements have been made for you. Just check out of your room and stop worrying. Now, here're your orders . . ."

That was three weeks ago. Since then I've been to Detroit and Dallas and now I'm on my way to Kansas City. They gave me a new name—Lloyd Jones—and credentials to match. Everywhere I go, I am met by contacts who give me instructions. I make the investments and I sit in my hotel room. I can see where it's going to be an endless, monotonous grind.

But I can stand that part of it. It's just that lately, something else has started to worry me.

You see, I remember how I got on the trail of Mr. Mariner. I was ambitious; I wanted to find a man who had the secret of playing the market. So I looked around, and finally I found him. As a result, I was responsible for his death. At the very least, precipitated it.

No, it isn't my conscience that's bothering me.

It's this.

Somewhere, someplace, there must be others like myself—little guys with big ideas. And somewhere, sooner or later, another man is going to start looking for a fabulous character who seems to have the golden touch. He's going to run across my name, and he's going to make up his mind, like I did.

And then he'll come looking for me.

If he finds me—well, I remember only too well what happened to Mariner.

There's no sense trying to run; I'm trapped in my new identity. I can only wait until the man catches up with me. And, meanwhile, I'll keep on making millions. Doing what I always wanted to do—make a killing in the market.

But the next victim might very well be me.

# Do It Yourself

## by Charles Mergendahl

"**P**lease, Norman, *please!*" Corliss' voice rasped through the earpiece. "I asked you a simple question, and all I want is a simple answer. Did you change the water in the pool or didn't you? Answer me now!"

"Listen, Corliss—"

"It was filthy last Saturday, and you *promised,* Norman. And today is *Tuesday*."

"I know I promised, and I know it's Tuesday, and that's what I want to talk about." Mr. Pimsley wet his lips, moved them closer to the mouthpiece, dropped his voice to a hoarse whisper. "Corliss, is—is Gregg coming with you tonight?"

"Doesn't he always?"

"Yes, but not *tonight,* Corliss. I have to talk to you. I mean it's been so long—"

"Goodbye," Corliss said.

The phone clicked.

Mr. Pimsley hung up and sat there at the telephone stand for a long, thinking time. He thought, "Yes, doesn't Gregg always?" and "When is it going to stop?" It was unheard of—absolutely shocking—a man's own wife bringing home a young swimming instructor three times each week, for lessons according to Corliss, though she and Gregg were always so quiet out there in the dark summer nights, while he waited alone in the living room, almost frightened, trembling all through him because he knew, of course, that the lessons were an obvious sham, and they were both out there taunting him from the still, dark water of the pool.

Mr. Norman Pimsley was a round, balding man. "Ineffectual," Corliss called him, though he was an excellent gardener, a near professional cabinet maker, a mason of the first order. He'd practically built this house himself—all for Corliss. He'd grown American Beauty roses and delicate orchids in his little greenhouse—all for Corliss. A terrace for Corliss; a badminton court for Corliss. And then last year, the crowning achievement—a beautiful kidney-

87

shaped swimming pool—for Corliss and for young, blond-haired, arrogant Mr. Gregg "Adonis" Muller.

"Please, Corliss . . . Not *tonight*, Corliss." Mr. Pimsley waddled his little body through the cathedral-ceilinged living room, out through the glass door to the terrace that fronted the huge picture window. Night was dropping slowly and the crickets scraped in the grass and dark clouds gathered fast, so that he thought perhaps it would rain and that would solve everything because Corliss and Gregg would not go swimming after all.

He moved to the pool's edge, stared down at the quick streaks of light on the black water, and tried to imagine exactly what happened down there on those Tuesday, Thursday, and Saturday nights. All he could see from his chair in the living room were reflections of light on the picture window. All he could hear was Gregg's wild "Yi-ee!" as he leaped on the end of the diving board ("He always does a one and a half," Corliss boasted), and then the splash, followed by Corliss' "Here I come, Gregg!" and the lighter, daintier twang of the board, the smaller splash, and then always silence . . . secret, interminable silence.

What did they *do* in that still black water? "Teaching me to float," Corliss smiled sometimes. Or "We're swimming under water, of course." But what did they *really* do? Where did Gregg get that scratch along his muscular shoulder, and once, that lipstick a half-inch below his lip? And worst of all, why didn't he himself have the personal, masculine, husbandly courage to stop them—or at least go out there and see once and for all what was going on?

Well, he did not have the courage. And accordingly, for a long time now, he'd been planning to install lights around the pool, so that he could watch them easily from the safety of the living room. "Everyone lights his pool," he'd suggested casually to Corliss. "I mean it's very fashionable, you know." But she'd only smiled in that taunting way and said, "You built the pool for me, so it's *my* pool, and I will *not* have any lights glaring down on *my* pool. That is final."

"Of course not. No, not you, Corliss." Mr. Pimsley pulled his eyes from the dark water that held its own dark secrets, listened again to the summer sounds, then went back to the living room.

He sat and waited. He thought and remembered. And after a while, when the frustration and rage had built up to tremble all through his round little body, he rose abruptly, opened the desk drawer, and removed a revolver. It was a Japanese war souvenir.

Bad workmanship, with a small calibre and low muzzle velocity. But it would kill a man—even a strong young man. It would also kill a woman.

A car swung into the drive, and Mr. Pimsley hastily returned the weapon to the drawer, relieved that he could think no further on the matter. For though he certainly hated Gregg Muller enough to kill him, and though Corliss *was* taunting him, teasing him, driving him ever closer to insanity, still he was not fool enough to put himself in the electric chair through some stupid act of unthinking jealousy.

The front door swung open. Corliss wore a pink afternoon dress. Her arms were bare and brown. Her hair was yellow and long above her young face with the light blue eyes and the pouting red lips. Behind her, Gregg Muller loomed large and curly-haired. He wore slacks and a sport shirt and the kind of loud jacket that only the young and handsome can ever wear with ease.

"You *know* it's Tuesday," Corliss snapped as she crossed the room toward the hall and the bath beyond. "You *know* the water was filthy on Saturday, so there was no reason to make such a fuss on the telephone."

"I wasn't making a fuss, dear."

"Yackity-yack."

"I just thought—maybe once—well, you'd come home alone."

"Well, I won't. And for heaven's sake, don't grovel in front of Gregg."

Corliss tripped off to change to her bathing suit, and Gregg said, "I presume you don't approve of me, Mr. Pimsley. But considering I'm giving your wife *free* swimming lessons—" He laughed, masculine, sneering, defiant, then whirled and shouted, "Be ready before you are, Cor!" and dashed from the room.

Mr. Pimsley waited. The crickets sounded faint and distant. The desk drawer was still slightly ajar, so that if he wanted to, if he *had* to, he could jerk it open and snatch up the revolver, all in one continuous movement. But "Don't *make* me," he thought. "Please, Corliss, please don't *make* me."

In a moment, Gregg appeared from the guest room. As usual he wore tight red bathing trunks. He looked like a piece of sculpture, Mr. Pimsley thought. Tanned and hard and muscular, and as unfeeling as any statuary. He scarcely looked at Mr. Pimsley. "Come on, Cor!" he shouted to Corliss, then abruptly stood on his hands in the center of the rug. He walked back and forth for a while in that upside down position. "As though he *lives* here," Mr. Pimsley thought, while he squinted one eye and wondered whether or not it would be difficult to shoot a man straight through the heart while that man was upside down. He decided the back of the upside down curly head made a far better target, really a very good target.

Then Corliss entered. She wore the white, two-piece suit that displayed all her smooth soft curves of flesh. She laughed and said, "Don't be such a silly fool, Gregg," and Gregg, still upside down, said, "Limbering up, Cor. Getting ready for some real action."

Mr. Pimsley saw the wet-lipped way that Corliss looked at the man's upside down body. And then Gregg dropped abruptly to his feet, gave Corliss a frankly appraising, boldly anticipatory glance, and bounded out the door to the terrace and the pool beyond.

Corliss started after him.

"Dear," said Mr. Pimsley. Corliss was tucking yellow hair beneath a white bathing cap, standing with her weight on one leg in a way that reminded him of those rare intimate moments a few years back, before they were married, when she'd made him promises that she'd never had any intention of keeping. "Please, dear . . . Don't leave me alone tonight."

She laughed. Outside the springboard twanged up and down as sure-footed Gregg limbered up. "Please," begged Mr. Pimsley. "Please, I think it's going to rain tonight."

"It's not going to rain."

"Well, just sit . . . a while anyway, just a while . . . "

"Perhaps if you could *swim*," Corliss jeered. "If you didn't sink like a rock—if you weren't so fat and you weren't so old and you could play tennis or do *something* like a man."

"But I can do lots of things," Mr. Pimsley protested. "Flowers, and I'm very good in the workshop, you know. I mean just because I'm older than Gregg—well, a man finds other amusements—"

"Old do-it-yourself." Corliss snorted and started for the terrace.

"Please, Corliss." He jerked up from the chair, took a step after her. "I'm *begging* you, Corliss. *Please*."

She turned, stared at him with open contempt. "Don't beg, Norman. Don't ever *beg*!"

The twanging continued, until in a moment Gregg's voice sounded high in the familiar "Yi-ee!" as he made one final spring, followed by a quick silence, and the faint splash of water.

"A one and a half," said Mr. Pimsley.

"Beautiful," said Corliss wistfully. "He does everything so beautifully." She turned away again, and in that moment Mr. Pimsley knew that nothing he could ever say would keep her from going to Gregg—exactly as she'd done last Saturday and last Thursday—week after week, while he'd listened to the silence and wondered and wondered—and he knew, too, that he could not let it happen again. "Corliss!" he said sharply, then swung, drew the revolver from the drawer, and pointed it square at his wife's bare midriff.

Corliss half turned, saw the revolver, then finished the turn while a slow smile crept along her lips. "Mustn't play with guns, dear. They can be dangerous."

Mr. Pimsley's hand was shaking. His eyes stared at the tanned bare skin between the two thin strips of her bathing suit, and he thought that if he really did pull the trigger, then an ugly bloody hole would appear right in the center of that beautiful soft skin. He closed his eyes, squeezed them tight, opened them again. His voice shook. He said, "Corliss . . . I've asked you . . . I've begged you . . . Now I'm threatening you. Don't go swimming tonight."

The smile and, "Why is tonight so very important?"

"Corliss . . . listen . . . things build up . . . over a period of time . . . until suddenly a man can't go on any longer."

"Oh, you'll go on, Norman."

"Corliss, I swear . . . if you make one more move to go out there, I'll . . . I'll—"

"You'll what, dear?"

"I'll kill you."

Corliss' eyes narrowed a moment as she studied him. Then suddenly she laughed, high, mocking, completely unafraid. "You want the truth, darling? Well, here it is: I'd rather be dead than stay here one minute longer with you."

Mr. Pimsley lowered the gun. "You want to be with him *that* much?" he said, and Corliss said, *"That* much," and backed slowly toward the door. Mr. Pimsley watched her through half-closed misting eyes, the gun dangling impotent from his index finger. He lowered his head into his hands and knew, finally, that even threats were useless, though he'd tried, God knows, he'd tried, as he heard her low, derisive laugh and the soft patting of her bare feet as she skipped out to the terrace. He heard her voice, "I'm coming, Gregg!" and "Watch this one, Gregg!" and the faint twang of the diving board and the faint following splash and then the long secret silence with the crickets again, making the silence deeper and deeper until he could not stand it a moment longer.

He rose, put the gun in the drawer, and edged softly toward the terrace. His legs felt weak. Perspiration broke out beneath his shirt. In the doorway he paused, listening, listening, then crept softly, unseen, across the terrace to the edge of the pool. He'd never done this before, because in the past he'd never dared invade their privacy. Tonight, though, was different. Everything had finally come into the open. He'd asked, pleaded, threatened, all to no avail. She would rather be with Gregg, rather dead than be with him. "Corliss," he whispered inside himself. "Oh, Corliss . . . Corliss . . . " He took the final step, paused in the deep aching silence, then peered over the edge of the night-darkened pool.

At first he saw nothing but the black water against the blacker night. But then, in a moment, he found the two figures.

He pulled back; he could not bear to see them. A sob choked into his throat, and he stumbled toward the house, heedless of the noise because Gregg and Corliss had each other now and would not be listening . . .

He sat in the living room. The silence deepened. The crickets hummed. He waited . . . waited . . . trembling, perspiring, sick, sick all through him, until finally, when the silence was sure to burst inside him, he rose, wavering, and stumbled toward the phone. His finger shook as he dialed, and at first he could not speak at all. Finally, though, the words came out, choked, stammering, all run together. "Oh, God . . . I tried . . . I did everything . . . But it was too late, you see . . . I mean I wanted to put in lights, but she wouldn't *let* me, and I'd been draining the pool, just like she wanted me to, you see, except it wasn't finished and there were only a few inches of water left, you see . . . only a few *inches*, and it's such a dark night, and they didn't *know* . . . "

The police sergeant said they'd send a squad car immediately. He said, "Don't blame yourself, Mr. Pimsley. You mustn't blame yourself."

"Thank you," sobbed Mr. Pimsley. He hung up and sat there motionless, then dropped his head into his hands, crying uncontrollably, reminding himself that he *had* done everything to save her . . . everything a man could possibly do. He'd pleaded and begged; he'd commanded and threatened. But still she'd preferred to be with Gregg. Rather dead than stay with him. So of course he must never blame himself. He must never blame himself for anything . . .

# Lost and Found

## by James Michael Ullman

Phil was turning away from the cashier in the coffee shop of a hotel just outside Chicago's Loop when something he saw made him stop.

A well-dressed man in a business suit and horn-rimmed glasses had just hung his hat and coat in an unattended cloakroom; and as the man pulled a handkerchief from a hip pocket, his wallet fell to the floor.

It landed right at the man's feet, but he did not look down. Apparently engrossed in thought, he wiped his glasses with the handkerchief and then joined a young woman in the lobby. Together, they strolled into the cocktail lounge.

The wallet just lay there, filled with who-knew-what treasures.

Fascinated, Phil stared at it. Then he glanced around. Nobody seemed to have noticed. Could he get his hands on that wallet before someone else saw it? Well, nothing ventured, nothing gained...

There was a newspaper vending machine nearby. Phil bought a paper, left the coffee shop and approached the cloakroom. When he reached it, he let the paper slip to the floor.

He scooped up paper and wallet together, straightened, and looked around again.

As far as he could tell, he'd been unobserved. Back in the coffee shop, the cashier was talking to a waitress, a woman at the counter was lighting a cigarette, and a burly man in a booth was thumbing through a racing form.

As casually as he could, Phil got out of there and hurried up the street toward the dingy little hotel where he and Doris were staying, one that even lacked eating or drinking facilities for its guests.

Phil was a slight, pale, sandy-haired man in his early thirties. The chill Lake Michigan wind cut through the well-worn suit covering his thin frame, but his heart began pounding with anticipation.

Just arrived in Chicago from Indianapolis, where the home improvement firm for which he'd been selling overpriced awnings had folded, he and Doris were down to their last thirty dollars. If the wallet held anything of value, it would be a timely break for them.

Alone in the elevator on the way up to their room, he finally took the wallet from under the newspaper and looked inside.

There was no money in it—no doubt the man kept his currency in a money clip—but far better than any small sum of cash, there were twenty-four credit cards, plus a driver's license, several business cards and a Social Security card. All bore the name of Felix K. Moore, who apparently ran a real estate brokerage business in St. Louis.

"Credit cards?" Doris seemed disappointed. She was blonde, with hips a little too big and shoulders too narrow. When Phil had met her, she was a clerk in the home improvement dealer's office. They'd been living together for nearly two months now.

"What good are they?" Doris went on. "If we tried to use them they'd catch us and put us in jail."

Phil had to smile. Doris was still woefully uninformed about some things. She'd have to learn a few tricks if she expected to go on sharing his lifestyle.

"Not if we work fast enough, they won't," he explained. "It takes a while for the charges on those cards to go through the billing system. Even if the man who lost the wallet reported the loss right away, we might have up to a week or more, if we're not too greedy and don't charge too much in the same place. All I have to do is practice imitating the guy's signature, and that'll only take a few minutes. Look, don't you understand what this means?"

"Frankly, no."

"It means we won't have to knock ourselves out finding jobs here right away."

"Are those cards worth *that* much?"

"You bet. We can do practically anything with them. Rent cars, buy merchandise, eat at the best restaurants, stay at the best hotels. We can even take them to a bank and borrow money. You can have anything you want—dresses, coats, negligees, the works."

"You mean it?"

"Sure. Get your purse, and we'll go down to the Loop and hit some of the big stores."

"I don't know, Phil. Suppose—"

"Look," he reassured her, "don't *worry*. It might be hours before the guy notices his wallet is missing. The last time I saw him he was walking into a cocktail lounge, where he'll pay with cash. And if he's like most people, when he does find it's missing he won't even remember what some of the credit cards are. If he ever bothered to make a list of them, the list is probably buried in a desk drawer back in St. Louis."

"All right." Doris was beginning to pick up some of his enthusiasm. Eyes bright, she started for the dressing table. "I've always wanted to go into one of those big department stores and—"

A knock sounded at the door.

They exchanged glances.

The knock was repeated.

Phil called, "Who is it?"

"Open up," a man said. "I wanna talk to you about what you found in that cloakroom. And if you don't wanna talk to me, maybe I'll discuss it with the guy who lost it."

Cautiously, Phil opened the door.

Waiting outside was the burly man he'd seen in the booth in the coffee shop, the racing form jutting from a jacket pocket.

As Phil closed the door behind him, he walked in and sized up the room and voluptuous Doris.

"Well, well," the man drawled. "So you're Mr. and Mrs. Philip Brown. At least that's who the desk clerk said you were, when I told him I was a private cop on a divorce case. Where are you two from, Phil?"

Phil's eyes narrowed. "I don't see that it matters. What do you want?"

Towering over Phil, the man moved closer. "I want a cut of whatever's in the wallet you picked up. Let's have a look." He paused, and then added: "You gonna let me see it? Or do I have to take it away from you? I wouldn't *want* to get rough, now, but . . ."

The threat needed no elaboration. He outweighed Phil by about a hundred pounds and obviously could have handled him with ease.

Chewing at her lower lip, Doris said, "Don't lose your temper, Phil. It isn't worth it. Just give it to him."

Sullenly, Phil handed over the wallet.

The man settled in a chair and began leafing through it.

"There wasn't any cash," Phil said. "Just—"

"Yeah, I see. Credit cards. Oh, boy! He had all the big ones, didn't he, and some oil companies, a few national retail chains—and his driver's license yet! I mean, this is real good!"

He closed the wallet and slipped it into his pocket.

"Look here," Phil began, moving toward the man.

"Don't worry," the intruder said reassuringly, "I won't stiff you. If I did, you'd run to that guy in the cocktail lounge and holler your head off—and the longer before he knows these cards are missing, the better."

"Okay." Phil sighed. "As the saying goes, fifty percent of something is better than a hundred percent of nothing. I'll deal with you. We both saw him drop the wallet. You'd have picked it up if I hadn't, so I guess that's fair. But if we're going to be milking those cards together, let's get started."

"That's too dangerous. Yeah, I know the odds are ninety-nine in a hundred we wouldn't get caught, but I can't take even that little risk. I been in stir before. The cops here would like to get absolutely anything on me, so they could send me away again."

"I'll use the cards, then."

"Uh-uh. I'd have to waste a lot of time running around with you. And even if I did, no one man could squeeze the most possible out of these cards. No, what I had in mind was, I'd sell the cards outright to some guys I know. They're organized—they'll do things with these cards you wouldn't believe. They got a nationwide jet courier system. By tonight, guys will be using some of these cards in New York, Miami Beach, L.A., Vegas and who knows where else."

The man got to his feet. "These people I'm tellin' you about," he continued, "don't deal with just *anybody,* only with people they know. They don't know you, but they know me. So the simplest thing would be for me to buy the cards from you, and then sell the cards to them."

"Buy them from me for how much?" Phil asked suspiciously.

"A hundred bucks."

"A hundred?" Phil was incredulous. "Why, that's—"

"A fair price, if you ask me." The man pulled a wad of bills from his pocket.

"It isn't fair at all," Phil said angrily. "On the black market, some of those cards are worth at least a hundred bucks *apiece.*"

"They are," the man replied blandly, "if you can *find* the black market. And if the black market will do business with you. Look at it this way: I can see from this hotel room that fooling around with all these credit cards is out of your league anyhow, and there's always the chance you'd get caught. But my way, you get the hundred for sure—no risk, no strain. You found the wallet about fifteen minutes ago. You're getting a hundred bucks for fifteen minutes of your time. That's four hundred bucks an hour, or thirty-two hundred for an eight-hour day."

"I don't think that's very funny."

"Neither do I. I'm just trying to tell you why it's a fair price. Here."
He held out a hundred dollars.

Phil just stared at it.

The man studied Phil. Then he shrugged and dropped the bills
onto a table.

"You'll feel better," he said, "after you think it over. I'll leave the
dough here. Just one thing: now that this organization I told you
about is involved, don't say a word about this to anyone. If you do,
you'll wind up with your arms and legs busted and maybe a hole in
your head." He turned to leave.

Phil was furious. It was so unfair! All the things he and Doris
could have done with those cards . . . The hundred would be gone
in a few days, and they'd be back on the same old treadmill.

"No, that's not enough," Phil said, springing forward and grabbing
the man's arm. "You can't just—"

"Let go." With ease, the man pushed Phil against the wall and
turned to leave again.

There was a heavy bronze ashtray on the table. In a rage, Phil
picked it up with both hands, stepped behind the man, raised it and
brought it down on the man's head as hard as he could.

The man crumpled.

Phil kept hitting him, again and again, until suddenly he realized
there was no point to it anymore.

His rage gone, replaced by a growing comprehension of the enormity of what he had just done, he stood motionless as Doris bent
over the man's limp form.

She looked up and announced, "He's dead."

"I didn't mean to . . . "

"Well, you killed him. You and that temper of yours." She was on
her feet, wringing her hands. "How'll I ever get out of *this?* Phil,
honey, I don't want to get you in trouble, but you know I didn't have
anything to do with it. *You* found that wallet, *you* brought it up
here, that man had the fight with *you.* I was just watching. To protect
myself, I'll have to call the police and tell them everything. If I don't,
they'll think I'm an accomplice, what they call an accessory. You
understand that, don't you?"

"Sure, but—"

"Anyhow," she went on, "it's not as though you *meant* to kill him.
It's what they call 'in the heat of passion.' And since he's so much
bigger than you, and probably some kind of gangster, they won't

send you away for long. Probably just for a couple years, although it would have been better if you hadn't hit him so many times."

She reached for the phone, but Phil grabbed her wrist.

"Listen," he said tensely, his mind racing as he tried to figure how to bring the situation under control, "don't panic. The police don't have to get either of us."

"Don't be silly, Phil. We—"

"Hear me out. We've only been in this city two days. Nobody here knows us. All they have downstairs at the desk is my name—Philip Brown. It's a real common name. They won't even know where to start looking for me. You ever been arrested or fingerprinted?"

"No."

"Neither have I."

"But the people in this hotel can describe us. And there's a dead man in this room."

"He won't be found until tomorrow morning, when the maid comes to clean. Oh, sure, if we were still in Chicago tomorrow, the police could track us down, but we won't be here. And I won't be Phil Brown anymore."

"What do you mean?"

"We'll be thousands of miles away, and I'll be Felix K. Moore. Our first stop will be that bank down the street. We'll borrow fifty bucks on one of Moore's credit cards, for walking-around money. We'll take a cab to the airport and charge tickets to L.A. And after we get to California, we'll clean up."

"With the credit cards?"

"Sure. We won't fool around buying clothes. We'll concentrate on airline tickets, lots of airline tickets, to places all over the world. Airline tickets are almost as good as currency, if we sell them below cost. We'll sell the tickets to some people I know out there, and unload the credit cards too. Then I'll pick some other name, and we'll wind up with at least four or five thousand bucks. Enough to take it easy for a while down in Mexico, where money goes a lot further, until we figure what to do next."

"I don't know . . . "

"Wouldn't you like that?" he persisted. "Nothing to do but lie around the beach all day, instead of spending the winter up here in Chicago? Without any money? Killing yourself in a dead-end job while waiting to testify at my trial?"

"You really think," she wondered aloud, "we could get away with it?"

"I *know* we can. We'll leave without luggage or anything. Just take your papers, and anything else that could identify you. You'll see how easy it is."

"All right," she said, suddenly thinking about the four or five thousand dollars. After they got to California, she'd have enough on Phil to make him give her most of that money, after which she'd dump him. "I'll do it."

Back in the coffee shop, the man in the horn-rimmed glasses, the young woman at his side, approached the cashier and said, "Excuse me, but did anyone find a wallet here in the last fifteen minutes or so?"

"No," the girl told him. "But you might try the desk in the lobby."

"I already have."

"Well, I'm terribly sorry, sir, but—"

"Oh, that's all right." He smiled. "Actually, I'm almost certain I left it in another suit. I just thought I'd check, in case."

He and the young woman walked outside.

"It worked," he announced with satisfaction. "The wallet's no longer in front of the cloakroom, where I dropped it, and nobody turned it in. That means whoever found it will try to use those credit cards."

"Confidentially," the woman said in an amused voice, "that was a dirty trick. We've already run up about fifteen thousand in phony charges on those cards ourselves. By now they must be at the top of every hot sheet in the country."

"Exactly," he told her. "The first time the guy tries to use one, he'll be arrested. And for a while, anyhow, the police and the credit card companies will assume *he* ran up all those phony charges. It'll take the heat off us. And when the money runs out, we'll steal another set of cards from some drunk in a bar, like we stole Moore's back in St. Louis, and start all over again."

# Passport in Order

## by Lawrence Block

**M**arcia stood up, yawned, and crushed out a cigarette in the round glass ashtray. "It's late," she said. "I should be getting home. How I hate to leave you!"

"You said it was his poker night."

"It is, but he might call me. Sometimes, too, he loses a lot of money in a hurry and comes home early, and in a foul mood, naturally." She sighed, turned to look at him. "I wish it didn't have to be secretive like this—hotel rooms, motels."

"It can't stay this way much longer."

"Why not?"

Bruce Farr ran a hand through his wavy hair, groped for a cigarette and lit it. "Inventory is scheduled in a month," he said. "It won't be ten minutes before they discover I'm into them up to the eyes. They're a big firm, but a quarter of a million dollars worth of jewelry can't be eased out of the vaults without someone noticing it sooner or later."

"Did you take that much?"

He grinned. "That much," he said, "a little at a time. I picked pieces no one would ever look for, but the inventory will show them gone. I made out beautifully on the sale, honey; peddled some of the goods outright and borrowed on the rest. Got a little better than a hundred thousand dollars, safely stowed away."

"All that money," she said. She pursed her lips as if to whistle. "A hundred thousand. . . ."

"Plus change." His smile spread and she thought how pleased he was with himself. Then he became serious. "Close to half the retail value. It went pretty well, Marcia, but we can't sit on it. We have to get out, out of the country."

"I know, but I'm afraid," Marcia said.

"They won't get us. Once we're out of the country, we don't have a thing to worry about. There are countries where you can buy yourself citizenship for a few thousand U.S. dollars, and beat extradition forever. They can't get us."

She was silent for a moment. When he took her hand and asked her what was wrong, she turned away, then met his eyes. "I'm not that worried about the police. If you say we can get away with it, well, I believe you."

"Then what's scaring you?"

"It's Ray," she said and dropped her eyes. "Ray, my sweet loving husband. He'll find us, darling. I know he will. He'll find us, and he won't care whether we're citizens of Patagonia or Cambodia or wherever we go. He won't try to extradite us. He'll . . ." her voice broke, "he'll kill us," she finished.

"How can he find us? And what makes you think. . . ."

She was shaking her head. "You don't know him."

"I don't particularly want to. Honey. . . ."

"You don't know him," she repeated. "I do. I wish I didn't, I wish I'd never met him. I'm one of his possessions, I belong to him, and he wouldn't let me get away from him, not in a million years. He knows all kinds of people, terrible people. Criminals, gangsters." She gnawed her lip. "Why do you think I never left him? Why do you think I stay with him? Because I know what would happen if I didn't. He'd find me, one way or another, and he'd kill me, and. . . ."

She broke. His arms went around her and held her, comforted her.

"I'm not giving you up," he said, "and he won't kill us. He won't kill either of us."

"You don't *know* him." Panic rose in her voice. "He's vicious, ruthless. He. . . ."

"Suppose we kill him first, Marcia?"

He had to go over it with her a long time before she would even listen to him. They had to leave the country anyway. Neither of them was ready to spend a lifetime, or part of it, in jail. Once they were out they could stay out. So why not burn an extra bridge on the way? If Ray was really a threat to them, why not put him all the way out of the picture?

"Besides," he told her, "I'd like to see him dead. I really would. For months now you've been mine, yet you always have to go home to him."

"I'll have to think about it," she said.

"You wouldn't have to do a thing, baby. I'd take care of everything."

She nodded, got to her feet. "I never thought of—murder," she said. "Is this how murders happen? When ordinary people get caught up over their heads? Is that how it starts?"

"We're not ordinary people, Marcia. We're special. And we're not in over our heads. It'll work."

"I'll think about it," she said. "I'll—I'll think about it."

Marcia called Bruce two days later. She said, "Do you remember what we were taking about? We don't have a month any more."

"What do you mean?"

"Ray surprised me last night. He showed me a pair of airline tickets for Paris. We're set to fly in ten days. Our passports are still in order from last year's trip. I couldn't stand another trip with him, dear. I couldn't live through it."

"Did you think about. . . ."

"Yes, but this is no time to talk about it," she said. "I think I can get away tonight."

"Where and when?"

She named a time and place. When she placed the receiver back in its cradle she was surprised that her hand did not tremble. So easy, she thought. She was deciding a man's fate, planning the end of a man's life, and her hand was as steady as a surgeon's. It astonished her that questions of life and death could be so easily resolved.

She was a few minutes late that night. Bruce was waiting for her in front of a tavern on Randolph Avenue. As she approached, he stepped forward and took her arm.

"We can't talk here," he said. "I don't think we should chance being seen together. We can drive around. My car's across the street."

He took Claibourne Drive out to the east end of town. She lit a cigarette with the dashboard lighter and smoked in silence. He asked her what she had decided.

"I tried not to think about it," she told him. "Then last night he sprang this jaunt on me, this European tour. He's planning on spending three weeks over there. I don't think I could endure it."

"So?"

"Well, I got this wild idea. I thought about what you said, about—about killing him. . . ."

"Yes?"

She drew a breath, let it out slowly. "I think you're right. We have to kill him. I'd never rest if I knew he was after us. I'd wake up terrified in the middle of the night. I know I would. So would you."

He didn't say anything. His eyes were on hers and he clasped her hands.

"I guess I'm a worrier. I'd worry about the police, too. Even if we managed to do what you said, to buy our way out of extradition. The things you read, I don't know. I'd hate to feel like a hunted animal for the rest of my life. I'd rather have the police hunting me than Ray, but even so, I don't think I'd like it."

"So?"

She lit another cigarette. "It's probably silly," she said. "I thought there might be a way to keep them from looking for you, and to get rid of him at the same time. Last night it occurred to me that you're about his build. About six-one, aren't you?"

"Just about."

"That's what I thought. You're younger, and you're much better looking than he is, but you're both about the same height and weight. And I thought— Oh, this is silly!"

"Keep going."

"Oh, this is the kind of crazy thing you see on television. I don't know what kind of a mind I must have to think of it. But I thought that you could leave a note. You'd go to sleep at your house, then get up in the middle of the night and leave a long note explaining how you stole jewelry from your company and lost the money gambling and kept stealing more money and getting in deeper and deeper until there's no way out. And that you're doing the only thing you can do, that you've decided, well, to commit suicide."

"I think I'm beginning to get it."

Her eyes lowered. "It doesn't make any sense, does it?"

"It sure does. You're about as crazy as a fox. Then we kill Ray and make it appear to be me."

She nodded. "I thought of a way we could do it. I can't believe it's really me saying all of this! I thought we could do it that same night. You would come over to the house and I would let you in. We could get Ray in his sleep. Press a pillow over his face or something like that. I don't know. Then we could load him into your car and drive somewhere and. . . ."

"And put him over a cliff." His eyes were filled with frank admiration. "Beautiful, just beautiful."

"Do you really think so?"

"It couldn't be better. They'll have a perfect note, in my handwriting. They'll have my car over a cliff and a burned body in it. And they'll have a good motive for suicide. You're a wonder, honey."

She managed a smile. "Then your company won't be hunting you, will they?"

"Not me or their money. *Gambled every penny away*—that'll throw 'em a curve. I haven't bet more than two bucks on a horse in my life. But your sweetheart of a husband will be gone, and somebody might start wondering where he is. Oh, wait a minute. . . ."

"What?"

"This gets better the more I think about it. He'll take my place in the car and I'll take his on that plane to Europe. We're the same build, his passport is in good order, and the reservations are all made. We'll use those tickets to take the Grand Tour, except that we won't come back. Or if we do, we'll wind up in some other city where nobody knows us, baby. We'll have every bridge burned the minute we cross over. When are you scheduled to take that trip?"

She closed her eyes, thought it through. "A week from Friday," she said. "We fly to New York in the morning, and then on to Paris the next afternoon."

"Perfect. You can expect company Thursday night. Slip downstairs after he goes to bed and let me into the house. I'll have the note written. We'll take care of him and go straight to the airport. We won't even have to come back to the house."

"The money?"

"I'll have it with me. You can do your packing Thursday so we'll have everything ready, passports and all." He shook his head in disbelief. "I always knew you were wonderful Marcia. I didn't realize you were a genius."

"You really think it will work?"

He kissed her and she clung to him. He kissed her again, then grinned down at her. "I don't see how it can miss," he said.

The days crawled. They couldn't risk seeing each other until Thursday night, but Bruce assured Marcia that it wouldn't be long.

But it *was* long. Although she found herself far calmer than she had dared to expect, Marcia was still anxious, nervous about the way it might go.

Oh, it was long, very long. Bruce called Wednesday afternoon to make final plans. They arranged a calling system. When Ray was sleeping soundly, she would slip out of bed and go downstairs. She would dial his phone number. He would have the note written, the money stowed in the trunk of his car. As soon as she called he would come over to her house, and she would be waiting downstairs to let him in.

"Don't worry about what happens then," he said. "I'll take care of the details."

That night and the following day consumed at least a month of subjective time for her. She called him, finally, at twenty minutes of three Friday morning. He answered at once.

"I thought you weren't going to call at all," he said.

"He was up late, but he's asleep now."

"I'll be right over."

She waited downstairs at the front door, heard his car pull to a stop, had the door open for him before he could knock. He stepped quickly inside and closed the door.

"All set," he said. "The note, everything."

"The money?"

"It's in the trunk, in an attache case, packed to the brim."

"Fine," she said. "It's been fun, darling."

But Bruce never heard the last sentence. Just as her lips framed the words, a form moved behind him and a leather-covered sap arced downward, catching him deftly and decisively behind the right ear. He fell like a stone and never made a sound.

Ray Danahy straightened up. "Out cold," he said. "Neat and sweet. Take a look outside and check the traffic. This is no time for nosy neighbors."

She opened the door, stepped outside. The night was properly dark and silent. She filled her lungs gratefully with fresh air.

Ray said, "Pull his car into the driveway alongside the house. Wait a sec, I think he's got the keys on him." He bent over Farr, dug a set of car keys out of his pocket. "Go ahead," he said.

She brought the car to the side door. Ray appeared in the doorway with Bruce's inert form over one shoulder. He dumped him onto the back seat and walked around the car to get behind the wheel.

"Take our buggy," he told Marcia. "Follow me, but not too close. I'm taking 32 north of town. There's a good drop about a mile and a half past the county line."

"Not too good a drop, I hope," she said. "He could be burned beyond recognition."

"No such thing. Dental X-rays—they can't miss. It's a good thing he didn't have the brains to think of that."

"He wasn't very long on brains," she said.

"*Isn't*," he corrected. "He's not dead yet."

She followed Ray, lagging about a block and a half behind him. At the site he had chosen, she stood by while he took the money from the trunk and checked Farr's pockets to make sure he wasn't

carrying anything that might tip anybody off. Ray propped him
behind the wheel, put the car in neutral, braced Farr's foot on the
gas pedal. Farr was just beginning to stir.

"Goodbye, Brucie," Marcia said. "You don't know what a bore you
were."

Ray reached inside and popped the car into gear, then jumped
aside. The heavy car hurtled through an ineffective guard rail, hung
momentarily in the air, then began the long fast fall. First, there
was the noise of the impact. Then there was another loud noise, an
explosion, and the vehicle burst into flames.

They drove slowly away, the suitcase full of money between them
on the seat of their car. "Scratch one fool," Ray said pleasantly.
"We've got two hours to catch our flight to New York, then on to
Paris."

"Paris," she sighed. "Not on a shoestring, the way we did it last
time. This time we'll do it in style."

She looked down at her hands, her steady hands. How surprisingly
calm she was, she thought, and a slow smile spread over her face.

# Moonlight Gardener

## by Robert L. Fish

"**A**nd the fights! Oh, the fights! Ah, the fights!" Mrs. Williams said piously, leaning forward, her ungainly flowered hat almost toppling, her small china-blue eyes intent upon the young sergeant's unrevealing face. "Awful! *Awful!*" She paused significantly. "Especially the terrible one they had the night before last—Wednesday, it was," she said, and paused again, almost breathlessly. "The night she disappeared," she added meaningfully.

"Disappeared." The sergeant started to write the word down on his lined pad and then stopped halfway to end it in a wiggly squiggle, culminated in an almost vicious dot. He wished, not for the first time, that he had chosen a different line of endeavor for his life's work; he had a strong feeling he knew what was coming.

"Disappeared. That's what I said," Mrs. Williams said sharply. "She hasn't been seen since—and that's disappearance, isn't it?" The edge of poorly concealed disdain tinged her voice. "And then *that man* trying to tell me, when I went over to borrow a cup of sugar—"

"You were out of sugar," the sergeant murmured politely, and carefully printed the word SUGAR on his pad. He hated busybodies of all types, but particularly those like the woman facing him, and not merely because they caused the police a great deal of work that almost inevitably was pointless. He wondered how life must have been in those delightful days before neighbors-within-earshot. Beautiful, without a doubt.

Mrs. Williams' little chin hardened. Her eyes defied him to attempt avoiding the responsibilities of his office with such flimsy tactics. Her well-tended hands clasped themselves more tightly about her purse, as if it might not be safe in this world of predators, even here in the local police station.

"*That man* was trying to tell me," she went on inexorably, a juggernaut not to be stopped, "that she was out shopping. Before eight in the morning, when the stores in town don't open until nine!"

The sergeant made a series of little 9's to border the mutilated DISAPPEARED and the intact SUGAR.

"And she wasn't home all day," Mrs. Williams declared flatly, "because I was watching. And then, this morning, I went over again, because I was worried about her, and *he* comes up with an entirely new story this time, about how she suddenly decided late last night to visit her sister. Which is a bit strange, since she doesn't have a sister and I know that for a gospel fact!"

The sergeant carefully printed NO SISTER on the paper before him, boxed the words neatly with his pencil, and began shading the enclosed parallelogram. He kept his eyes from the rather pretty face of the woman across from him. At the moment, she wasn't all that pretty.

"And how could she possibly have gone away in the middle of the night the way he said—without my hearing, I mean?" Mrs. Williams demanded, "My house is the only one nearby and I'm sure, if Mr. Jenkins had come for her in his taxi—or even if he drove her to either the train or the bus station—I would have heard."

"I'm sure," the sergeant said, and added under his breath, "at any hour, day or night," and he made a series of tiny loops to border the shaded box on his pad. They intertwined with the curved 9's very nicely.

Her blue eyes studied the expressionless face across from her and then dropped to the artistic calligraphy on the pad. Her jaw tightened dangerously, but she kept her voice under control as she brought up her heaviest artillery.

"And then last night," she said, her tone almost vicious, "after two in the morning, he digs up one of the small peach trees in the garden, and then, fifteen minutes later—or maybe a half-hour, no more—I can hear him out there replanting it. And her gone—disappeared—more than twenty-four hours! Now," she said, her tone, her angle of incidence, her entire bearing daring him to downgrade her testimony, "what is your smart-aleck answer to that, young man? Does it make sense for a man to dig up a tree in the middle of the night, and then replant it a half-hour later? Does it? Well?"

The sergeant laid aside the pencil with a certain sense of reluctance and for the first time really studied the woman facing him. The spiteful expression spoiled what he knew might have been beauty under different circumstances; the faint sneer disgusted him. But he couldn't deny the substance of her arguments.

"No," he admitted in his drawl. "No, it doesn't."

"Well! I'm glad you finally realize it, young man. And the money was all hers, too," Mrs. Williams added, almost as an afterthought. She was quite aware that the statement was anticlimactic, but she definitely wanted it included in the record of evidence.

"Money?"

"In the safe-deposit box with her jewels. The money that bought the house, even though everything is in both their names. You wait and see," she added, leaning forward again. "He'll be having it up for sale within a week. He never did a day's work since they married—if he ever did one before, which I seriously doubt!"

There were several moments' silence. The sergeant made the first move, bringing his considerable bulk to his feet, indicating the interview was over. He waited as she came to her five-feet-two-inches of height, looking up at him defiantly.

"I'll take the matter up with the sheriff, ma'am," he said.

"I should certainly hope so, young man," she retorted coldly, studying him once again with eyes that were quite unimpressed. Then she marched from the station house, the fur piece about her neck seeming to hurry to catch up with her.

"I suppose we'll have to check it out," the sheriff said wearily. "I don't know too many people in this town—most of my time is spent over in Bellerville at the county seat—but I do happen to know Charley Crompton. The idea of him doing away with that battle-axe he married is simply ridiculous. If he has a temper, I've never seen it. He's a mouse. If it was the other way around, I might believe it. But Charley! Impossible. At any rate, it's just a rumor from that nosy woman at this stage."

He glanced up at the husky young sergeant. "I don't suppose you've had time to do anything about it yet?"

"Well," the sergeant said, considering, "old Sol Jenkins—he's our taxi here—he didn't pick her up, last night or any other time. He laughed and said he didn't believe she ever took a taxi in her life. They cost money. And if Charley drove her, or if she walked across the fields to the station, nobody caught either the eight o'clock or the midnight train, and that's the last one. And the ticket men at both the train and the bus station don't remember her on any train or bus in the last two days, afternoon or night."

"What about this Mrs. Williams' husband?" the sheriff asked. "Mr. Williams? Does he confirm or deny it?"

"There *is* no Mr. Williams," the sergeant said. His tone commended the shade of Mr. Williams for his wisdom in being the nonexistent spouse of the meddling Mrs. Williams. "She's been a widow over four years." He shook his head. "She's only forty, but I think she's been forty all her life. Doesn't have anything to do all day except sit on the telephone or write letters to the editor of the *Bugle*. She's a feminist. I gather she even had Mrs. Crompton all worked up on the stuff."

The sheriff smiled. "But not your wife?" he said.

"Not yet, at any rate," the sergeant said, and grinned back.

The sheriff's smile faded. "Any other neighbors?"

"About a half-mile away, the nearest. Those two houses stand all alone at the end of the road. Around a curve from the others, as a matter of fact. They're pretty isolated."

"I see." The sheriff drummed his fingers and then looked up. "What about that statement regarding money?"

"Well," the sergeant said slowly, frowning, "the money was Mrs. Crompton's—*is* hers, I mean. Everybody in town knew that, but if every man who marries a dollar or two killed his wife for it, we'd be in real trouble. And as far as Charley Crompton telling that busybody neighbor of his that his wife was out shopping, or visiting a sister that doesn't exist, I don't see where he had a duty to tell her anything. If it had been me, I'd have told her my wife was off to Timbuktu, and let her make something of it."

"That's just what she's been doing," the sheriff pointed out. "Still, a man replanting a tree in the middle of the night—well, it seems rather—"

"I know," the sergeant said unhappily, and sighed. "We'll have to look into it a lot deeper, I know."

The man who opened the door of the large old-fashioned house was a nondescript person with thin brown hair pasted against his head and large brown eyes swimming behind thick lenses. He was dressed in slacks and a sweater, neither impressive, and carried a hatchet in a hand one finger of which was heavily bandaged. A honing stone had been tucked under his arm to allow him a free hand with the latch. He took the honing stone from the pit of his arm and allowed the two implements to dangle; they seemed to weigh down his thin arms.

"Hello, sergeant. What can I do for you?"

"Hello, Charley. Actually, it was your wife I'd hoped to see."

"Well, you can't," Crompton said apologetically. "She isn't here. She's gone away."

"Oh? To visit her sister?"

The smaller man turned his head to stare reproachfully at the house across the road, and down a bit from his. His eyes came back to the patient face of the sergeant.

"Her brother. She has no sister."

"And his name and address?" The sergeant produced a pad and pencil.

"Brown. John Brown." No muscle moved in Crompton's thin face, nor did his hesitant voice reveal anything. He sounded as if he were repeating something by rote. "I don't have his street address or telephone. Chicago is all I know."

"John Brown, Chicago," the sergeant repeated genially, and wrote it down, not at all perturbed. He looked up from his pad. "I say, Charley, would you mind a lot if we went inside to talk. I mean, standing here in the doorway . . ."

"Do you have a warrant to enter these premises?"

The young sergeant was surprised. He managed to turn his expression into one of slight hurt. "A warrant? To visit an old friend for a few moments? Although," he added, considering it, "I suppose one could be arranged, but it seems a bit foolish."

Crompton's thin lips compressed. He hesitated a moment and then, with a shrug, led the way inside, laying the hatchet and hone in a shelf in the entranceway and continuing into the living room. The sergeant picked the hatchet from its resting place and followed. He lowered his bulk into a chair and studied the instrument in his hand, touching the edge gingerly.

"Quite sharp," he observed.

"I like my tools in order," Crompton said evenly, and continued to watch the other man through his thick glasses.

"Oh? It's a shame it's so stained, then. Other than the honed edge, of course." The sergeant peered more closely. "These brown blotches, for example . . ."

"They're blood, if you want to know," Crompton said abruptly. "I cut my finger yesterday while I was honing it."

"Fingers do bleed like the devil," the sergeant admitted, and placed the hatchet on the floor beside his chair. He looked about the sunlit room and nodded. "A nice place you have here, Charley. I envy you. My wife was saying just the other day how small our house was getting, with two kids here and another on the way. But it's so hard to find a house near enough to the station house not to spend a week's pay on gas, or one that's a decent size any more. A house for sale, that is." A sudden thought struck him. "I don't suppose—well, I don't suppose you have any idea of selling, do you?"

There were several moments of silence as Charley Crompton appeared to gauge the man seated across from him. A mantel clock above the fireplace filled the quiet with a loud and steady ticking.

"I might," Charley Crompton said at last.

"You're sure your wife wouldn't object?"

"No." It was a flat statement, expressionless. Crompton seemed to feel that the discussion had taken enough of his time. He came to his feet. "Well, sergeant, I'm rather occupied, and if that's all the business you had in mind . . ."

The sergeant rose dutifully and smiled.

"If there's any possibility of the house being up for sale in the near future," he said, "I don't imagine you'd mind greatly if I looked it over? We're really interested, you know." He turned and walked into the kitchen with Crompton on his heels. "Say! This is a nice-sized kitchen. My wife puts a good deal of store by the kitchen. Me, I'm more fussy about the cellar and the yard, the places I spend most of my free time." He opened a door, saw brooms, and closed it. He opened another door. "Stairs to the basement, eh? Do you mind?" He flicked a light switch without awaiting permission, and descended with the smaller man right behind him. He stood and shook his head forlornly. "What a damned shame! What happened to your nice concrete floor?"

"Line under it burst," Crompton said in a rather constricted voice. He cleared his throat. "Line from the sinks over to the septic tank. Had to dig it all up and replace an elbow."

"Tough luck," the sergeant said sympathetically. "Guess contractors weren't much better in those days than they are today. But, other than that, it's a nice dry cellar. Gas heat, too, I see. Well, let's take a look at the back yard, while I'm here. I'm sure you won't mind."

They climbed the steps and walked through the kitchen to the back porch and the enclosed yard. One of the peach trees did, indeed, list slightly, and the fresh earth packed about its base was cleared of grass, reddish-brown in color, like a bad bruise. But the sergeant had been expecting that. What he had not been expecting was to see a second peach tree lying on its side beside a deep excavation, its root ball wrapped in canvas, or a third with a hole begun at its edge and a shovel thrust into the soil there. He glanced at his host.

"Trouble with your peach trees?"

"Tree roots need air," Crompton said. His voice was unnatural, as if he, too, needed air. "My own idea, but it's a valid one. I dig up trees and replant them quite frequently. I—" He paused a moment, eyeing the sergeant as if pleading for belief, and then continued, "It's the truth! They really do, you know. Need fresh air, I mean. They're living creatures; they can't stand not having air. The branches and the leaves get their share, but that's not enough." He shook his head, and behind his thick glasses, his eyes were impossible to interpret. "It's the roots, you see. That's the important part! They need air. It's the truth."

He leaned back, balancing himself on his heels, a trifle breathless, staring at the excavated peach tree and the dark hole it had left behind in the earth.

"A few more hours," he said as if to himself, "and the roots will be fine. Ready to bury again."

The large young sergeant sighed and turned toward the gate leading to the street and his parked patrol car.

"I'll probably be back again," he said conversationally. "I'm sure you won't mind. I'm really quite interested in this house."

"Are you trying to tell me Charley Crompton is a nut?" the sheriff asked. "The last thing from a nut! He's pulling our leg. A policeman shows up at his house and asks where his wife is, and he doesn't even ask why! And that mound in the basement, and that hatchet bit! Cut himself honing the thing the day before, and he's still walking around with the hone the day after!"

"It really was blood, I suppose? Not ketchup, or paint?"

"It was blood, all right. The same type as his. We don't know his wife's type; she never gave anything away, not even blood."

The sergeant turned and paced the room, his large hands locked behind his back, his face grim. He paused and faced the sheriff. "And he *did* have a bad gash under that bandage. I think I'd have preferred to believe him if he didn't." He shook his head, frowning. "More than ten days, and we're where we were when we started. Even further behind, in fact. He's having fun with us, I tell you!"

The sheriff bit at an outcropping of fingernail. "You got your warrant, though, didn't you? I spoke to Judge—"

"Oh, we got the warrant, right enough," the sergeant said darkly, and dropped into his chair, putting a knee against the edge of the desk. "And we dug up the cellar floor. And all we found was an elbow."

"An *elbow*?" The sheriff sat more erect.

"A plumber's elbow," the sergeant said grimly. "Exactly as he told us. New. We dug another three feet down, too, down to solid rock—just in case. She certainly isn't buried there, I can tell you that."

"Could she have *been* buried there?"

"That I don't know," the sergeant said bitterly. "There was more than enough room, but we didn't find any signs. All I know is that she isn't buried there now."

"Nor under the peach trees, either, I gather."

"Nor under anything in the whole damned back yard, and we gave his tree roots all the air they could handle! Ten days and nothing at all!" He shook his head broodingly and then looked up. "Oh, yes. He put the house up for sale this morning. I spoke to Jimmy Glass at the bank; Crompton and his wife exchanged powers of attorney the day they got married, so that's that."

The sheriff frowned. "So what's *his* explanation as to his wife's disappearance?"

"He finally broke down and confessed," the sergeant said bitterly. "According to Charley, they had this big quarrel he was ashamed to admit, and she just up and walked out on him—and of course his pride would never allow him to tell perfect strangers like us about it. They fought and she just upped and away, like that."

"And disappeared into thin air?"

"His idea—or what he says is his idea—is that she probably got to the highway and some kindly soul in a car or a truck picked her up and gave her a lift. That was his second idea. His first was that she caught a Greyhound bus, until I told him we'd checked all the buses. He says he has no idea where she'd head for, but he doesn't expect her back because she's stubborn. He says maybe she went to her brother's, but he honestly doesn't know the address. Just John Brown, in Chicago." He snorted. "And all we got from the cops there, when we asked, were a couple of wisecracks. For which I don't blame them."

The sheriff drummed his fingers. "So what's your idea?"

"My idea," the sergeant began slowly, and then stopped as the telephone at his elbow rang. He picked it up. "Hello?" He cupped the receiver and shook his head dolefully at the sheriff. "Our man on the scene." He uncupped the receiver. "No, Mrs. Williams. No,

Mrs. Williams. Yes, Mrs. Williams. Yes, we are, Mrs. Williams. As much as we can, ma'am. Yes, Mrs. Williams. Yes, we will, Mrs. Williams." He put the receiver back in its cradle and sighed.

"Mrs. Williams," he said, and raised his eyes to the ceiling. "What a woman! She called the other day, all excited. It seems Charley Crompton thought she wasn't home, because he came over and rang her bell and tried to look in the windows. She kept out of sight and then he went back to his house and came out with something bulky and big and put it in the trunk of his car and drove off, and she called us at once. And when we got there, Charley was back, and he had mud all over his tires, red clay like we have down at Wiley Creek, and we searched his trunk, but we never came up with a thing."

"So what's your idea?"

"My idea," the sergeant said, staring at the girly calendar on the wall without seeing it, "is that Charley Crompton has gotten away with murder. My idea is that his wife is buried somewhere in the woods and that, if we ever find her, it will be sheer luck. And that without her body we're in trouble. We don't have a case and we don't have a chance of holding him. My idea is that he went through that rigamarole of digging up trees and ruining a perfect concrete floor because he wanted to rub our noses in a perfect crime."

"Or because it gave him a chance to misdirect your attention while he had her body stored away somewhere else." The sheriff shook his head. "I still can't believe a mouse like Charley Crompton would have the nerve, though, to do a thing like that."

"Believe it," the sergeant said shortly.

"So what do we do?"

The young sergeant swiveled his chair, staring through the window at the deserted square before the old courthouse.

"We wait," he said heavily. "We wait until some Boy Scouts on a hike, or some gang out on a picnic, or some kids necking, or some curious dog, makes what the newspapers call 'a gruesome discovery.' Because one thing is certain: whether she was buried in that house or in that yard at one time or another, she isn't buried there now. That's about the only thing that *is* certain."

The sheriff sighed and swung around and back in his swivel chair.

The mean, petulant, whining voice carried through the still night, threading its way from the garage through the back yard to the house, out-cricketing the crickets. There was an air of continuity

about it, as if it had been going on for some time and would continue
to go on indefinitely, or until a stop were put to it.

" . . . certainly pure nonsense to pick me up in Joliet three stations
down the line when the train stops here just as well, same as it was
silly to put me on the train there, as if gasoline grew on trees, but
of course that wouldn't bother you none—none of it comes out of
your pockets and why you insisted on my visiting your mother in
the first place heaven only knows, there isn't a thing wrong with
her except she's spoiled the way old women are spoiled and she dotes
on her darling Charley—darling Charley this darling Charley
that—and how her darling Charley could have had any girl he ever
wanted, which simply goes to show she doesn't know her darling
Charley as well as I do and three weeks with her in that horrible
house was no pleasure, locked in that mausoleum with no newspapers, no radio, no television, I don't know how she stands it but
you never care what I go through just as long as you get your
way—well, that was the last time and if I find you've been up to
your usual tricks with girls while I was gone, you'll regret it and
you'll regret it where it hurts the most, in the pocketbook."

The gate from the garage to the back yard was opened and closed
again.

" . . . and for heaven's sake what on earth has happened to that
peach tree excavated out of the ground and that lantern alongside?
I hope you realize that Chaber's Hardware doesn't give kerosene
free and if you want to transplant a tree, the least you can do is do
it during the daylight though why you should want to do it at all
I can't imagine, the peach trees have been fine ever since I remember—in any event, I want it replanted immediately tomorrow, do
you hear? I don't want it lying around and I don't want all that dirt
to be tracked into my clean house—"

The kitchen door was swung back; the voice continued, an acid
eating through Charley's eardrums.

" . . . and leaving the lamp on in the house while you were coming
to pick me up all the way to Joliet, electricity costs money but you
don't care—why should you, you don't pay the bills, and leaving that
ugly hatchet on the kitchen counter, I've told you a thousand times
the place for your dirty tools is in the cellar—well, at least I see you
had the decency to set out two cups of coffee, I only hope you didn't
use the electric percolator and leave it on while you were out, electricity isn't free, but you wouldn't think of that, and—"

A sudden pause, and then—"Charles! These cups are dirty—they've

been used. If you've been entertaining people in this house while
I've been away, that Mrs. Williams from across the street, don't
think I'm blind, I see the way you two look at each other. Charles,
wait, wait! Charles, who's that in the shadow there? Charles, do you
hear me? Charles . . ."

"Hello, dear," said Mrs. Williams quietly, and reached for the
kitchen counter and the hatchet there. "Welcome home."

# Courtesy Call

## by Sonora Morrow

small-town police chief like me has a lot more leeway than a big city cop. We don't have a fancy lab or a far-flung communication system but, heck, we don't need it. We get a few apple-stealers and a little rock-throwing, local kid stuff; and some speeders, transient-tourist stuff. Once in a while we knock over a farmer's still, but only if it's real dirty. Good, clean, cheap whiskey is hard to come by, and even though all of us on the force know Lars Kipple is making the stuff, we don't bother him. He's very sanitary, and only charges five dollars a gallon.

This is all beside the point, but I wanted you to know that Chitterden, California, is a nice place to be chief of police, or was, until a couple of months ago.

We were all sorry when Eliza Chitterden died. The eldest of the four Chitterden girls whose father had founded the town, she had lived with her sisters in the mansion on the hill, and lived well on the money the old man had left. His mine had petered out thirty years before, but he'd invested his profits wisely. He had ruled his home with an iron hand since his wife died during the birth of Kate in 1920. He lived to be ninety-two without a trace of senility, and no young man who had ever come courting found favor with him. "They're all after my money," he'd say.

Eliza was sixty-two, Janet was fifty-eight, Sarah, fifty-five, and Kate, forty-seven. A heart attack took Eliza, was Doc Kilton's diagnosis.

It was a beautiful funeral and afterward, naturally, I had to make a courtesy call. I knew the girls by sight but had never met them socially. The Victorian home was surrounded by ten acres of trees, grass, and flowers. A wrought iron spiked fence enclosed it, but the gates had always been open since I could remember.

I took Sergeant, my German shepherd, who's been my sole companion since I got him seven years ago. He's usually very well behaved, but he couldn't resist the trees and the grass. I let him run and romp for a few minutes, then ordered him to lie down on the porch, which he did with reproachful brown eyes.

The Misses Janet, Sarah, and Kate, dressed in black, greeted me. I was invited in for tea and cookies and we all sat in the huge living room dominated by the twelve foot fireplace. It was November, and while it never really gets *cold* in California, the blazing log felt good.

A maid and a butler tiptoed in and out, bringing messages to Miss Janet and refurbishing the tea tray. I hardly knew what to say after extending my condolences, which were quietly received.

"Uh, Miss Kate, I understand you're the gardener in the family—the flowers are beautiful."

She had a nice smile in an unlined face topped by soft brown hair. "Thank you, chief. I do hope you'll let me give you a bouquet of my best fall flowers before you leave."

I nodded my thanks and bit into a flaky apple tart. "These tarts are excellent, so light."

"I made them," Miss Sarah said shyly. "I do all the baking of bread, rolls, and pastries, and on Thursdays, cook's day off, I prepare all the meals. I do so love a kitchen." Sarah did not look her fifty-five, probably through all good habits and no vices, but some makeup and a hairdresser could have done a lot for her. I thought, too, a belt of Kipple homemade probably wouldn't have hurt.

As I looked at the three of them, I decided that a night on the town would do all of them some good.

Miss Janet stood up. "So nice of you to come, chie ' It was a dismissal, and I wondered if having a fifty-two-year-ld bachelor around made her nervous.

I stood too. "Thank you for your kindness. You know I am always at your service."

Miss Kate followed me out to the front yard with shears and a basket. "I'll just cut you a few flowers."

Sergeant trailed us, sniffed at Miss Kate, and growled a little.

"It's all right," I assured Miss Kate. "He's not used to women. Probably a little jealous."

Twenty minutes later I left with a large basket of pink and white oleander, red roses, marguerites, and a small potted holly. Miss Sarah, too, had rushed out with *her* contribution. The bread was wrapped in a fresh tea towel and the half dozen apple tarts showed through neatly folded wax paper. Miss Janet didn't even wave at me, but you can't win them all.

I thought a lot about the Chitterden sisters, that beautiful big house, all that money. They would be easy prey for fortune hunters, so anxious were they for male companionship. However, I felt Miss

Janet was equal to the occasion; *she* had enough Chitterden in her
to protect the younger two. I determined to keep an eye on them
myself and instructed my officers to let me know of any newcomers
to our town. Wealthy spinsters, even in remote towns like ours, are
usually discovered in some devious way by con men and marrying
drifters.

On the day I returned the flower basket and the tea towel, laun
dered and ironed by my landlady, I found Miss Kate in her garden

"Oh, chief," she called out to me as I walked up the path to the
porch, "how nice to see you. Do come and see my flowers." Taking
the basket, she set it on the ground, then led me along a brick walk
"My hydrangea has such large blossoms, don't they look like snow
balls?"

I mumbled in the affirmative and continued to admire bushes and
flowers I'd seen, but never knew their names—pyracantha, lupin
star anise, wild grape, and wisteria.

Finally, we sat down on a cement bench under a large pepper tree

Miss Kate was wearing the Chitterden uniform, a dark blue, long
sleeved dress, dark stockings, and sensible black shoes. However
she was not unattractive, although because of her life she was not
over-endowed with personality.

She looked at me out of clear blue eyes. "I would like your advice
on something."

"Of course, Miss Kate."

"Do you think forty-seven is too late to see the world? I mean the
*real* world. Father took us to San Francisco thirty years ago and we
enjoyed it so. I watched the ships come and go from our hotel windows
and I thought then how wonderful it would be to get on one of those
ships and travel all around the world." Her eyes shone with the
thought.

I had to smile. "Ma'am, you have the money, the time, and the
inclination—there's nothing to stop you. But if you go, please let me
caution you about making friends. Criminals of all kinds gravitate
to wealth like pins to a magnet."

"Oh, I know about that kind of thing."

I was surprised. "You do?"

"Two whole shelves of Father's library contain information about
murderers, confidence men, swindlers, phony stock and real estate
methods and, oh . . . all kinds of things."

The old man had been as smart as I'd thought.

"Then I say you should go. You know the old saying, 'It's later than you think'."

She gave me a thank-you smile. "Come on, I'll take you to the kitchen to see Sarah. It's her cooking and baking day."

"How about Miss Janet?"

"She's gone to see our lawyer and the minister. She won't be back for at least an hour or so."

The kitchen smelled of baking bread, simmering meat, and onions. It was a huge room, clean and full of sunshine, with copper pots and pans and utensils hanging everywhere. It was old-fashioned in some respects. The large stove must have been forty years old, but a dinner for one hundred could easily have been cooked by it. Sarah, almost completely enveloped by a large white starched apron, stood before a large table in the center of the room, rolling out large rounds of dough. When she saw me she wiped her hands on her apron.

"Chief, how good to see you. Please come and have some coffee."

The three of us sat around the middle table, sipping delicious coffee.

"Chief," Sarah looked at me as a small child looks at a Christmas tree, "has Kate mentioned our thoughts on going around the world?"

"She has, and I think it's a great idea."

They smiled and nodded at each other. "I think we can even talk Janet into it," Sarah said.

Kate shrugged. "We can try."

A few minutes later, as I was regaling them with a story about a still we had destroyed, a stentorian voice rang out. "Ladies, we do *not* entertain visitors in the kitchen." It was Miss Janet looming in the doorway.

Both Sarah and Kate looked stricken.

"I—I had hoped to invite the chief to dinner tonight, Janet," Sarah said. "I'm making my special lamb stew with dumplings."

"Perhaps some other time," the eldest sister canceled the invitation.

I made as graceful an exit as possible, after thanking them for their hospitality.

At nine the next morning Doc Kilton called to tell me Janet Chitterden had died of a heart attack.

"Are you sure?" I asked.

"Of course I'm sure," he retorted rather testily. "Been treating her and Eliza for a couple of years, giving them proper doses of digitalis,

supervising their diets and activities. Her manner of death had a
the symptoms of a heart that just got tired of pumping."

Now I'm a small-town cop, but I'm not stupid. It's one thing fo
a family to have a medical history of heart disease, but when tw
of the members, hard-core spinsters with no wish to make change
die, well . . . Survivors where millions are concerned are alway
suspect whether anything can be proved or not.

However, everyone knew the sisters shared equally, that the
were well over twenty-one and could do as they pleased, so I couldn
figure a motive. I also found it hard to suspect flower-loving Kat
and baker-cook Sarah of foul deeds of any kind. Consequently
attended the funeral, extended my condolences to the two remainin
sisters, and let it go.

Over the ensuing months I spent every Thursday evening at th
Chitterden mansion, enjoying Sarah's gourmet dinners, Kate's flora
displays, and three-handed cribbage. Sometimes Kate played th
piano and we all three sang the old songs everyone knows. Consid
ering there was no television or radio, it wasn't bad at all. I alway
brought Sergeant, but he refused to come into the house, and curle
up on the front porch to wait for me. Sarah had instructed the cool
to save all bones for him, but he'd never touch them.

One evening as we enjoyed our coffee and pastries made by Sarah
I asked, "When are you ladies taking off for Europe?"

They looked at each other in confusion. "Soon, I think, chief," Kat
replied. "It's hard to plunge into something different no matter hov
long you've thought about it and wished for it."

Sarah nodded agreement. "There are so many things attached t
it. We have to get passports, buy clothes, arrange for the house t
be kept up. We don't know any foreign languages, and we have t
put our trust in so many strangers." Sarah looked solemn. "Kat
told me about your warning. I guess being rich can have its prob
lems."

I shook my head. "Ladies, people don't have to *know* you're rich
Just travel as any average citizen. I doubt that anyone outside o
California knows your name. You wouldn't have any trouble."

Sarah seemed ecstatic. "Of course, Kate, he's right, you know. W
could do it, we really *could*."

Kate nodded. "And we shall."

That was how I left them. At one o'clock in the morning Doc Kilto
phoned me.

"Sarah and Kate are in convulsions, chief. One of the servant

alled me half an hour ago, and I've got them in the hospital having
their stomachs pumped. Seems like poisoning of some
ind—accidental, I'm sure. Toadstools mistaken for mushrooms or
omething, most likely."

I rushed to our small hospital immediately.

It was a long three hours. They couldn't save Sarah, but Kate was
oing to make it.

"I just don't know," Doc told me in the doctor's coffee room. "I wish
had the laboratory for this kind of thing." He looked at me. "I even
ave to send my cancer possibility specimens fifty miles away. I can
andle cuts and breaks, births and appendicitis, give preventive
hots, but anything out of the way . . ." He shook his shaggy head.

"It'll be all right, Doc," I patted his shoulder. "Give me the spec-
nens and I'll take them to the city."

I had to stay two days in the city, which I didn't mind. It gave me
chance to roam around and be thankful I didn't have big city traffic
roblems. I visited the main police station and was treated nicely.
also found out I could have had the analysis on Sarah and Kate's
tomach contents done for nothing instead of paying fifty dollars to
he fancy private laboratory.

Anyway, the report came through and I went home and showed
t to Doc Kilton.

"Do you suppose I made a mistake on Eliza and Janet?" He seemed
ery perturbed.

"If you did, it was a natural one," I replied. "I'll never believe any
f the Chitterden girls capable of murder. They *had* to be accidents;
here was absolutely no motive." I thought a few minutes. "I'm going
o find out where the Chitterden money goes if all the girls die." I
tormed out of Doc's office and made for Mr. London, the Chitterden
amily's old lawyer.

He'd been the town lawyer for so many years he was like the trees
hat get lost in the forest. Everybody knew he was there, but nobody
eally noticed him. I guess Doc Kilton and I fit into that category,
oo, as do the butcher, the hardware store man, the postman, and
ust about everybody who does the same thing day after day, year
after year.

At first he was reluctant to disclose what he considered secret
nformation, but when I confronted him with three deaths and one
ear-death, he relented.

"Chief, is it understood that this information goes no further?"

"If it involves murder, Mr. London, I can't hold it back. If it doesn't,

I can promise it won't go any further." That was the best I could d◆
It seemed to suit him.

An hour later I understood the disposition of the Chitterden fo▮
tune. Coupled with the lab analysis, I knew I had my answer.

Miss Kate was sitting on the cement bench in the garden whe▮
I walked up the path to the house. She didn't call out to me, but ▮
walked over and sat down beside her.

I spoke softly. "I know what has happened, Miss Kate. I kno▮
that Eliza and Janet and Sarah all died from a strong potion ◆
oleander leaves. It's a poison that gives the symptoms of a hea▮
attack, and therefore is not treated correctly and the patient dies▮

She didn't say anything.

"I also know that you sisters did not share equally in your father▮
estate. Complete control was assumed by the eldest, in succession▮

She sighed. "I had so hoped to fool everyone by taking a sma▮
dose myself." She grasped my hands. "Do you know what it mean▮
to live as I have the past forty-seven years? I thought when Eliz▮
and Janet were gone that I could begin to live a life of my own. Bu▮
then Sarah didn't want to leave, *and* even if she did, who wants t▮
travel with her sister?" She put her face in her hands. The rest cam▮
through muffled. "I did so want to know the love, the arms of a ma▮
I wanted to see the rest of the world. Chitterden isn't the beginnin▮
and the end, is it?"

She took her hands away and looked at me.

Mr. London and Doc Kilton were easily convinced of accident▮
death and went back to their businesses satisfied. While I admit i▮
makes me nervous to be married to a murderess, as long as I kee▮
her happy in our travels and in all other ways, I'm safe. Howeve▮
I may take up gardening myself one of these days.

# Restored Evidence

## by Patrick O'Keeffe

Captain Somme views it, with no little amusement, as one of the closest-kept secrets of the war. It was purely by chance that he became privy to it, almost twenty-five years after the incidents surrounding it occurred. He was returning from a visit to a crew member lying in the Marine Hospital on Staten Island and, walking up State Street from the ferry in the sharp, spring air, he turned into the newly opened Seamen's Church Institute building, feeling a sudden desire for a cup of coffee.

While sipping it beside the cafeteria windows facing Battery Park, his gaze wandered over the other tables. It was midafternoon and not many were in use, but at one sat an old man who was staring at him intently. Captain Somme stared back vaguely feeling that there was something familiar about the deep-furrowed face and cropped white head.

The old man suddenly rose and came over. "Ain't you Cap'n Somme, master of the *Delcrest* during the war?"

"That's right." The captain's face lit up in sudden recognition. "Old Pop Seymour! I was just thinking I'd seen you somewhere."

"I figured it was you, Cap'n." The old man looked pleased. "I wasn't sure, though, with them sideburns and mustache."

The captain smiled. "I keep up with the style of the mod crews we get nowadays. What have you been doing with yourself all these years, Pop? Still sailing, I'll bet."

Pop Seymour shook his head sadly. "I had to quit after the war. Pension rules. Too old, they said. So now I do odd jobs around the Institute. Get my room and board here, too." The old man eyed the captain quizzically. "You must be about ready to swallow the hook yourself."

"Another two years or so, Pop. But sit down and tell me what's been happening to you all these years."

"Let me get another cup o' coffee first, Cap'n."

As the stoop-shouldered former steward ambled over to the serving counter, Captain Somme's thoughts drifted back to the coffee incident aboard the refrigerated ship *Delcrest*. She was discharging

125

Army meat cargo in Naples at the time, shortly after the city ha[s] been captured by the Allied Fifth Army. It was his first trip a[s] captain, relieving the regular captain for his vacation. When Po[p] Seymour was serving the Army security officer at lunch, Pop Se[y]mour's hand accidentally knocked against the lieutenant's cup i[n] avoiding a sudden movement of the officer's arm, and a little coffe[e] splashed down onto the flap of a side pocket of his khaki jacket.

The stain was hardly noticeable, but the lieutenant, fastidiou[s] about his appearance, muttered, "Clumsy old fool! My only clea[n] blouse."

"I'm sorry, Lieutenant," said Pop, distressed.

The lieutenant looked across at Captain Somme, on the other sid[e] of the table. "He should be kept ashore out of harm's way."

Captain Somme offered no comment. Lieutenant Harmson wa[s] quick-tempered and would probably regret his hasty outburst. H[e] was a young, wartime-commissioned officer, assigned to the *Delcres[t]* as Army security officer in charge of the meat cargo. The inciden[t] worried Pop Seymour, knowing that the Navy held a certain wartim[e] veto over merchant-marine personnel it regarded as unfit or un[-] desirable. If the security officer turned in a bad report about hi[m] to the Navy he'd perhaps be barred from sailing again.

He wasn't a clumsy old fool, he told himself, resenting the remark[.] A bit jumpy, maybe, from the war. Going on sixty, he wasn't a[s] nimble and steady-handed as in the days when he was a first-clas[s] waiter in big liners like the old *Leviathan* and the *America*, but h[e] was a lot better at the job than most of these war-trained kids sailin[g] as officers' messmen.

Pop was still smarting over the spilled coffee as he prepared to g[o] ashore after lunch. The Allied Military Government permitted shor[e] leave to twenty percent of the personnel of each merchant ship be[-] tween one and five in the afternoon, but because of the shortage o[f] official launches, ships had to provide their own liberty-boat servic[e.] This was necessary because all quays had been blocked with ship[s] scuttled by the retreating Germans, forcing Allied supply ships t[o] anchor in clusters inside the breakwaters and discharge into am[-] phibious "ducks" and lighters. Ships not equipped with a motorboa[t] such as the *Delcrest*, had to depend on bumboats and other oare[d] craft to ferry their crewmen ashore.

Pop Seymour left the ship in a bumboat along with three othe[r] crew members, young men who were bent on a lively time ashor[e] in the few hours available to them. Pop wandered on his own throug[h]

he docks area and the bombed-out waterfront streets to Via Roma.
The thoroughfare was heavy with military traffic, and the sidewalks
were thronged with soldiers, sailors, and nurses in the various uniforms of the Allied forces and collaborating Italians. Most of the
shops were closed and dark, but street vendors had set up displays
of cheap cameos, shells, and religious articles.

Pop Seymour wandered about aimlessly, having come ashore
chiefly to stretch his legs on the last day in port; the ship had finished
discharging at noon. He ignored the cries of picture-postcard vendors
and small boys offering sticky, nutted candy for sale. At one intersection, a swarthy young Italian policeman wearing an Allied Military Government brassard followed him with his eyes as he passed,
no doubt thinking that this old man in striped shirt, serge trousers,
and felt hat was an American seaman and an easy mark for way-
laying and murdering for his clothes and dock pass and any seaman's
papers he might have on him.

Pop Seymour finally came to rest in a small wineshop down a
steep side street. He had spent almost an hour strolling through the
narrow and hilly streets of the squalid neighborhood on the other
side of Via Roma, and he was tired and thirsty.

A few civilians were sitting at tables and except for one big man
who scowled, they glanced indifferently at Pop Seymour as he entered. He took a vacant table by the door, heeding notices posted
around the *Delcrest* warning personnel against talking to strangers
ashore, in or out of uniform. He ordered a glass of Marsala from a
waiter, paying for it with Allied Military Government lire.

Pop lit his pipe and sat gazing out into the quiet street. He thought
the Marsala didn't taste anything like it did before the war. After
a while, his pipe went out. When he relit it, he looked up in time
to see two men in American Army officer uniforms enter a shop
across the street. One was the *Delcrest's* security officer, Lieutenant
Harmson. Pop wasn't surprised to see him going into such a shop,
for a sign outside included the words, "Objets d'art," and he knew
from the officers' conversations at mealtimes that Lieutenant Harmson ran a similar business with his father on Sixth Avenue, New
York City. Pop Seymour had heard him remark that he hoped to
pick up a rare piece or two as bargains while in Naples.

The glimpse of the security officer revived Pop Seymour's fear
over the likelihood of having to dump himself onto his youngest
daughter at the end of the voyage. She was constantly urging him
to live a quiet and safe life ashore with her and her family, but ever

since his wife died just before the war, it had been his hope to remain
at sea to the end and be put over the side in a piece of canvas, with
little trouble or expense to anyone.

Pop presently glanced at his wristwatch and then ordered another
glass of wine. It was getting near time to start back toward the
waterfront. He glanced across the street at the art shop. The security
officer hadn't come out yet. The window was empty, and Pop couldn't
see beyond it into the unlighted interior.

The door suddenly opened and two men came out. One was the
officer who had entered with Lieutenant Harmson, but even before
his companion turned his face in the direction of the wineshop, Pop
Seymour could tell by his ill-fitting jacket that he wasn't the fas-
tidious Lieutenant Harmson, although roughly of the same height
and build. The other officer, he saw, wore the two silver bars of a
captain.

The security officer had not left the art shop by the time Pop
Seymour knocked out his pipe and pushed back the chair. The lieutenant, mused Pop, would, with his quick young stride, reach the
docks in half the time he himself would take. The late afternoon
chill was setting in, and Pop stepped along briskly. It was four thirty
by the time he reached the gate at the foot of Piazza Municipal. An
M.P. eyed him closely and scrutinized his pass before waving him
on.

When Pop Seymour arrived at the quayside, two of the ship's Navy
armed guard and an oiler were hailing a bumboat. There was no
sign of the security officer. Already most of the bumboats peddling
wine and souvenirs to the anchored ships were starting to head back
for the quays, fearful of being caught out in the open during the
expected hail of bombs and anti-aircraft shrapnel after nightfall.
The white plume rising from Vesuvius would glow red at intervals
in the darkness, providing a natural beacon to guide the Nazi planes.

While the little group was waiting for the bumboat to come alongside, black smoke and debris shot into the sky above a nearby waterfront street. The men gave it only passing notice, for time bombs
and booby traps left behind by the enemy had been exploding almost
daily since the ship's arrival.

The security officer still had not appeared when the bumboat
owner plied his oars in the direction of the *Delcrest*. Pop figured that
Lieutenant Harmson would have to stay ashore all night, unless he
were lucky enough to get a ride in an Army launch after the expected
air raid.

There was no air raid on the port that night, however; two attempts ended when the bombers were turned back by fighter planes. The *Delcrest* moved out past the breakwater at dawn and anchored in the open bay among several other vessels awaiting convoy. At breakfast time, Pop Seymour heard Captain Somme remark to the chief engineer that the security officer was still ashore. "If he doesn't show up by noon, I'll blinker a message reporting his absence."

During the forenoon coffee break, Pop happened to go out on deck in time to see a launch heading back to shore from the *Delcrest*. Standing in the stern and looking back at the ship was a man he recognized as the Army captain he had seen enter the art shop with Lieutenant Harmson.

He turned to one of the armed guards standing beside him at the rails. "Did the security officer just come aboard?"

The guard nodded solemnly. "But it wasn't Lieutenant Harmson. He was killed yesterday afternoon when a time bomb blew out the wall of a building he was passing. That Army captain brought out a replacement for him."

Pop Seymour was shocked, telling himself that it must have been the explosion he heard while waiting for the bumboat. "He was one of the unlucky guys," he remarked sadly.

"The new officer is one of the lucky guys," said the Navy sailor. "I heard him tell our officer he was just off a torpedoed ship, landed here yesterday with nothing but the uniform he was wearing. He was the only officer available to take Lieutenant Harmson's place. The lieutenant's clothes were left aboard for him to use till he gets outfitted."

Pop did not see the new security officer until lunch time. When he went to take the Army officer's order, Captain Somme said, "Lieutenant Sanford, that's Pop Seymour, the Methuselah of all stewards and past master of the art. A wise old sea gull, too, even if he does decorate your uniform with a splash of coffee once in a while."

Pop Seymour grinned. After several years with Captain Somme as chief mate of the *Delcrest,* he was used to his kidding.

Sanford laughed. "As long as he doesn't go beyond scalding the back of my neck and pays my laundry bill, I won't object."

Pop Seymour was pleased. Lieutenant Sanford sounded like a better officer to get along with than Lieutenant Harmson, and he might be good for a favorable report. He stared at him for a moment. Sanford was a little older-looking than his predecessor, darker and with a jutting forehead and square jaw. "Ain't I seen you someplace before, Lieutenant?"

Sanford looked up quickly, scanning the old steward's lined face. He smiled. "You must be confusing me with someone else, Pop. Looking across at Captain Somme, he chuckled. "As though I could have run into old Pop before and not remembered him!"

Pop Seymour hurried off to the galley, shaking his head as if to stir up his memory. He was sure he'd seen the man somewhere. On his way back to the table, it suddenly came to him. Setting a plate of soup before Sanford, he said, "I knew I'd seen you someplace, Lieutenant. It was coming out of that art shop yesterday afternoon.

"Art shop?"

"Sure. I forget the name of the street. I was sitting in a little wine shop across the way and saw you come out."

Sanford shook his head in slow motion. "Pop," he said patiently, "I was nowhere near any art shop yesterday afternoon. I was at Army headquarters all day, trying to get outfitted and finding out what was to be done with me."

"That's funny, Lieutenant. My eyes ain't too good for reading, but they're fine for distance. You came out with another officer."

"Are you insinuating I'm a liar?" demanded Sanford, in a sudden show of anger.

"No, sir," said Pop hastily. "I didn't mean it that way. Don't get me wrong. It's just that—well, maybe my eyes are getting bad for distance too."

"Perhaps Pop had a glass of wine too much," said Captain Somme, smiling.

"When an old man starts seeing things, it's a sign of approaching senility," growled Sanford. "I had no permission to leave headquarters yesterday at any time."

Pop Seymour backed away from the table in misery. After lunch, he went out to the afterdeck with his pipe. He sat alone, pulling dismally on his pipe. He'd started off on the wrong foot with the new security officer. If the lieutenant reported him as going senile, this could be his last voyage.

Pop told himself angrily that Lieutenant Sanford was a liar. He'd seen him come out of that art shop as sure as he'd seen Lieutenant Harmson go in. He'd recognized that Army captain this forenoon, so why should he be wrong about Lieutenant Sanford?

Why was the lieutenant saying it wasn't he who came out of the art shop? It was queer, too, Lieutenant Harmson going in with that

:aptain and Lieutenant Sanford coming out with him, and the two
of them coming aboard together this forenoon, with Lieutenant Sanford as the new security officer.

From mealtime conversations among the officers, Pop had heard
that Naples was swarming with Nazi and Fascist spies and sabo-
teurs, some masquerading in Allied uniforms. One with a Southern
accent had been caught passing himself off as an American Navy
lieutenant, he had been raised in Texas by German parents and was
living in Germany when war broke out. He and other agents had
been left behind after the fall of Naples to harass the Allies by
taking advantage of the confusion and lack of coordination that
would exist among Allied units until the stocked electric-power and
telephone services had been restored and all time bombs and booby
traps removed.

After pondering at length on the art shop and the new security
officer, Pop Seymour decided to take his ruminations to Captain
Somme. He always served coffee to the officers around three thirty,
and when he went into the captain's cabin that afternoon, Captain
Somme had just wakened from a brief nap. He sat up as the steward
placed the tray on the desk, and then watched curiously as Pop,
instead of withdrawing, closed the door and turned to him.

"Cap'n, it was Lieutenant Sanford I saw coming out of that art
shop yesterday afternoon. I didn't mix him up with nobody else, and
it wasn't too much wine. And I ain't going senile either."

Captain Somme smiled. "It's nothing to get worked up about, Pop.
I was joking, and Lieutenant Sanford said that without meaning it.
You're a long way from being senile, you wise old sea gull."

"That ain't what's bothering me, Cap'n. It's because Lieutenant
Sanford's lying when he says it wasn't him I saw come out of the art
shop."

"It was possibly a look-alike, Pop. That sometimes happens."

"It didn't happen yesterday. Another thing bothering me is that
Lieutenant Harmson went into the shop with that other officer, a
captain and Lieutenant Sanford came out. Don't that look kinda
queer to you?"

"Well, what might have happened is that Lieutenant Harmson
got into conversation with the Army captain about art shops, and
he took him to one. You've heard Lieutenant Harmson say that that
was his line of business. An officer looking like Lieutenant Sanford
happened to be in there at the time and came away with the captain.

It's unfortunate that Lieutenant Harmson didn't leave with them.
He'd be alive now."

"That ain't the way I figure it, Cap'n," Pop said stubbornly. "You're
figuring it your way because you don't think Lieutenant Sanford's
lying. And something you don't know is that the Army captain who
brought the lieutenant aboard this forenoon was the same officer
who came out of the art shop with him. Don't that look kinda queer
too?"

"If that is so, it does seem odd," admitted Captain Somme. "But
it may be nothing more than a coincidence. The way conditions are
in Naples at present, nothing would surprise me."

"You know what I think, Cap'n: they're a couple German spies.
That art shop's some kinda Fascist joint. They killed Lieutenant
Harmson in there. That's why Lieutenant Sanford's lying. He knows
if I saw him come out of the art shop, I maybe saw Lieutenant
Harmson go in."

The look of mild amusement faded from the captain's face. Pop
Seymour continued. "You know what else I think? I think Lieutenant Sanford came out of that art shop in Lieutenant Harmson's
uniform. Maybe you noticed the jacket ain't a good fit. And that's
why Lieutenant Harmson's clothes are being left aboard. It ain't
because Lieutenant Sanford lost his aboard a torpedoed ship. It's
because he's a German spy, with only the uniform Lieutenant Harmson was murdered for."

Captain Somme stared gravely at his wise old sea gull. If what
Pop Seymour had said were true, it would seem that German agents
had seized an opportunity to put one of their number aboard the
Delcrest. He had perhaps been too easily duped with a forged letter
as signing the new security officer to the ship and by the possibly
bogus captain accompanying him. With the ship secured for sea,
convoy orders aboard, all contact with shore ended, there was little
likelihood that the assignment of a new security officer would become known ashore and lead to inquiries. Lieutenant Sanford may
have brought a secret radio transmitter aboard; one such had been
used in the outward-bound convoy, enabling U-boats to home in on
the ships. The bogus security officer would disappear the moment
the ship arrived in the home port, to operate as a spy ashore, taking
with him knowledge of secret codes and convoy procedure.

"Pop, you've really got me worried now. You could be right."

"What makes you figure maybe I ain't right, Cap'n?"

The captain's young face took on a distracted expression. "Look

t what I'm up against, Pop. If I blinker ashore for a confirmation
f the death of Lieutenant Harmson and the assignment of Lieu-
enant Sanford, heaven knows how long under present conditions
t'll take for the message to reach the right quarter, and perhaps
ven longer to get a reply. If the convoy gets under way on schedule
t five o'clock and there's no word from shore, I'll have to hold back.
There's a shortage of refrigerated ships, so if you turn out to be
wrong, Pop, and we're delayed a week waiting for the next convoy,
he Navy would crucify me. I'd never get command of another ship
vhile the war lasted. They'd say I'd listened to the wild imaginings
of an old steward, because he was an old shipmate, instead of taking
he word of a United States Army officer."

"Cap'n," said Pop Seymour sympathetically, "I know how it is. It's
your first trip as master and you don't feel you can risk sticking
your neck out like some old-timer would. I ain't trying to tell you
what to do, but it's okay by me if you want to play safe. Maybe you
could figure out a way after we get to sea of showing up Lieutenant
Sanford as a phony and put him in irons."

"If that art shop is an enemy agents' hideout and that Army
captain is one of them, something should be done about it now; the
military authorities here should know about it at once. Pop, if I
could be sure you're not mistaken about Lieutenant Sanford . . ."
The captain broke off with a helpless gesture.

"I wish I could help you out on that, Cap'n," Pop said sadly. "All
I can do is say I ain't mistaken." He turned toward the door. "I'd
better be getting on with the coffee for the officers."

Pop Seymour went out. He came hurrying back within a few minutes, looking excited. "Cap'n," he said, almost slamming the door
behind him, "I've got something to tell you. When I took coffee into
Lieutenant Sanford's cabin, he was out on deck somewhere. His
jacket was hanging up. I couldn't miss seeing the coffee stain on it,
right where I made it yesterday, on the pocket flap, same side. Don't
that prove it's Lieutenant Harmson's?"

Captain Somme, sitting with coffee untouched, gazed at the old
steward as if still unconvinced.

"Cap'n, you don't have to believe me this time. You can go in and
see it for yourself, just to be sure."

The captain suddenly stood up. "Pop, it looks as if it's about time
I started believing you."

When old Pop Seymour returned to Captain Somme's table in the

cafeteria of the Seamen's Church Institute building, the captain wa
smiling reminiscently. As the former steward put down the cup an
saucer and drew out a chair, the captain remarked, "I was jus
thinking about that coffee stain years ago. What a sweat I was in
waiting for an answer to my blinker message and watching th
convoy preparing to get under way. The grandest sight of my lif
was seeing that launch heading for the ship with the M.P.s. If tha
coffee stain had turned out to be another coincidence, I think I'
have jumped overboard."

Pop Seymour gave an odd smile. "I knew for sure it wasn't."

"Pop, you couldn't have been really sure at the time."

"I knew for sure because there was no stain on the jacket."

The captain looked puzzled. "What do you mean, Pop? I saw it
Everybody saw it."

Pop Seymour grinned. "When I saw the jacket hanging up, I re
membered the stain. So I looked for it. It wasn't there. I figure
Lieutenant Harmson must have sponged it off before going ashor
the day before, or maybe that phony security officer had done it.
didn't think figuring it out that way would be enough to make yo
stick your neck out. So I dabbed a little coffee in the right place."

Captain Somme seemed speechless. Still grinning, Pop Seymou
said, "With everybody making me out to be some kinda hero ove
spotting that stain, and me sitting pretty with the Navy, I didn'
see any sense in letting on that it didn't happen that way."

Captain Somme drew in a long breath, as if about to explode. "Pop
if I'd known that when I was waiting for an answer to my message
I think I'd have had you keelhauled." He broke into a laugh. "I use
to call you a wise old sea gull. But you were really a crafty ol
buzzard."

# The Standoff

## by Frank Sisk

**L**ast call at Marvin Morrell's was 12:45 by the beer-ad clock over the bar. The clock was always set five minutes fast, which gave the necessary leeway for weaning the slow drinkers and he drunken ones away from their glasses by legal closing time. At :05 Morrell and Pete Lavelle, the night bartender, usually had the lace all to themselves. The dining room lights were out and the nly light in the bar-and-lounge section came from the gooseneck amp beside the cash register. The back and front doors were locked.

The routine rarely varied. Morrell read the register tape, then no-saled the cash drawer open and began counting the money. He some-imes nibbled his hairline mustache with an air of concentration, and his deft fingers with their manicured nails flashed like a ma-gician's under the pale circle of light.

Lavelle busied himself with clearing glasses and ashtrays off the lounge tables and sponging spillage off the formica surfaces with a dry towel, then performed the same service for the bar. After that he cleaned the ashtrays and placed them in a self-nesting stack on the back shelf. He dipped the glasses in lukewarm water and de-tergent and gave them a cold rinse in a jet spray. When the last glass was set on the drainboard, he dried his hands on a clean towel, rolled down his sleeves and reached his jacket off a nearby hook, all in nearly one continuous motion. With a final look around at the angular shadows, he then said as usual, "Want me to mix you one before I leave, Marv?"

Stuffing the day's receipts into a canvas bag, Morrell made the customary reply. "Thanks, Pete. But don't bother."

"Everything balance out?"

"Seems so. Some odd change over, maybe."

"Well, okay then, Marv. I guess I'll shove."

"Night, Pete. Be sure to snap the catch on the back door."

"Right, Marv. See you tomorrow."

The unvarying routine varied tonight. Lavelle vanished into the darkened dining room where the back door was situated, but he reappeared within several seconds. His shadow lay strangely long against the wall. He was holding his hands above his head and seemed to be throwing another, more solid shadow directly behind him.

Morrell was in the act of reaching for his very best cognac when he saw the blurred hint of Lavelle in the bar mirror and said without turning, "Forget something, Pete?"

"Not really," Lavelle said in a tense voice.

"What gives then?"

"We got company, Marv."

Morrell replaced the bottle of cognac. "You don't say," he said. Peering into the murky shadow, he saw that the solid shadow behind Lavelle was not a shadow at all. Slowly he turned around. "A thirsty friend, Pete?"

"I hardly think so, Marv."

"That's cool thinking, pal," the shadow said in a muffled voice.

"He's got some kind of weapon on my backbone, Marv," said Lavelle.

"A big thirty-eight with man-size slugs," the shadow added in that same muffled voice. "So don't do anything too cool, Marv, or the joint might close down overnight."

Morrell glanced covertly at the .32 caliber automatic slung in a leather holster that was nailed to the inside corner of the bar under the cash register.

"Don't do nothing rash, Marv, please," Lavelle cautioned.

"Don't worry, Pete. I'm a gambler but no sucker."

"That's the way to talk, man." The shadow detached itself from Lavelle and became a man about five-feet-eight weighing perhaps one hundred and fifty pounds. He wore a rubber mask caricaturing a demon, which accounted for the turbid quality of his words, and rubber gloves. Otherwise he was dressed normally for the summer season—sports shirt open at the neck, dark slacks, and thick-soled sneakers.

"You're holding the cards, mister," Morrell said.

"And the gun," the masked man pointed out.

Morrell noticed that the gun was not in the hands of an expert. The realization gave him incipient jitters, but his face remained impassive. "Well, what can we do for you?"

"Pass over the day's take is all."

"That's easy," Morrell said, turning toward the back shelf to get the canvas bag.

"Not another move, Marv," the masked man said, a nervous note
in his muffled voice.

"I'm only going—"

"Steady, Marv, or I'll drill that silly mustache right off your lip."

Morrell slowly faced about. *The stupid jerk,* he thought. *His first
job and he's itchy enough to blow it sky high.* "All right, mate," he
said patiently. "You name it and I'll do it. I like money but I'm not
in love with it."

"The dough," the man said. "Pass it over."

"That's what I started to do."

"From the register."

"It's not in the register now," Morrell said. "It's counted and sacked
for the night deposit."

"Sacked?"

"I can see you've been around," Morrell said.

"Cut the cracks, Marv, and hand it over."

"I've got to turn around to do it."

"Make it slow motion."

Morrell complied. With the bag in hand, he momentarily calculated the odds in favor of hurling it into the masked face, then ruled
it out. The guy was just nutty enough to shoot and he might even
be lucky enough to hit something or somebody. "Shall I toss it across
to you?"

The fool almost nodded assent but checked himself midway. "Just
set it on the bar, smart guy."

Morrell obeyed.

The masked man elbowed Lavelle. "Go get it."

In three cooperative strides Lavelle reached the bar and grabbed
the canvas bag.

"Now back up," the man ordered.

Lavelle shuffled into reverse.

The man relieved him of the bag and said, "Keep backing to the
front door and when we get there, unlock it."

Lavelle did as bid.

In the frame of the open door the masked man issued some advice.
"Stay inside at least five minutes. Or else." He slammed the door
hard. They could hear his feet hurrying across the parking lot and
beyond it.

"If he's got a car," Lavelle said, "it's parked down the road somewhere."

Morrell nodded and reached for the telephone. "Get me the police, he told the operator.

While they waited for the police to arrive, Morrell asked, "Wher the hell did he come from, Pete?"

"He must have been in the men's room when the waitresses close up shop."

"He come at you from the men's room?"

"No. When I started to walk through the dining room he wa sitting in the corner booth. Like waiting for the money to be counte and all."

"He's no pro, though."

"How can you tell, Marv?"

"Something about him that's familiar. I don't know what, bu something."

"You think he might be a customer?"

"Something like that. You sure you didn't notice that sport shir around earlier?"

"It's like a hundred other sport shirts, Marv. And this was pretty busy even for a Friday night. I hardly had time to notice what anyon was wearing."

"And the sneakers," Morrell said musingly, more to himself than to Lavelle.

"Sneakers are a dime a dozen around here in the summer, Marv You know that."

"Yeah, I suppose so." A light swept past the front windows. "The police. Better open up, Pete."

The holdup man had taken $483.28. It was enough to hurt Morrel a little, but it didn't hurt him half as much as being taken cold by an obvious bubblehead. He'd been braced a few times in his life by experts, and he had nothing but a grudging respect for that type. The man in the rubber mask was another matter, even to the thick-soled sneakers. Rope-soled, could be; the kind worn on highly pol-ished boat decks . . .

It was nearly 3 A.M. when Morrell unlocked the front door of his cottage and let himself in. Tillie was standing at the end of the hall, an ample silhouette in housecoat against the night light of the kitchen.

"You're later than usual," she said.

"I was held up," Morrell told her.

"By what?"

"By what? No, I mean I was literally held up by a man with a gun."

"Oh, gee, doll, that's terrible. When did it happen?" she asked.

"About a minute after closing." Morrell, his voice sounding weary, started up the stairs.

Tillie hustled after him. "Did he get much, Marv?"

"Everything we took in after the afternoon deposit."

"You weren't hurt or anything?"

"Nope."

"Well, that's something." They were at the top of the staircase now, outside the open door to a lighted bedroom. "Why don't you come in and tell me all about it, honey?"

"Not tonight, Tillie. I'm dragging."

"I didn't mean it that way, Marv." She was actually blushing, at her age. "I'm only interested in hearing the details of the holdup."

"If that's all you want," Morrell said twittingly, "tune in the local news tomorrow morning. Good night."

Tille opened her mouth to express mild reproach but her husband's supple back was vanishing through the doorway of his own room.

Morrell had been rather fond of Tillie five years earlier, but that wasn't why he married her. She was thinner then, of course, and a lustrum younger, but the determining factor was money. Tillie had a good bit of it. She wasn't rich in the big sense of the word, but she was well off. More than that, she had a willingness to set him up in business under certain conditions. Morrell, who had instinctively evaded marriage for thirty-five years, at last settled for those conditions.

Now that the business was a success and wholly in his name, he didn't really need Tillie any longer, and his tempered fondness for her had dwindled to an indifferent familiarity. Still, she had quite a sockful of money remaining and he, being a natural gambler, liked to feel the security of a reserve, just in case he ever again got to the tapping-out stage. Besides, he found Tillie a useful foil against the serious encroachments of other females.

One such female was a honey-haired morsel of exquisite palatability named June Reeve. She phoned him the following afternoon around four. She phoned him about that time every afternoon except Fridays and, even after three months, the spicy wantonness of her voice still touched him where he lived.

"You all alone, sweetie?" she began.

Morrell leaned back in the swivel chair and planted a suede loafer on the office desk. "All alone by the telephone, baby."

"The coast is clear up here, too."

Morrell smacked his lips theatrically. "I'm tempted, baby. Believe me, I'm tempted."

"And the people next door have gone to the mountains for the weekend."

"I've fallen, baby. What shall I bring?"

"Just your great big self. And a couple of jugs of champagne would be nice, too."

"Chill nothing but the glasses," said Morrell.

June was the first person whom he'd talked to that day who hadn't mentioned the holdup. It was typical of her to consider such an event secondary to the principal theme of her life. She had a one-track mind and, at his convenience, he loved her for it. But he never envied that shadowy figure, her husband.

A few hours later, as they were finishing the last of the champagne, June said, "I wish we'd met before, Marv."

"Before what, honey?"

"Before we hitched up with the wrong people."

He was standing in front of the dressing-table mirror, buttoning up his shirt.

"Look at it this way, baby—a half a loaf is better than none."

"Not for a woman it isn't."

"Well, there's nothing we can do about it now."

"I could always get a divorce. And so could you, Marv."

Smiling, he turned to face her. "Funny thing, baby, but my old lady doesn't give me any grounds. How about your old man?"

"I could figure something out, with a little encouragement."

"That's a woman for you." Giving her a broad wink, he walked to the chair on which he'd draped his jacket. As he was taking it off the back, his foot kicked something and he looked down. An expression of surprise flickered over his face, but his voice was matter-of-fact. "By the way, June, does your old man suspect anything about us?"

"I wouldn't be surprised."

"What makes you say that?"

"Well, hell, sweetie, he probably notices the empty champagne bottles around. And he doesn't even give me beer money."

"So he asks how come and you tell him?"

"So what, Marv? Don't worry. He's harmless."

Driving back to his business, Morrell tried to fit the pieces together. Reeve had been pointed out to him a few months earlier. Morrell retained a clear image—a man just about the size of the holdup man. Six nights a week Reeve drove an empty truck to Rockland, Maine, and returned with it full of live lobsters. He'd be around boats—could wear heavy-soled sneakers. His one night off was Friday, which made him available for the job. And then there was that crack about shooting "that silly mustache right off your lip." If that wasn't a gibe straight from a jealous cuckold, Morrell hadn't been tuned in right.

If any doubt remained in Morrell's mind, it was dispelled a few days later by June during one of their afternoon phone conversations.

"I got something terrific to show you, sweetie," she said. "Hurry over."

"I've seen about everything, baby."

"Oh, *you!* This is something else. Just delivered. A color TV."

"From Santa Claus?"

"From Fred, believe it or not."

"I believe it."

"His boss gave him a bonus for getting a shipment of lobsters way below the market price. Come on over, sweetie. I'm kind of thirsty."

"I guess I owe it to myself," Morrell said, more to himself than to June.

He was enough of a realist to regard the situation as a standoff. He couldn't turn Reeve over to the police without risking a scandal. As sure as God made big yaps, the stupid jerk would sing to high heaven about the affair between his wife and his victim. The resultant embarrassment might even be enough to mortify Tillie into divorce, and Morrell didn't want anything like that to happen while he was still so vulnerable to June. He needed a buffer between himself and his ungovernable yen and Tillie was solid and legal.

A month later Marvin Morrell's place was held up again. Again it was at the close of Friday's business. Again the holdup man paraded Pete Lavelle at gun point from the darkened dining room.

This time, though, Morrell heard them coming. Instinctively he reached for the automatic tucked in the holster nailed to the inside corner of the bar, but then he realized that he wouldn't shoot Reeve tonight any more than he would have him arrested. To kill him would be to free June of her marital ties; and a free June, he was afraid, would be irresistible.

"This time he was waiting outside the back door, Marv," Lavelle said, almost apologetically.

"He doesn't want to get in a rut," Morrell snapped, "if he can help it."

"None of your lip, Marv," Reeve said, his voice muffled by the same rubber mask and blurred with Dutch courage. "Just pass the sack over, thass all."

Morrell wordlessly set the sack on the bar. It was not as heavy as the last time, but heavy enough. Morrell resolved each Friday hereafter to prepare the night deposit at 10 P.M. That would reduce the amount of cash on the premises at closing time to an amount more in keeping with the value he placed on June's favors. He could stand the gaff to that extent until he worked her out of his system.

Reeve took the sack from the bar with his back carelessly turned to Lavelle. For a moment Morrell was afraid the bartender might be inspired by a flash of courage, but Lavelle stood, mute and pale, while Reeve turned and tottered to the front door, once again a sitting duck. Morrell glanced at the concealed automatic and sighed regretfully. *Patience, the time will come,* he counseled himself, and reached for the bottle of his best cognac.

# A Fine and Private Place

## by Virginia Long

It was one of those big curved swords—scimitars, I think they're called—like in Arabian Nights, and it was suspended by a chain from an iron eyebolt set in the stone ceiling. I couldn't see any mechanism that kept it moving, but it was swinging in a wide, regular arc. On each pass it came a little closer to my bare belly. I could feel the rope cutting in where it passed across my stomach, looped my wrists and passed on under the scarred wooden block on which I was spread-eagled. With each deadly swoop, from somewhere to my left I could hear the mind-shattering clangor of a bell which hushed and held for a moment as the sword hesitated at its apogee, then jangled again louder and louder as the sword came back. I gauged the distance the blade lowered with each pass, and when I knew the next swing would gut me like a fish, I tensed my muscles and threw myself to one side, snapping the heavy rope as if it were string. As I rolled off the side of the block a bare fraction of an inch ahead of the murderous blade, my left elbow struck with numbing force against—the bedside table.

It took me a while to orient myself, and I sat there on the side of the bed shuddering, not so much from the lingering horror of the dream as from the writer's horror of unconscious plagiarism. The sword was gone, but the bell still kept up its hellish tempo.

Finally I reached for the telephone, with the sneaking suspicion that it was old Edgar himself, telling me that he was suing me for everything I had; or half of what I had—after all, I didn't steal his Pit.

It wasn't Edgar's voice, but a soft, hesitant half-drawl I hadn't heard often for six years and not at all for two, and the heart that hadn't so much as stirred in me those past two years slowly turned over and started pounding like a trip-hammer.

"Max?"

I held my breath for a minute and let the room settle back down around me, and then I said, "Julia." It was all I could manage, and it wasn't a question.

143

"Max—" She said it urgently and stopped. "Max, does the name Marvell mean anything to you?"

I hadn't seen her for two years, but it would have taken longer than that to turn her into the moronic sort of woman who calls at ungodly hours to ask stupid questions. If she called me at this time of night—I looked at the clock and saw that it was eleven, then at the window and saw that it was light. All right, so it wasn't an ungodly hour except to a writer who had gotten back in town late the night before and then stayed up for the rest of it to finish a story. Anyway, if she'd called me at all it was for a good reason and, as far as I was concerned, she didn't even need that.

*Marvell*, I thought, and my mind took over for a while to give my heart, which was still doing calisthenics, a rest. "Well, there's a lawyer in town, Louis Marvell; old guy, been practicing for forty or fifty years. Fellow named Buck Marvell runs a service station across from the auditorium. There's a Little Marvell Manufacturing Company out on South Loop."

No reaction from the other end of the line, so I dug deeper. "There was a girl in college, Marvell Hudson. Big girl—"

"No. No, it has to be a Marvell that means something to *me*! Oh Max, I'm being so rude. How are you? I've read dozens of your stories and I'm so proud of you!"

"Thanks," I said, but she hadn't broken a two-year silence to tell me she liked my stories, which aren't all that good anyway. They keep the refrigerator full of beer and cheese while I write my novel.

Julia's voice was unsteady, and I was sure it wasn't for the same reason my own was. I asked, "Is something wrong? What's this Marvell business?"

There was a long silence and I heard her draw a deep breath. "I'm frightened, Max. I got this letter—not really a letter—could I see you?"

"Do you still live in the same place? I can be there in half an hour."

"Oh, please! Yes, the same apartment. It will be so good to see you again."

After I hung up, I sat there on the side of the bed remembering the last time I'd seen her; thin and pale, her eyes dark and shiny with tears she hadn't been able to let go, telling me she didn't want to see me for a while. There were a lot of pieces she had to try to put back together, and it was something she had to do alone. She'd known for a long time that I loved her and I knew she knew, but it was something we'd never talked about. There are things you just don't say to your best friend's wife, or even to his widow—at least until after a decent interval.

A week isn't a decent interval, and it was only a week after Lang Winters died that she'd told me in effect, "Don't call me, I'll call you." I'd already done all I could to help. It was me she called when a highway patrolman broke the news to her that Lang's car had gone off the road into a gully, rolled over maybe half a dozen times and then burned to a twisted black mess. Part of the twisted black mess was Lang, and I went with her to the morgue to identify the monogrammed ring, money clip and the batch of keys that were about all there was left to identify, but there was never any doubt in anyone's mind that it was Lang. His favorite bar on the edge of town provided plenty of witnesses who'd seen him stagger out alone not long before closing time, thirty minutes before the accident, and get in his car. They weren't surprised to hear about the wreck, but only that he'd been able to drive twelve miles before he had it.

Lang was sort of an oddball in college, and I suppose maybe I was too. We lived in the same dorm, and we had hit it off right from the start. We were both taking a lot of literature and creative writing courses, but his interest was poetry and I knew I was destined to write the Great American Novel. He showed me quite a bit of his stuff, but it was too undisciplined for my taste.

I remember the night he decided on a pen name. "Lang Winters," he said, giving it the German pronunciation. "Kurt Sommers. What could be more logical for the other half of me, my alter ego? Long winters and short summers make a nice rounded whole. What do you think?"

I assured him it was an inspired choice.

During our junior year he started sending off poems, signed "Kurt Sommers," to different magazines, but I don't think he ever had one accepted. I always knew when he got a rejection slip, though. He'd come to my room, lounge around for a few minutes playing at being casual, and then say suddenly, "What we need is a *beer!*"

During our last year, Julia was in one English Lit class with us. We started going around together, the three of us at first and then it gradually narrowed down to the two of them. I didn't hear any more invitations for beer and, as far as I know, he never wrote another poem. At midterm, he changed his schedule to get as many journalism classes as he could, and that would have told me, even if he hadn't, that he was dead serious about Julia. Rejection slips don't go far toward supporting a wife.

They were married right after graduation, as soon as he'd landed a job writing copy for an advertising agency. He was good at it, too, and within a couple of years he made account executive.

At first, they had me over to dinner often. I enjoyed the evenings, the good food and the good conversation. Trouble was, I gradually found myself looking forward to those evenings too much and not for the food or conversation, so I started finding excuses to turn down the dinner invitations, even to the point of taking out girls I didn't care anything about, just to be busy when Lang called. Through friends, I heard that things weren't going well with them. Lang started drinking heavily and lost his advertising job, but he took a couple of big clients along with him and set up an agency of his own. It was a shoestring affair, but he was able to keep his head above water because Julia ran the office and saw that he was sober enough at the right times to keep the small stable of clients happy.

I still went by for an occasional Sunday dinner, but it was pizza now instead of steak, beer instead of wine. I couldn't bring myself to a complete break, but I made a deal with myself that I'd look at Julia only when she spoke to me, and I'd confine most of my conversation to Lang. It got harder and harder to do, though. There was a bitterness building up in him, along with his increasing reliance on the bottle. Most of his hostility was aimed dead at Julia, who would sit there with a bruised, helpless look in her eyes after one of his tirades. I was getting pretty close to hating him.

The last time I saw him, just a couple of weeks before the accident, was at the end of a particularly unpleasant Sunday evening. I helped Julia get him to bed after he'd taken a drunken swing at me for no good reason, and then passed out. As I was leaving, I brushed aside her apologies and took both her hands in mine.

"Julia, if you ever need me for anything, call me. But whatever friendship we had—" I glanced toward the bedroom where Lang was snoring heavily, "I think it got drowned somewhere along the way."

She nodded, clasping my hands like a frightened child, and when I bent to touch my lips to her forehead, it was like kissing a little girl; but netiher of us was a child, and I knew that was why I had to leave and not come back.

I did come back, of course, but it was only when I got a frantic call in the night two weeks later . . .

Now I pulled my thoughts back to the present. I put some coffee on to perk while I shaved and showered, and then burned my mouth trying to drink it and dress at the same time.

It was exactly thirty-five minutes after I'd hung up the telephone that I wheeled my elderly car into a parking spot at her apartment house, and I was cursing myself for being five minutes late; but when she opened the door it didn't matter. Even two years didn't matter. There she was, tall and slim and completely lovely, the short blonde hair done a little differently, but those incredible violet eyes just the same.

We stumbled through our greetings. I tried to tell her I was glad to see her without telling just *how* glad, and she was trying to observe the amenities but obviously wanting to get to the point. I apologized for being so slow to answer the phone, explaining that I'd been out of town until late and then up the rest of the night writing, and then she apologized for waking me.

Finally, she walked over to a desk where she took a folded sheet of paper from an envelope, turned and held it out to me.

I took it and glanced at it. Three words, scrawled in a heavy masculine hand, jumped out at me. "Marvell was wrong!" That's all it said.

I met her eyes and saw there a sort of waiting terror. There was nothing so frightening about the words, but obviously it wasn't the words themselves that had her on the edge of hysterics.

"You still can't make any sense of it?"

"No, I have no idea what it could mean. But, Max, don't you notice anything about it?"

I studied the paper again and shook my head. She started to speak, then took a cigarette from a box and lit it with trembling hands. With her back to me, her voice was almost inaudible and completely without inflection.

"It's Lang's handwriting."

I stared at the back of her head, then down at the paper and wondered if she'd grieved herself into some kind of lunacy.

"Julia, it can't be. It's impossible, you *know* that!" But I didn't sound convincing, even to myself. I was comparing the harsh scrawl with what I remembered, and I knew she was right. The "ng" on the end of "wrong" was the same flattened waves with a mere hook at the end that I'd seen a hundred times when Lang signed his name.

She turned to see how I was taking it, and nodded slightly in answer to the stunned look on my face. "A voice from the grave," she said, still in the same lifeless tone.

When she said that, something started buzzing in the back of my mind, something about Lang and Julia and me and graves and Marvell. Finally I had it.

"Julia, remember English Lit in college, the class we three were in?" I saw her hesitate, thinking, and then nod. "We studied Seventeenth Century metaphysical poets: John Donne, George Herbert, Andrew Marvell."

Her eyes widened and some life came back into her voice. "Of course! Marvell was one of Lang's favorites. He was always quoting from something—" She rose and went to a bookshelf near the fireplace and ran her hand slowly along a row of books. She found what she wanted and brought it to me. We didn't need to see the "Lang Winters" written on the flyleaf, but I held the paper in my hand up beside the name. No doubt about it; the very same hand.

She leafed through the book, found Marvell and we started running through poems rapidly. She reached to turn another page, then suddenly slapped her hand down.

"Here. This is the one he quoted so often. *To His Coy Mistress.*"

It was familiar enough to both of us, now that it was right in front of us, but we read it slowly.

*"Had we but world enough and time,*
*This coyness, lady, were no crime . . . "*

It's a clever piece of work, but we were as puzzled as ever until we got a little past the middle of it, and then we both saw it at the same time.

*"The grave's a fine and private place,*
*But none I think do there embrace."*

She closed the book and put it on the coffee table, shoving it away from her as if it were a live and threatening thing.

For a few minutes it had been a challenge, a strange game of Twenty Questions, but now it hit her. She dropped her face into her hands. "Oh, Max, who was that man in the car? *Who did we bury?"*

I was as shocked as she was, but I tried to discipline my thoughts. I went over to the desk where she'd left the envelope. Her name and address were printed, a little shakily, and the ink was blurred and streaked as if it had gotten wet. No return address, and the postmark was blurred as well. I brought it over to the light to try to make it out. At first I couldn't read it—I was pretty shaky myself—but gradually the letters steadied enough that I could see "Overton." I couldn't make out the state, but the zip code was clear. I knew where it was.

Julia still sat in an attitude of despair. I reached for her hand but it was cold and still in mine. I could guess at some of the things that were going through her mind; at best, that Lang had deserted her and let her think he was dead; at worst, that he'd killed a man and was in hiding. While I was aching for her, a plan was shaping in my mind. I knew I had to do something. I had a lot at stake in this too.

"Julia." She looked at me dully from a long distance away, then blinked and came back. "I'm between stories and there's nothing I have to do for a few days. I'll go to this Overton and have a look around. Okay?"

She shook off the numbness with an effort, and with some of her old efficiency found an atlas of road maps. She checked for Overtons and found several, but only one in the right zip code zone, about three hundred miles away. She wanted to go with me, but I convinced her that I should do the preliminary scouting, then call her if I had any good leads.

A couple of hours later, after packing a small bag and stopping for a hamburger I couldn't eat, I was on my way. My car is old, but I keep it in good condition and I made the drive in an easy five hours, including a couple of gas stops.

Overton wasn't much of a city. The city limits sign said, "Pop. 35,427" but I don't think it had been changed with the last census or two. I checked into a motel, cleaned up a little and went out to look around.

I found a bar in a decent neighborhood and ordered a Scotch on the rocks. As I sipped, I saw a telephone at the end of the bar and asked the bartender if a directory went with it. He pulled a stained, dog-eared book from under the counter and slid it along the bar to me.

I opened it to the W's and automatically looked for Winters. There wasn't much chance that he'd be using his own name, but in fact as well as in fiction, most people who change their names stick with the same initials. I had to start somewhere. I found a Lloyd Winton and a Lawrence Walters. There was an L. Robert Winters, but it was followed by an M.D., which ruled him out.

My first dime bought me a recording that said the number I had dialed was no longer in service, and when I fed back the dime to try Lawrence Walters, a woman answered. I asked for Mr. Walters, she said, "Just a minute," and then a creaky voice that must have been eighty years old came on. I apologized for getting the wrong Mr.

Walters and hung up. I sipped my Scotch thoughtfully, without any
clear idea of what to do next. I was absently flipping the pages of
the phone book when one of those alphabetical page headers caught
my eye. I turned back to it quickly, and a surge of electricity went
through me. "Short-Summers."

It was too much of a coincidence to ignore. Kurt Sommers—Lang
would very likely have used his old pen name. I ran my finger down
the listings and felt only a slight letdown that there wasn't a Kurt
Sommers. I checked quickly for Curt Summers, just to make sure,
and then dialed Directory Assistance to see if there were a new
listing for either name. There wasn't, but I still felt I was onto
something halfway solid—a ghost still, but at least one with a name.
Lang Winters was dead, and it made a lot more sense to be hunting
Kurt Sommers.

After a fine steak I headed back to my motel. It was too late to
do anything else, and morning would come soon enough. I read for
a while and then slept uneasily, with Julia's face slipping in and
out of my dreams with tantalizing regularity.

The next morning I stalled around over breakfast, trying to think
how one of my fictional private detectives would handle an investigation like this. Not through the police, that was sure. I was hoping
it would never turn into a police matter, and right now it was strictly
a personal affair.

A man can change his name, his living habits, his whole identity,
but he can't change his basic nature easily. Lang had always been
an insatiable reader, and I knew that wherever he lived, as long as
he lived, he'd have a rut worn in the steps of the public library. I
got directions to the library, and was waiting when the door opened
at nine. There was a stern-faced, frizzy-haired woman at the desk.
I arranged my face into a shy, stranger-in-town expression and went
up to her.

I told her I was just passing through town and trying to look up
an old Army buddy. He wasn't in the telephone book, but I just knew
if he were around, he'd have a library card. It worked and while she
was explaining the rules that made it impossible for her to help me,
she was flipping through a card index to "Sommers, Kurt." I saw
"1323 W. 16th, 2B" and fitted it into a mental slot while I assured
her I understood, and thanks anyway.

I had a name and address now, and it almost scared me that things
were moving so fast. I considered calling Julia but decided against
it. Maybe it was all coincidence, and this Kurt Sommers would turn

out to be a fat, middle-aged butcher with a wife and six kids. I'd better narrow things down more before I called.

I found a city map in a drugstore and drove out to West Sixteenth Street. It was a run-down neighborhood, with a scattering of small businesses mixed in with old, two-storied houses and apartment buildings. I located 1323 in the middle of a depressing block, and parked across from it.

I watched the dingy entrance while I smoked a cigarette, reluctant to go in. It was sad to think of an old friend living in such a place, and even sadder to think of the reasons he would have for living there.

When I did get up the courage to go into the building, I rang the bell of apartment 2B a couple of times, and then was turning to leave when I heard movement inside. It was a soft scuffling, as of a man stepping back from the door, trying not to make any noise. I held my breath and listened. I thought I could hear breathing on the other side of the door, but it could have been my imagination. Then there was a faint mewing kind of sound, and I almost laughed out loud at myself. Someone's cat. But still—

Obviously the cat or anyone else there didn't intend to come to the door, so I went back to my car. As I started it, I glanced across and it wasn't my imagination that twitched a curtain back into place. It could have been a cat jumping onto the window sill, but I didn't think so.

I felt that I was at some sort of dead end, so I did just what I do when inspiration deserts me in the middle of a story. I put the whole mess out of my mind, and turned to other things that needed to be done. I got some lunch, had a haircut and shine, and checked over the paperbacks and magazines at a bookstore. I was pleased to see three mystery mags that carried stories of mine. It comforted me to think of how competently I'd solved the problems in those. On that upbeat note I went back to the motel and slept for a while. When I woke up, it was getting dark and I didn't have any better plan than to go back to 1323 West Sixteenth and try again.

This time, as soon as I rang the doorbell I heard heels clicking across a bare floor, and the door opened about six inches, showing me a young, big-eyed girl with dark hair tied back in a ponytail. She appeared to be about seventeen from her hair and her clothes, but her eyes gave her another five years or so.

"Mrs. Sommers?" I hadn't expected a girl at all, but that seemed like a natural assumption.

"Yes, I'm Mrs. Sommers. What do you want?" The question wasn't abrupt or unfriendly, just businesslike.

"I'm looking for an old friend from college days, Kurt Sommers. Someone said he lived here." I watched her closely, not knowing quite what to expect. What I got was tears.

She didn't burst into tears. She just stood there while two huge tears slowly made their way down her cheeks. It was odd that neither her expression nor her voice changed.

"He's not here."

"When will he be back? I'd really like to see old Kurt again."

"When did you say you knew him?" She still held the door open a scant six inches.

"We lived in the same dormitory at college. Does he still write poetry?"

Her expression changed, and she slowly stepped back as she opened the door all the way. I could see the room now—shabby, with cheap furnishings and a sink and stove at one side. It looked clean and neat though, as did the girl. I walked in and she waved me to the only big chair in the room. She drew up a straight kitchen chair and sat down facing me.

"What is your name?"

"Oh, I'm sorry. I'm Maxwell Mannington. I don't know if he's ever mentioned me."

"Mannington," she repeated, her solemn eyes never leaving my face. "He's never talked much about the past. What did you want to see him about?"

"Just wanted to say hello to an old buddy," I said heartily. "I heard he lived in Overton and thought I'd look him up while I was in town."

"When did you last see him?" Fine investigator I was. She was asking all the questions.

"Just about two years ago, I think it was." I knew it was a mistake as soon as I said it. She stood up suddenly and her face was closed and cold.

"He's not here, and I'm very busy."

I stood too, and as I did, I saw a door at the side of the room move imperceptibly. I heard a faint crinkling sound which I couldn't quite place, and I knew that someone stood just inside the door, watching through the hairline crack. I've heard of people's scalps crawling, but this was the first time my own did.

I realized that she hadn't told me a damned thing really. Maybe

here was a Kurt Sommers in the next room and he wasn't Lang at
ll. One of my heroes would have jerked the door open and hauled
he watcher out into sight, but I wasn't about to do it.

She had gone to the door and was holding it open. I had no choice
ut to leave, but I made one last stab. "When Kurt gets home, would
ou tell him I'm at the Starlite Motel on North Central?" She stared
t me stonily, and I left.

I stood by my car uncertainly for a few minutes before I reached
or my keys to unlock it. It was good and dark now, and the dim
ight from the street corners didn't reach the middle of the block.
 had the key out and was making a blind try at finding the keyhole
vhen I sensed, rather than heard, movement behind me, and at the
ame time I got a whiff of something sweet and pungent. Before I
:ould turn, something slammed into the back of my head and the
ast thought I had before I hit the pavement was that it was too
rite; people don't *really* see stars. But I did—novas, supernovas, the
vorks.

I don't know how much later it was when I woke up. I was flat on
ny face on the street, luckily right next to my car, so I hadn't been
run over by any passing vehicles. Maybe there hadn't even been
:ime for any to pass. My head hurt like hell and I was nauseated.
 pulled myself up and found that I still had the car keys clenched
in my fist. I managed to get the car door open and collapsed into the
seat. I cranked the window down and drew some deep breaths of the
night air, and the nausea started to recede a little. I felt the back
of my head. No cuts or scrapes, just one big circle of pain.

I turned on the dome light and checked my wallet. Nothing was
missing, but I didn't expect there would be. If it had been a run-of-
the-mill mugging, I could have hollered cop, but I sure didn't want
them in on this case. One thing was certain: someone didn't want
me to find Kurt Sommers, and that slip of a girl couldn't have packed
the wallop that put me down.

As soon as I felt steady enough, I drove to the motel, took a long,
hot shower, then propped myself up on the bed, set a bottle of Scotch
and a glass within easy reach, and pulled the phone to me. It was
time to let Julia know what was going on.

She listened quietly while I filled her in. I didn't editorialize, I
just reported. I felt a little foolish telling her about getting clobbered,
but I gave her the whole story. When I was through, she was silent
for a moment and then said with soft certainty, "Then Lang *is* there!"

I told her I was inclined to agree but wondered why she was s
sure.

"You said it was after you asked if he still wrote poetry that sh
let you in. So her Kurt Sommers is a poet. And it was when yo
said two years that she turned you out. Isn't it asking too much c
coincidence for there to be two Kurt Sommers who write poetry an
had some shady event in their lives two years ago?"

"Seems like it, doesn't it?" I said, and started to tell her I'd cal
her again the nest day. She had other ideas.

"I've already checked the airlines, and I can get a commuter fligh
out at 7:40 tomorrow morning, arriving in Overton at 9:30. Can yo
meet me?"

"Of course I can, but I don't know if you should be here. I
someone's going to play rough . . . " I touched the back of my necl
gingerly.

"I'm not afraid of anything as much as I am of staying here, no
knowing. See you in the morning?"

I still didn't like the idea of her walking into what was bound t
be unpleasant, however it came out, but I did like the idea of seein
her again. I told her I'd be waiting at the airport.

I'd just hung up, hadn't even taken my hand off the receiver, whe
the phone rang. I picked it up again, and it was a woman's voice.

"Mr. Mannington, this is Elsie Sommers."

I thought about it and decided the girl naturally would have
first name, even if her last name wasn't what you'd call real legit
imate. I was pretty abrupt, which I thought was excusable unde
the circumstances. "Yes?"

"You really are an old friend of Kurt's, aren't you?"

"I told you I was."

"I wasn't sure. I thought you might be looking for him for—fo
some other reason."

"What other reason?" I was curious about how much the girl knew

"No reason, I guess. But I was just looking through some of hi
papers and found an envelope addressed to you."

That really threw me. It was a little too pat. I come around askin
questions, and she conveniently finds a letter that might answe
them for me.

She went on, "If you could come by again, I'll give it to you. I
really am sorry I acted like I did."

I looked at my watch. "It's late now, and I have to meet someone

n the morning. But afterward—would you be home at about
leven?"

"I'll be here, Mr. Mannington." She hung up without saying good-
ye, and it was a long time before I could get to sleep.

This was a puzzler, might even be a trap of some kind, and if it
vere, I'd have to walk right into it. Julia had to have some answers,
nd I had to find them for her. At least this time I'd be awfully
areful about who got behind me. I knew Julia would insist on going
vith me, and she was the one person in the world to whom I couldn't
ay no.

I was at the airport early. When the small plane eased down onto
runway, she was the only passenger to get off at this stop, and
started for her. When she saw me, she broke into a half-run and
rom the look in her eyes I thought for the first time that whatever
egal technicalities our search might stir up, its object no longer had
any emotional claim on her. We both stopped a step short, a little
incertain what to do. Then I put an arm across her shoulders and
she touched her cheek briefly to mine. I led her to the car and we
drove the few miles into Overton.

As we went, I filled her in on the girl's phone call about the letter
and, as I'd anticipated, she wanted to go with me to get it. We stopped
by the motel, got a room for Julia, and I waited while she freshened
up. Then we headed for Sixteenth Street.

It was half an hour earlier than I'd told Mrs. Sommers when we
pulled to the curb across the street and down a couple of doors. I
started to get out, glanced across the street and sank back into my
seat, sliding down as far as I could and motioning to Julia to get
down.

Elsie Sommers was coming down the steps of the apartment building, carrying a man's dark suit across her arm. There was a green-
and-black-striped tie looped around the neck of the hanger, and in
her other hand she carried a paper bag. She walked quickly off down
the street in the opposite direction from the one the car was pointed.
Just as she approached the corner, a large moving van blocked our
view so that we couldn't see which way she turned.

I started the car and drove around the block to the corner where
we'd lost sight of her. I kept circling blocks for ten minutes or so,
but we didn't get another glimpse of her. At last we gave up and
went back to park in front of her apartment. While we waited for
her to come back, Julia speculated: Lang had moved to some other

place nearby, and Elsie was keeping him supplied with fresh clothe
while she got rid of me with a trumped-up letter of some kind.

At five to eleven, we saw her come back, empty-handed. We waite
a few minutes and then went in. She opened the door immediatel;
and seemed only moderately surprised that I wasn't alone.

"This is Julia Winters. Mrs. Sommers." I made the brief intro
duction without attempting an explanation, but I put my arm aroun
Julia to give the impression that I'd just brought my girlfriend along
Things were tangled enough without bringing in more complica
tions. I sure wasn't going to say, "Mrs. Sommers, this is your hus
band's wife."

Julia, very calm and polite, said, "How do you do?" like she reall;
wanted to know, and under the cover of her poise she was studyin;
the girl and the room carefully. My old anger at Lang ballooned. I
was a painful position for her.

Elsie Sommers didn't ask us to sit down, but went straight to th
kitchen counter and picked up a thick envelope. She handed it t
me without a word. I knew she expected me to take it and leave
but I was listening, and it came—a very slight movement from th
other room that I'd have missed if I hadn't been tuned for it. I sav
the tilt of Julia's head, and knew she'd heard it too. It didn't fit wit
the theory Julia had worked out earlier, but I decided to go for broke
since it wasn't likely we'd be invited back again.

Resisting an insane impulse to call, "Lazarus, come forth!" I fixe
Elsie with what I hoped was a steely-eyed look and gestured towar
the bedroom door. "Tell him to come out here!"

She had half turned from us, but she spun back to face me an
she looked startled and puzzled but not frightened, as far as I coul
tell. Then a curious look of resignation took over, and she walke
to the door, opened it a little and said something very quietly. Sh
came back to stand near us and we waited, all three of us, with ou
eyes riveted on the door.

He walked out slowly and reluctantly, looking at the floor, acros
the room, everywhere but at us. He was tall, heavy, and soft-lookin;
through the middle. As we stared, he fumbled in his pocket, took
out a peppermint drop, unwrapped it with the utmost concentratior
and popped it into his mouth.

That brought me out of my paralysis. I'd heard the crinkling o:
a wrapper like that before, and the sharp sweet aroma of peppermint
That's what I had smelled just before I caught it in the back of the

ead. I took three steps, grabbed a handful of shirt just under his
hin and pulled him up onto his toes.

"I ought to break *your* head!" I yelled.

Julia was pulling ineffectually at my arm and Elsie was pounding
n my back, screaming something, when I suddenly realized that
omething was wrong. The man—no, he was just a boy, eighteen or
ineteen—was finally looking at me, and I saw the blankness in his
yes, the slackness about his mouth that mark the mentally re-
arded. I let go of his shirt, feeling foolish as hell.

A defensive Elsie was by him now, her arm around him, and
aying, "This is my brother, Jodie. He's my big, strong helper." She
aid it with the forced brightness of a mother trying to make her
our-year-old feel good. "He's a little shy around strangers."

He was clinging to her, crying, but he sneaked a look at me. "I
idn't want to hurt you. But you scared my sister. She was already
ad, and you *scared* her!"

She kept patting him as one comforts a child, and I guessed it was
he first she knew about him slipping out and clouting me when I
eft the night before. I told her about it, minimizing it now that I
aw it for what it was. She merely nodded as if it weren't important,
vhich of course it wasn't.

There was a soft mewing, whimpering sound from the bedroom
uddenly, and the boy Jodie stopped crying, straightened up and
urried in, to return immediately carrying a sleepy-eyed-baby.

Things were going too fast for me, and I just stood there staring
tupidly. Elsie took the baby, got a bottle from a pan on the stove
nd sat down to feed it. She seemed oblivious to our presence, but
ve weren't about to leave with so many loose ends dangling. I found
ome chairs for Julia and me, and we sat down to wait. Jodie was
eaning against the kitchen counter, watching his sister and the
aby like a big, protective puppy.

Finally the girl looked up, and her face was transfigured. "This
s Amy," she said dreamily. "Amarantha, really—Kurt named
er—but Amarantha is such a big name for such a tiny little
irl . . . " Her voice dwindled off.

"*Amarantha*," I heard Julia breathe, as she put out a tentative
and to touch the golden fuzz on the little head. My mind supplied
a couple more lines: " . . . *Sweet and fair, Ah, braid no more that
hining hair!*" Lovelace, also Seventeenth Century English Lit.

As if she'd read our thoughts, the girl said suddenly, "Kurt has written a lot of things lately. There's a pile of it over there by Jodi if you want to see it."

I found a stack of notebooks on the counter, brought them bac to where Julia and I were sitting and handed the top half to he We started glancing through the closely written pages. I don't kno how it struck Julia—she seemed almost in a trance—but I realize the stuff was good; not great, but very, very good. It was the recor of a poet finally finding his voice. I felt a twinge of sympathy. Whe he was at last writing good poetry, he didn't dare publish.

"I'm not much for reading, but they sounded so pretty when Ku read them out loud to me." Elsie held the baby to her shoulder an patted its back gently. "I don't think he'd want me to give them t you, but I know he wouldn't care if you read then."

We sat silently reading through the six notebooks, then I gathere them up and put them on the counter. Jodie gave me a friendl smile, accepting me now that his sister did, but all I wanted was t get out of there and read the letter that hung like lead in my jacke pocket. I reached for Julia's arm and she stood.

As we turned to go, Elsie looked at me appraisingly. "You reall didn't come here to make any trouble for Kurt, did you?"

That was a hard question to answer, so I just gave her what hoped was a reassuring smile. Julia was an automaton at my sid

"I'll bet it was *you* he wrote to last week!" Elsie said. "I'll bet sounded crazy and you were worried about him."

I looked at her sharply and hedged. "It wasn't very clear."

"He had this awful headache and started drinking to kill the pai But it just got worse, and he started yelling and acting crazy. H tore up the whole apartment to find a stamp, and went out in th rain to mail that letter. I said I would, but it just made him ma He said it wasn't anything to do with me. He wasn't used to drinkin so I guess that's what made him act like that."

I could almost see Lang, out of his mind from drink and pain an maybe a gnawing conscience, sending up one little smoke signa like a hunter who was lost but not at all sure he wanted to be foun We turned again to go.

"Come back in an hour, and I'll take you to him." Elsie droppe the bombshell casually and walked off into the bedroom, hummin softly into the baby's ear.

We got in the car and I waited for Julia to say something. I'd don what I promised to do. I'd found Lang for her, and in an hour we' see him. For better or for worse, whatever we did now was up t ner. Against all logic, I was hoping she would say, "Let's leave it alone. Let's go home." But of course she didn't.

"Are you hungry?" she asked, not looking at me.

"No."

"I'm not either, but I'd like a cup of coffee." Her eyes tried to stay away from the edge of the letter that stuck out of my pocket, but couldn't quite manage it.

I started the car. "Okay. Let's get some, and see what Lang has to say for himself." I was getting scared. I didn't want to know what was in that letter. There were a lot of lives just about to get messed up, and I was sure mine was one of them.

Over our coffee, we started reading. I'd finish one page and hand it to her, while our coffee got cold and was replaced with hot by a hovering waitress. Finally, Julia gathered the seven pages together, folded them carefully, and slipped them back into the envelope. She placed it precisely in the middle of the table between us.

"Well," I said. "Now we know."

"For two years I've felt almost like a murderess. I thought I'd failed him and he drank to get the confidence I couldn't give him." She took a sip of her coffee, which was cold again. "He says I tried to make a businessman out of him. I didn't, did I? He could have written poetry or driven a cab or volunteered as an astronaut. I wouldn't have cared."

"No. He just was frustrated and it's easier to blame you. And picking up that drunk drifter at the next bar is just the sort of thing Lang would have seen as a big joke—switching identities with a stranger, even trading jewelry and everything they had in their pockets to make it seem real. Ordinarily they'd have sobered up later, swapped back and you'd never have heard anything about it." I gave Julia a cigarette and lit hers and my own.

"He was in no shape to drive, so the other guy did and he was probably in no better condition. And when Lang was thrown clear of the wreck, he was still drunk enough to be cunning. He had a perfect chance to be a different person, so he just started walking. He must have walked a long way. No one ever reported picking up a hitchhiker in the vicinity that night."

"It's sad to think the man who died was never missed by *anyone.*" She touched the letter with one slim finger. "But Lang says that's what appealed to him, the complete anonymity of the man: no ties, no relatives, no responsibilities. Pretending to be him, Lang was

free to be anything he wanted to be. And he decided to be Kurt
Sommers."

"I guess he met Elsie fairly soon after he settled down in Overton.
He says they are married, and that he managed to get some identification so that his name was never questioned." I was puzzling
over this. He'd have had to be fingerprinted to get a driver's license,
so he probably didn't have one, but anyone can get a Social Security
number and a few credit cards.

"He wrote the letter to you and hardly mentions me, so obviously
he doesn't want to come back. He has Elsie and Amarantha. Oh
Max, that sweet baby would be illegitimate if—Then why did he
send that strange note to me?"

"Conscience, I suppose. Gave you one cryptic clue and if you didn't
follow up on it, it was your fault and he was home free. Or maybe
he was just needling you, like he used to when he got tanked. Elsie
said he was drinking that night, and wasn't used to it."

I picked up the envelope. "This letter is dated almost two months
ago. Maybe he just couldn't make up his mind to mail it. Says he
wants it all on record with 'someone close enough to understand but
not involved enough to interfere.' "

"If he wrote it just since you've been in Overton, surely he wouldn't
have gone into so much detail. After all, you're here, and he could
just tell you all of it." Julia looked at her watch. "Let's give him a
chance to now."

Her voice was heavy with reluctance. I felt it too, but the hour
was up, and we had to see this thing through.

As we walked into the hallway, Elsie was at her door, giving last-
minute instructions to Jodie, who was holding the baby carefully
against his big shoulder and frowning with concentration. She
turned to greet us.

"We can walk. It's only a few blocks." She turned to her left outside
the doorway, and we fell into step on either side of her. I kept
glancing over at Julia, but her face was unreadable. My feet felt
heavier with every step. I didn't want to see him. I just wanted to
take Julia and go home. Lang Winters was as dead as we'd thought
him to be, and it was Kurt Sommers who was waiting for us—husband,
father, poet, and stranger. But there wasn't any easy way out of this
awfulness.

Elsie turned to climb some steps into a gloomy building, and we
followed obediently in her wake. We entered a long, dimly lit hall
where a thick, sweet smell hung in the air, faint incense or the

mingled odors of a hundred kinds of stale flowers. She paused at a door, and I was only vaguely aware of an elderly man coming toward us, his footsteps muffled by the worn carpet. Elsie shook her head, and he retreated as she opened the door and we went in.

We stood in complete silence, staring at last at Lang Winters. His face was thinner than it was two years ago, more sensitive, and there was a little gray in his hair that was out of place in a man only twenty-eight years old; but it was Lang, or Kurt—or both. He wore the dark suit we'd seen Elsie carrying, the green-striped tie, and an expression of impenetrable serenity. I involuntarily put one hand against the casket to steady myself and the other arm around Julia, who had gone as white and still as marble.

Elsie was speaking in a soft monotone. "The morning after he went out in the rain to mail that letter—Thursday, it was—his head was still hurting so much I talked him into going to a doctor. They took X-rays and said he had a cerebral aneurism, a weak spot in an artery in the brain." She said the words carefully, as if she'd learned them by rote. "The doctor gave him something for the pain, but said he had to be careful not to exert hinself or get real excited about anything. He was supposed to go to the hospital for tests the next day, but—"

I was sweating and my ears were ringing. I hadn't counted on seeing him like this, but I didn't miss a word of her explanation.

She went on. "We went home and he just sat in that big chair for a long time, I guess thinking about how bad things looked for him. Then he said he had to go out for a while. That was about noon Thursday, and at eight thirty that night some people found him dead by the door of a bar downtown. He'd been drinking, and they say the aneurism just burst."

Her eyes left his face reluctantly and moved to mine. "I always thought he did something real bad just before he came to Overton, but he didn't tell me about it and I never pestered him to find out. I was afraid you were a policeman, and I didn't know what to do. It was too late to hurt him, but there's Amy—"

I put my hand to her cheek and said shakily. "You did right, Elsie. And thank you for letting us see him."

"Would you want to stay for the funeral? You, too, Miss Winters?"

I waited for Julia to answer that one, and it took her a minute. She looked deep into the girl's eyes and made a decision. "I'm afraid we won't be able to stay, but thank you. And it's *Mrs*. Winters."

"But I thought—" Elsie looked from Julia's ringless finger to me, a little embarrassed. "I thought—"

"I'm a widow." Julia said it slowly. "I lost my husband several years ago."

We left Elsie and Kurt Sommers there together, and walked out into the sunlight, which almost blinded us after the gloom of the mortuary.

Julia was quiet and so was I, for a while, but the silence got too heavy for me. It was stepping up the shakes I'd had ever since we had walked into the room and seen Lang. I had to say something, anything.

"That was a shock, but maybe now you can finally forget him. He looked good, didn't he, in spite of the nasty fall?"

"Nasty fall?" She turned and stared at me blankly. "Elsie didn't say—"

Something in my face must have made her stop, and I saw a curious expression come into her violet eyes—that uncanny mind-reading of hers again. She backed away from me and when she spoke again, her voice was like shaved ice. "You *knew!* And yet you let me walk in there expecting— You said you were out of town Thursday night. *Where were you?*"

"Julia, Julia—" I reached for her but she jerked away from me, right off the curb into the path of a cruising cab. It screamed to a stop, and when she saw what it was, she ran around to the far side and climbed into the back seat.

I stood there on the sidewalk with the smell of exhaust fumes in my nose and a taste like ashes in my mouth, thinking. Probably they could find out that Lang had called me Thursday a little after noon, asking me to come to Overton. Maybe they'd even find the service stations where I'd gassed up on that first trip. I hadn't tried to cover my tracks; I was half-numb from the shock of finding out he was alive. The numbness went away and a sort of cold fury took over when he asked me to help him put things in order. He said he didn't know if Julia would want him back, or even if he wanted to go back, but it was very important to him to get everything straightened out. He didn't mention mailing anything to Julia—he never had remembered things he did when he was drunk—and he didn't tell me what name he was using. So both my shock when Julia called me and the search itself were genuine. I just figured he was having a bad run of luck and wanted me to pull him out of his depression as I did in college. The beer in front of us was the same, but my feeling had changed considerably since those days.

With Lang dead, I'd always figured I'd eventually get Julia if I played my cards right and didn't rush her. I'm a patient man and I knew she was worth waiting for; but with him alive, I wasn't so sure. I knew I couldn't stand losing her to him again.

When we left the little basement bar where he'd had me meet him, we climbed up fourteen or fifteen steps to street level. I was ahead of him and when I reached the top step, there wasn't anyone in sight on the street. I didn't plan it at all—I just turned, put my hands against his chest and gave him a quick, hard shove. I remembered his eyes, wide and unbelieving as he went over backwards and down, and then he lay without moving at the bottom of the steps, just short of the bar door. I went down quickly, with the idea that cracking his head a time or two against the cement would finish it, but when I saw his eyes still wide open and staring in blind astonishment, I knew there wasn't any need. No one saw any of it, I'm positive of that.

If he just hadn't written that damned thing to Julia . . .

Looking after her cab now, I couldn't even guess what she would do; let the dead past bury its doubly dead, or blow the whistle on me. It didn't matter, one way or the other. Once she'd figured it all out, she was lost to me for good, and that's about all the punishment I can handle.

Besides, what can be done to a person for killing a dead man?

# Dead, You Know

## by John Lutz

**D**ale Buzzly had stopped in at the lounge of the Hockley Building for a pre-dinner cocktail when he spotted him, the same suave and dashing Phillip Curtendon of college yesteryear. Buzzly surveyed his old acquaintance from his vantage point in a corner booth. Curtendon had put on a bit of weight in the five years since Buzzly had seen him, but there was that same imperturbable yet somehow eager look in the pale blue eyes, the perfectly straight, too-pretty nose. It was the look of a winner, and Buzzly knew immediately what Curtendon was doing in the Hockley Building lounge.

Curtendon spotted Buzzly, looked astonished, then recovered his composure and walked over to join him in the booth. Buzzly stood, smiling, and held out his hand.

"Why, Dale Buzzly!" Curtendon said as they clasped hands warmly.

"Phil Curtendon," Buzzly said. "What the heck are you doing *here?*"

Curtendon's face remained composed as he sat down. "Oh, I stop in here every once in a while in the evenings."

Buzzly finished his martini, saw that was what Curtendon was drinking and signaled Billy, the bartender, for two more of the same. "What are you doing now, Phil?" he asked.

"I'm a sort of manufacturer's representative," Curtendon said. "The occupation is hard to describe but the pay is good."

Buzzly smiled. "That's what counts."

The barmaid brought their martinis and both men were silent until she'd left.

Buzzly took a sip of his drink and began slowly revolving the glass by its slender stem. "Funny we never ran into each other before. I'm in here pretty often myself."

Curtendon shrugged. "Coincidence works both ways, I guess."

"You don't live around here, do you, Phil?"

"Nope. Over on the west side of town." Curtendon averted his eyes as he sipped his drink. "Where you living, Dale?"

164

"I live upstairs," Buzzly said. "The building has apartments from
he fifth floor up. I'm on the seventh."

Curtendon looked appropriately surprised. "Say, nice address."

"Yes, nice number," Buzzly said slowly.

Curtendon cleared his throat. "Far cry from our rooms at old State
University." He smiled into his drink. "Some days, those . . . "

"Almost ten years ago."

"Remember Professor Newcombe?"Curtendon asked. "And Molly
Wallace?"

"Couldn't forget Molly Wallace," Buzzly said. "You know, Phil, I
never really liked you much in those days."

Curtendon looked surprised, and more hurt than Buzzly imagined
he would.

"Why, that's a hell of a thing to say, Dale. We were even room-
mates for a while."

"True," Buzzly said. "Maybe that's why we were friends. You always seemed to get the better of me in those days, Phil: better at
sports, better grades, better car, better looking . . . I lost more girls
to you than I can remember."

Curtendon laughed, but not very humorously. "Well, you didn't
lose the one that counted." He twisted the cheap diamond on his left
ring finger. "How is Babs?"

"I'm surprised you didn't ask sooner," Buzzly said, "considering
you were engaged to her once."

"Well, buddy boy, that's one you stole from me, and it's been six
or seven years ago. It's over and done with now."

"You forget pretty easily, Phil."

Curtendon shook his head. "I just know how to chalk up my losses
and not eat my heart out. That's something you should have learned,
Dale."

Buzzly shrugged. "Some people are born grudge holders, I guess."

"I guess," Curtendon said. "So how is Babs?"

"She's dead, you know," Buzzly said. "Committed suicide two years
ago."

Buzzly watched Curtendon's face carefully as he said this. The
handsome features registered shock, and Curtendon even began to
grin with incredulity. Then the implications of Buzzly's statement
began to sink in and the expected sadness came over Curtendon's
face, but not quite enough sadness.

"She'd had some nervous trouble," Buzzly went on, "suicidal ten-
dencies. Saw every kind of doctor and took every kind of medicine

for three years. Tried to do away with herself several times, and then one day she succeeded."

"That's hard to believe," Curtendon said with unconvincing grief "She was so—"

"So full of life so recently?" Buzzly interrupted.

Curtendon stared at him with unmistakable anger. "Yes," he said "I can't believe she's gone."

"Well," Buzzly said, "every step was taken to prevent it, but—" he lowered his palms on the booth's cool table top with finality "—it happened."

"A pity," Curtendon said. The barely concealed anger had completely displaced the grief, and Buzzly was satisfied.

Curtendon tossed the rest of his drink down and stood, buttoning his well cut sport jacket. "I'd better be going, Dale. Work to catch up on tonight."

"Sure you won't stay for another?" Buzzly asked, noticing that Curtendon's shirt needed pressing and his tie was slightly rumpled.

"No," Curtendon said, shuffling sideways out of the booth. "Like to but I can't."

"Drop by sometime now that you know where I live," Buzzly said, standing. "Apartment 742." He pulled a pen and a slip of paper from his pocket as he talked.

"I can remember it," Curtendon said dryly. "Be seeing you, Dale." He forced a smile and left.

Still standing, Buzzly finished his martini. Then he went over to the bar.

Billy was wiping off the bar top with a white towel.

"That fellow I was over there with," Buzzly said, "you seen him around much?"

"Ain't seen him around at all."

"He says he stops in here pretty often."

Billy stuffed the towel on a rack invisible behind the bar. "Maybe he just means the building. If he stops in the lounge, here, it ain't while I'm on duty, and I work from three to midnight. Far as I know, he's just been in this once."

"Once too often," Buzzly said under his breath.

"What say, Mr. Buzzly?"

"Nothing," Buzzly said. "I was just wondering about him; he's an old college friend." Hr turned and left the lounge, walked across the lobby and pressed an elevator button.

The elevator let Buzzly out on the seventh floor and he walked

he few feet down the tiled hall to apartment 742. The door was
unlocked, as he knew it would be, and he entered without hesitation.

Babs was just finishing setting the table for supper. "Hello, daring," she said, coming out of the kitchen with two glasses of iced
tea. "Be ready to eat in a few minutes."

Buzzly smiled at her. She was an attractive woman in her most
attractive years, marred only by the thin, permanently etched lines
of nervousness on her pale forehead.

While waiting for her to finish setting the table Buzzly walked
idly about, looking at the apartment with new insight. Things were
as usual, maybe a bit too much as usual. He went into the half-bath
of the master bedroom and washed his hands.

Buzzly sat across from Babs at the dinner table, exchanging pleas-
antries, stealing admiring glances at her bright eyes and soft blonde
hair, waiting until they were halfway through supper before he
broached the subject. Then he spoke casually, lowering a bit of steak
that he'd speared with his fork and was just lifting from his plate.
"You remember Phillip Curtendon, don't you, dear?"

Her eyes seemed even brighter as her face paled. "Of course. It's
been . . . how long since we've seen him?"

"Oh, five or six years, at least."

She took a sip of iced tea, lifting the glass quickly and jerkily so
Buzzly wouldn't see that her hand trembled. "Whatever made you
think of him?"

"He's dead, you know," Buzzly said. "Thought you might have
heard about it on the radio. As I was driving home tonight I noticed
a crowd and the police just a few blocks down the street. Two of
those radio station roving news cars were there, too, and lo and
behold I hadn't driven a block past when it was on the news on the
car radio. Phillip Curtendon, thirty-three years old, struck and killed
by an automobile at Fourteenth and Brent. Nasty business, too.
Head got caught between the tire and fender and he was dragged
almost a block. Police were sprinkling sawdust all up and down the
street."

Buzzly stopped talking as he heard Babs' fork clacking noisily
against her wooden salad bowl. She was biting her lower lip so hard
that it must bring blood and her eyes were wide and strange. She
seemed completely unaware of the fork in her quaking hand.

"Of course," Buzzly went on, "it might not have been our Phillip
Curtendon, but then there aren't too many Curtendons."

Babs tried to take another drink of tea but the glass slipped from

her hand, bounced off the table edge, and the cold tea spilled ont
the carpet. She only stared at it.

Buzzly rose and walked to her side, placing a comforting hand o
her shoulder. "Here, here, now," he said gently. "I didn't think thi
would upset you so. I'll run down to the pharmacy and get some c
your medicine." He crossed the room and slipped into his jacket
Pausing at the door he looked back at her, sitting white and shake
at the table. "I'll be back quick as I can," he said. "Perhaps I'll hea
something more about the accident while I'm at the pharmacy."

However, Buzzly didn't go to the pharmacy. He got out of th
elevator and instead went directly to the lounge. He sat at the ba
and ordered a martini.

He was still sitting there a few minutes later when he heard a
woman in the lobby near the lounge entrance gasp. Then a man'
voice said, "Oh, my God!" and behind him Buzzly heard a rush o
feet crossing the lobby floor to the main entrance, then silence.

Buzzly sat calmly sipping his martini, waiting for them to identify
the body. It wouldn't be easy, after seven stories. Allowing himsel
a faint smile into his upraised glass, he wondered what Phillip Cur
tendon would say when next they met

# A Certain Power

## by Edward D. Hoch

I had been on the island close to a month, hanging in that sort of nameless void that seems to affect all stateside soldiers in wartime. My duties, within sight of the slender television mast that topped the Empire State Building, were both light and routine, and sometimes whole days would pass without a thought of that steaming jungle halfway around the world where men were dying in the same uniform that I wore.

Duty on Bankers' Island was good duty. We were a Headquarters Unit, which meant lots of typewriters and mimeograph machines, and even pretty young secretaries taking the morning ferry from the mainland. I worked in the office of the Provost Marshal, handling routine clerk's duties, overseeing the two civilian girls who did most of the typing. On weekends I took the ferry to shore and then the bus to the train station for the half-hour ride into Manhattan. Sometimes I dated the girls in the office.

The first month was good like that, with very little extra duty and lots of free time. Often on my lunch hour I'd wander about the island's hundred-odd acres, studying the shore birds that perched on the breakwater, examining the great old homes that once had catered to Long Island's yachting society and now served as officers' quarters. At other times I'd wander up to the north end of the island, where the Castle stood.

The Castle was a gloomy fortress of a place, with walls of brick and mortar more than a foot thick in spots. Some said it had been built originally as a bastion against pirate ships sailing up Long Island Sound, but in truth it had been constructed just after the Civil War for exactly the purpose it was now used—as a military prison.

Some two hundred soldiers were serving their time behind the solid walls of the Castle, adjudged guilty of offenses ranging from drunken driving and insubordination to desertion and manslaughter. Some would serve their entire sentence on the island, others were merely awaiting transfer to a federal penitentiary.

I'd see them occasionally on work details around the island, always

accompanied by one or two "chasers"—military policemen or prison
guards or just plain soldiers, always carrying the M-2 carbines that
were standard issue for such a detail. The prisoners in the pale green
fatigues were a sorry lot, policing the area for dampened cigarette
butts, raking up the few September leaves which were already beginning to drift from the trees. I noticed almost immediately that
they never seemed to smile. Even on occasions when they attempted
a joke with their guards, there was a false ring to it. They never
forgot that they were the prisoners.

I thought about them a lot during that first month, and especially
about one young blond fellow in particular. I'd first noticed him in
a work detail down by the ferry dock, smiling and chatting as he
helped hoist rotting driftwood from the water. He seemed to have
a particularly easy-going manner for a prisoner, unlike that blank
grimness of the others. I wondered what he had to be so cheerful
about.

The war dragged on seeming, by turns, very close and then quite
far away. Autumn was in the air, and already some of the fellows
were dating the civilian girls, taking them into town for college
football games on a Saturday afternoon, or the pro grames on Sunday. Though I didn't have a girl yet from among the local crop, I'd
been debating making the trip alone.

It was on a Friday afternoon the captain ruined whatever vague
plans I had for the weekend. "You are on duty tomorrow, Kenton,"
he said. "We're short of guards for the work details."

"You mean guarding prisoners, sir?" I'd never done it before, and
somehow never imagined I could do it.

"Can't spend all your time behind a desk, Kenton." He lit one of
his customary cigars and looked through the papers on his desk.
"Nothing to worry about. If they try to escape, you just shoot 'em."

"And then what happens to me?"

The captain shrugged. "I think it's customary around here to give
you a carton of cigarettes and a transfer to another post. But it
doesn't happen very often. Nobody tries to escape when he's on an
island like this. Don't you worry."

So that was it. I turned out at eight o'clock Saturday morning,
waving to a few of the fellows who were already on their way to the
ferry dock. It was my first visit inside the thick stone walls of the
Castle, but I was to see nothing but the courtyard where we assem-
bled.

There were four of us assigned to guard prisoners that morning, and I was teamed with a military policeman named Craig. He was tall and tough looking, just back from the war, where he claimed to have acquired the slight limp that was more noticeable when he'd been drinking. His conversation was sprinkled with the more obvious obscenities, and I had made a point of avoiding him whenever possible during my month on the island.

"Pick up your carbines at the supply room," the sergeant of the guard instructed us. "And don't be afraid to use them, if necessary. You'll be taking two crews out to work on cleaning and painting officers' quarters for some new occupants. At no time should any prisoner be out of sight of a guard."

We marched them ahead of us, with one guard assigned to each pair of prisoners. I had two who were familiar to me; a stocky balding career soldier who'd been a cook in the mess hall the first week I arrived, and the blond fellow I'd noticed before on work details. Each of them had a large white "P" on the back of his fatigues, the only obvious symbol of status.

"All right," Craig told our four-man detail as we reached the big empty house at the far end of the island. "Fall out here!"

We put them to work at the tasks assigned, but it soon became obvious that orders could not be followed to the letter. Three prisoners had to work outside the house, painting, raking leaves, and generally policing the area, while one, the blond fellow, was assigned to indoor work.

"You can't watch both your prisoners," Craig decided finally. "Go inside with that one and I'll keep these three under control." He fingered the trigger of the carbine as he spoke, and I had the distinct impression he was itching for a chance to use it. Perhaps for him it was like the war all over again, and these were the enemy.

I could do nothing but agree, and so I motioned my single prisoner into the house. It was a big old place with a beamed ceiling in the living room and a built-in bar in a corner of the den—a colonel's quarters at the very least.

"Okay," I told him, "get to it. The floor needs scrubbing first."

He got down on his knees to scrape away some gummy deposit, then looked up at me, smiling, from that position. "What's your name, soldier? Mine's Royce. Tommy Royce."

I shifted uneasily. "Kenton," I replied, not bothering with the first name. There was no point in getting friendly.

"I haven't had you for a guard before," he said.

I thought I wanted a cigarette, anything to keep from the necessity for conversation, but I didn't know how I'd light it without showing a degree of awkwardness with the carbine. I decided against it and answered him instead. "I have a desk job. They were short for the weekend."

He rose from his knees and went to the kitchen for a bucket of water. I followed close behind, the carbine ready. "You don't have to be so nervous," he said, returning to the living room with a bucket of water. "I won't bite you. Go ahead and smoke or something." He was starting to wash down the walls.

"I don't smoke," I lied, then wondered why I'd felt it was necessary.

"Been overseas?"

"No."

"I have. Got shot at once. Bullet nicked the heel of my combat boot. Damn! Never thought I'd come back to something like this—washing down the walls of an officer's quarters."

I grunted and tried to keep from answering him, but I felt almost drawn into conversation against my will, forced into an odd semi-intimacy with this man I guarded. I wanted to know more about him, to know, perhaps, why he always seemed to smile. "What are you in for?" I asked, and the step was taken.

"That's a long story," he said, still smiling. "It would take me all day to tell you."

"I guess we've got all day, at least till you finish this work."

His eyes shifted down to the gun, just for a moment and then rose again to meet mine. "I clipped a sergeant with a shovel," he said casually. "Damn near killed him. Why I did it is the long story."

"How long you in for?"

"Six months hard labor, though this isn't very hard. Maybe they'll find a rock pile for me somewhere."

"You're lucky you didn't get five years."

"I had a good lawyer." He paused in his task and eyed the gun once more. "Would you shoot me if I tried to escape?"

"Probably." I felt uneasy at his question, and wondered why he'd asked it. "They say a guard who lets a prisoner escape has to finish serving his term."

"That's just talk."

"I guess it happens sometimes." I was beginning to wish that Craig would come inside with the others, but he showed no sign of it. I could see him through the front windows, lounging against a tree with a cigarette he'd somehow managed to light, probably by the simple act of leaning his carbine against the tree or cradling it in his arm for a very risky moment.

"That gives you a lot of power, doesn't it?" Royce asked.

"What? The gun?"

"Didn't they ever chew you out for calling it a gun? Rifle, carbine—but never gun!"

I felt myself flush at his correction. "It doesn't give me power," I retorted. "Actually, I don't like the thing."

"But you'd use it against me."

"If I had to."

"You like the army?" he asked after a moment.

"I'm in it. I'm making the best of it."

"What do you think about the colonel who's moving in here? You think he likes it?"

"I suppose so, if he's a colonel."

He'd completely stopped working now, and was facing me from across the room. "Maybe they feel a certain power too, like you when you're holding that carbine. Maybe if the button is just beneath your thumb, there's always a great desire to press it."

"Maybe," I agreed dryly. I wasn't in the mood for philosophy on a Saturday morning.

"This sergeant I hit, I suppose he was like that. Power can be a terrible thing. Somebody said it, 'All power corrupts, and absolute power corrupts absolutely.'"

"Lord Acton said it, but not exactly like that."

"You know a lot, don't you?"

"Not really."

"The power of life and death, that's a pretty absolute power. You could pull that trigger right now, put a half-dozen bullets into me in a couple of seconds. You'd just say I was trying to escape, and nobody'd question it."

I motioned with the carbine. "You'd better cut the talk and get back to work."

"If I don't?"

I was beginning to feel the sweat forming up around my hairline. It was as if he were deliberately goading me. "What do you want, Royce? Do you want trouble?"

He smiled that same smile I'd noticed the first time I saw him, and now it was almost as if I knew the reason for it. He held the power, not me. His words were somehow more powerful than the carbine in my hands.

"You're shaking, Kenton," he said slowly.

"I'm going to get the other guard."

"Can't handle it yourself?"

"*What?* Handle *what*?"

"Me."

I realized in that instant how much he hated me. I don't know why it was me, maybe just because I was guarding him this day, but the hate was true and real and so strong I could almost feel it with my fingers. Perhaps I was the sergeant to him all over again.

"Why are you doing this?" I asked. "Why did you do it to him?"

"With the shovel, you mean?"

"Yes."

"I guess it was just that the shovel gave me a sense of power, like that carbine gives you."

"But he didn't do anything to you?"

"He talked to me," Royce answered. "He was talking to me just the way I've been talking to you, and I wanted to kill him for it. I had the power, and I used it."

I knew then that he'd probably talked to all the guards like this, taunting them, goading them as he'd been goaded, to the point of murder. "I'm not like you," I said, but my mouth was too dry.

"Sure you are. Don't you see, somebody has to be. I suppose I'd go mad if I thought only I could be goaded into murder. I've tried the others. You're the last one." He stretched his arms wide and started walking toward me.

"I'm not the last of anything."

"Sure you are. You have the power. The power."

He was still walking toward me when I flipped off the safety and fired a quick burst of the carbine into his stomach and chest. He didn't even look surprised.

The sergeant of the guard stared unhappily at the blood that had streamed and splattered about the walls. "Damn! We'll have to work all night to get this place cleaned up!"

"He tried to escape," I mumbled. "I had to kill him."

"Yeah."

"I suppose that means a transfer."

The sergeant stared bleakly at the covered body as it went by on the stretcher. "Afraid it means more than that, Kenton. We'll have to call a full investigation. Tommy Royce wouldn't have tried to escape, because he was due to be released tomorrow."

# Hunters

## by Borden Deal

I try to stay out of the woods on the first day of deer season. Any distiller is going to hide his still and keep his feet in his fireplace on that day; besides, there's always people with grudges against the sheriff and that's a mighty good time to pay off any shooting debts. You can always claim it was an accident.

So I had plenty of reasons not to be doing exactly what I was doing now. But there I was, just this side of dawn, wearing a red jacket and walking quietly up the thickly brushed side of a hill, because of the biggest job a sheriff can have. I was trying to prevent a murder from happening.

What's even more important, I was trying to keep a good man from becoming a murderer. He was up there ahead of me and I knew he wasn't out for deer. I topped the ridge and looked down the other side, seeing Webb below me crossing a clearing. He was young, in his late twenties, and I knew he could handle the rifle in his hand. I'd seen him kill his first deer when he was thirteen years old and I remembered his grinning face. And, thinking about it, I knew grimly inside me that he was going to be hard to stop. When murder comes into the mind of a good man, all the good parts of him are twisted to that bloody end.

I got off the crest of the ridge, down into the brush again. I could tell that Charley Woodring, the man that Webb was following, was working toward the bottoms. So I wasn't too anxious yet, knowing that the time for decision hadn't arrived. I had to stop Webb at just the crucial moment, for I'd tried before to talk him out of it without success.

It had started with Webb's wife, a pretty woman with too much youngness and not enough sense. Why women like Charley Woodring I don't know, but he's had a lot of success—especially with other men's wives.

Some men just make a career out of meanness. Charley Woodring was a good man with a gun, and he had guts and bravery. I had hired him once as deputy, but within six months I fired him for bringing in too many arrests with the blood of their beating on them.

Charley liked to pistol-whip a man. So I took his gun and his badge away from him. No deputy of mine is going to pistol-whip people under arrest for the fun of it, or for any reason.

I kept moving, catching a glimpse of Webb once in a while. Even if Charley was as mean as a yard-dog, I had to keep Webb from killing him. I've never been one to step around my duty, even if I didn't like Charley. You can't enforce the law according to your personal likes and dislikes.

The hills were flattening out now into the river bottom. Charley was something of a hunter and I figured he'd get his deer today. If Webb didn't get him first. I could have locked Webb up until the first day of the season was over, I thought. But it would only have postponed the problem. Sooner or later Webb and Charley would come face to face, with murder between them, and this was my best chance to be there, to save Charley and Webb both.

I remembered the day before in the pool room. Charley was shooting a game when Webb walked into the place. I was standing in the back drinking a Coke when he walked up to Charley and put his hand on his arm. Webb is a little man, neat and well-put-together, and he had to look up into Charley's face.

"Charley," he said quietly. The words reached out into the room, stopping the talk, turning the listening faces toward the two men. "Charley, I want you to leave my wife alone."

Charley shook off his hand. I was already moving from the back of the room, but it happened too fast, before I could get to them.

"If a man can't keep his wife at home," Charley said, a mean grin on his face, "I don't know why I should worry . . ."

Webb hit him in the mouth. Charley rocked back with the blow and I could see the blood on his teeth. He chopped at Webb with the pool cue, knocking him down. He butted the cue, aiming it at Webb's face, and Webb was rolling on the floor, trying to get away. It was sudden, ruthless, completely cruel. Chances were Charley could have hand-whipped Webb because of his size. But he used the cue stick.

I put a hard grip on Charley's shoulder. "Hold it," I said. I didn't even have to raise my voice, because he knew who I was.

Charley stopped, looking down at Webb getting slowly to his feet. Then I looked at Webb. I can smell murder, taste it, when I look at a man with killing in his blood. And Webb had it.

"Get on out of here, Charley," I said, not taking my eyes off Webb. "Get on, now."

He had sense enough to go. He walked away, not hurrying, not walking fast. But he was going. I looked at Webb.

"Come on," I said. "Let me clean you up."

He was watching me. "Are you taking me in?"

"No," I said mildly. "Come on. You got a pretty bad place there on your head."

He came with me then. We walked out of the pool room together and up the street to the courthouse. I didn't say anything until we were in my office.

"Charley's right, you know," I said finally. "If a man can't keep his wife . . ."

Webb was looking at me, the hurt in his eyes as naked as an animal's hunting. "What's a man going to do?" he said. "Elsie's young. She likes to go to those dances. What's a man going to do?"

I sighed, sitting down at my desk. "I wish I could tell you, son," I said. "But fighting and killing is no answer."

Webb stopped then, looking at me. "You know I'm going to kill him."

I could feel my eyes and my face going hard. "Not if I can help it, Webb."

He watched me. "I know you don't like Charley Woodring any more than I do." He paused a moment. "Nobody in his town would mind seeing him dead. You know that." He stopped again, looking at me.

I nodded my head. "Yes," I said. I could feel a tiredness in me. I looked at Webb, feeling the futility you get in a job like mine.

"Webb," I said. "Charley Woodring is a human being. When you kill a human being it's murder. And murder is never in season. There's always another way, a better way. I wish you'd understand that."

"Speaking of seasons," Webb said, and his voice was almost light. "Tomorrow is the first day for deer. You going?"

"I never go into the woods on the first day," I said. I tried to match his lightness. "Too many accidents can happen."

His voice was still light when he spoke, but there was that look in his eyes again. I could see it, feel it, but I knew I couldn't reach him, talk him out of it. He was beyond reason.

"I think I'll go," he said. "I might be lucky enough to get me a deer."

He turned and walked out of the office.

I sighed, remembering it. I was walking easier, the brushy undergrowth opening up. I had hoped to show Webb the foolishness of throwing his own life away to kill Charley. But I had failed and now the only thing left to do was to stop him in the moment when Charley Woodring was in his sights. I had to stop him if it took killing to do it.

I turned my head, listening to a racket up on the ridge. A gang of those city fellows was trying to drive the game into stands. I hoped they wouldn't come this way and get tangled up with my own little operation. I speeded up, trying to close in on Webb. There was an old trapper's cabin, empty now and falling down, ahead of us. I knew Charley had killed more than one deer there by waiting until a group of city hunters started driving the game toward the bottoms. I topped the last little ridge and could see the still-empty clearing.

I circled around to the east so I could locate and get to Webb before the shooting started. When I edged up in the brush, Charley was sitting on the rotted steps of the cabin, his rifle between his knees, lighting a cigarette. I swung my head, looking immediately for Webb. He was not in sight. I'll have to work around, I thought, hoping that Webb wouldn't ambush him right away. But he's got something smarter than that figured out, I thought. Something he thinks is smart, anyway.

I started to move around the clearing, hunting Webb, when I saw him coming toward me, walking lightly among the trees. I stiffened, afraid that he saw me, but he stopped a short distance away and worked toward the clearing. He was still in sight when he stopped behind a tree and I knew that he had seen Charley.

Webb was not wearing a red coat or a red cap. He was dressed all in brown, the color of the leaves, and except when he moved he was hard to see. He was a good woodsman. And I knew he was a good shot with the rifle. After all, I'd seem him make his very first kill and develop his skill as a hunter.

Charley sat on the front steps of the cabin, the rifle in his hands now, watching the edges of the clearing with quick flicks of the eye. The waiting stretched out and the sun began to take the cool snap out of the air. I stood quietly, knowing the time was not yet ripe to try to stop Webb. And I had to stop him without hurting him . . . or letting Charley get hurt. I looked at Charley again in the clearing. Somebody ought to have shook you down like a mean dog, I thought, and somebody will one of these days. I brought my mind back to calmness again. But it's not going to be Webb, I told myself. Not if I can help it.

I heard something moving in the brush behind me. I stiffened and turned, very slowly. It was a big buck, with as pretty a set of forks as I've ever seen. He carried that rocking chair high and proud, walking like drifting smoke through the dead-leaved brush. I could have killed him with my pistol from where I stood.

I watched him, thinking, I've seen a better head today than any of these hunters will ever see. And I can't take him, thinking, I don't know if I would take him if I could. For he's seen a lot of hunting seasons come and go. He's got a calendar in his deer-mind marked in red for this day. He's looking for a place to lay up until the season is over, moving without fear ahead of the guns and the men.

I watched him meld into the undergrowth. The seeing of him caught at me. But I didn't have time to think about deer, not even a buck like him. I looked back at Webb, checking his position. He was watching Charley so hard he hadn't even seen the buck.

Then I saw Charley stiffen, lifting his gun. My eyes swept the edge of the clearing, looking toward the place he was watching, and I saw the doe standing in the underbrush. You fool, I thought. Can't you see it's a doe? But he was lifting the rifle, turning slightly in his seat, lifting and firing in one movement, and there was a sudden thrashing where the doe had been. Charley didn't move for a full minute after the sudden crack of the shot, listening for the sound of someone who might possibly be coming to the kill. He knew it was a doe, I thought coldly, watching him. And he shot anyway.

Charley got up, going quickly toward the doe, and stooped over her. A knife flashed in his hand and I knew he was bleeding her. My eyes flicked to Webb. He was standing still, frozen, and I could see his face set tight and hard, watching Charley. I could smell the murder in the clean morning air, tainting it like a polecat does.

Charley stood up, looking around cautiously. He'll take her to the road, I thought, and stash her in a thicket. Tonight he'll come in his car to get the meat, the doe meat that's always out of season, too. Charley stooped again and lifted the carcass. The body flowed over his shoulder in a limp brownness. I looked at him, seeing the design in an instant. There wasn't a spot of red in his clothing to be seen; it was covered by the deer; and Charley was blended against the dead leaves of the brush.

I looked quickly at Webb. He had the gun to his shoulder and I could see the tightness in his face. I knew he was going to kill. It was going to be a premeditated accident. And he hoped to make it stick, in spite of the fight he'd had with Charley, for nobody liked

Charley and lots of accidents happen on the first day of deer season. When Charley was found crumpled under the dead doe . . .

Now was my time. If I could get him over this moment in which he was keyed to the killing, I knew that Webb would be okay, that he'd never want to go through emotionally what he had gone through. But I had to be right . . . for I could get killed, too.

He centered the sights on Charley, his hands smooth and clean in handling the gun. He knew guns. He knew killing. But he didn't know that this killing would follow him the rest of his life—even if I hadn't been there to see it happen.

"Webb," I said. My voice was quiet, just reaching him. "Webb. It's not going to be an accident."

He jerked, stiffened, at the sound of my voice. I had my pistol ready in my hand now. I'd kill him if I had to. I knew that I'd kill him. And he knew it too.

"You can't stop me, Jess," he said. His voice was ragged with tension. "You can't move fast enough to stop me."

"No," I said softly. "But I can hang you for it, Webb."

He turned his head, still holding the gun to his shoulder. His face was white, looking at me.

"You know he deserves it," he said bitterly. "Let me kill him. It's an accident. He's under that doe he killed. And then he won't hurt anybody any more."

I didn't even listen to him. "No," I said. "Put that gun down, Webb. Now."

I could hear his breathing. Charley was in the clearing now, staggering under the weight of his illegal meat. If I didn't have Webb to deal with right now, I thought grimly, I'd arrest you. I'd put you in jail for shooting that doe, even if it isn't my job. But I couldn't think about Charley Woodring, and the unsavory kind of person he was.

No matter what, I couldn't forget that he was a man, a human, and that his killing would be murder.

Webb still hadn't moved his gun. I knew he could pull the trigger before I could stop him. I lifted my pistol, thinking. If I could just wound him, knock him down.

"You ought to let me do it," he said, his voice still soft from the tension in it. "You ought to."

"Webb," I said just as softly, "You saw Charley kill that doe. It hurt you, didn't it? Because it was murder. If you kill Charley Woodring, even if you get away with it, it's going to hurt, too. The rest of your life. Listen to me, Webb. I know what I'm saying."

I had the pistol on him, the hammer back, and I could feel the steel of the trigger under my finger.

"Somebody's going to kill him," Webb said. "It might as well be me."

"Charley'll get his," I said. "He'll bring it on himself."

"And he shot that doe," Webb said. "He killed her . . . murdered her . . ."

He turned to look at me again and this time he was lowering his rifle.

I could see his lips move, and then the shaking went through his whole body like a hard chill.

"All right, Jess," he said, almost whispering the words. "You win. All right, Jess."

I moved then, going toward him, putting my gun into the holster. I wouldn't need it now. I put my hand on his arm, feeling the trembling of the muscles, knowing the turmoil that he was going through now.

"Come on," I said gently. "Let's get back to the car."

He didn't even turn to glance at the clearing where Charley was still unaware how close he had come to death. He went ahead of me, stumbling, as if his feet could not feel the ground.

We climbed toward the ridge, the last ridge from which we could see the clearing. I heard someone coming toward us and stopped, standing in the open where the red of my jacket could be seen. Then I relaxed.

"Hello, Jim," I said to the game warden. "I thought you might be one of those blasted city hunters."

"Hello, Jess," he said. "Just checking around."

We started to move on, and then I stopped suddenly, turning. "Listen," I said. "I think you'll find something interesting down there. If you hurry."

He looked at me sharply. "Yes?"

"Yes," I said carefully. "I think you'll find a dead doe down there in the clearing."

He looked at me, at Webb, and I knew what he was thinking. "Just a doe?" he said. "A dead doe?"

"And the man who killed her," I said quietly. "I saw him do it. I'll testify to it."

"All right," he said. "Thank you, Jess."

He was gone then, moving fast, and I went on up the ridge with Webb.

We reached the top and stopped, panting a little with the sudden, sharp climb. I looked at Webb, seeing his eyes were clearer, his hands steadier.

He stopped and looked at me, drawing a deep breath. "I'm glad you did it," he said. His voice still had a shake in it. "I must have been crazy. To kill a man like that . . ." His voice stopped, shuddering.

"All right," I said. "Forget about it. It's all over now." I looked at him. "And try to go dancing with Elsie yourself once in a while. How about it?"

He smiled at me sheepishly. "I never liked to dance," he said. "But I guess I can try."

"That's all it takes," I said. "Let's go on to town."

He watched me for a moment. "Are you going to . . ."

I shook my head. "We'll just forget about it. There'll be no charge against you. You can't hang a man for what he's got in his mind."

He was looking past me, not even listening to my words. I saw him lifting the gun, the tension in his face again, and blackness whirled in my mind as I started to move, too late to stop him. *I thought he was all right,* my mind gasped at me. *I thought it was all over.* I threw myself at him, but he shoved me away, knocking me off my feet. He steadied himself again and fired in one clean movement.

The shot cracked and I was up again, my pistol in my hand. "I ought to kill you," I said tightly. "I ought to blow a hole in you. After I . . ."

I looked at his face. It was calm. "I didn't kill him," he said slowly. "Look."

I turned and looked down into the clearing. Charley was sprawled on the ground, his gun near him, and Jim was wavering groggily to his feet.

"He hit Jim with the rifle," Webb said. "And then he was going to shoot him. I had to do something . . . I had to try."

I looked, trying to arrange things in my mind. It was a long shot, but he had knocked the gun out of Charley's hands, knocked him down with the shot, giving Jim time to recover. Jim was on his feet now, standing over Charley, moving on the ground.

I studied Webb. "You could have killed him then," I said. "You know that."

He looked at me steadily. "Yes," he said. "I thought of it, in that second I had the gun to my shoulder. And then I knew I couldn't. knew I . . ."

He stopped in confusion. I grinned at him, slapping a hand on his shoulder. "Come on," I said. "Jim will need help. Let's go down there."

We started back down into the clearing again together.

# The Driver

## by William Brittain

The driver would have found it hard to explain, even to himself, why he offered a ride to the man standing with thumb extended at the side of the road. He'd heard story after lurid story about individuals and sometimes whole families that had picked up hitchhikers who had turned out to be dangerous. The lucky ones lost only their cars and personal belongings. The unlucky ones ended up on a slab in the morgue, some with bodies marred only by a single neat bullet hole and others horribly mutilated.

Perhaps it was loneliness. He'd been driving since five o'clock that afternoon, and it was now after nine. The car was almost new, with only a thin layer of dust dulling the glistening exterior, but something was wrong with the radio; it only hissed and popped when he turned it on, so there was no human voice to relieve the tedium. There was just the ribbon of cement, coming into the beam of the headlights and passing out of sight beneath the wheels, mile after brain-numbing mile of it.

Then again, maybe it was the memory of how he himself in his younger days used to thumb his way around the country. There were times when he'd have given the shirt off his back for somebody to stop and give him a lift, and he remembered how rough it was when darkness fell and he still hadn't reached his destination.

The driver had just passed the Thruway tollgates at Spring Valley. According to the attendant, the road was clear at least to Albany. A little rain was expected between there and Utica, but nothing to worry about. The driver grasped the offered ticket, tucked it above the sun visor, and pulled out into the darkness that was punctuated only by the reflecting mileage indicators on posts at the edge of the road. Four to every tenth of a mile, they seemed to zip by him like glittering cats' eyes. For the next four hundred miles, he'd have no worries about traffic lights, oncoming cars or crossroads; just the reflectors, four to every tenth of a mile.

As the Thruway narrowed beyond the tollgates, the car's headlights illuminated the man standing at the edge of the road. There

184

vas a cheap cloth bag at his feet. As the car passed, the man waved
his thumb, a questioning expression on his face.

On a sudden impulse, the driver braked his car to a halt. Before
he could put it into reverse, the man had run up beside him and
poked his head in through the open window on the passenger's side.
"Ride, mister?" he asked.

The driver turned on the overhead light and looked at the man.
He was wearing a jacket and tie—that was good—and even though
he needed a haircut, he wasn't too shaggy, not like those hippie kids
with their knapsacks and bedrolls. The man smiled shyly.

"Hop in," said the driver.

Opening the door, the man placed his bag on the floor and relaxed
onto the seat with a weary sigh. The driver switched off the overhead
light and pulled the car out into the center of the three northbound
lanes. The speedometer needle crept quickly up to 60.

"How far are you going?" asked the driver.

"Albany," the man said. "That is, if you're not getting off the
Thruway before that. I've got a job up there, but I've got to make
it before eight o'clock tomorrow morning."

"You'll make it. I'm going clear through to Buffalo. I'll have to let
you off at the exit ramp, though."

"That'll be fine. I'm sure I can get a ride into the city from there."

In silence, they sped through the night for several minutes.
"What's your name, young fellow?" asked the driver finally.

"Sam. Sam McCullough. And I'm not so young. I'm almost twenty-
five."

"To me, that's young," said the driver. "You know, Sam, I'm glad
to help you if you've got a job waiting in Albany, but don't you know
it's against the law to be hitching rides on the Thruway?" He heard
McCullough twisting uneasily in his seat.

"Are you going to turn me in?" McCullough asked in a small voice.

"No. Matter of fact, I don't know why I said that. I've had to thumb
rides a few times in my life, too. But people trusted each other more
then, I guess. I seldom had trouble getting where I wanted to go."

"I was waiting in that spot where you picked me up since it got
dark," said McCullough. "I dodged into the bushes when I spotted
anything looking like a police car. What I mean is, I had to get
moving tonight. I couldn't take any chances on getting picked up
for hitchhiking."

As the car hummed onward, bright specks of light in the darkness
indicated that they were approaching a village. "That's the Suffern

exit," said the driver. "Tell you what. There's a restaurant just be
yond here. Suppose we stop for a few minutes. Stretch our legs an
get a cup of coffee."

"I don't want any coffee," said McCullough.

"A bit down in your luck, are you? I'll buy for both of us. How'
that?"

"No coffee," McCullough repeated. "I don't want anything."

"Oh. Well, I hope you don't mind waiting while I have a cup. I
won't take long. I like to drink it while it's hot."

There was a rustling of cloth, followed by the sound of a zippe
being pulled. *Maybe McCullough has got some money in that bag o
his,* thought the driver. *Maybe . . .*

"We're not stopping, mister." McCullough's voice grated harshl;
in his throat.

"Listen, this is my car. I'll do what I want to. What right hav
you got to tell me—"

"I got this right, mister."

The barrel of the pistol ground painfully into the driver's ribs
Involuntarily, he jerked at the wheel and the car lurched toward th
center divider.

"Careful," snarled McCullough.

The driver yanked the car back into the center lane and tappe
at the brake.

"Don't stop," McCullough went on. "Just keep driving, not to
fast, not too slow. Nice and normal, get me?"

They flashed by the restaurant and out into open country. For th
fifteen miles to the Harriman interchange, neither man said a word

"The Thruway narrows to two lanes here," the driver finally whis
pered hoarsely.

"So? We haven't seen more than half a dozen cars. Just don't star
getting cute if you spot a police car. No tricks with the lights o
anything. I'm holding all the aces right here in my hand." Mc
Cullough waved the pistol in front of the driver's eyes.

"How—how far are you going to take me?" The driver felt the fea
knotting his stomach muscles, and he wondered if he were going t
be sick. Keeping one hand on the wheel, he used the other to loose
slightly the safety belt and shoulder harness which were clampe
about his body.

"Far enough. The farther I go, the less likely it'll be that the polic
will spot me. It's too bad. I really liked that place." He tapped th

dashboard loudly with the butt of the gun. "Damn that old lady," he added softly.

"Old lady? You mean your mother?" asked the driver.

"No. I mean the old broad in the house back there near Spring Valley. When I saw the man and his wife go out with the kids, I figured the house would be empty, right? Just ripe for the picking. And with the back door unlocked, too. How'd I know they'd leave granny home? I went through the whole first floor and picked up a bunch of great stuff. Portable TV, typewriter, even a good-sized roll of cash. I got this gun out of there, too. Then, just as I was ready to leave, there she was, standing on the stairs in that old nightgown, looking like she should have died ten years ago, but there was nothing wrong with her lungs. She screamed loud enough to wake up everybody in town."

"What—what did you do?" asked the driver.

McCullough rubbed the pistol thoughtfully with his free hand. "Let's just say she won't do no more screaming," he said.

"So you've gotten away," said the driver. "What happens now?"

"That depends on you. Just play it cool, the way you've been doing, and maybe you come out of this alive. Try something, and they'll be picking your body out of the ditch. I got nothing to lose."

"I won't try anything. I—I don't want to die."

"Not many people do, mister."

As the car gathered up the miles, the driver tried unsuccessfully to control the trembling in his body. He wanted to live but that, after all, was the reason McCullough was holding the gun on him. McCullough wanted to live, too.

At the Newburgh interchange, a tractor-trailer truck suddenly lurched out in front of them from the entrance ramp. The driver jammed on his brakes, and McCullough drew in a sharp breath, slamming his feet against the floorboard as if he could stop the car by force of will alone.

"Idiot!" snapped McCullough as the truck, doing at least eighty, growled off into the darkness and the car rocked back under control again.

The driver didn't respond. Instead, he peered thoughtfully at the pattern the headlights made on the highway ahead. Then he twisted a knob which turned on the instrument-panel lights. Darting a glance toward his passenger, he saw McCullough fingering the shoulder harness which was clipped to the roof of the car, just above the door.

"Don't touch that!" barked the driver. McCullough, startled by th
commanding tone, instinctively drew his hand away. Then he smile
slowly.

"You got it all wrong, mister," he muttered softly. "I'm giving th
orders, not you."

"Listen to me and listen carefully, or neither of us will be worryin
about who's giving orders. Because the highway patrol will be scrap
ing our bodies off a tree or a highway abutment."

"Keep talking, mister. It helps to pass the time."

"First of all, keep your hands off the seat belt and shoulder har
ness. Don't try to buckle them on."

McCullough shrugged elaborately. "I've gotten this far withou
them with no trouble," he said.

"Okay. Keep your hands where I can see them. Because if yo
don't, I'm smashing this car against the first solid thing I can find.

"You don't worry me much," said McCullough. "After all, you'
die, too. Even that safety harness wouldn't do much good in a ca
doing seventy."

"But that's the difference between your situation and mine. I'n
going to die anyway. Isn't that right, McCullough?"

"Look, I told you if you didn't pull any smart stuff, I'd let you go
All I want is the car."

Slowly the driver shook his head. "I don't buy that," he said
"You've already murdered once. Your only chance to get away is t
vanish somewhere the police can't find you. And if you let me go
I might be able to give them enough information to pick up you
trail. What's another killing to you now?"

"Hell-fire! Can't you slow the thing down? We're doing almos
eighty."

"Speed, that's my weapon, McCullough. At eighty miles an hour
you won't dare shoot." The driver jammed his foot on the accelerator
and the car jumped ahead even faster.

"Watch it. If your tires drop into that loose gravel at the side an
you lose control, we'll turn over."

"Don't worry about my driving. Ever read the sport pages, Mc
Cullough? The columns about automobile racing?"

"I don't dig that stuff."

"Too bad. You might have run across my name. 'Lucky' Algood
that's who you're riding with tonight. Two-time winner of the Gran
Prix, Le Mans and Watkins Glen. I never spun out on a racing circui
in my life, and I don't intend to do it now."

"What are you gonna— Look out! You almost clipped that car we passed."

"The gun, McCullough."

"What about the gun?"

"Throw it out the window. That's my price for slowing down."

McCullough chuckled slightly. "You must think I'm crazy. If I throw this gun away, you turn me over to a cop and I face a murder rap. But if you crash, maybe there's a chance I walk away. I'll keep the gun."

"Besides racing," said the driver, "I'm also a safety consultant for an automotive company. I'll bet you didn't know that, either."

"So?"

"So you might try figuring your chances of walking away from a head-on crash at eighty miles per hour. Maybe I can help you. We did some tests, out at the test track. Of course, fifty was the fastest any of our test cars went, but it'll give you some idea of what'll happen to you.

"In the first tenth of a second after the car hits, the front fenders, the grille and the radiator are mashed into crumpled metal. In the next tenth of a second, the hood smashes and pops up in front of the windshield, while the back wheels lift off the ground. You see, the front of the car will have stopped, but the rear keeps right on coming forward. By instinct, you stiffen up, just the way you did when that truck swerved in front of us. The bones in your legs break clean through at the knees."

"Cut it out, Algood!"

"Don't you want to know how you're going to die? During the third tenth of a second, your body rockets forward. The dashboard mashes your knees. At the fourth and fifth, both you and the rear of the car are still traveling at about thirty-five miles per hour. Your head collides with the instrument panel.

"At six-tenths of a second, the car's frame bends. The instrument panel has crushed your skull by this time. Your feet crunch their way through the floor. The force of the sudden stop yanks your shoes right off your feet."

The driver paused. "That's about it," he finished. "Then doors pop open and hinges tear away. The front seat rips loose and crushes your body from behind. But you don't have to worry about that. Because by that time, you're dead."

"You—you've seen this happen?" asked McCullough.

The driver nodded. "Slow-motion pictures of wax dummies on the

test track. Of course, in doing the amount of racing I have, I've see
the results of some bad accidents. It isn't pretty, McCullough."

McCullough forced a thin laugh through dry lips. "You know, yo
had me going there for a while," he said. "But you're not going t
crash this car unless you have to, Algood. What happens if I outwa
you? You've got to run out of gas sometime."

"I'm way ahead of you. I'm a racing driver, remember? Thes
machines are my meat and potatoes. Why do you think I didn't allo
you to put on the safety harness?"

"What are you getting at?"

"There's a certain speed—not very fast, really—where I can h
something solid and this harness I'm wearing will keep me safe. Ol
it'll bruise my chest, but I'll be held in the car. You, on the othe
hand, will be shot forward. There are a lot of interesting possibilitie
Maybe you'll just be knocked unconscious against the dashboar
On the other hand, you could stick your head through the windshie
and either fracture your skull or slit your throat on the glass. I
any case, I'll be safe, and you . . . Please don't touch the safety belt.

The car swerved alarmingly, and McCullough slid his hands ont
the top of the dashboard.

"Now the gun, McCullough. Throw it away."

McCullough gripped the pistol tightly. "I oughtta . . ." He pointe
the weapon at the driver. Neither man spoke, and the only sound
were those of the tires on pavement and the air rushing by the ca
The driver could sense McCullough's mind weighing the alterna
tives. Capture meant an easily proved accusation of murder and th
rest of his life spent in a small cell; years wasted because of an ol
woman's screams. There was a click as McCullough took up th
slack in the trigger, and the driver's sweaty hands tightened on th
steering wheel.

Yet to shoot was to risk the awful carnage of a crash at nearly
hundred miles an hour, the shriek of jagged, twisted metal cuttin
through flesh and bone, the mangling of living bodies as the wreck
age compressed them into a bloody, formless mash.

With an oath, McCullough rolled down the car window. A stron
wind stung the driver's face as McCullough threw away the gun. A
shower of sparks appeared in the rear-view mirror as it hit th
surface of the road. The driver slowed the car to a lawful sixty-fiv
miles per hour.

At an underpass just beyond Kingston, he located a police car, it
door open and its red dome-light revolving. He wheeled in besid

he gray automobile, placing his own car close enough so that it was mpossible for McCullough to open his door and make a run for it.

"Lucky Algood, a racing driver!" spat McCullough as the trooper napped handcuffs onto his wrists. "Out of all the cars that travel he Thruway, I had to get you. You don't even look like a racing lriver should. Too small and skinny."

"It doesn't take strength, McCullough. Just quick reflexes."

"If you weren't a professional driver and didn't know all that stuff about crashing cars and such, I'd have been home free," growled McCullough. "The cops never would have found me—or you either."

None too gently, the trooper yanked McCullough to the gray car and placed him inside. Then the trooper returned to where the driver was standing.

"I heard McCullough mention Lucky Algood," the trooper said. "I've seen him a few times on TV, and there's one thing I'm sure of, mister. You aren't him."

"No," was the soft answer. "My name's Entwhistle—Ernest Entwhistle. I run a small bookstore in Philadelphia. I was on my way to visit my daughter and her family in Buffalo. As a matter of fact, I was bringing a gift to my grandson, a book. I found it fascinating reading. But perhaps Mr. McCullough would be interested in it. I can always get another copy somewhere."

From his pocket, the driver drew a slim, paper-backed volume. The trooper took it, glancing at the title: *Safety on Wheels* by Charles W. "Lucky" Algood.

From the front cover, a photograph of a handsome young man in the act of donning racing goggles looked back at him.

# Class Reunion

## by Charles Boeckman

The banner across one wall in the Plaza Hotel banquet room welcomed "Jacksonville High, Class of '53." The crowd milling around in the room was on the rim of middle age. Temples were graying, bald spots were in evidence.

Tad Jarmon roamed through the crowd. At the bar, he found his old friend, Lowell Oliver, whom he had not seen since graduation. "Hello, Lowell," he said.

Oliver drained his glass. "Hi, ol' buddy," he said with a loose grin. He shoved his face closer in an effort to focus his eyes. Suddenly, he became oddly sober. "Tad Jarmon."

"In the flesh."

"Well . . . good to see you, Tad. You haven't changed much." He held his glass toward the bartender for a refill. His hand was shaking slightly.

"We've all changed some, Lowell. It's been twenty years."

"Twenty years. Yeah . . . Twenty years . . ."

"Have you seen Jack and Duncan?"

"They're around here someplace," Oliver mumbled.

"We'll have to get together after the banquet and talk over old times," Tad said.

Oliver stared at him with a peculiar expression. Beads of perspiration stood out on his forehead. "Old times. Yeah . . . sure, Tad."

Tad Jarmon meandered back into the crowd. Soon he spotted Jack Harriman with a circle of friends in another corner of the room. Jack looked every inch the prosperous businessman. He was expensively dressed. His face was deeply tanned, but he was growing paunchy. He'd put on at least forty pounds since graduation.

"Hello, Jack."

Harriman turned. His smile became frozen. "Well, if it isn't Tad Jarmon." He reached out for a handshake. "You guys all remember Tad," he said, a trifle too loudly. His hand felt damp in Tad's clasp.

One of their ex-schoolmates grinned. "I remember how you two guys and Duncan Gitterhouse and Lowell Oliver were always pulling off practical jokes on the town."

192

"Yeah," another added. "If something weird happened, everybody figured you four guys had a hand in it. Like the time the clock in the courthouse steeple started running backward. Took them a week to figure out how to get it to run in the right direction again. Nobody could prove anything, but we all knew you four guys did it."

The group chuckled.

"I saw Lowell over at the bar," Tad said to Harriman. "I told him we should get together after the banquet and talk over old times."

"Old times . . ." Harriman repeated, a hollow note creeping into his voice. "Well . . . sure, Tad." He wiped a nervous hand across his chin. "By the way, where are you living now?"

"Still right here in Jacksonville, in the big old stuffy house on the hill. After my dad died, I just stayed on there."

Tad excused himself and went in search of Duncan Gitterhouse. He soon found him, a man turned prematurely gray, with a deeply lined face and brooding eyes.

"Well, Duncan, I guess I should call you 'Doctor' now."

"That's just for my patients," Gitterhouse replied, his deep-set eyes resting somberly on Tad. "I was pretty sure I'd be seeing you here, Tad."

"Well, you know I couldn't pass up the opportunity of talking over old times with you and Jack and Lowell. Maybe after the banquet, the four of us can get together."

The doctor's eyes appeared to sink deeper and grow more resigned. "Yes, Tad."

The banquet was followed by speeches and introductions. Each alumnus arose and told briefly what he had done since graduation. When the master of ceremonies came to Tad, he said, "Well, I'm sure you all remember this next guy. He and his three buddies sure did liven up our school years. Remember the Halloween we found old Mrs. Gifford's wheelchair on top of the school building? And the stink bombs that went off during assembly meetings? They never could prove who did any of those things, but we all knew. How about confessing now, Tad? The statute of limitations has run out."

Tad arose amid laughter and applause. He grinned and shook his head. "I won't talk. My lips are sealed . . ."

After the banquet, the four chums from high school days drifted outside and crossed the street to a small, quiet town-square park. Jack Harriman lit an expensive cigar.

"It hasn't changed, has it?" Duncan Gitterhouse said, looking up at the ancient, dome-shaped courthouse, at the Civil War monument, the heavy magnolia trees, the quiet streets. "It's as if everything stopped the night we graduated, and time stood still ever since."

"The night we graduated," Jack Harriman echoed. He pressed a finger against his cheek which was beginning to twitch again. "Seems like a thousand years ago."

"Does it?" Tad said. "That's odd. Time is relative, though. To me it's just like last night."

"We don't have any business talking about it," Duncan Gitterhouse said harshly. "I don't know why I came here for this ridiculous class reunion. It was insanity."

"Don't know why you came back, Duncan?" Tad said softly. "I think I do. You couldn't stay away. None of you could. You had to know if anyone ever suspected what we did that night. And you wanted to find out what that night did to the rest of us, how it changed our lives. We shared something so powerful it will bind us together always. I was sure you'd all come back."

"Still the amateur psychologist, Tad?" Harriman asked sourly.

Tad shrugged.

"It was your fault what we did that night, Tad," Lowell Oliver said, beginning to blubber in a near-alcoholic crying jag. "You were always the ringleader. We followed you like sheep. Whatever crazy, sick schemes you thought up—"

"We were just kids," Gitterhouse argued angrily. "Just irresponsible kids, all of us. Nobody could be held accountable—"

"Just kids? We were old enough in this state to have been tried for murder," Tad pointed out.

There was a heavy silence. Then Tad murmured slowly, "I used to go past the place on the creek where old Pete Bonner had his house-trailer. For years you could see where the fire had been. The ground was black and the rusty framework of the house-trailer was still there. It was finally cleared away when the shopping center was built, but every time I go by that place I think about the night old Pete Bonner died there. And I think about us. A person acts; the act is over in a few minutes. But the aftermath of the act lives on in our emotions, our brains, perhaps forever. We committed an act twenty years ago. The next day, they buried what was left of old Pete. We're stuck with that for the rest of our lives."

They fell silent again, each thinking back to that night. It was true that Tad had been the ringleader of their tight little group, and the night of their graduation, it was Tad who thought of the final, monstrous prank: "Let's set Pete Bonner's trailer on fire."

"But Pete's liable to be in the trailer," one of the others had said.
"That's the whole point." Tad had grinned, then explained, "After
onight, we'll be going in different directions. Duncan is going into
iedical school. Lowell's going into the Army. Jack's going to busi-
iess college. I'll probably stay here. We need to do something so
tupendous, so important, that it will weld the four of us together
orever. So, we'll roast old Pete Bonner alive."

Tad had pointed out to the rest of them that Pete was the town
Irunk, an old wino who had no family. It would be like putting a
vorthless old dog out of his misery.

Because of the hypnotic-like hold Tad had on the others, they had
Igreed—sweating and scared—but they'd agreed.

That night after graduation exercises, Tad led them to Pete Bon-
ier's trailer with cans of gasoline and matches. As they ran away
rom the blazing funeral pyre, the screams of the dying old wino
ollowed them.

"I can still hear that old man screaming," Duncan Gitterhouse
iaid, his hands shaking as he chain-lit another cigarette.

"Tad, you said we're stuck with what we did for the rest of our
ives," Jack Harriman sighed. "It's true. I've made a pile of money,
iut what good is it? I can't go to sleep without pills. I eat too much.
My doctor says I'm going to have a coronary in five years if I don't
quit eating so much, but I can't stop. It's an emotional thing, a
:ompulsion. Look at poor Lowell there. He's spent the last five years
in and out of alcoholic sanitariums."

Duncan Gitterhouse nodded. "My practice is a success. Compen-
sation, I guess. I have the idea that if I save enough lives, I'll make
up for the one we took. I do five, ten operations a day. But my private
life is a shambles—my wife left me years ago; my kids are freaked
out on drugs." He turned to Tad Jarmon. "I suspect you didn't get
off any better than we did, Tad. You never married. You're stuck
here, in the home you grew up in. I don't think you *can* leave . . ."

They sat in the park for a while. Then they got up and went off
to their respective motel rooms—Tad to his big, old-fashioned house
with white columns.

In his study, Tad took down one of his journals from a bookshelf.
In his neat, precise hand, he carefully described the events of the
evening, recording in detail all that Jack, Duncan and Lowell had
said. Following that entry, he added his prognostication for their
future. "I would estimate that Jack will be dead within ten years,
probably suicide if he doesn't have a stroke first. Lowell will become

a hopeless alcoholic and spend his last years in a sanitarium. Duncan will keep on with his practice, but will have to turn to drugs to keep himself going."

He sat back for a moment. Then as an afterthought, he added, "I will continue to live out my life here in this old house, on the inheritance my father left me, eventually becoming something of a recluse. Duncan was right; I can't leave. It is a psychological prison. But I am reasonably content, keeping busy with my hobby, the study of human nature, that will fill volumes when I am through."

He put the journal away. Then he turned to another bookcase. It was lined with similar neatly bound and dated journals. He went down the line until he found one dated 1953. He opened it and flipped the pages, stopping when he came to the date of their graduation, then he started to read:

"Tonight being graduation," he had written, "I decided we must do something spectacular. A crowning achievement to top any previous prank.

"Early in the afternoon, I stopped by Pete Bonner's trailer. I had in mind giving him a few dollars to buy us some whiskey for the evening. Being under-age, we couldn't go to the liquor store ourselves, but Pete is always ready to do anything for a small bribe.

"I was surprised, indeed, when I walked into Pete's trailer and found him sprawled out on the floor. He was quite dead, apparently from a heart attack. If I hadn't found him, he'd probably have stayed there for days until someone accidentally stumbled upon him as I had done.

"I immediately got a brilliant idea for a colossal joke and a chance to test a theory of mine. They say time is relative. I think relativity is relative. If someone believes he has committed an act, it's the same to him as if he *has* committed the act. The consequences, as far as they affect him, should be the same.

"This time the joke would be on Jack, Duncan and Lowell. They're so gullible, they'll do anything I tell them. I hurried home and swiped the wire recorder out of Dad's study. I recorded some agonized screams and put it under Pete's trailer, all hooked up so it would take only a second to turn it on. I then went over to talk to Jack, Duncan and Lowell. I convinced them it would be a great idea to burn up Pete's trailer and roast Pete alive. Of course, they had no way of knowing Pete was already dead.

"Tonight, after graduation, we slipped down to Pete's trailer with gasoline and matches. I went around the other side, pretending to

losh my gasoline around, and reached under the trailer and
witched on the wire recorder. As soon as the flames shot up, we
egan hearing some very convincing screams. It will be most interesting, in future years, to see what effect tonight's act will have on
he lives of Jack Harriman, Duncan Gitterhouse, and Lowell Oliver."

Tad Jarmon closed the journal and leaned back with a cold,
houghtful smile.

# Mean Cop
## by W. Sherwood Hartman

**H**arry's Lunch isn't the fanciest restaurant in town and i
certainly hasn't the greatest location. If you'd take hot dogs
hamburgers, and beer off the menu, we'd be out of business
but we keep the place clean and stay open all night, so it makes
Harry a good living and it keeps me off the streets. I've been nigh
man for a little over two years, from nine at night until six in the
morning. As a three-time loser in a state where it's four times and
you've lost for life, I've always been grateful to Harry for giving me
a chance, and I try to run the place like it was my own when I'm
on duty. It isn't always easy.

An all-night restaurant in a rough neighborhood doesn't attract
the highest class of clientele. The toughest part of the night is after
the bars close. Then musicians, bartenders, bouncers come drifting
in, along with an assortment of drunks, milkmen, and garbage col-
lectors having breakfast before going to work, and a vague, faceless
group who come out at night and disappear with the first light of
day. For the most part, they're well behaved, laughing and joking,
or quietly eating and going on their way. Sometimes a couple of
drunks get to squabbling, but there's hardly anything that ever
happens that could be called real trouble. Perhaps part of that was
due to Hemphig, but I'd always wished for a little more trouble and
a lot less Hemphig.

Leo Hemphig wasn't an ordinary cop. He stood six four, and at
two hundred and thirty pounds his muscles packed the sleeves of
his uniform. If there was any fat on him, the only place it showed
was on his face. His lips were thick and there was a puffiness under
the iciest blue eyes I've ever looked into. His cheeks were like slabs
of bacon hung over a bull neck, and a roll of muscle over his eyes
rippled under black brows that met when he talked. His voice was
high, not effeminate, but with a hard shrillness like a power saw
ripping oak. He walked the night beat in the neighborhood and
would usually get into the restaurant at the peak of the late rush.
Conversation would die before the door had closed behind him. Then
the only sounds would be the clink of stainless steel knives and forks

198

gainst cheap china. He'd sit at the end of the counter near the register and wolf three doughnuts, slurp two cups of coffee, then get up without any motion to pay for his food and turn toward the people lined up on the stools. "Good night," he would sneer, "you *crud*, you *lobs!*" Then he would spit his departing epithet, *"PUNKS!"* With that, he would turn and leave.

The silence would continue for a few minutes more until someone invented a new obscenity to celebrate his departure and conversation slowly returned to its normal pitch.

My first meeting with Hemphig had been right after I got out for the third time. I have no excuses. I have no one to blame but myself. The first two times I was wrong and I paid. The third time was a mistake too. I'd been at the wrong place at the wrong time. It was a bum rap, but we won't go into that here. When I was eligible for parole, the parole officer had gone to bat for me and Harry had given me a job. I had every intention of sticking with it. Hemphig had walked in on me the first night I was back of the counter alone.

"You the con Harry hired?" he asked.

"I'm on parole."

"Keep your nose clean," he said, and his lips pulled back in a grin that was so evil that the air suddenly smelled sour. "There's nothing I like better than to stomp on punks. Don't ever forget it."

He ordered his doughnuts and coffee and ignored the check I put in front of him. I shivered after he left. The unpaid check was still tucked under his empty coffee cup. I wrote "Cop" across the front of it and put it in the register.

Harry found it there when he was checking me out in the morning. He looked at it for a long time, then tore it up and threw it in the waste basket. "He give you a rough time?" he asked, rubbing blunt fingers through his gray hair.

"No," I hedged. "I guess he just forgot to pay his check."

"I should have warned you, but I didn't think. Don't write any more checks for him. Just give him what he wants and forget it. And please don't make any trouble with him. He's not a nice man."

I started to leave and Harry put his hand on my shoulder.

"You'll be all right, boy. Just be careful."

I nodded and left with a warm feeling.

I heard a lot about Hemphig in the months that followed. Most of it would have to be discounted as rumor, but the night people were sure. It was more than rumors to them. They traveled in pairs, afraid to be alone on the streets in the wee small hours. Their fear sprang from the fact that hardly a week went by without some drunk being found beaten to death in an alley. Once, a pensioner who walked with a cane was found with his back broken from a kick in the spine. Through it all, Hemphig continued to humiliate my patrons with his fervent curses.

Most of the people who lived in the neighborhood operated just outside the law, and what law could they turn to without risk of ending up face down in the gutter? Hemphig was the law. Hemphig was life or death. No one had the guts to file a complaint on mere suspicion. Who wants to sign his own death warrant?

That's the way things were when my cousin Joe came in from the coast to see me. I say cousin, but we were always more like brothers. After my folks died, I lived with Joe and his parents until they were killed in a car accident. Then we were put in different orphanages, but we always kept in touch. He never got in any trouble and he'd write giving me seven different kinds of hell for the scrapes I got into. He had a great thing in his mind about how we could work together after he made us a stake.

He stomped into Harry's Lunch at the peak of the night, grinning like a big tom with a chew of catnip. As much as I'd have liked to throw away the apron and jump over the bar and kiss him, I couldn't. The place was jammed and I was trying to wait on people and take orders and listen to him. I was so happy I was damned near bawling ... "Four hundred and sixty acres," he said, "and some of the most beautiful timberland you've ever seen."

Hemphig walked in and the room chilled in a pall of silence, but Joe continued, his voice rich and strong in the electric tension he never noticed. "And some of the finest grazing land in the world! We can run three hundred head of cattle, and they'll be fatter than ticks! We're finally gonna make it, Buddy!"

Hemphig left his stool and walked to where Joe was sitting. "Let me see your driver's license," he said. The room turned dead calm. Not even a spoon turned in a coffee cup.

I tried to warn Joe with my eyes, but he swung around and faced Hemphig. "Look, mister," he said. "I'm sitting on a bar stool in a restaurant. What kind of nut are you, asking for my driver's license?"

"I'm a police officer," Hemphig shrilled, his voice an octave higher than usual. "I want to see your identification!"

"I arrived by plane and I came here in a taxi," Joe said. "Now go find yourself a corner and polish your tin badge. And let me alone!"

Joe turned back toward me and the back of Hemphig's hand sounded like a slab of ham smashing against the counter top as it slashed against Joe's mouth. He tumbled backward against a booth and came up with blood dripping from his lips. He rubbed his arm against his face as he got to his feet. Then he shook his head. "Mister," he said, "do you have the guts to take this out on the street without that badge and the gun? Man to man and the hell with the rule book!"

Hemphig looked happy. He stripped off his gear and folded it in his coat and we all went outside. That happy grin didn't last long. Joe stood five-ten and carried a light hundred and eighty, but his left hand flicked out with all the authority of a jackhammer, and every time he'd cut Hemphig with a left, the right would follow like a pile driver into his middle, cutting into his wind like a knife until he was wheezing like a bellows. Twice Leo caught Joe, but before he had a chance to squeeze him, Joe did a little dance and leaped into the air, the top of his head catching Leo on the chin and sending him reeling backward at the mercy of Joe's following punches. Then Joe sent five hard rights and lefts to Leo's jaw and he went to his knees, sagged forward, and fell with his face on the front step of the restaurant. We dragged him into the alley and let him sleep it off.

A week went by and Hemphig never once showed himself in the restaurant. The night people were starting to joke about it, but I couldn't feel easy. I tried to get Joe to stay away, but he wouldn't.

It was after the late rush, and Joe and I were sitting alone after the crowd had gone, talking about how great it would be with just the two of us working together and building for something. There was only one more week until my parole was up and I'd be free to go back out west. Then Hemphig walked in. His face still carried the black and blue from the fight he'd been in, but his lips were smiling. He walked up to Joe and put out his hand. "You're a good man, friend," he said. "It was a fair fight. No hard feelings . . ."

Joe shook his hand, then Leo patted his breast pocket absently. "I'm out of smokes. You have a cigarette I could borrow?"

Joe never had a chance. As he reached under his coat an explosion rocked the restaurant and a gun was smoking in Hemphig's hand. There was a hole in Joe's hand cut by the bullet, and what was left of his chest could never be repaired. He was dead before he hit the floor.

"You saw it!" Hemphig screamed. "You saw him try to draw on me!"

"He was reaching for a cigarette!"

"You want to put your word against mine?" he said and the pistol was wavering in my direction.

I went to Joe and pulled his coat away as he lay on the floor. "He wasn't even wearing a gun!"

"I'm a cop," Hemphig said, "not a mind reader. He reached inside his coat like he was going to pull a gun on me."

"He was reaching for a cigarette! You *asked* him for a cigarette!"

"I don't remember anything like that," Hemphig said. "I walked in here and he made like he was going to pull a gun on me. Isn't that the way it looked to you?"

After I thought about it a little, that's the only way it could look to me. Being a three-time loser, my word would be like a breath of honeysuckle in a steel mill when we got to court, and after that, Leo would be sure to find a way to frame me for the final rap. "Sure, Leo," I said, "it sure did look like he was going to pull a gun on you."

The inquest was laughable. Hemphig told his version of what had happened, and I agreed. The verdict was justifiable homicide. I cried that night.

My parole ended three months ago and now I'm free to go wherever I want, but I'm still working the night shift at Harry's. The boy brought the newspapers in tonight during the late rush and I didn't have a chance to read them until a few minutes ago. There's a story on page three that says Patrolman Leo Hemphig was struck and killed by a hit and run driver at an intersection only five blocks from where I work. The police are looking for a late model dark sedan with broken headlights.

They'll find the car soon—it's parked within two blocks of Harry's Lunch—but it won't do them any good. It was a stolen car and there are no fingerprints. I was wearing gloves.

# Kill, If You Want Me!

## by Richard Deming

On the hundred-mile drive back from Morganville I kept priming myself to tell off Mathews the minute I walked into the office. I was using martinis for priming fluid, one about every ten miles.

Since I was going to be fired anyway, I didn't have anything to lose. Maybe it's childish to tell off the boss when you're fired, but I had reasons.

I don't think I tend to blame others for my own mistakes. When I was bounced off the Raine City police force as a rookie for drinking on duty, I never held it against the lieutenant who caught me. Six months later, when I lost my agency job for trying to shake down a client, I didn't blame anybody but myself. And I didn't hold any resentment against the inspector who caught me gimmicking my cab meter when I was hacking.

But now I was a reformed character. Since shooting angles had never gotten me anything but trouble, I'd been square with the Schyler Tool Company during the six months I'd been with it. I didn't even pad my expense account. And I'd worked my head off.

Only I couldn't seem to sell tools. Not enough of them anyway. I knew the axe was going to fall this time the minute I turned in my scanty order book.

I wouldn't have resented losing the job so much if my opinion of George Mathews had been higher. But to be fired by an incompetent was rubbing it in.

Rating the president of Schyler Tools as an incompetent wasn't just sour grapes. It was an opinion held throughout the plant. George Mathews held his position because his wife owned controlling interest. Without her vote he couldn't have been a stock boy. He spent about three hours a day at the office, the rest golfing, boating and discreetly chasing females. Discreetly, because his wife's tolerance of his shortcomings ended with extra-marital activity.

The real brains of the company was the force of assistants old Lyman Schyler, Helen Mathews' father, had built up before he died.

It went on functioning automatically under its figurehead boss just as efficiently as it had under Schyler.

I was pretty well primed by the time I reached Raine City. Not drunk, just courageous as a lion.

The little blonde who served as George Mathews' receptionist gave me a nice smile and trilled, "Good afternoon, Mr. Cavanaugh."

The smile turned to a look of alarm when, without even answering, I pushed through the swinging gate and headed for Mathews' private office.

"You can't go in there!" she squealed. "Mr. Mathews is in conference."

By then I had my hand on the knob. The sound of scurrying feet as I pushed open the door made me glance back. The secretary was rushing after me with an expression of horror on her face.

I winked at her, stepped inside and shut the door.

My unannounced entrance brought on a flurry of activity. With a flash of white legs a shapely brunette bounced from Mathews' leather couch, swept up her dress and darted into his private washroom so rapidly I didn't even glimpse her face.

But I didn't have to. I recognized the small pink birthmark just above the swell of rounded hips. George Mathews wasn't the only man at Schyler Tools who knew file clerk Gertie Drake. However, he probably did have the distinction of being the first to get acquainted on company time.

Mathews' look of consternation changed to a threatening frown when he saw who had interrupted his conference. But he delayed saying anything until he got himself readjusted.

Then he asked in a cold voice, "What do you mean bursting in here without being announced?"

I had intended blistering his ears with my personal opinion of him, but the situation changed my mind. Giving him a chummy smile, I took one of his padded guest chairs and lit a cigarette. Mathews glared at me.

"I don't seem to be much good on the road," I said. "I think I'd like district sales manager better."

Striding around the desk, he looked down at me with clenched fists. I wasn't very impressed. At thirty-two George Mathews was lean and hard and well-muscled, but at twenty-eight I was leaner and harder and better muscled. Besides outweighing his one seventy-five by twenty pounds.

"Of all the unmitigated—"

"Would you rather have me discuss the promotion with Mrs. Mathews?"

He opened his mouth and closed it again. After staring at me wordlessly for a few moments, he managed in a slightly high voice, "Are you trying to blackmail me?"

I gave him a pleasant nod.

He stared a while more, unclenched his fists and rubbed the back of his neck. His gaze strayed to the closed washroom door.

"I'll make as good a district sales manager as you do a company president," I said reasonably.

Looking back at me, he sniffed. "You've been drinking," he said.

"A little," I admitted. "We all have our minor indulgences."

"You're drunk."

"You're an adulterer," I countered amiably.

His fists clenched again, then unclenched. Instead of getting mad, he decided to make me a fellow conspirator.

Summoning a rueful smile, he said, "What the hell, Tom. We don't have to insult each other. You'd get a little sore if I barged in on you at a time like this. And don't tell me you've never had a time like this."

"I won't. But I'm single."

He dismissed this with an airy wave. "According to Kinsey, fifty percent of all married men cheat a little."

"How many of them have wives who could pitch them out in the street without a nickle?"

He flushed. "You want to be nasty about this?"

"No," I said. "I just want to be district sales manager."

"Don't be ridiculous," he said testily. "There's no opening."

"Ed Harmony retires in two weeks."

"You know very well Harry Graves is scheduled for that spot. Moving you over his head would create an office scandal."

I knew I was in by the way he was arguing instead of just telling me to go to hell.

"Then create one," I said. "I don't feel like going on the road any more, so I'll take a two-week leave until the job opens. With pay, of course."

For a long time he examined me coldly, the false camaraderie gone from his eyes. Then he said in a curt tone, "All right, Cavanaugh. Now get the hell out of my office."

If there was any scandal over my appointment as district sales manager, most of it had died down by the time I returned from my two-weeks' leave. In the interest of harmony Harry Graves, who had expected the promotion, had been moved to another district so that he wouldn't have to serve under me. And while congratulations on my appointment from my sales force struck me as rather perfunctory, there was no indication of resentment.

Possibly one of the reasons I was accepted with so little furor was that during my absence the plant found a more interesting tidbit to gossip about. The affair between file clerk Gertie Drake and the company president had become an open scandal.

Because I was too new in an executive position to be on gossiping terms with my staff, I didn't learn this at once. As a matter of fact I guessed it from observation before anyone got around to mentioning it to me.

Beyond reporting in to George Mathews my first day on the new job, a short and frigid meeting, I made a point of avoiding him, not caring to push my luck. Except for an occasional glimpse of Gertie Drake in the main office, I didn't see her either the first few days I was back, which set me to wondering if she were avoiding me. We'd had some pretty smoky sessions at my apartment on occasion, and while both of us regarded them as casual interludes I thought she might at least pop her head in long enough to admire my new office. Suspecting she might be embarrassed by my catching her dallying with the boss, I took the trouble to look her up.

I arranged to get her alone by the simple device of asking my stenographer for the file on a dead account. The storage files were part of Gertie's province, and I knew the request would be relayed to her by phone. After waiting ten minutes, I went to the file room.

This was a perfect place for privacy, because no one aside from Gertie had any reason to enter it. Even she used it rarely, as it contained nothing but tier upon tier of stored records seven years or more old.

I found her in a rear alcove formed by twin rows of file cabinets. Startled by my unexpected appearance, she looked up from the drawer she was searching.

She made a face at me. "You're developing a bad habit of sneaking up on people, Tom."

The complete lack of self-consciousness in her tone, coupled with the oblique reference to the last time I had startled her convinced me it wasn't embarrassment which had kept her away.

"Sinners ought to lock their doors," I said. "How have you been, Gertie?"

"All right." She turned her attention back to the drawer.

For a few moments I admired her in profile. She had a nice one all the way down from her pert little nose to her tiny feet.

Finally I asked, "How'd you like to get together some night soon?"

She shook her head without looking at me. "Sorry, Tom. I'm pretty busy these nights."

The answer surprised me. Gertie had always been a healthy animal with the moral outlook of an alley cat. About the only men in the office she hadn't favored were the ones who hadn't suggested it.

I said, "You must not have understood the question, honey." Lightly, I gripped her arm and pulled her against me. Momentarily her round breast pressed into my chest, but before I could encircle her with my arms, she twisted away. The almost prim look on her face astonished me.

"I'm not like that any more," she said. "I only play with one man, Tom."

"Oh? Who's the lucky fellow?"

"None of your business." She closed the drawer she'd been searching and began to search another.

"You're serious about this guy?"

She barely nodded.

"Serious like marriage?"

She glanced at me, then away again. "Eventually, maybe. Not right away. It hasn't gotten to that point yet."

"Oh?" I couldn't think of anything more to say, so I finally murmured lamely, "Well, I wish you luck, Gertie," and retreated.

It wasn't until later that same day when I happened to spot her coming from George Mathews' office with a radiantly happy smile on her face that the incredible thought hit me that Mathews was the man. If she expected eventual marriage from him, she was in for a jolt, I thought. George Mathews would never divorce his meal ticket, no matter how much he was in love.

The next day I learned that my guess was right. My stenographer apparently decided I was going to last as her boss and tested our future relationship by cautiously dishing me up some office gossip. Included in it was a passing reference to the affair between Gertie Drake and Mathews. When I accepted this without comment, but with an encouraging smile, she needed no more urging to unload the whole story.

I gathered that half the plant was buzzing over the love affair because the principals made so little effort to keep it secret. Gertie Drake moved in and out of Mathews' office at will, often remaining in it as long as an hour, while the president's secretary-receptionist barred entry to all visitors with the excuse that Mathews was "in conference." What the little blonde's opinion of this sentry duty was remained a secret, she apparently being the only non-gossiper in the office.

Gertie made no bones about being the boss's mistress, my stenographer told me, seeming to take considerable pride in the position. She didn't exactly brag about it, the girl said, but her attitude left no doubt in the other female workers' minds that she considered Mathews her private property.

"As though any of the rest of us would be interested in a married man," my informant inserted virtuously. "She even refers to him as George, though she makes a point of calling him Mr. Mathews to his face when any of us girls are around."

I learned that Mathews himself seemed unaware of the gossip. Outside his private office he was as politely formal to Gertie as he was to the other help. But inside . . .

As that part was obviously mere guessing by the grapevine, I stopped listening at that point and became engrossed in my own thoughts.

The whole thing left me vaguely uneasy. It was common knowledge to everyone but his wife that George Mathews did a bit of philandering now and then. But he'd never been this open. If word of the affair got to Helen Mathews my hold over Mathews was gone, and I was reasonably certain he'd fire me at once. If he himself lasted long enough after the exposé to fire anyone.

I decided after some thought that with the gossip as extensive as it was, Helen Mathews was certain to get wind of it eventually. The minute that happened my job was in danger, but it would be considerably less in danger if I had some support from Mrs. Mathews.

I would have preferred the status quo, with the company's majority stockholder never learning of her husband's infidelity. But if it was inevitable that she find out, I thought it best that she find out from me.

If I approached it just right, I believed I could insure my job against any eventuality.

I decided to visit Helen Mathews the first evening I was sure her husband wasn't home.

My opportunity came the next night. The morning paper announced that there was to be a community chest banquet that evening, and that George Mathews was to be the main speaker. The banquet was scheduled for eight o'clock, so I timed my arrival at the Mathews home for eight thirty.

The Mathews lived in a large rose-granite home on Sheridan Drive, one of the most exclusive sections in town. With Mrs. Mathews' money I imagine they had servants, but apparently they were gone for the evening, because Helen Mathews answered the door herself.

I had seen Helen Mathews only once, on one of her rare visits to the plant; we hadn't been introduced at the time. But I had been sufficiently impressed by my single glimpse to wonder why George Mathews chased other women when he had something so nice at home. It had occurred to me that possibly he strayed because his wife was frigid, for though she was a beautiful woman, her beauty was of a cool, regal sort, not the warm, animal beauty of Gertie Drake.

She was a slim, poised woman of about my age, with a delicately sculptured face framed by loose golden hair. She looked at me inquiringly.

"I'm Tom Cavanaugh, Mrs. Mathews," I said. "One of Schyler Tool's district sales managers. May I speak to you for a minute?"

"Of course," she said, moving aside to let me enter.

She led me into a large front room expensively equipped with Louis XIV furniture, indicated a handsome chair with clawed feet and seated herself on a sofa with similar feet. When we were both seated, she gave me a second inquiring look.

I said, "This is a rather delicate matter, Mrs. Mathews. I'm risking my job by coming here "

Her fine eyebrows raised, but she made no comment.

"As it happens, I would have been risking my job by not coming too. I've been sort of between the devil and the deep blue sea."

She merely waited expectantly.

"It concerns your husband, Mrs. Mathews."

A wary expression flitted across her face, was gone, and her features became expressionless. "Before you go on, Mr. Cavanaugh, maybe you should know that I love my husband very much."

"I'm aware of it. Which is why I hesitated so long to do anything which might hurt your relationship. But it's reached the point where it's inevitable that you're going to hear what I have to say from some source. I'd rather you hear it from me."

"Why?"

"Because your husband thinks I'm the only one who knows it. The minute he discovers you've learned of it, he's going to assume I told you. And he'll fire me on the spot."

She said coolly. "Won't his assumption be right?"

"Not if I waited a few more days. The matter's become common gossip. Practically every person in the plant knows it. You couldn't possibly escape hearing of it from some source."

"I see. And you hope by telling me first to enlist my aid in keeping your job."

"Is that wrong?" I asked. "Consider my position, Mrs. Mathews. I happen to have some knowledge I didn't want to have and which I never intended to use against your husband. It's not my fault the knowledge has become widespread. Of course I hope to enlist your aid. It's my only chance out of an impossible situation. If I waited for someone else to tell you, I'd be certain to lose my job. Without your support I'll lose it anyway, but that's the calculated risk I had to take."

For a time she studied me without expression. Presently she said, "Having gone this far, you may as well tell me the rest of the story, Mr. Cavanaugh."

I took a deep breath. "Your husband has a mistress."

What she expected . . . news that Mathews was dipping into the company till, perhaps . . . I don't know. But it obviously wasn't this. Her face didn't change an iota, but the suddenly pinched look about her eyes indicated shock more definitely than if she had screamed.

"Who?" she asked with unnatural quietness.

"A file clerk named Gertie Drake. A girl about twenty-three years old."

"It isn't just office gossip? Perhaps because he's been over-friendly?"

I shook my head. "They practically flaunt it in front of the whole plant. She does, anyway. Apparently he's unaware of the gossip. Besides, I *know* it's an affair. The reason Mr. Mathews thinks I'm the only one who knows about it is that I accidentally walked in on them at a crucial moment."

Her face still contained no expression, but I noted it was appreciably paler. "You think it's just philandering, Mr. Cavanaugh? Or is he serious about this girl?"

I shrugged. "She's serious. She's been heard to say that she hopes for eventual marriage. How he feels, I can't say."

"She expects to marry him!"

Her voice was so sharp it startled me. I said, "I didn't say, 'expects'. I said, 'hopes'. There's a considerable difference."

She stared at me for a long time, then moved her gaze to the fireplace and stared at it for a longer time.

Eventually, without looking at me, she said, "I love George enough to forgive a physical infidelity, Mr. Cavanaugh. Providing he ended the affair. But I'd never stay with a man I thought loved another woman. I have to know."

Silence built between us until she turned to give me a level look. "Are you willing to do me a favor to win my support, Mr. Cavanaugh?"

"What kind of favor?"

"Find out for me exactly how much this woman means to my husband."

"How?" I asked. "I can't read his mind."

"There are other ways. Learn how much time they spend together. Where they go and what they do. How he treats her. A woman could tell by observation if another woman loved a man. Can't you diagnose a man's attitude toward a woman?"

"You mean follow them?"

She made an impatient gesture. "That's up to you. I don't care what method you use. But I have to know how he feels. It's important enough to me so that I'll guarantee your job if you find out what I want to know."

I rose from my chair. "All right, Mrs. Mathews. I'll try to find out."

She followed me to the front door. As I turned to say good night she laid a hand on my sleeve and looked into my face. "Tell me, Mr. Cavanaugh, was protecting your job the sole reason you came to me?"

"What do you mean?" I asked.

"How well do you know this Gertie Drake?"

I hesitated a moment, said reservedly, "We used to go out together some."

She smiled a little bitterly. "I suspected as much. It seemed you might just have suggested more discretion to my husband if you hadn't had a personal interest. That makes us a little closer allies, doesn't it?"

I didn't deny the charge that I had a personal interest in Gertie. If she was sharp enough to pick a hole in my story which I hadn't even considered, I was glad that her woman's intuition had so neatly patched the hole.

My six months' agency experience as a private investigator came in handy now because I knew all the procedures to follow, and I knew how to tail a man without being detected. I enlisted my stenographer's unwitting aid by letting her pour gossip in my ear so that I learned of contacts Mathews and Gertie Drake had in the plant which I otherwise would not have known about.

Outside the plant I began to tail Mathews night and day. This wasn't as difficult as it sounds for as a junior executive I didn't have to punch a time clock and was free to come and go pretty much as I pleased. I developed the habit of parking my car on the street near the main gate instead of on the plant parking lot where I had a reserved place. Fifty bucks to the downstairs receptionist in front of the main entrance bought me a phone call every time Mathews left the building. By the time he could get his car from the lot and drive through the main gate, I was seated in mine all ready to tail him.

For three days this netted me nothing. Mathews spent the first afternoon at the golf course, the second fishing from his sailboat with a male friend, and the third playing golf again. On the fourth day he left the plant at noon, met Gertie Drake at a quiet backstreet restaurant on the East Side at twelve thirty, and kept her there in a booth until two, when presumably she returned to the office.

Mathews himself spent the rest of the afternoon playing golf again.

Evenings I had a little more luck. The first night he attended a party with his wife, but the other three he went out alone. Each time he drove straight to the rooming house where Gertie lived, picked her up and headed south out of town. Their trysting place turned out to be a roadhouse named the Flying Swan about ten miles from the city line on Route 60.

All three evenings followed the same pattern. They would have a few drinks, dance once, then disappear upstairs where the management maintained rooms for the convenience of patrons who wanted privacy. After an hour or so they'd reappear, have a nightcap, and go home.

On Saturday afternoon, after tailing Mathews to the Yacht Club and watching him sail off alone in his boat I phoned Helen Mathews and suggested we meet somewhere so that I could deliver a report. She picked a small bar and grill named the Top Hat about a mile up Sheridan Drive from her home.

When we were seated in a back booth with drinks before us, I said, "Friday at lunch was the only time they've met outside the plant all week during the day. But he saw her Wednesday, Thursday and Friday at night. They go to a place called the Flying Swan out on Route Sixty. Have a few drinks, dance a little, then spend an hour to two hours upstairs."

She winced slightly. "Have you formed any opinion of how he feels about her?"

I said dryly, "Not emotionally, but she must have an overpowering physical attraction for him. They also had 'conferences' in his private office on Wednesday, Thursday and Friday."

Red spots appeared in her cheeks, she drained her highball at a gulp and asked for another. I ordered her a double and myself none as I hadn't even touched the first yet.

While we were waiting for the order to be filled, she said, "I think he plans to spend next weekend with her. He wants me to go up to our cottage on Weed Lake next Friday to get it ready for a few days' vacation. He doesn't plan to join me until Monday."

"Going?" I asked.

"Why not? I may as well speed up this thing by giving him all the rope he wants."

The waiter temporarily interrupted our conversation by bringing her second drink.

She drank half of it before saying, "If you can manage to keep them under close observation the whole weekened, I'll appreciate it. You can understand that I have to know soon or I'll go crazy."

"All right," I said. "I'll do my best."

We left it at that.

Monday nothing unusual happened. On Tuesday Mathews left the plant at two P.M. and plenty happened.

He first led me to a pawn shop on Franklin Avenue where he spent about fifteen minutes. Next he stopped at a sporting goods store downtown, and finally at a neighborhood hardware store. Only from the last did he emerge with a visible package.

It was about a foot square, and so heavy he had to heave it into the trunk of his car with both hands.

After following him back to the plant, I returned to the pawn shop. The proprietor was a wizened old man in his seventies.

"Police," I said, flashing a wallet identification card which denoted that I'd been a volunteer fireman four years previously, but which resembled the card detectives carried if you didn't examine it too closely. I put the wallet back in my pocket before he could get a good look.

"Yes, sir," the old man said.

"A man came in here about an hour ago. Around thirty-two, black, curly hair, slim and well-dressed. Deeply tanned."

He nodded. "Yes, sir. A Mr. McClellan, I think. Just a minute." Picking up a ledger, he peered at it nearsightedly. "McClelland, rather. John McClelland. What about him, officer?"

"What did he want?"

"He bought a secondhand thirty-two. Twenty-five dollars. He looked quite respectable. He isn't a criminal, is he, officer?"

"He isn't yet," I said slowly. "Maybe he's planning to be."

From the pawn shop I drove to the sporting goods store, and from there to the hardware store. At the former I learned that Mathews had purchased a box of .32 caliber shells, and from the latter he'd bought six sash weights and fifty feet of sash cord.

I didn't jump to any hasty conclusions. Returning to the plant, I used the same device I had once before to get Gertie Drake into the dead file room. When I joined her there for a second time, she looked a little irked.

"Are you calling for these dead accounts just to see me alone?" she demanded.

Assuming an air of mock shame, I said, "You've found me out. Gertie, I want to talk to you."

"About what?"

"About us. Why can't we get together again?"

"I told you why," she said impatiently. "I'm going steady."

I shook my head pityingly. "I know who you're going with, honey. Everyone in the plant knows. Why waste your time on a man who's never going to be able to take you anywhere but to backstreet taverns?"

"That's all you know about it," she flared at me.

"He'll never marry you, Gertie, because he'll never get a divorce."

Balling her fists on her hips, she faced me with an angry look on her face. "Won't he, smarty-pants? Well, for your information George loves me. He is going to get a divorce, and marry me."

That clinched it. I'd felt all along that George Mathews would never turn loose of his wife's money by getting a divorce, or letting her get one.

That evening I tailed Mathews from his home only far enough to make sure he would be gone for some hours. When he picked up Gertie Drake and headed south, I returned to his house.

Again I found Helen Mathews at home alone.

When we were seated in the front room, I asked, "Are any of your windows here out of repair? Won't slide up or down, for instance?"

She looked puzzled. "Not that I know of. Why?"

"Does your husband own a pistol?"

"Several. What are you getting at, Mr. Cavanaugh?"

"It'll hold a minute," I said. "Mrs. Mathews, today I needled Gertie Drake a little by telling her she was a sucker to play around with your husband, that he'd never take her anywhere but to backstreet taverns. She got mad and told me they were in love, he intended to divorce you and marry her."

She paled slightly. "You think she was telling the truth?"

"She thought she was. But your husband isn't going to divorce you."

Her eyes widened. "How do you know?"

"Because prior to my talk with Gertie he bought a .32 caliber pistol, a box of shells, six widow-sash weights and fifty feet of sash cord. He bought the pistol under an assumed name."

Her eyes widened even more.

"Since you say he already owns several pistols, I'd say he bought this one so it couldn't be traced back to him. And if none of your windows need repair, I'd guess he intends to weight something and drop it in the lake. In short, it means he intends to kill you."

For nearly a minute she looked at me steadily without any expression at all on her face. Then she tumbled forward in a dead faint.

I couldn't get across the room fast enough to catch her before she hit the floor. But the carpet was too soft for her to hurt herself in falling. I laid her on the sofa and began to massage her wists.

After a few moments her eyes slowly opened and she looked up at me dully.

"Maybe I should have broken it more gently," I said.

Withdrawing her hands from mine, she pressed the back of one to her forehead. In a wondering tone she said, "That's why he wants me alone up at the cottage. To kill me."

I didn't say anything to her.

She lay there, one hand still raised to her forehead, lost in her own thoughts. Rising, I went back to my chair. After a time she sat up, deathly pale but in control of herself.

"I think I want to be alone for a time," she said. "Will you please go?"

"Of course," I said instantly. "I'll let myself out. Don't get up."

As I started from the room, she said in a dead voice, "I'll phone you at work tomorrow, after I've had a chance to think."

Since I had learned what Helen Mathews wanted to know, there was no further point in tailing Mathews. For the first time in more than a week I put in a full day's work for the company. Mrs. Mathews phoned just before five P.M.

"I'd like to see you tonight," she said. "Somewhere we can be alone."

"How about my place?"

She said that would be fine, and I gave her the address.

"Expect me about eight thirty," she said, and hung up.

My apartment has only three rooms, but the combination living and dining room is large and comfortable, with a brick fireplace, smart modern furniture, and a thick pile rug twelve feet wide by eighteen long. After dinner I gave it a brisk going over, checked my liquor supply, then showered and dressed as carefully as a high-school student getting ready for his first dance.

It wasn't until all these preparations were finished that it occurred to me I was behaving exactly as though I expected an evening of drinking and romance. Which seemed unlikely.

She arrived exactly at eight thirty and I was surprised to discover she had dressed in line with my subconscious thoughts. I had never before seen her in anything but simple street dresses, but tonight she wore a daringly low-cut gown which clung to her slim body like wet tissue paper, outlining every curve.

As I took her light cape I smiled down at her and said, "It's been a long time since so much beauty has graced this hovel."

She smiled back a little strainedly, and moved into the center of the room. As she looked about in womanly curiosity I got the impression she was so tense that she was preventing herself from trembling only by supreme effort.

"Would you like a drink?" I asked.

She gave me a grateful smile. "Please."

I mixed two double bourbons.

I seemed to have guessed correctly about her taut nerves, for she worked through her highball before a quarter of mine was gone. By the time she got down the second she began to relax.

"What did you want to see me about?" I asked as I handed her a third.

She turned a trifle pink. "Nothing, really. I just couldn't stand to be in the house alone another night. I . . . I suppose I thought I wanted to talk about this horrible plot of George's. But that was just a mental excuse. I really don't want to talk about anything."

I said, "You can't just brush it from your mind. He means to kill you."

"I can brush it from my mind tonight. I thought of nothing else all last night. And I came to a decision."

"What?" I asked.

"I hate him," she said without emotion. "Every bit of love I ever had for him is gone. I want to hurt him in any way I can."

I considered this, finally asked, "And how do you plan to hurt him?"

She gave me a slow smile, all of her previous nervousness now gone to be replaced by a slightly alcoholic sleepiness. "What's the best way a woman can hurt a man? And enjoy herself at the same time?"

Our eyes locked and I smiled back at her. Apparently my instinctive preparations for the evening had been right after all. Setting down my drink, I walked over to the sofa where she was seated.

She set her glass down too, turned to move against me. Her lips were on mine before I even started to reach for her.

My guess that George Mathews' straying might be due to his wife's frigidity turned out to be one of the poorest guesses I ever made. It was beyond my comprehension what Mathews was looking for in other women when he had a human bonfire awaiting him at home.

Helen decided she had better leave about midnight. I had never before spent such a pleasantly exhausting evening. While we waited for her cab, she suddenly gave me a tender kiss completely lacking in passion.

"Was this just an interlude, Tom?" she asked. "Or does it have any meaning?"

"It does for me," I said. "My head is spinning like a top."

"My heart is spinning the same way."

I looked down at her, started to open my mouth, but she pressed her fingers against it.

"Don't say anything. I don't want to hear a bachelor evasion, and I wouldn't believe you if you said you loved me. Let's let it rest."

"I wasn't going to give you a bachelor evasion."

"I still don't want to hear it tonight. Let's sleep on the whole subject."

But I couldn't sleep on it. After she left, I lay awake most of the night visualizing the future prospects the evening made possible.

I didn't try to fool myself into thinking I was in love with Helen on such short acquaintance. But I could be, if I put my mind to it. What more could a man want in a woman? Beauty, passion, money. Particularly money. It was enough to make even a confirmed bachelor like myself consider marriage.

It would be nice to be president of the Schyler Tool Company, work three hours a day and spend the rest of the time sailing that lovely boat of George Mathews'.

I might have known there would be a catch to any prospect as pleasant as the one I visualized. Helen gently let me know what the catch was the next night.

She phoned me at the office again just before five, and again appeared at my apartment at eight thirty. The early part of the evening followed the same pattern as the previous one.

"Were you serious last night about being in love?" I asked as we sat side by side on the sofa, sipping drinks.

She gave me a level look. "I don't joke about love."

"Is it the marriage kind of love?"

She grinned at me. "Is that a proposal, or just a request for information?"

"Some of both, probably."

Her face became serious. "It's the marriage kind of love if you reciprocate. I'm not interested in another philandering husband."

I said, "I'm the monogamous type."

"That's not quite enough, Tom. Do you love me?"

I pulled her head against my shoulder and said into her hair, "I love you."

"Completely?"

"Completely."

She was silent for a time. Presently she said in a withdrawn voice, almost as though speaking to herself, "Marriage to me would mean a big change in your life. Money, social position. George's present job, if you wanted it."

"Hey," I said, "you don't have to parade your wares. It's you I love, not the side products."

"Is it?" she asked.

Cupping her chin, I tilted her head upward. "What do you mean by that?"

"Nothing," she said. "Only there's the factor to consider that I already have a husband. George has to be disposed of."

I dropped my hand from her chin. "I didn't intend making you a bigamist. That's a simple problem. After you divorce George, we'll get married.

"I don't intend to divorce George."

"What?" I asked.

"I want you to kill him."

I sat up straight. "Kill him! What in the hell for?"

In a voice suddenly so cold with venom it nearly hissed she said, "Because I hate him. I want to do to him what he planned to do to me. I want to watch him die, and make sure he knows I planned it."

I looked at her with my jaw hanging open. A little stupidly I said, "But divorce is so simple, baby. You have all the evidence . . ."

"You don't know me very well," she interrupted. "I don't do things halfway. I gave George all the love there was in me. And now he has all the hate I'm capable of feeling. If you want me for your wife, you're going to have to kill him. Because you're not going to get me any other way."

She wasn't any more in love with me than I was with her. She was offering herself and the material things which went with her in exchange for vengeance.

I guess it's true that Hell hath no fury such as that of a woman scorned.

I got up and poured myself a straight shot. Then I mixed fresh drinks for both of us.

"So it isn't love after all," I said. "It's just hate for George."

"I told you I love you," she said levelly. "You'll never find any indication that I don't, even if we live to be a hundred." She added with faint mockery in her voice, "In return I expect you never to let me feel you married me just to get George's sinecure, instead of just for myself."

There wasn't any point in further discussion. It was clear from her manner that it was a take-it-or-leave-it proposition.

"I've never committed a felony," I said. "Though I've been guilty of a few misdemeanors. This is a thing I'm going to have to think over long and carefully."

"Then I'll go home and give you time to think," she told me, rising. "Tomorrow is Wednesday, you know, and Friday I leave for the cottage. It doesn't give you much time to plan out details."

For the second night I didn't get any sleep. I didn't even go to bed until nearly time to get up again. I spent the whole night pacing and smoking cigarettes while I balanced in my mind the attractions of being a rich murderer against the attractions of being poor but relatively sinless.

After weighing all the pros and cons, I came to a decision at six thirty A.M. Then I fell into bed for an hour, rose again, showered and shaved, drank three cups of black coffee and went to the office.

Helen phoned me as usual just before closing time.

"Come to any decision?" she asked.

"Yes," I said. "Want to drop by tonight about the same time?"

"Is it yes or no?"

"I'll tell you when I see you."

She said, "Why can't you tell me now? If it's no I can save myself the trip and you your bourbon."

I decided it was time to let her know that I had no intention of being a yes-dear husband for the rest of my life. "Be there at eight thirty," I said, and hung up.

As always she arrived right on the dot. When she came in, she didn't offer me a kiss. She stood just inside the front door, examining me coolly.

"Well?" she asked.

"You win," I said. "I'll kill him for you."

Instantly she was in my arms. Her lips came up to mine with all the fire she had exhibited the first night.

"I love you, darling," she whispered. "You'll never regret it. I'll love you as no man was ever loved before."

Having reached my decision, the problem now was how to perform the act without getting caught. Helen's insistence on being present at the kill, plus her insistence that Mathews know why he was going to die, complicated matters.

I said, "We're not going to make any of the mistakes your husband would have made if he'd actually gotten around to killing you. He's an utter jerk."

"How do you mean?" Helen asked.

"Buying a gun under an assumed name, for instance. If the gun had ever been located, they'd have traced it back to him within hours."

"How?"

"Because that's all the time it would take to trace it to the pawn shop. And from there on it would be routine. The husband is always automatically a suspect when a woman's murdered. With you as the corpse they'd march George down to the pawn shop and the proprietor would instantly identify him as the buyer."

"But suppose my . . ." She paused to grimace. ". . . my body had never been recovered?"

"Possibly it wouldn't have been," I admitted. "With six sash weights tied to it. There are a couple of hundred-foot holes in Weed Lake. But if it had been, the weights and cord would have been as easily traceable back to him as the gun. We won't take that sort of chance."

"What will we do?"

"There's only one sure-fire murder method," I said. "A planned accident. The cops can never prove murder in an accident case, even if they suspect it."

"You mean something such as running over him in a car?"

"I mean something such as his falling out of a boat and drowning. While you and he are out fishing."

She frowned. "How could I get him out in a boat? Anyway, it's too dangerous. Suppose he pulled his gun and shot me before you came out of hiding?"

"You don't actually have to go fishing with him," I said. "We just have to make it appear that's what happened. I think I have an idea, but I want to stew over it a while. Why don't you go home and I'll phone you tomorrow?"

"Tomorrow's Thursday," she reminded me. "We'd better have things worked out by tomorrow night. Because I leave the next morning."

"They're practically worked out now," I told her. "Don't worry about it."

She seemed content with that; she left a few minutes later. I didn't even attempt to think any more that evening. After two sleepless nights, I was interested in nothing but bed. I was asleep fifteen minutes after Helen's departure.

The next day I kept only half my mind on my job, the other half on the problem of how to stage a convincing accidental drowning.

By five o'clock, when I phoned Helen, I had all the details worked
out in my mind.

"You won't have to drop over tonight," I said. "Everything's set."

"Shouldn't we talk it over?"

"No," I said. "We can discuss it at the cottage."

"When are you coming up?"

"Friday night after work."

She said in a dubious tone, "Suppose he arrives before you do?"

I hadn't thought of that. With Mathews' habit of taking off at two
P.M. or earlier, he could drive to the cottage, perform his murder and
be gone again before I got there.

I said, "Would he think it funny if you changed plans and didn't
start for the cottage until Friday night?"

"He might."

I considered for a moment, then said, "Suppose you leave as
planned, but don't drive to the cottage together. Where is your
place?"

"Beyond Dune Point, on the west side of the lake."

I placed Dune Point on a mental map. "There's a roadhouse called
Gill's Grill on Route Seventeen about a mile past Dune Point. I'll
meet you there about seven P.M. By the time I stop home for a bag
it will take me that long, even if I get away from here at five on the
dot."

"All right," she said. "I won't see you before then?"

"No," I said. "Let's not chance someone seeing us together."

At five I drove home to pack a weekend bag. I put two articles in
it aside from clothing and toilet supplies: a length of strong clothesline and my army automatic.

I reached Gill's Grill at five minutes of seven and found Helen
there. We had dinner at the roadhouse before driving back to the
cottage.

She led the way in her car. We passed under the white wooden
archway marking the entrance to the public beach at Dune Point,
turned right on the gravel road which circled the lake, and followed
it past two small private beaches clustered with summer cottages.
A half mile beyond the second cluster she turned left into a dirt lane
which ended in a strip of white sand at the lake edge.

A white cottage was situated a dozen feet back from the strip of
sand. I knew Mathews had not been there because the powdery dust
of the lane would have shown his tire tracks.

Weed Lake gets its name from the tremendous amount of seaweed in it, which makes it an excellent breeding ground for muskalonge. Horseshoe-shaped, it is only about five miles long, and nowhere wider than a couple of hundred yards. Yet its average depth is fifty feet and it contains holes over a hundred feet deep. I've seen fifty and sixty pound muskie pulled from it.

The Mathews' cottage was on the west side of the horseshoe in a relatively isolated spot. While several other cottages were visible from it, the nearest was a good four hundred yards away on the opposite side of the lake. Heavily underbrushed timber screened it from view of the cottages on this side.

I made use of the latter to conceal my car fifty yards from the cottage so that when Mathews drove in he wouldn't suspect that Helen had company.

The car hidden to my satisfaction, I checked the small boat Mathews used for muskie fishing, a twelve-foot skiff turned bottom up on the beach. The seams all appeared tight enough. Helen showed me its outboard motor, which was stored in a shed attached to the cottage. While she watched for his possible arrival I tinkered with it until it ran smoothly.

The only other immediate preparation necessary was to make sure Mathews couldn't walk in on us unexpectedly while we were asleep. As the cottage contained only one window in each of its three rooms, and there was only one outside door, this didn't present much of a problem. The windows were heavily screened and the door had an inside bolt.

We sat back to wait for him to walk into the trap.

Before we went to bed that night, I went over my murder plan again with Helen. It was a good plan, having the twin virtues of being simple and foolproof. It's the elaborate plans which put murderers in the electric chair. There's not much the police can do about an apparently accidental drowning even if they suspect murder.

"Can you swim?" I asked her.

When she said that she could, I explained how we could make it seem that she and her husband had been night fishing, tipped over the boat and he drowned.

"We'll pick some lighted cottage," I said. "Tip the boat about fifty yards from it and then yell your head off. You swim toward the cottage; I'll swim back here, jump in my car and take off. It can't fail."

"Suppose he manages to drown you instead of you drowning him?" she suggested.

I grinned at her. It was the one detail I hadn't previously given her. "He's going to be drowned before we go out in the boat. In the bathtub."

While we waited for Mathews to show up Helen was kept pretty busy getting the cottage ready for occupancy. All we did Friday night was air the place out and start the electric water pump. But Saturday she had a lot to do. In the morning she drove to the shopping center at Dune Point to lay in a supply of groceries. She spent the afternoon thoroughly cleaning the cottage, even washing the windows.

All this was necessary because I wanted it to look as though she was planning on her husband and herself spending a several-day vacation there.

Mathews arrived Sunday evening.

I was lolling on the beach in swim trunks only a few yards from the cottage when I heard his car engine. Helen was inside preparing dinner. The instant I heard the car turn into the lane, I leaped up and headed for the cottage at a dead run.

I was inside before he came into view.

Helen, wearing nothing but a bathing suit, nervously wiped moist hands on her stomach and peered out the kitchen window to where her husband was parking his car next to hers. She was deathly pale.

"Take it easy," I cautioned, quietly moving into the bedroom.

Getting my automatic from my bag, I checked the load, then pressed my back against the wall next to the door and waited. After a few moments I heard the screen door slam as Mathews came into the house.

"Hi, honey," I heard him say. "I decided to run up tonight instead of tomorrow. What are you fixing?"

"Just cold cuts and potato salad," she said in a steady voice. "It's too hot to cook. Go put something comfortable on and I'll feed you. I was all ready to sit down."

"Be with you in five minutes," he said cheerfully, and headed toward the bedroom whistling.

He walked right past me without seeing my figure flattened against the wall alongside the door, dropped his weekend bag on the bed, and struggled out of his suit coat. He dropped his coat on the bed, started to loosen his tie, and then, turning, spotted me.

He froze in position, his gaze on the automatic leveled at his belt.

"What's this?" he asked. "What are you doing here?"

"Just keep undressing," I said. "Right down to your shorts."

"Are you crazy?" he asked. "Have you switched from blackmail to housebreaking? How'd you get in here without Helen seeing you?"

I grinned at him. "She knows I'm here. Do what I tell you, or I'll put a bullet in your gut."

Flipping off the safety, I let the grin fade from my face. He raised a hand, palm out.

"Don't get excited, Cavanaugh. I'll do what you say."

He stripped off his shirt and trousers.

"The shoes too," I ordered.

Stooping, he unlaced his brightly polished shoes and kicked them off.

"Now get into your favorite fishing clothes," I said.

For a moment he looked at me blankly, then turned and walked to the closet. He put on a faded T-shirt, worn denim trousers and some scuffed loafers. In this outfit he no longer looked like a business executive.

"Now let's go sit down to dinner," I suggested.

Helen was backed against the sink when we entered the kitchen with my gun pressed into Mathews' back. In a high voice he said to her, "What's this all about, honey?"

There was the same high tension in her I had noted on her first visit to my apartment. She gave the impression that if she didn't restrain herself, she would go into a violent fit of trembling. She said nothing, merely stared at her husband without expression.

I said to Mathews, "Sit at the table and don't ask questions."

Seating himself, he looked puzzledly from one to the other of us.

"All right," I told Helen. "Serve him up some dinner."

Quietly she filled a plate with cold cuts, potato salad and sliced tomatoes. Putting it in front of him, she moved butter and rolls within his reach and poured him a cup of coffee. Then she moved back against the sink.

"Eat," I ordered.

"Why?" Mathews asked. "What is this?"

"A game," I said. "Either eat or get shot."

He looked at me a little belligerently, decided I meant it and reluctantly began to eat.

Halfway through his plate, he asked with an attempt at nonchalance, "Aren't you two going to have anything?"

"Later," I said. "Just keep quiet and eat."

I didn't see any point in informing him that the reason I wanted food in his stomach was in the event of an autopsy. It might just strike the medical examiner as strange that Mathews had skipped dinner entirely and had gone night fishing on an empty stomach. I suspected Mathews might lose his appetite if he knew why I was so insistent that he eat.

All the time he was eating, Helen stood with her back against the sink, watching him from unwinking eyes. Aside from her paleness and rigid bearing, there was no indication of emotion in her.

By then Mathews must have figured out that his wife and I were lovers; but I believe he thought I had pulled a gun because I panicked when he caught me alone in the cottage with her. I don't think it occurred to him that we'd deliberately set a trap. Possibly he thought I was holding him under a gun merely as a time-gaining device while I tried to decide what to do about being caught in a compromising position.

I'm sure he didn't suspect for a moment we meant to kill him, or he would never have eaten as well as he did. He seemed puzzled rather than frightened, and more amazed at his wife's infidelity than angry.

When he finished eating, I ordered him back into the bedroom. Helen followed us to the doorway and watched as I commanded Mathews to lie face down on the bed.

When he had complied, I said, "Put your hands behind your back."

Thrusting the gun under the belt of my swim trunks, where I could get at it instantly if Mathews made any unexpected move, I securely tied his hands and feet with the clothesline I had brought along.

When I finished, he inquired in a pettish voice, "What do you two expect to accomplish by all this nonsense? Maybe I'd be willing to discuss a reasonable divorce settlement if you weren't behaving so idiotically."

Ignoring him, I said to Helen, "It's only a little past six thirty and it won't be dark until nine. We ought to wait until an hour after dark, which gives us three and a half hours. Those knots are tight enough to keep him. Let's get things ready."

Something in my tone seemed to tell Mathews for the first time that his treatment wasn't just spur-of-the-moment action on our part. He twisted around to stare at his wife with growing understanding. His eyes had a strained look.

"What's gotten into you, honey?" he asked in a voice which cracked slightly. "You're not planning anything foolish, are you?"

Without answering him, Helen turned and left the room. I followed, pulling the door closed behind me and leaving Mathews alone with his thoughts.

Leading Helen down to the beach, I had her help me heave the boat over right side up and slide the stern into the water. Then I sent her after fishing gear while I clamped on the outboard motor and laid a set of oars in the bottom.

Helen returned from the house with a tackle box and two fishing rods.

"Do you have a Coleman lantern?" I asked.

Entering the shed attached to the cottage, she brought me a gasoline lantern which had a bolt welded to its bottom to fit into one of the oarlocks. Pumping it up, I lighted it, then shut it off again as soon as I knew it would work.

Helen spoke for the first time since I had forced her husband into the kitchen at gunpoint. "Why do we have to do all this now, if we aren't going to need the boat until ten?"

"I want it all set to shove off," I said. "I want George in the lake as soon after he's dead as possible. We can't risk an autopsy showing he drowned an hour or more before you yelled for help. Now, the large bucket."

My abrupt change of direction befuddled her. She gave me a confused look and asked, "What?"

"The bucket. For carrying the water. To carry water from the lake. To fill the bathtub."

She looked even more confused. "Not from the tap?"

I said, "An analysis of the water in his lungs would show he drowned in tap water instead of lake water. I told you. This is going to be a foolproof murder."

Some of the confusion left her and her expression became one of grudging respect. "I wouldn't have thought of that."

She brought two four-gallon buckets from the shed. Wading knee-deep into the lake, I filled both and carried them ashore. I refused her offer to carry one, preferring to have her go ahead of me to open doors.

When we walked into the bedroom, we found Mathews lying on his stomach as we had left him. His eyes followed us as we marched to the bathroom.

When Helen had inserted the drain plug, I emptied both buckets. It was a long, old-fashioned tub on legs; the nearly eight gallons of water filled it only a couple of inches.

"This is going to take a number of trips," I said.

It took five, nearly forty gallons of water, before it came up to the level of the overflow drain. And each time we walked through the room, the look of horror on George Mathews' face increased.

It was obvious to me that Mathews had figured out why we were filling the bathtub, and the way Helen's eyes glittered at her husband each time we trooped past made it equally obvious that she obtained considerable sadistic pleasure from his mental suffering. She even tried to prolong the ordeal by suggesting, ostensibly out of concern for me, that it would be easier if I carried only one bucket at a time.

But Mathews' murder was only a job to me, not a mission of revenge. In spite of my dislike of the man, I found myself feeling a little sorry for him. I continued to carry the double load.

The whole procedure was carried on in dead silence, neither of us speaking either to each other or to Mathews, and Mathews not once opening his mouth. At least not while I was present.

When the tub was full, I returned the buckets to the shed. Reentering the cottage, I discovered that Mathews had finally broken the prolonged silence. Helen stood in the bedroom doorway looking at him.

"He knows what's coming," she said to me in a flat voice. "He's been pleading with me to untie him. He thinks this is all your idea."

I checked his bonds and found them as tight as ever. Apparently he'd done a little struggling for his wrists were slightly chafed, but he hadn't succeeded in loosening the knots. I loosened them somewhat, not enough for him to pull his hands free, but enough to allow freer circulation, kneaded his wrists for a minute and tightened the bonds again.

This wasn't solely out of the goodness of my heart. I didn't want the rope marks to show after he was dead.

Suddenly Mathews said with a peculiar mixture of eagerness and despair, "Listen, Cavanaugh, I'll give Helen a divorce, if that's what you want."

"She doesn't want a divorce," I told him. "I suggested that myself. She wants revenge."

"Revenge for what?" he asked on a high note. "Helen, I never did anything to you."

The glitter I had periodically noted before appeared in Helen's eyes again. Approaching the bed, she squatted on her heels so that her face was nearly level with his.

"Think about your hot little mistress, Gertie Drake," she nearly hissed at him. "Maybe it will make you feel better when you begin to suck in water."

Mathews' gaze moved sickly from his wife to me, then back again. Knowing it was useless to deny Gertie's existence, he tried another tack.

"Cavanaugh told you about Gertie just to turn you against me, honey. Because he wants you for himself. I admit I played with her a little, but it's all over. I swear it. After this past weekend I never intended to see her again. You have to believe me."

Helen's lips curled in the expression of a cat getting ready to spit. Reaching down, I drew her to her feet before she could speak.

"It's only seven thirty," I said. "We've two hours to wait and we're not going to spend it goading the man. Come out of here now."

Her eyes continued to glitter back toward her husband, but she let herself be led from the room.

"Wait!" Mathews called desperately as we reached the door. "Can't we talk this over?"

Propelling Helen into the kitchen, I closed the door behind us. But not in time to cut off the long, drawn-out sob that came from the doomed man.

In the kitchen Helen stared at me almost accusingly, as though I had somehow spoiled her pleasure.

"How about a couple of sandwiches, or at least a cup of coffee," I said tactfully. "We haven't had any dinner."

Wordlessly she turned toward the stove.

She fixed a plate of sandwiches, but the prospect of the task ahead had driven the appetite from both of us. A couple of nibbles was all I could manage, and Helen didn't even attempt that. We settled for coffee.

The next two hours dragged interminably. After that one short period in the bedroom when she had momentarily lost control and started to upbraid her husband, Helen showed no desire to go near him. Periodically I went in to loosen his bonds for a moment, but otherwise we left him to his own thoughts.

These didn't seem to be very pleasant. He had sunk into a sort of hopeless lethargy, just lying inert and waiting for the inevitable. He made no attempt to speak to me when I was in the room, or even to look at me.

At nine thirty I said to Helen, "Better put on whatever you customarily wear fishing."

Her face grew still. Then she rose from the table and moved toward the bedroom. Following, I stood in the doorway and watched as she took a blue cotton blouse and a pair of blue jeans from her closet and laid them on the bed next to Mathews. From a dresser drawer she obtained a bra and panties, laid them with the other clothing.

For a time she stood looking down at her husband expressionlessly. Then, slowly, deliberately, she peeled off her swimming suit.

It was an exquisite bit of torture such as only a feminine mind could conceive. She was fully conscious of the beauty of her body, and was giving Mathews a last look at what he no longer possessed. At the same time, by so casually stripping in front of me, she was flaunting our relationship in his face.

The demonstration succeeded in rousing Mathews from his hopeless stupor. Momentarily his nostrils flared in shocked and impotent rage. Then the flame died and he only looked sick.

Taking her time, Helen dressed in her fishing costume. She didn't put on shoes, apparently in the habit of fishing barefoot.

Approaching the bed, I got an arm under Mathews' chest and another around his legs. Understandably enough he refused to cooperate, wriggling in his bonds so much that I couldn't lift him.

"I guess you'll have to help," I told Helen. "Take his legs and I'll take his head."

Together we managed to get him off the bed. He began to plead: "Don't do it, for God's sake," he said in a near whimper as we carried him into the bathroom. "Please, Helen! For God's sake, Cavanaugh! Don't do it. I'll do anything you want. I'll disappear, never bother you again."

We got him suspended over the tub, when suddenly he began to scream. He renewed his struggles too, so violently that we nearly dropped him.

Falling to one knee, I lowered the upper part of his body into the water while Helen, desperately holding onto his thrashing legs, tried to help guide him downward. The screaming stopped abruptly as I shoved his head under the water.

I was conscious that behind me it was only with effort that Helen was able to hold his legs still as he fought for his life.

After what seemed an eon, but was probably only a matter of seconds, there was a rather horrible gurgling sound, and his thrashing grew weaker and weaker until it stopped altogether.

I stood up and looked at Helen. Releasing Mathews' legs, she backed unsteadily to the door and leaned against it, needing its support. Mathews slid a little father forward into the tub. His knees flopped past the inside edge and his legs made such a loud splash that we both jumped.

Helen kept staring at the tub. She began to shake uncontrollably.

I found that I didn't want to look at her. Leaning over Mathews, I untied his hands and feet, put the rope in my pocket. A slight choking sound made me look up.

Helen still leaned against the door, and now tears were streaming down her face. "He's dead, isn't he?" she said in a near-hysterical whimper.

"You wanted him that way," I said sharply. "Get hold of yourself. It's a little late to cry now."

"He's dead," she repeated dully. "I'll never see him again."

Walking over to her, I took her by her arms and gave her a slight shake. "If you go to pieces now we're both finished, Helen. You've still got a big role to play."

She gazed at me sightlessly and repeated again in the same dull tone, "He's dead. We killed him."

Deliberately I brought my palm across her face in a stinging slap. Shock replaced the dullness in her eyes and she looked at me incredulously.

"Sorry," I said. "Just an antidote for hysteria. You all right now?"

Her hand felt her cheek and she continued to stare at me. Then, abruptly, her shoulders slumped and she said in a small voice, "I'll be all right."

"Then let's get moving. The faster we work now, the better our chances are of beating the electric chair."

That completed her recovery, which is why I said it. Up to now Helen's mind had been too full of vengeance to think of consequences. A gentle reminder of what we were both up against if we didn't make this a perfect job might keep her mind on her work.

It did. All of a sudden she became eager to help me.

It proved unexpectedly difficult to get the body down to the boat. Even when he was struggling, alive, Mathews had seemed lighter than he did as dead weight. In addition it was too dark out to see where we were going, for there was no moon. Twice during the short trip Helen stubbed her bare toes on rocks, fell to her knees, and dropped Mathews' legs, nearly jerking me off balance.

We were both panting and covered with perspiration when we finally got him settled in the bottom of the boat.

"You bring any matches?" I asked.

Helen shook her head.

That necessitated my first trip back to the cottage. I had Helen seated amidship and was just getting ready to shove off when I noticed two lights on the water three or four hundred yards north of us. I hadn't taken into consideration the possibility that there might be other night fishermen out tonight, but now it occurred to me that we would be in a fine fix if another boat came close enough to see in ours.

I made another trip to the cottage for a blanket to throw over the corpse.

Then, finally, we were away from shore. I lit the Coleman lantern and started the outboard motor. I would have preferred to move in darkness but was afraid that an unlighted boat would attract more attention than our light.

At slow speed I headed offshore and south, away from the two stationary lights to the north. Some five hundred yards south on the far side of the lake I spotted a lighted cottage. I headed toward it.

We hadn't moved fifty yards when a gasoline lantern suddenly flared fifty yards ahead of us on our own side of the lake.

Then a voice called, "Hey, Mathews! That you?"

In panic I glanced toward the small boat just leaving shore, then was relieved to see that I couldn't make out the appearance of either occupant in it. It followed that they couldn't make us out clearly.

"Who is it?" I whispered to Helen.

"John Blake, our nearest neighbor," she whispered back. "And probably his oldest son."

"Hey, Mathews!" the voice repeated, and the boat headed toward us.

Slightly revving the motor to hide the tone of my voice, I shouted, "Hi, John. Bet I land one before you do." Then I threw the throttle wide and sped away.

Even with the lighted cottage, I cut the motor in the center of the lake, which left us about a hundred yards from it.

"Sure you can swim a hundred yards?" I asked Helen.

She merely nodded.

"All right," I said. "Let's capsize it."

Cautiously I moved until I was seated on the gunwale, then motioned for Helen to follow suit. She moved just as cautiously, and her added weight caused that side of the boat to tip until water began to drip over the side.

I rocked forward gently, and Helen rocked in rhythm with me. On the back rock quite a lot of water was shipped.

"Now!" I said.

Together we threw all our weight forward, then backward, and the boat upturned. When I came to the surface, Helen's head bobbed up within three feet of me.

"You all right?" I asked.

She blew water from her mouth, gasped, "Yes."

"Then start screaming," I said. "Then swim for that lighted cottage. Phone me at my apartment when things quiet down."

With a strong stroke I headed back toward the Mathews' cottage.

Before I was a dozen yards away Helen began to cry for help. By the time a searchlight near the lighted cottage went on and began to sweep the water, I was a good fifty yards away. I had to dive once, when the probing beam threatened to touch me, but then it picked up Helen and the overturned boat and stopped searching.

I looked back to see a boat leave shore and Helen begin to swim toward it.

No one spotted me during my long swim back to Helen's cottage, though a couple of boats speeding toward the cries for help passed not very far off. Twenty minutes after capsizing the boat I was dressed, had my bag packed and was headed for my car concealed in the underbrush.

By midnight I was safely in bed in my own apartment, with no one but Helen aware that I'd stirred from it during the entire weekend.

Monday when I went to work the plant was in an uproar. The news of Mathews' drowning had been in the morning paper.

My stenographer couldn't wait to tell me about it. I had no more than walked in the door when she thrust the paper at me and said with a mixture of sadness and relish, "Did you see this about the big boss, Mr. Cavanaugh?"

Mathews' social importance made it a page-one item, but the story got routine handling. It simply reported the drowning, added that Mrs. Mathews had nearly drowned at the same time.

There was no intimation that his death might have been anything other than an accident.

I made some discreetly appropriate sounds of regret to my stenographer, then shut up to let her do the talking.

"I wonder how Gertie Drake's taking it?" the girl speculated. "I'll bet she saw the item, because she hasn't come in yet."

Later in the day I learned that Gertie never did come to work. Ordinarily someone from the office would have phoned to inquire why an employee didn't show up, but in tacit conspiracy Gertie's absence was simply ignored. Everyone at the office assumed she wanted to be alone with her grief.

By Tuesday the plant started to get back to normal. Having been only a figurehead boss, Mathews' absence failed to disrupt operations in the slightest, old Lyman Schyler's team of assistants carrying on as efficiently as usual. Aside from a little speculation as to who would inherit Mathews' title of company president, discussion of his death pretty well died down.

On Wednesday it revived again because a half holiday was declared for the purpose of allowing company employees to attend the funeral. I went myself but stayed at the rear of the church, not even going forward to offer the widow sympathy.

I saw no point in it since as far as anyone knew, Helen and I had never met.

I looked for Gertie Drake at the funeral but failed to spot her.

Thursday the plant was operating just as though George Mathews had never existed. Gertie Drake still had not showed up.

And I hadn't heard a word from Helen.

When I still hadn't heard from her by Friday evening I took the chance of phoning. Her voice sounded cool and distant.

"I thought you were going to phone me," I said.

"So soon?" she asked. "You said when things died down."

"Everything went smoothly, didn't it? You weren't asked any unpleasant questions?"

"No," she said. "There wasn't any trouble."

"Then things *have* died down. Why don't you drop over?"

"Tonight?"

"Of course tonight."

She was some time answering me, and when she did, the delay may have made me imagine the reluctance in her voice. However, the words were agreeable enough.

"Eight thirty, as usual," she said.

For the first time she failed to be prompt, arriving ten minutes late. When I kissed her hello, her response was about as torrid as a bronze statue's.

"What's the matter?" I asked, examining her closely. "Thinking of reneging on our deal now that I've done my part?"

"Of course not," she said quickly, moved into my arms and gave me a more enthusiastic kiss.

But I could tell it was simulated enthusiasm.

I thought: *It isn't going to work. She doesn't want to keep her bargain.*

I asked, "How soon do you think it would be safe to marry?"

She answered so quickly I knew she had the reply all prepared. "A year is conventional, isn't it?"

"I was figuring about three months," I said. "A year of widow's weeds went out with Queen Victoria."

"Do we have to discuss it now?"

"I guess it can ride for a few days," I told her.

When she was ready to leave, I said, "You know, we never looked in George's car for that .32 and the sash weights. Or have you?"

She shook her head. "One of the sheriff's deputies drove George's car back to town for me. It's in the garage at home. Should I take the gun and weights out and dispose of them?"

I shrugged. "They don't point to anything. Do as you please."

Later that night, well past midnight, she phoned me.

In a worried voice she said, "Tom, there isn't any gun or sash weights in George's car. What do you think happened to them?"

"He must have had them in the car when he arrived at the cottage," I said. "Could that deputy who drove the car back to town have removed them somehow?"

"I don't see how. He followed me into town. He wasn't out of sight of my rear view mirror all the way."

"Well, it isn't anything to worry about," I assured her. "The stuff only points to George's unfulfilled intentions, not to us."

"I suppose," she said dubiously. "But it's certainly mysterious."

After she hung up, I brooded over it a long time. Despite my telling Helen it was nothing to worry about, it worried me considerably. In the back of my mind, I began to form an uneasy suspicion about where the items were.

The Schyler Tool Company was closed on Saturday, but nevertheless I was up early. By nine A.M. I was at the rooming house where Gertie Drake lived.

The stout, middle-aged woman who answered the door said, "Gertie Drake? Sorry, mister. She's home on vacation."

"Oh?" I said. "Where's home?"

When the woman scowled suspiciously, I gave her my most charming smile and said, "I'm not a bill collector or a process server. I'm a personal friend. I just wanted to ask her out to dinner."

"Oh," she said. After examining me carefully, she seemed to decide I was all right. "Coral Grove's her home. Four twenty-three Warsaw Drive. I imagine the phone number's in the book. It'd be under her father's name. Henry Drake."

Coral Gove was practically a suburb of Raine City, being only ten miles away. Instead of driving there, I phoned. A man answered.

"Gertie there?" I asked.

"Gertie? She hasn't lived here for years. Rooms in Raine City."

"Yes, I know. But she isn't home, and I thought she might be visiting you."

"Well, she ain't," the man said. "I ought to know. I'm her father."

"Sorry I bothered you," I said, and hung up.

I know where Gertie Drake is. There's only one possible explanation for her telling her landlady she was going home for a time, when her father knew nothing about the proposed visit. She must have made the excuse to cover a contemplated secret vacation with George Mathews. And since Mathews had no intention of being with her beyond the weekend, he must have suggested that she make the excuse in order to delay the report that she was missing.

Gertie Drake is somewhere in the lake with six sash weights tied to her body.

Even if the body is never recovered, eventually she is bound to be reported missing. And then Helen is going to realize what I already know: that her husband meant to kill to retain her—to keep her love—not to get rid of her.

Whether we're married or not, what then? Will she go to the police with the whole story? I'm afraid she will. I've got to be afraid that she will. How else be sure of my own neck?

How else except to kill Helen? Kill her before Gertie Drake is reported missing.

# Welcome to My Prison

## by Jack Ritchie

I gave Big Jim Turley the usual routine. You're here because of the debt you owe society. If you make trouble for us, we'll make trouble for you, but if you cooperate, one of these days you'll walk out of the gates a free man.

Turley smiled and looked at the ceiling.

Ed Pollard, my chief of guards, glared at him. "Wipe the smirk off your face when the warden's talking."

I paused a moment to light a cigar. "Your first three days here will be your orientation period. You'll be given a physical examination and various psychological and aptitude tests."

Turley looked a big man, and the two hundred dollar suit helped to cover the fact that not all of the bigness was muscle.

I studied him objectively and wondered how he had ever become so important. I could see the weakness in him, the flaws that I saw in so many others.

I folded my hands on the desk. "If you've got any questions, now is the time to ask them."

Turley grinned and glanced at Pollard. "I like privacy when I talk, warden."

I was aware that Pollard's eyes were on me. I shook my head. "Anything you might have to say can be said right now."

Turley chuckled. "I guess I can wait. I'm going to be around for five years."

When Turley was gone, Pollard paced back and forth in front of my desk. He was an intense man, with the bitter fanatic eyes of one who has found that the justice of this world is not as harsh as his own. "Five years," he snapped. "He gets a lousy five years, and I'll be damned if he doesn't get out in half the time."

I leaned back in my chair. "All he did was steal money, Ed. He didn't kill anybody." I took a few puffs on my cigar. "You got a fine anger there, Ed, but I'll tell you what I just figured out. Turley robbed us taxpayers of about twenty-two cents per square head."

Pollard put his knuckles on my desk. "You're looking at it from

237

the wrong end, warden. Turley lined his pockets with a million dollars of the public's money."

He regarded me steadily. "Where does Turley spend his time in here, warden? Does he start in the laundry like the poor people, or do we get him a feather bed and let him sleep?"

I glanced at the records on my desk. "He's just one person, Ed. You don't have to hate him like he was a regiment."

Pollard snorted. "He's just one of the crooks who was unlucky enough to get caught. He's covering up for the whole rotten upstate gang. He's taking the rap for Costa and his organization and he's doing it with a smile."

Pollard's face was a dark flush. "He'll be taken care of. *All along the line.*"

I looked up at him and wondered whether it was worth the effort to show anger. I kept my voice quiet. "How far along the line, Ed?"

His mouth tightened. "I'd better get back to the job."

I grinned slowly. "Just a minute, Ed. Your face and your voice tell me that you're wondering if the organization got to me. Did Costa maybe slip me a little something to make this a heaven for Turley?"

Pollard was at the door. "I didn't use the words."

I nodded. "But you got their meaning across. You know that my job depends on politics and you know who's knee-deep in the politics of this state."

He waited, saying nothing.

"Ed," I said. "Nobody's got to me, politics or no politics. I don't know Costa and I don't know anything about his organization. I got this job before anybody ever heard of him and I still got a few friends in the capitol who can see that I keep it. Turley will get a number, just like anybody else."

Pollard managed a crooked smile. "You make me happier, warden. Real glad."

At the end of three days I got the results of Turley's tests and examinations. I studied them carefully for more than an hour before I tore out one page and crumpled it. I burned it in my ashtray and sent for Turley.

He waited until the guard left the room and then sat down. "Some of those tests were downright interesting. I'll bet I didn't do too bad either."

I spoke softly. "On your feet, Turley. I didn't tell you to sit down."

A flush came slowly to his face. "Do you know who you're talking to?"

I smiled. "I think I'm talking to a prisoner. You've got five seconds to get up or I'll arrange for some special persuasion."

His jaw sagged slightly. After a moment he got to his feet.

That's the first part of it, I thought to myself. I'm the boss here and you're going to know it. I picked up his records and tamped the edges even. "I'm starting you in the laundry. We'll see if we can work off some of that lard."

Confusion flickered in Turley's eyes and he licked his lips. "I don't get it. Mr. Costa promised he'd fix everything."

"I don't care what your Mr. Costa promised. I don't take orders from him, you understand." My smile was thin. "Did he guarantee you that this would be just like a rest home? You'd have everything you wanted? Maybe even a couple of days outside the wall every month?"

I laughed. "Costa is just a dirty name to me."

Turley blinked indignantly. "They won't get away with it. I can blow the lid off. I'm not just anybody. I'm Big Jim Turley."

You're not big anything, I thought, when you're wearing that uniform.

"Costa's fingers don't reach this far," I said. I paused significantly for a few moments. "But that doesn't necessarily mean that you've got to suffer."

I gave him sufficient silence to work on what I'd just said. He watched me, his eyes narrowed cautiously and waited for more.

I studied my cigar. "You don't have to lead a rough life here, Turley. Not if you're prepared to help yourself. I think I can be reasonable."

After a few moments he began to chuckle. "You scared me for a while there, warden. I thought I was looking at an honest man."

You scare easy, I thought. You quiver fast if somebody puts a thumb on you.

I smiled and looked at the ceiling. "You took a million, Turley."

He laughed shortly. "I spent it too."

I shook my head. "It's hard to get rid of that much money, Turley. I'd guess that you got a few pennies left."

Turley frowned. "Ten thousand. That's the best I can do.

I leaned back in my chair. "I was thinking of twenty-five."

He glowered. "Go to hell!"

I was watching him when he said it. The words were positive, but I could tell he'd go up to twenty-five.

"Turley," I said quietly, "you don't know how dead and buried you are here. I can be God to you or Devil. You got your choice."

He ran his fingers nervously through his hair a couple of times and scowled. "All right. Twenty-five. I'll have to get a letter out."

I pointed to my ink stand. "Write it here and make it this way. You want the money in hundreds. You want it thrown out of a car in a nice tight bundle at the junction of 42 and JJ at ten in the night. You name the day, but make it soon."

He raised an eyebrow and grinned faintly. "You didn't stumble over the words. I guess you've done some thinking about this."

"Yes," I said. "I put in a little time on it."

He began writing. "It'll take at least a couple of days for my wife to get the cash. How about Friday?"

I nodded and stood over his shoulder as he wrote. "Don't mention why you want the money and don't write any names."

When he finished, I took the letter from him and put it in the envelope he addressed. "I'll mail this outside. I don't think we want anybody to censor it."

I sat down and relaxed. "You're assigned to the library for the time being, Turley. But if things don't work out Friday, you're going to be made uncomfortable."

On Friday I left the walls and was at the junction before ten. There was no trouble.

I took a hotel room in the city for the night and counted the money. In the morning I put it in my safety deposit box at the bank and drove back to the prison.

When I got there, Pollard was waiting, his face splotched red with anger. He followed me into the office and came directly to the point. "I'd like to know why you put Turley in the library," he demanded.

I studied Pollard while I removed the wrapper from a cigar. You'd be fool enough to resign if I let Turley stay in the library. You're built like that and you're a fool. It's taken you twenty years to get where you are now, but you'd probably throw it all away because you like to feed your righteous indignation.

I lit the cigar. "Turley scored good on his tests, Ed. You know I like to put a man where I think he'll do the best job."

Pollard's eyes glowed. "You're treating him like a guest." He leaned over my desk and his voice was harsh as he asked, "Is he a paying guest?"

I sighed heavily. "Ed, suppose you were sitting in this chair? Suppose you had to make the decisions? What would you do? Think about it fully, Ed."

His laugh was caustic. "I've been thinking about it. I've been thinking about it a lot."

I know you have, I thought. But it's just a dream, Pollard, old boy. You'll never sit in this chair. You're too brittle. You have to learn to bend with things to get to the top. It's that way everywhere, Ed. Not just here. But people like you never learn that.

I smiled faintly. "You'd make Turley sweat?"

"You're damn right I would," he snapped. "I'd stand over him personally."

I rapped my fingers thoughtfully on the desk and then looked up. "I could have made a mistake about Turley, Ed."

Pollard's eyes were suspicious and he waited.

I got to my feet. "We'll do it your way, Ed. If you want him in the laundry, that's where he'll be."

Pollard nodded with sharp satisfaction. He started for the door, but turned before he reached it. There was some color high in his cheeks. "I'm sorry—about—about what I said, warden. I talk faster than I think sometimes."

Don't apologize too much, Ed, I thought. I'm not doing anything for you.

I smiled tiredly. "That's all right, Ed. Forget it."

Even though the medical report on Turley had sounded serious, I figured it might take some time. But at four-thirty that same afternoon Pollard came to me. His face was gray. "He just keeled over, warden. He just dropped."

I looked up from the papers on my desk and frowned. "Who keeled over?"

Pollard's voice was shaky. "Turley. He's dead. I guess it was his heart."

I kept staring at him.

He shifted nervously. "I kept him sweating and hauling in the laundry. I stood over him and told him where he could go, when he complained that he was feeling sick."

I rubbed my forehead and said nothing for a while. Then I flicked the switch on my intercom. "Novack, bring in Turley's records."

When they came, I slipped out the medical forms and read them. I pointed to a scrap of paper remaining under one of the staples.

"It looks like that was one page somebody didn't want me to read. Maybe it's the one that tells about Turley's heart."

I glanced at Pollard.

His eyes went wide. "You can't think that I'd do something like that?"

I looked away. "No. You've been with me a long time, Ed. I guess I can believe you if you say you didn't."

Pollard's voice was tight. "Sure I hated him. I hate all his kind, but I wouldn't deliberately get rid of him." A tic appeared on the side of his face. "One of the clerks could have destroyed that page."

I smiled sadly. "You want an investigation, Ed? Is that what you want?"

He hesitated. "Why not? I've got nothing to hide."

"Of course not, Ed," I said soothingly. I rubbed my jaw. "Turley had a lot of important friends and they can make things rough. If I started an investigation, it would eventually get out to the newspapers and a lot of people would be looking over our shoulders. They'd want a goat, Ed. They'd want to know who hated Turley enough to want him dead." I met his eyes. "They'd find one, Ed."

I got out of my chair. "Ed," I said quietly. "I think it would be better for . . . better for both of us, if this thing died right here. In this office."

Pollard was silent, not looking at me.

"Ed," I said softly. "You've got a wife and two kids."

He stood there for a good three minutes, working his hands into white-knuckled fists. Finally, he looked at me. "There's the doctor. He might want to know why we put Turley in the laundry if his heart was bad."

I shook my head. "He knows that we all make mistakes, Ed. Honest mistakes. I've known him long enough to ask for a favor." I patted Pollard's shoulder. "He's a good friend of yours too, isn't he, Ed?"

I left before the gates were sealed for the night and drove to the lake shore section of the city.

Mr. Costa fixed the drinks himself. He shook his head sadly. "So it was his heart?"

"Yes, sir," I said. "I don't think he ever knew how bad it was himself."

He handed me my drink. "Jim looked so healthy."

"You can never tell, sir," I said. "He died in his sleep. Well . . . it was a peaceful way to go."

Costa shrugged. "At least we tried to make it easy for him. The organization prides itself on that. We like loyalty and Jim had it."

"Yes, sir," I said. "He lived like a king in there. He had everything he wanted—I saw to that." I looked at Costa over the rim of my glass. He didn't seem so big to me. Not now.

He sipped at his drink. "Too bad about Jim. We try to take care of our own."

"Yes, sir," I said. "We always do."

# Come Into My Parlor

## by Gloria Amoury

In the luxurious hotel room overlooking the Bay of Naples glistening in the setting sun, two middle-aged ladies chatted pleasantly. Surface talk, their conversation gave no hint of their reflections.

The hostess, thin and dark in prim black, with a youthful face of one who nibbles at life rather than devours it, appeared innocent and passionless compared to the other. Yet it was Marcia who regarded her guest as a spider might an unwary fly. Vivienne, in girlish pink which accented her plumpness, and with gray-black roots marring her yellow hair and the sensuous face of one who constantly participates in life and is soiled by it, seemed relaxed.

"What a coincidence that we met in the square," Vivienne murmured, as a small maid, olive-skinned and peasant-skirted, cleared the remnants of the *piccata* from the candlelit table and brought in a bowl of apples and almonds.

"It's never a coincidence when Americans meet in Italy," Marcia answered. "We all cluster around the same squares and fountains. Too, I'd heard from home that you were touring near here. Your sister told Mother." She didn't add that she'd had her parents keep her posted on Vivienne's whereabouts, which they'd thought good sportsmanship; nor that during the past week she had been actively searching for Vivienne.

"Touring is a word used by the successful," Vivienne said wistfully. "Wandering is what I do."

The slight sympathy evoked in Marcia by the words evaporated at the sight of Vivienne's still round bosom and shapely legs. Possibly Vivienne had had it rough, financially, since Tom's death, while she herself had made money. Still, there were other ways of being successful than the most obvious, and a restless spirit, not a roaming body, made a wanderer.

"*You* tour," the guest went on, "with your music."

Marcia glanced at the talisman of every hotel room she occupied, her rented grand piano with the embroidered covering protecting its gloss, like a shawl a delicate person. Thanks to Vivienne, the piano had been a person to her through the years, the only constant companion, friend and mate she'd had. "I was lucky to click with it."

"I read about your last concert. The critic said you interpreted Chopin as well as Rosalind Turek does Bach. I don't know who Rosalind Turek is, but that's a compliment, isn't it?"

That compliment, like others about her singing tones and the nuances of her shadings, as always, whirled through Marcia's head meaninglessly. She suspected that musical talent, like other such gifts, was more admired by those who heard it from box seats than by those who, happening to possess it, had to use it as a life-substitute. "Let's not talk about music. Let's talk about us."

"That's the subject I've been hoping to avoid," Vivienne said, embarrassed.

Marcia's expression hardened. "At this point, the—circumstances —are just something you and I shared."

Vivenne looked at her curiously. "I should have known a woman as—great—as you are, from the music, would feel that way. But when you stopped me tonight, my first thought was that you felt toward me the way most women in your place would and I—got scared."

"Scared?" Marcia forced a laugh. "Of me?"

"I harmed you long ago. Another in your place might think—of harming me now."

"Let's not use ambiguous words like 'harm.' You were a divorcee living next door to us, and my trusted friend. Somehow, possibly helped by such stimuli as the moonlight on the nearby Wabash, you managed to run off with my husband—"

"It didn't happen the way you put it," Vivienne said.

"How did it happen? I've always been curious."

"I can't explain it," Vivienne said, "especially to someone as—self-controlled—as you've always been. But Tom and I had to do what we did."

"If Tom was driven by a wild passion for you," Marcia said, "he successfully hid it from me."

"But from no one else," Vivienne said, artlessly. "I guess because you're the artistic type, with your thoughts always above the flesh, we did surprise *you*."

This artistic type, Marcia reflected, was now going to claim her revenge—a life for a life. Vivienne had taken hers and left the hulk to exhaust itself pushing an ordinary talent to an undreamed-of potential. For with Tom gone and no appetite for other men, what could she have done with her years but follow the instructions of piano coaches, practice eight hours a day, and finally smile woodenly over concert-stage footlights at the audiences of the world? She had planned this action for seventeen years. Now, the victim had been relatively easily found, had come with her readily, and was unconsciously goading her to it. "Now that you realize my thoughts *are* always above the flesh," she said, disarmingly, "you trust me, don't you?"

"I came with you, didn't I?"

"Why? To find out how I've managed without Tom?"

"No," Vivienne said, in a low voice. "Because you talk with the accent of home, and I was sure you'd give me good food. I haven't heard the one or had the other in some time. But now that I've heard your talk and had your good food, I hope Tom and I didn't hurt you too much."

"You didn't hurt me at all. Witness the piano. How many women pianists make it big? Dame Myra Hess, Turek, Novaes—only a few. With Tom I'd have been an ordinary housewife; without him I've touched the stars."

"I guess you have," Vivienne said.

Marcia shivered. Failures always had their dreams of success as an opiate against loneliness, but no one was lonelier than the successful, alone. What was hollower for a performer than a concert stage before an audience with no one in it cared for or caring? If she'd been a failure, she might have forgiven Vivienne, but success made the revenge more necessary. "The past is past," she said, smiling. "Now, we're Americans far from home and you're visiting me. I've a treat for you." She rang for the maid.

The maid came in with a pitcher.

"Lemonade," Vivienne said delightedly. "Made the American way. Lemony, with lots of ice."

"Made the Indiana way. I remember you loved lemons. You used to suck lemon halves with sugar."

"Imagine your remembering! The veal was flavored with lemon too. How considerate you are, and what a fool I was to worry."

"You were foolish indeed," Marcia agreed as she turned away from her guest and took a tall glass from the cupboard, a certain glass containing a few powdered grains which, when mixed with lemonade, Marcia knew, would kill.

It takes six weeks for the poison to close the kidneys of its victim and cause death from uremia, the book on poisons in the Rome library had said. By then she'd be safe behind the Iron Curtain on a Budapest stage, this encounter with Vivienne forgotten by its only other witness, the small maid.

Turning back to Vivienne, Marcia asked conversationally, "How long have you been in Europe?"

"Ten years. But we traveled around in the States before that."

Traveling with Tom . . . Marcia thought of sidewalk cafes in Paris she'd sat in, alone, of the car ride through the grandeur of the Amalfi mountains taken with a fellow passenger, a German woman who couldn't speak English but had smiled with irritating recognition that they were both those pitiable objects, women alone; she thought of Bavarian Alps, seen alone, of the Mediterranean at night, seen alone. Only once had *she* traveled with Tom.

"Tom and I," she couldn't help saying, "went to San Francisco on our honeymoon. We rode cablecars and ate at wharf fish-places. There was a baby grand in our hotel lobby which overlooked the Golden Gate. I'd play Debussy and he'd recite Francois Villon's poems to me, in French, to the music."

Vivienne smiled. "Those poems are effective even without Debussy."

"I should have realized," Marcia said bitterly, "that you'd be familiar with them too. Stupid of me."

"I had them fifteen years to your two," Vivienne said. "They sounded impressive in the States but ridiculous in Paris, with his American accent. But who could stop him from spouting the only French he knew?"

Marcia realized with a slight shock that she hadn't known Tom had had a poor French accent. That wasn't something one noticed when one was young and in love. What did a poor accent matter? She filled Vivienne's glass with lemonade. "Didn't Tom get a good job with an engineering firm in Kansas City right after—he left with you?"

"That's right. A good job."

Until Vivienne's sister had babbled that news to her one bright, hot morning as she'd dusted Tom's big chair, she'd convinced herself that it was a fling and that he'd be back. But the words "good job" made it permanent and had sealed her doom as this concoction would Vivienne's. "All the while he was a teller at that bank in South Bend, he talked about finding some opening in engineering. He was lucky to find one so quickly after he went with you."

"We'd driven off in the car, *your* car," Vivienne said, somewhat sheepishly. "It was summer, you remember. When we got to K.C., Tom bought a newspaper and saw an ad for an engineering trainee. He answered it in his shirtsleeves, with the sweat from the road on his face. Maybe if he'd cleaned up he'd have looked like the other applicants and he mightn't have got the job, but as it was, the boss probably figured he was so—dedicated—that he put wanting-the-job even before cleanliness."

Marcia, too, had traveled that summer. Numbed beyond tears, she'd passed flat Indiana towns on the small electric train and then had made her way through Chicago to Professor Hoelick's studio overlooking Lake Michigan. Unawed by the giant grands back to back, or by the electric metronome sternly overhead—so different from Miss Claver's prim parlor-with-upright—she'd played a Beethoven Sonata and then said, "I've studied the piano casually, under a local teacher, most of my life. I'd like to do something important with my music now. I've heard your name. Will you teach me?"

"The maximum talent, application, and luck," the bushy-haired German answered, "is still no guarantee that the possessor of them all will accomplish anything artistically. In your case, your timing is execrable and, obviously, you've never been taught that a sustaining pedal exists. Still, you have the beginning of a singing tone. If you can meet my price . . ."

Unhelped by Tom, she'd met it through her steno and typing.

"Tom clashed with his boss after three months in K.C.," Vivienne was saying, "and that ended the engineering. Then he tried sales promotion."

"I can't believe he gave up engineering that easily," Marcia said. "He kept talking about a series of tunnels he wanted to build some day."

Vivienne smiled. "If I didn't know which two years you had him, I could figure out the dates from that brainstorm."

"What do you mean?" Marcia asked uneasily.

"His notions lasted about two years apiece and produced their own job-kicks. I went through at least seven. I didn't mind the insurance salesman bit or the TV producer bit, in the States, but in Europe his ideas got wilder. The worst was the hotel in Yugoslavia in which he wanted to invest, without knowing the language."

Marcia glanced sharply at her guest, jolted by the words. After Tom had left her, she had continued to have images of him: Tom, a thin, dignified thirtyish, a gray-templed, distinguished fortyish, ever onward and upward in engineering and, recently, even wonderful in death. It was jarring to realize that Vivienne had so unsettled him. "I'm surprised he was so—unstable."

"He wasn't exactly unstable. Just restless in jobs. The two-and-a-half-year stint with that bank, when he was engaged to and then married to you, was the longest he ever had in one place, he told me."

She was lying, Marcia decided. Tom had been as solid as stone in the old days, his head filled with dreams of one career, engineering. Still, a remark of her father's popped into her head. "He's as solid as a five-letter word beginning with 'S', all right. Sieve, not stone. Your love's blinding you, daughter." Her father had been jealous of Tom. Weren't all fathers of their sons-in-law?

"I suspect he'd have exploded in some other way," Vivienne went on, "if he hadn't met me."

"I never saw signs that an explosion was coming."

"They just weren't visible to you. For example, you never got that fifty dollars back, did you?"

"What fifty dollars?"

"The money that was stolen from your purse the day of the picnic."

"Oh, that money. No. But our cleaning girl took it. She admitted it, and said she'd spent it."

"She was protecting Tom," Vivienne said. "She'd had an affair with him."

"I don't believe you!" Marcia burst out. "You can say anything here, after all this time and with Tom dead. You know the only way you can boost yourself in my eyes is by making him seem bad. Next you'll tell me that rotten Tom corrupted innocent you."

"No," Vivienne said, softly. "We deserved each other."

Marcia couldn't deafen herself to the ring of truth in the tone.

Shaken, she gathered memories once precious and suddenly seeming soiled, and searched for consolation in them. "The—fifty dollars. How did you know about that? No one but Tom and the maid— But of course. Tom probably told you about it later."

"No," Vivienne said. "At the time. *He* took it and spent it on me. We had a lovely drunk on it at the Three Bay Bar. You were awake when Tom got home, he said. He told you some tale about a lonely bank examiner promising him a promotion if he drank with him until three A.M.—"

In Tom's arms, Marcia remembered, painfully, despite the reek of his breath, she'd consoled him after the dead hours spent with the bank examiner. There'd been other nights when he'd said he'd been delayed with other bank examiners, or scouts for engineering firms. And times when he'd driven the cleaning girl home and had got lost on the way back, he'd said. He'd been such a silly, Marcia had murmured fondly, getting lost for an hour on a straight road. Other money had disappeared, and the pearl ring, an heirloom of her mother's. Once the memories started souring, Marcia, still holding Vivienne's glass, was powerless to stop them.

"You must have had quite a life with him," Marcia said, "because presumably when *you* lived with him, you knew him."

"It wasn't bad," Vivienne said, seriously. "We had our ups and downs, like most couples."

One's lot, Marcia reflected, was indeed tailored to suit one.

"When he didn't work," Vivienne said, "I did. I had some weird jobs, from hash slinging to hat checking."

"He let *you* work! He wouldn't even let me give piano lessons!"

"So he told me. But that was because he couldn't stand kids around. Which was why we never had any, and probably why you didn't have any."

The golden wraith of the child who might have been and whose coming, Marcia'd thought, had been only temporarily postponed by Tom, left its perch on her conscience and vanished into oblivion.

Vivienne was still talking of her jobs. "The one job I had that I never let him forget was the time *he* arranged for me to—well— It was very dignified. Tom had met a rich New Yorker in a London pub. We were broke, and the fellow wanted a date for the night. Tom told him he knew an English girl—I was so good with the limey accent that the guy never noticed my midwest twang. But later, whenever Tom and I fought, I'd say, 'You've done the worst a man can do, by your woman.' "

For the first time, Vivienne's eyes clouded with pain. As insensitive as Vivienne seemed, Tom had hurt her, too.

"People are like icebergs," Marcia breathed, her hand tightening on the glass. "Nine-tenths submerged beneath the surface. I never knew Tom at all."

Vivienne shrugged. "He wasn't a bad guy. And shaved, dressed-up and sober, he had enough charm to win a queen, right to the end. With that baby face and tousled hair, he *was* handsome when he was young, wasn't he?"

"Yes," Marcia said, "he was." And she let her earliest and most sacred memories of him sour with the rest.

"He grew enormously fat before he died. In my opinion, his weight brought on the heart attack, not the brawl he was in. But maybe you never heard how he died."

"No, I never did."

"He died in my arms," Vivienne said.

"Oh?" Marcia didn't resent it in the least.

"In Paris, some months ago. Tom had been drinking, and this fellow came up to him and said— It's a long story. Are you sure you're interested?"

"On second thought," Marcia said, "I'd rather hear it some other time. I've absorbed enough about Tom for one night."

"I guess a woman as—great—as you are, with the music, can't waste her time on small talk about a man she knew for only a little while. My throat's dry from all this talk. I suppose that gorgeous glass is for me. May I have it?"

"Glass?"

"The lemonade."

"Oh, *this* glass," Marcia said, staring at it. "There seems to be a spot on it. I'll get you a clean one."

"Don't bother."

"I insist." And Marcia poured the contents of the glass down the wash-basin drain.

Vivienne had three glassfuls of lemonade. Then she rose and said, "Guess I'll tootle off to my digs, as crummy as they are."

"Don't go!" Marcia cried, impulsively. The leaden feeling inside her for seventeen years had melted. She was appalled at what she'd almost done to this woman, this—human being, this fellow-sufferer at the hands of Tom. How could she make it up? "I have twin beds. Stay here while I'm here. My next concert isn't until next week, in Vienna."

"I couldn't bear to," Vivienne said. "It'd be too painful to leave it all when I had to. I'm not doing badly now. A friend I had left me a few lira to get by on."

Marcia studied Vivienne momentarily, then offered, "I can spare some lira too."

Vivienne protested, but not strongly, and then left richer than when she'd come.

Marcia stood at the window and watched the other leave the plushy hotel entrance and then walk tiredly past dusty street urchins and animals toward wherever cave dwellers live.

"There but for the grace of God," she murmured, and quietly began to weep. Then, carefully, she took the covering off the piano, sat down and began to play Chopin nocturnes, all nineteen, followed by the lesser known twentieth, posthumous, in C-sharp minor, and never had her trill been so exquisite nor her crescendos and de crescendos so gradual.

# Lend Me Your Ears

## by Edward Wellen

**N**ow and again a spy has to get away from himself for a while—away from his false self and back to his true self. Or else . . .

You've seen Marcel Marceau do his pantomime of the mask becoming the face—the clutching hands desperately trying to tear loose the clownish smile, and failing. Well, before it gets to that with me, every so often I take the mask off, just to make sure I still can.

I have to tell someone what I do, what I've done.

The need usually comes on me after I've gone through a bad one, when the reasons for going through it are not mine to know. What does the cog know of the machine? Or the pawn of the end game?

Your own government—or governments, if you're a double agent—must disown you. You can never be sure your own people aren't using you as human bait. There have been times when, on orders from above, I've had to throw comrades to the wolves.

So I often stop to remember I'm a pawn too. I'm a thinking pawn, though, and I realize I face torture if I fall into enemy hands. So I find myself waking up sweating. Could I stand up to it? Would I talk? Could I kill myself first?

Yet I can't let myself brood. If I got the blues thinking of all these things, my superiors would see that as a sign of weakness and would liquidate me. And rightly so.

Likewise, a spy can't take to drink or drugs. Even if his people never get wind of it, it's bad. It affects his judgment and makes him careless. A spy can misjudge badly, bungle badly, only once.

The answer—at least for me—is the confessional, but not the church confessional booth. Wasn't it the Croppy Boy, the captured Irish rebel in the ballad, who spilled all to a British soldier disguised as a priest? So to whom can a spy talk?

A spy has no friends. The deadening of feeling, the diminishing of trust, these occupational hazards see to that. No, I pick a perfect stranger, someone I'll never meet again.

Let me tell you about my latest assignment, the one from which

I'm just returning. It was to dispose of an enemy agent whose cover though he himself did not yet know it, had been blown. It turned out pretty bloody.

The mission before that had been a bad one too, and so I wondered as I planed in whether I was up to snuffing him out. I had not yet had a chance to discharge the build-up tension from the earlier mission. Luckily for me, my superiors didn't know how shaky I was.

There would be no time for games, for keeping him under long surveillance, or for attempting to turn him around, or even for bringing him in to a safe house and working on him to talk. It was to be in; do the job; and out. It was up to me to make the most of the few hours they gave me before I had to plane back.

I found him right off. He was at the atmospheric—low wattage to hide the dirt—cafe where they said he hung out. I picked him up as he paid and left, and followed him down the dark street. I came even with him, made as if to pass, then clapped him on the shoulder, like so, and he jumped.

He turned pale when I said his name, showed him the bulge of my gun and told him to come along with me.

Of course he composed himself quickly, tried to play dumb, then indignant, but he knew it was all up with him. At last he let his shoulders sag and gave a shrug and a smile.

We walked our shadows along the empty street toward my rented car. At the last minute, as we passed an alley, he broke away, shoving me to the ground. He then ran away into the alley.

Without getting up, I drew my gun and rested both elbows on the cobbles, gripping the wrist of my gun hand with the other one. He was zigzagging away, and a silencer throws you off, but my second shot got him in the leg before he wrenched around out of sight. I got up but was in no hurry to give chase. There was no need to, not merely because I was sure the man would be limping badly and would be weakening fast from loss of blood. I could have caught up with him easily and killed him, but I held back, kept out of sight.

The thing I had clapped to the back of his coat, placing it just under his collar, beeped in my inconspicuous earphone and gave me a constant fix on him. What I really wanted was not the man alone but as many of his contacts as I could get him to lead me to before it was time to finish him off.

Now, this may seem strange to you, but I knew his thinking as though I had planted a bug inside his head.

*They're right behind me and I'll never shake them off,* he told himself. *They know who I really am, so I'm no more use to our side. Where can I go? Who can I turn to? Someone had to give me away or I wouldn't be in this fix. Who did it? My girl? My comrades?*

I tell you, he was a bitter, jealous, hopeless man by then, and he began thinking about who he might bring down with him. Now he took a kind of perverse pride in having blown his cover. Now he was a Typhoid Mary who carried guilt by association, who bestowed the kiss of death. His touch, his glance were fatal.

By simply making ambiguous contact with someone he knew to be a valued agent of ours, he could make us think the man had sold out to the other side. In the same way, he could destroy a personal enemy, gratify a private grudge. He could put the finger on his girlfriend just in case she had tipped us off anonymously, or just to keep her from living on to enjoy another man. He could pick anyone at random and place on that person the mark of wrath. What power he had!

As it happened, he did all of those things. I know, because I followed his trail and found out to whom he went for bandaging and money and documents and a car.

Of course I had to dispose of all his contacts. Couldn't take a chance on passing up any, could I?

The really strange thing was, he was actually wearing a look of hope at the end—when it came time to finish him off—till he saw me again.

So, as I say, this was a particularly bad one. That's why, maybe once a year, I pick a conversation with a perfect stranger and tell him all. Each time, of course . . . but I see you understand. If it's any comfort to you, I promise you won't feel a thing, though you may have felt the tiniest pinprick a while back when I clapped you on the shoulder. It will pass as a heart attack. No, no, don't try to move. It's too late.

There, I told you.

Oh, stewardess! Over here, miss, please. I'm afraid my seatmate isn't feeling well. He seemed to go funny all at once and slump over like that. I think it might be serious . . .

No, a perfect stranger.

# Killer Scent

## by Joe L. Hensley

The small man came into my courthouse office in the afternoon just after yet another report of *someone* spotting Joe Ringer. The man waited patiently while I ordered a car dispatched to the sighting area.

"Could I speak with you privately, sheriff?" he then asked politely.

I examined him. He was so thin that he could be called emaciated. I thought him to be about my age, early forties. His handshake was soft and so somehow reserved. He wore rumpled, conservative clothes, thick glasses, and sported a small beard. He looked all right, but my sensitive nose smelled desperation and death, and I was distrustful of him. Most men trust something. I trust my nose.

"Edward Allen Reynolds," he said, introducing himself.

I nodded shortly. My long dead father once told me never to believe well of anyone who used three names.

"Sheriff Spain," I replied. "Things are busy. If you came to talk to Joe Ringer I'm sorry to report he somehow walked away from my jail last night."

He looked stricken. "I'd like to have talked to him, but not for what you probably think. My only interest is how he got to your town, sheriff." He gave me a sharp look. "How'd he manage to just walk away?"

"If I knew, I'd be a happier man," I said, still not sure of his intentions. I'd thought at first he might be another reporter like the many who'd appeared in Crossville like wolves drawn to bait when we'd picked up Joe Ringer.

"If you aren't a reporter then what are you?" I asked.

"I'm a psychology professor at a small college in the East, but I'm on sabbatical just now. If you'd like to check on me, you can call the head of the psychology department at your state university. He'll tell you I'm bona fide."

I considered doing that for a moment and decided against it. "I'm very busy," I said pointedly. "This is an election year." I tried to read his eyes behind their thick glasses, but nothing solid happened. There was only the faint smell to him of hurt or injury or desperation.

"If you want to talk more about Joe Ringer I can recommend my deputy, Chick Gaitlin. He spotted Ringer in the bus station and arrested him." Gaitlin had been very popular with the disappointed newsmen all day.

"I think it's you I need to talk with, sheriff," he said, lowering his voice. "I've got a theory that Joe Ringer was lured to your town for some reason I don't understand."

I smiled a little at that. "I've got an election opponent who's screaming all over the county today about my inefficiency, and I've got an escaped multiple murderer. I don't need wild theories. I do need to find Joe Ringer. Take your theories to the press. Perhaps they'd like them. They've turned Ringer into a folk hero instead of a cold killer."

"Please let me have a few moments of your time in private," he said. He looked around. The gum chewing deputy who was operating the radio was listening curiously. I'd heard he was the one who'd leaked things to my opponent all through the campaign. He'd probably been promised more rank and a better job after I was voted out. I knew he disliked me because I'd put him on the radio. Maybe he was the leak, maybe not. Election years make for chronic paranoia. I'd spent a lot of time getting where I was. I didn't plan to lose it. I had no wife, no family. I had only the job and the opportunities it brought.

"All right. Come into my private parlor, Edward Allen Reynolds," I said. I got up from the littered desk and led him into my dingy private office, closing the door behind us.

"First off I need to know how Joe Ringer got here," he said.

"Routinely enough. On a bus. A deputy saw him get off a bus and picked him up at the station. That was yesterday morning."

"But why would Ringer appear here? Why to this town, of all places?"

"Why not? Crossville's a nice town. Thirty thousand plus and growing. Industry, power, and farming. Read our Chamber of Commerce handouts."

"A lot of trails I've followed may have ended in your Crossville in the past few years, sheriff. Did you ever hear of one Peter Green?"

"No," I said. I had, but I wanted Reynolds to talk, not me.

"I traced him here. He has a sister in Florida. I started there. He was a heavy suspect there and in some other states on maybe a dozen rape murders. She showed me his picture. Handsome young man who made his living as a long-distance trucker. Somehow young women died almost every time he was very long around a town. His sister told me he came to Crossville because of a very good job offer from some firm called Multiple Trucking Incorporated. I checked them out earlier today. There isn't any company by that name around here and never has been. This sister hasn't heard from him since he left Florida. I've reason to suspect she never will again."

"I've sure never heard of the company," I said stolidly. "And I've lived all of my life around here. But so what?"

He shrugged. "Only that Green's missing in your town. I ran down one more certain, a construction worker named William Kole. I believe he killed for kicks, getting some kind of sick joy out of it, a butcher boy. He came out of Pennsylvania originally, but lived in San Francisco until he came here some months back. He was tried once in California for murder, but there wasn't enough evidence to make it stick. After the trial he moved here to work on your new power plant. I've got a copy of his work application. But when they tried to call him for work he'd disappeared. No one's seen him since." He shook his head, very intent, a man obsessed with his quest. "There have been some others I can't document as well yet. They apparently wound up here, but I can't prove it." He nodded positively. "I think they did. So I'll continue to check."

"All this is most interesting," I said, "but right now I'm a political candidate with a bad problem. I need to find Joe Ringer or start looking for a new job after the first of the year. And I like this job and also like to think I'm competent at it."

"I've heard around that you are, sheriff. All I want is permission to stick close. I think Joe Ringer may have also been lured here. If I can talk with him then maybe I can find out exactly how."

"I don't need or want anyone in the way."

"A trade, then. I've an idea or two about where Ringer might be found." He gave me a quick look. "All based on my research. I need to know something else first. Could he have been aided in his escape?"

"It's possible," I said, not liking to tell it. "He got away right at shift change time. He came out for a call after talking with his court-appointed attorney. Somehow he then just walked away."

"Who'd he call?"

I hesitated, not knowing how much to tell him. "We don't listen to prisoner phone calls."

"Come now, Sheriff Spain. Let's be truthful with each other. Ringer's a man suspected of at least thirty murders, men, women, children. He's a professional burglar and robber who enters homes and coldly kills anyone he finds inside, steals only the untraceables, and moves on. He's bright and careful and merciless. He's never been well caught. He's been tried twice and found innocent. I've got to think you cut a few corners on him. Who'd he call?"

I shook my head.

"What if I could name some names and one of them was who he called?"

"I'm not here to play games with you, Mr. Reynolds," I said, worried a little now.

"It's Professor Reynolds, really. Don't you want to find out what's happening in your town? What if Joe Ringer was lured here?"

"For what reason?" I asked.

"To be killed," he said.

"Then good riddance," I said, out of temper. "That won't bother me as long as it doesn't keep me from winning reelection."

"Nor me," he agreed softly. "But your problem is complicated because you've never found the bodies of any of the others, sheriff. You won't find Ringer either unless you level with me. Please, let me give you my names."

I nodded reluctantly. He seemed sincere. But somehow I could still scent death on him.

He dug a piece of paper out of his pocket and began reading. I stopped him on the fourth name. Quinn Cowper. A farmer, a raiser of beef cattle. I knew him well.

"How'd you get your names?" I asked curiously.

"My list contains the names of everyone in your town that I ran onto in my little investigation. Cowper isn't the name I ran onto most. That one I won't share with you now. But apparently Cowper's the name we should be watching to catch Joe Ringer." He nodded at me. "Shall we go?"

I hesitated and then nodded. I led him out of the courthouse and past the old men who continually whittled their sticks on the wall. Some of them nodded at me, others did not. *Election year.*

Cowper lived north, down an old gravel road, miles from the interstate. I took Reynolds, but no one else.

We hid the marked car out of sight and walked up a hill. I carried my best high-powered rifle.

From the top of the hill you could see most of the Cowper place. There was a ramshackle old house, a fallen-in barn, and a few other out-of-repair outbuildings. There was a good fence tented at the top with barbed wire strands. We repair the fences first in my part of the country.

We sat in the dry, cool fall grass and watched. There was no immediate sign of life from the house, no movement, no smoke.

"I'll bet your man is there," Reynolds whispered beside me.

"Maybe, maybe not. I don't know why he would be there, and I still don't completely understand your interest. Why are you here?"

He gave me a strange look. "I need to know how it works. How does Cowper get multiple murderers to come here, perhaps die here? How does he know or recognize them, contact them, entice them?"

I sniffed the air. Soon the cold days would come.

"Why do you care?"

He gave me a peculiar look, and I knew I wasn't getting it all. "I'm a psychologist. All my life I've had some minor interest in the criminal mind. In the last few years that interest has been forcibly turned to mass murderers and multiple killers as a class. There seem suddenly to be more of them, as if because more people are being born, there needs to be a doubling or tripling of their ratio among us. I've got some figures . . ."

"Forcibly turned?" I asked, stopping him.

He held up a paper-thin hand. "Someone's come onto the porch down there. See?"

I looked at the farmhouse. There was someone.

"Is that Joe Ringer?" he asked.

The man below moved into better light. It was Ringer. I could see his pinched face and cold eyes. I nodded. "That's him."

He shook his head and whispered. "Not the one."

"That's Ringer," I said, perplexed. "Not which one?"

"Let's go down after him," Reynolds said, ignoring my question. He had a bad habit of doing that, and so puzzled me.

"Wait a while," I said. "He looks as if he's waiting for someone. I'd like to know who." I wasn't ready to retake Ringer yet. I had too many questions unanswered about Reynolds.

"He's probably waiting for Cowper," Reynolds said.

"No, not Cowper," I said positively. "I know Cowper well, know he's in a hospital in a city forty miles from here. He was also there last night. I checked that out earlier." I smiled. "I thought maybe you might know who else it could be that Ringer's waiting for?"

He shook his head. "I truly don't. I swear it. We wait, then?"

"For a while. Someone helped him out, someone answered his call.

I wish I knew who. What with civil rights, the Miranda case, and Supreme Court decisions on wiretaps, I can't let my deputies take chances on bending the rules these days."

"But maybe you took a chance?"

I shrugged noncommittally. I pointed downward through the red and yellow fall foliage, somehow wanting to move things along. "There's a cattle tunnel under the road. We'll go through it and get closer."

"Maybe we ought to do like you said and stay right here until we spot his helper," he said, hesitant now. "We've surely not been seen so far. He might see us if we start moving in on him."

"I'm running this show, professor. I want to wait for your mystery man, but I've decided to do that waiting up close. So follow or stay here. Up to you."

He followed. We stayed behind trees and bushes and moved carefully. In a while we were within fifty yards of the house in a copse of trees. Joe Ringer, in the meantime, had disappeared back inside the house, but I could see movement now and then when he came to the front window and watched the road.

Insects whined about us voraciously as we waited out the long afternoon. Cars intermittently passed on the gravel road that paralleled the front fence. Professor Reynolds stiffened in anticipation each time one approached, but always the cars continued onward.

When the sun was almost down I made Reynolds move even closer to the house. Still no one came. Joe Ringer, now more confident as the light dimmed, came back onto the porch and impatiently watched the road.

"I'm going to have to go ahead and take him," I whispered finally. "It's getting dark. He could get away from us into the night."

"I need to know who he's waiting for," Reynolds whispered back angrily. "Remember that I found him for you."

I shook my head. I leveled my rifle and got Ringer in its sights.

"Stop right there, Ringer."

"Sheriff?" he called.

"Don't move."

He did what I'd thought he'd do and moved. He threw himself to the left and pulled desperately at his waistband. I bounced one errant shot through a window and hit him squarely with two more.

"No," Reynolds called, stricken. "No! I needed him."

"So did I," I said softly, thinking about my coming election. I moved cautiously to the porch, Reynolds following. Ringer lay unmoving. I'd aimed for his head. I foot-turned him. Already he smelled dead. A small caliber pistol lay beside him. I wrapped it in a handkerchief.

"You might have taken him without killing him," Reynolds accused.

I shook my head. "Not without taking bad chances. And not with you along. You saw his reaction when I called out. He went for his gun. He tried to get away."

"Where'd he get a gun?"

"Maybe the house," I said. "Maybe he found it inside the house."

I searched the body while he watched. I found the familiar note with Cowper's number on it, directions crudely printed to the farmhouse.

Reynolds said despondently, "Whoever it was could have been waiting out there for full dark, sheriff. You've scared him off for good now." He shook his head. "This won't stop me. I'm going to go on looking. Someone in your town somehow got Ringer to come here. Someone didn't want him caught. *Someone.*" He watched me.

I knew he was adding too many numbers in his head, and so I aimed the rifle at him.

He nodded, sure now. "Your name was on my list also. Top of the list."

I shook my head. "I've never had to kill anyone other than one of them. Cowper's my cousin. I take care of this place sometimes for him. I'm not going to be able to take a chance on your running around, talking. I've slept good until now. I'm thinking you'll keep me awake nights, professor. I don't hate you like I do them."

He gave me an unafraid smile.

"How do you do it? Tell me how you spot them. How do you get them here?"

I shook my head. "I don't know where it came from, but I've had a very sensitive sense of smell all my life. A gift. A gift of smell. People like Ringer and Peter Green and the several others planted out there in ailing cousin Cowper's fields have an odor I can smell." I nodded. "I smell them out, acrid and pungent. It hurts me inside when I smell them. I got it first when I was only a kid. I wanted to kill that first one who smelled so bad, but I didn't because I was only about eight years old. Then, when I was deputying for Frank Stickney, we caught one who'd killed five people, and he smelled just like that first one. All he got from the law was thirty days for vagrancy because we couldn't prove a thing on the murders, and he just laughed at us when we asked him questions about them. When he was released I got him and put him in deep here."

"You smell them?" he asked.

I nodded. "Now, every year I go on vacation, plus the job takes me places. There aren't any more around here, but last year I was in San Francisco and this year it's supposed to be New York. I tell the police in the cities that I've got a man supposed to be in their city. I ask where's a good place for someone hiding to hang around. Sometimes I just wander. And you're right. There seem to be more of them all the time." I smiled. "It's not hard to find someone who has the smell, sometimes more than one someone."

"And so you kill them?" he asked, somehow eager to hear about it.

"Not then. I find out what I can about my candidates. I do it carefully. Most of them are as wary as old foxes and also very bright. Sometimes, after I learn what I can about him or her, for there are females of the species, I can figure a way to get them here, a ruse, a subterfuge. Joe Ringer fancied himself a writer. I found him and sent him a letter offering to publish his stuff. I paid his way here. It was just bad luck my deputy saw him and arrested him in the bus depot. So I had to let him escape. It was easy enough. I wrote him a note to meet me here and smuggled it to him. I intercepted his call."

"And Peter Green?"

"He came to manage my trucking company."

He nodded, apparently delighted. I leveled the gun reluctantly.

"Not yet, please. You need to hear a few more important things before you decide on killing me." His eyes sparkled behind their thick-glass shields. For the first time they seemed alive. "Your deputies saw me leave with you for one thing."

"You tragically got in the line of fire," I said. "That's one of the reasons I missed with one shot. A sheriff doesn't have to answer many questions, especially with Joe Ringer dead." I shook my head. "Somehow you knew he was here and you led me to him. You died. I'll make you a hero, professor, if that's any consolation."

He nodded approval. "That might work, but I've been tracking multiple murderers for a while. Others, all over the country, know about me and my fixation. I've never been as open with any of them as I was with you, but I never suspected any of them as I did you. I don't think any one of them took me seriously. You can hope not, anyway. I'll hope so, too. But someone could get very serious if I wound up dead."

That was something to think on, and I pondered it.

He waited patiently.

"I'm sorry. I don't have a choice. If I can win my election then, with luck, I'll have another four years of hunting them. And somehow I have to hunt them. Maybe I'm different, maybe I'm their specific for dying. I hate them as they hate us." I nodded at him. "Sometimes I think they're mutants, the coming race for earth. I've thought on it lots. Maybe they came along to wipe us out, take our places, be the survivors of the cities, mercilessly preying on each other after we're gone." My voice trembled a little.

"Easy, Sheriff Spain," he said soothingly. "I told you I got into multiple murderers forcibly. Three years ago a man got into my house when I was away. He killed my daughter first. She was ten years old, quite pretty. He then beat my wife and left her for dead. She did die, but not before she told us—me—what he looked like. When my family died I also mostly died." He smiled without any humor at all. "Out there in your field would you perhaps have a man with a white patch of hair on the right side of his head, six feet or so tall, early thirties, hawk features?"

I shook my head. "No one like that. Not yet."

"I see," he said, disappointed.

I waited. I'd lowered the gun.

He asked, "Did you ever think how much more efficiently you could work this if you had someone who knew psychology, who could figure out ways to bring even the cleverest of them within reach? A trained person?"

I considered the possibilities. There were hundreds of them out there, maybe thousands, enough for a lifetime.

"You could help me live again," he said softly, deciding for me. "I tracked you down to be your assistant."

# Dear Corpus Delicti

## by William Link and Richard Levinson

**C**harles Lowe looked down at his wife. She lay on her side, the silk scarf knotted under her neck like a small, red flower. He held his hand near her mouth, but she had stopped breathing. Then he checked his watch—there was still plenty of time.

Moving carefully around her, he opened the French doors and stepped out on the flagged terrace. A light wind from the East River cooled him, dried the sweat on his forehead. He steadied himself against the glass door for a moment, then closed it behind him. On the edge of the terrace, near the railing, stood a row of flower pots. They had been purchased by his wife, and every morning she gave them a ritual watering. Lowe picked one up, tested its weight, and moved back to the door. It took only a light, gentle tap to shatter one of the panels; the glass shards tinkled on the study floor.

Lowe returned the pot and went back into the apartment, leaving the French doors partly open. Now if he could find her purse everything would be ready. Where did she keep it? Married six years and he didn't even know.

He searched the study and the bedroom before finding it on the hall table. Good. Very good. It was now virtually perfect. The maid would come the following morning and find her body in the study. It would look like a simple case of robbery. A sneak thief had climbed up on the terrace and broken in. But Vivian had caught him and he had strangled her with her scarf. He had fled, taking the purse.

Lowe whistled softly and opened his wallet. The two airline tickets. The most important part of all was still to come. He buttoned his tan raincoat, replaced the wallet, and stood at the door. Inside, in the darkened study, he could see his wife's outflung hand. The wedding band twinkled.

Lowe took a deep breath and left the apartment.

When he reached the street, he looked up toward the terrace. It was lost in darkness, impossible to see. He stepped into the street and hailed a cab. "96th and West End," he told the driver.

It was growing colder when the cab left him off. A thick river mist smudged the street lights. Where the devil is she? he thought. I told her six on the dot.

He waited nervously under a hotel canopy, glancing at his watch. His wife had always been punctual; Sue was always late. His wife was quick and dependable, as meticulous as a man; Sue was slow and childishly helpless. He smiled suddenly and looked up. She was crossing the street, moving against the wind, her blonde hair blowing loose.

"Am I late?" she asked, breathlessly.

"Yes, as usual. But it doesn't matter."

"I tried to get the early bus, but it didn't stop. I don't know—"

He put a finger on her lips. "It's all right. We've got plenty of time. So stop worrying."

He took her arm, guided her into the street. "Did you remember the glasses?" he asked.

"The glasses?"

"For God sake, Sue, I *told* you a thousand times. Your sunglasses. Now we've got to——"

"But I have them," she said. "I thought you meant my reading glasses. I only wear those when I read."

Lowe shook his head, wearily. "Put them on."

He studied her in the dark spectacles. She resembled Vivian now—the small, well-formed figure, the blonde hair. It was enough to fool a casual observer, and that was all that mattered.

"How do I look?" she said.

"Like my ex-wife."

Her lip trembled, but he couldn't see the eyes behind the glasses. "Charles. Did you—?"

"We agreed not to talk about it. Remember?"

She nodded. He flagged a cab and helped her in. The driver had a Hungarian name and spoke broken English. Another lucky break, Lowe thought.

"Take us to Idlewild," he said. "As fast as you can."

Sue snuggled next to him; her hand groped over his. "Here," he said, handing her Vivian's purse.

"What's this?"

"You'll need it for identification at the airline desk. Now no more questions. I'll tell you what to do—step by step."

She laid her head on his shoulder, staring up at his face. "Maybe we shouldn't," she whispered. "Charles, it's a terrible thing. We—"

He bent down and kissed her. "We're committed," he said. "We have to go through with it. Now relax."

He put his arm around her and looked out over the highway. Traffic was sparse, but they were moving well under the speed limit. "Hurry it up," he said. "Faster."

Soon the buildings were behind. They moved through shopping centers and along boulevards. Lights swung past, swollen with mist. Overhead, a huge airliner droned by, its wing tips blinking.

"How much farther?" she whispered.

"A few more miles."

Minutes later they were on the periphery of the gigantic airfield. There were more planes in the black sky, circling, climbing. "Let us off at the Trans-Continental building," he told the driver.

He sat, relaxed but watchful, as clumps of buildings rushed up in the windshield. The taxi swerved ahead of a line of cars, heading for the main entrance. Finally they stopped, skidding, at the entrance door. The driver looked back at them, smiling.

Lowe paid the fare and helped her out of the cab. "I gave him a heavy tip," he said. "He'll remember us."

The airline terminal was brightly lit and crowded. Lowe stopped just inside the entrance and moved close to her. "All right. It's up to you now."

"What?"

"Go over to the counter and check us in. If they ask for baggage tell them we're traveling without it."

Her eyes blinked at him. "But—but I don't know what to do. I never did this before."

"It's simple. The man will do all the work. Go ahead." He squeezed her arm and shoved her forward, feeling vaguely sorry for her. She looked back helplessly, then turned and hurried toward the counter.

Lowe glanced at the airline clock, checked it against his watch. They had thirty minutes until take-off time. He took out a cigarette.

"Charles!" The voice cut sharply through the room. He looked up quickly. She was standing at the counter, her face white, staring at him. He felt that everyone in the room was watching. "What is it?" he called.

"The tickets!"

He went quickly to the counter. The airline attendant was smiling.

"Oh yes, I forgot to give them to you." He removed his wallet, his hands perfectly steady, and slid the two envelopes across the counter.

The attendant checked the tickets, phoned for confirmation, and handed Lowe a small card. "Give this to the hostess when you board. Thank you, sir. Enjoy your flight."

Lowe nodded and turned away. He grabbed Sue tightly by the arm and led her toward the lounge.

"Was I all right?"

"Fine. Just fine."

"Where are we going?"

"The lounge. We'd better have a drink. I think we need one."

They stood at the gate leading to the field. Lowe's two drinks had gone to his head; he felt sleepy and less excited. Sue's face was flushed, almost feverish.

"Charles," she said, lightly. "I think I—I had a little too much . . ."

"That's all right. It's good for you." He put his arm around her waist. She seemed perfectly relaxed, weightless.

The crowd jostled them as the gate swung open. They walked out along the night runway, following the airline attendant.

Lowe tightened his grip on her arm. "Do you know what to do?"

"I'm . . . not exactly sure."

"As soon as we get settled in our seats we'll begin to argue. Loud—so that everyone can hear. And you won't take it. In fact, you get up and leave."

"But what can we argue about?"

"It doesn't matter. I'll start it off. Just follow my lead."

A cold wind shook at them, carrying a little pocket of rain. Ahead, the long, silver airliner gleamed wet in the darkness.

"After you leave the plane," said Lowe, "what do you do then?"

"I take a taxi straight home. And I stay there all weekend."

"Right. And you don't call anyone. I'll be back Monday. I'll try to come and see you."

"I want you to call me, Charles. Please. I don't know how I'll get through the weekend without hearing from you."

"I'll try."

They reached the boarding platform and Lowe helped her up the first step. It was beginning to rain now in heavy, blowing gusts. The hostess, standing at the door, gave them a professional smile.

"Nice weather," Lowe said, wryly.

"Just over New York," the hostess said. "We'll be out of it as soon as we're airborne."

"Famous last words." He smiled at her and entered the cabin.

Sue was taking off her raincoat, her teeth chattering. "I think I caught a chill."

"Maybe you better keep your coat on." He held it open for her, and she slipped into it. "You take the aisle seat," he whispered.

They sat down in the deep, upholstered chairs. The second hostess came by and leaned over them. "We'll have some hot coffee right after takeoff," she said.

"Fine," said Lowe. "We can use it." He looked down the long, lit cabin. The plane was almost filled; people were standing in the aisles, hoisting overnight cases in the racks, ducking down into their warm seats. Rain beat on the window, blurring the field.

"Charles," Sue said, "I'm frightened. I don't like flying in this kind of weather."

He looked at her, coldly. "Always complaining. I'm getting sick and tired of it."

She glanced at him, hurt and surprised, before she realized what he was doing.

"You didn't want to come along in the first place," he continued loudly. "You don't want to do anything with me any more."

"That's a lie!"

"Is it?" He watched an old man in the forward section turn to look at them. "The only thing you want from me is money. Out buying clothes, going to the theater—anything to keep away from home. You spend more time with your friends than with me!"

She began to cry. Excellent, he thought. Keep it up. Other people were watching.

"I thought we could take a trip together for a change, maybe get to know each other again. But you don't even want to come along!"

She stood up in the seat. "No, I don't," she said, sobbing. "And I'm not!"

"Fine! Go home. Go to your friends. I don't particularly give a damn." He looked at her. "What are you waiting for?"

She hurried to rear of the plane. Her voice was sharp and clear in the whole cabin. "I'm getting off."

"But ma'am," said the flight attendant, "we're almost ready to taxi."

"I don't care. Let me off!"

Lowe turned his face to the window. There were muffled words and more crying from the rear. The attendant had opened the door and was shouting something into the rain.

The hostess came over to his seat. "Mr. Lowe," she said softly. "Perhaps I could talk to her. Maybe—"

"No," he said bitterly. "If she wants to leave, fine. I don't care."

The hostess nodded, somberly, and went away. Lowe looked through the window. They were wheeling the aluminum platform back to the door. It made a sharp sound as it connected to the body of the plane.

He watched as Sue came down the platform and huddled under the attendant's umbrella. She looked up at his window for a brief moment, her face streaked and lonely, then turned and went off.

Lowe rested his head against the soft cushion. Perfect. At least twenty passengers had seen Mrs. Vivian Lowe leave her husband in a rage and return to the terminal. From there the police would construct a rough timetable. She had gone back to the apartment, just in time to catch a thief breaking in. He had killed her and fled. And her husband? Where was he? Thousands of feet in the sky, sulking over his wife's behavior. A perfect, perfect alibi.

The hostess, warm and sympathetic, was back at his side. "We'll have coffee in a few minutes, Mr. Lowe. Will you want some?"

"Yes," he said. "Lots of it."

The weekend was relaxing and uneventful. Lowe spent it at a hunting lodge a few miles from Montreal. He shared most of his time with some vacationing businessmen, playing bridge, fishing, and discussing politics over mellow Canadian whiskey. It was a shame that after two pleasant days of rest, he'd return to be told of his wife's unfortunate death.

During the flight back to New York, Lowe speculated on his new life. He'd be unencumbered, free to travel, relieved of his wife's financial drain. There was Sue, of course, but he could take his time with her. Eventually they'd be married. She was docile enough; she wouldn't be a burden.

He looked through the window. The plane was circling above Idlewild, beginning its long descent. The *Safety Belts* sign glowed red. He smiled as the plane tipped imperceptibly forward.

Later, in the airport grill, he had a steak sandwich and a beer. He read a copy of the *Times* with his meal; there was no sense hurrying. He was surprised to find that very little had happened in the world during the past two days.

On the way back to the city he told the taxi driver to take his time. It was a long, leisurely ride with the sun on his face. "This is the way to do it," the driver said. "Everybody's always in such a hurry."

"They ought to learn to slow down," said Lowe expansively. "Take life easy."

The cab let him off in front of his apartment building. The doorman was talking on the phone. That's good, Lowe thought. I don't want any phony condolences from him. He took the self-service elevator to his floor and walked slowly down the hall.

"Mr. Lowe?"

He turned from the door, digging in his pocket for his key. "Yes?"

A slight, insignificant little man stood near the stairway. He came forward, holding his hat. "Lieutenant Fisher," he said, "45th Precinct."

Lowe frowned. Well, here it comes, he thought. Let's hope I can react properly. "What can I do for you, Lieutenant?"

"It's, well, it's bad news, Mr. Lowe. We tried to contact you all weekend, but your office said you were out of town."

Lowe smiled. "Yes, I was in Montreal. Fishing trip. Doctor's orders." He looked down at the doormat. There was a slip of paper pushed under its edge. He bent down and picked it up.

"It's about your wife, Mr. Lowe. She—she was killed Friday night."

Lowe didn't look up at him. He stared at the slip of paper, his heart swelling against his chest. It was a scribbled note from the maid: "Mrs. Lowe—my sister took sick so I couldn't come in. I will come Tuesday instead."

Lieutenant Fisher fingered his hat. "She was coming from the airport in a taxi. It crashed into a furniture truck . . . "

In a daze, Lowe turned the key in the lock, pushed the door open. Standing in the hallway, his eyes moved toward the study.

"We found her purse in the cab," Fisher continued, "and got her identification . . . "

Lowe felt faint. He stared at the outflung hand in the study doorway. The wedding band glinted in the light from the French doors.

"There'll be a few details," Fisher said. "It won't take long." He looked at Lowe's frozen face. "May I come in?"

# Knight of the Road

## by Thomasina Weber

**H**e followed her as she pulled out of the diner's parking lot, being careful not to appear conspicuous. Her car was fire engine red, so he could safely allow other cars to pass him and still keep her in sight. Since he didn't want to show himself too early, Arthur Trimble relaxed behind the wheel of his silver-gray sportscar and prepared to enjoy the remainder of the afternoon.

He had been watching her all morning as she traveled south on the highway. Her short red hair was casually waved and the pale green button-type earrings she wore matched the suit jacket. But it wasn't until she went into the restaurant that he was able to see the slim neat figure in the rest of the tailored suit. This job promised to be more pleasant than the last one. That had been a maiden schoolteacher who had scoffed at the warnings of friends about ladies who traveled alone on long auto trips. Her gibbering disintegration before his eyes had make him feel uncomfortable. As a boy, he had always had a great respect for lady schoolteachers. But when you considered the fact that she had never faced such a situation standing before row after row of little faces, her reaction was quite understandable. By now she was undoubtedly back in class again, poorer but wiser.

Arthur decided the time had come to pass the girl's car, so he began his approach. He didn't look at her as he sped by, but kept the pedal to the floor for another mile. When he came to a service station, he slid smoothly up to the pump and watched the cars whisk by as the attendant filled his tank. After she passed, he used his credit card and took off behind her.

He played his game of leap frog until the sun began to set and he knew she had become accustomed to seeing his car. It had been on a trip to Florida years ago that he first got the idea for this, after noticing that you passed the same cars all the way down, and they in turn passed you, and by the time you all got to Florida, you felt you knew each other, even though you had never spoken. Sometimes you waved at each other though, and if there were children in the car, they would press their faces to the rear window and grimace after Daddy had passed you. Arthur had learned to watch for the lone travelers, the ones who used cash instead of credit cards.

As the sunlight faded, he noticed the girl's car slow slightly as motels began coming into view. She was looking for a place to stop. Smart girl. Stop early, relax and get a good rest. She was probably a pre-dawn starter. He really preferred the late sleepers, but with a good-looking one like this, you could make concessions.

He stayed as far as possible behind her, and when she turned in at a blinking neon sign that said *Swimming Pool,* he pulled to the side of the road and stopped. He waited ten minutes, but her car didn't come out. Back on the road, he drove slowly toward the motel, letting the other cars pass him. As he reached the driveway, he saw her car at once, parked before a lavender door. The motel didn't look crowded; plenty of vacancies. Smiling to himself, he drove on. After a hamburger and milkshake at a drive-in, he went back to the motel and got a room three doors away from the girl.

Leaving his suitcase in the car, Arthur placed a comfortable chair by the window, tilted the blinds so he could see out without being seen, and waited.

He had guessed right. She soon emerged in a sleek, sea-green one-piece and headed for the pool. She wore no bathing cap. The management probably didn't like women who went in without caps, but her hair was short, and from the way she walked, he could tell she wasn't the type to be cowed by the management. But on the other hand, she wasn't the type the management picked on either, unless the management happened to be female.

He waited until she was in the water, then went outside and took his suitcase out of the car, making sure he spent enough time there for her to recognize him as the owner of the car she had seen several times during the day. He was careful not to look her way.

It was a pity his occupation didn't afford him more opportunity to display his muscles, Arthur thought ruefully as he observed himself in the mirror. But muscles were so seldom necessary when the job was handled right. However, it seemed wasteful to keep such a physique covered up. He had worked hard to develop his body, and he was justifiably proud of it. Bless the redhead for choosing a motel with a pool!

The water was comfortable but contained too much chlorine. By the time he had crossed the pool four times, she was seated in a webbed chair with a cigarette in her hand. There was no one else in the pool, so he knew she was watching him. Since they were alone, it was the most natural thing in the world for him to pull himself up, the water sliding off his healthy tanned skin, step out of the pool and, with the controlled gait of the athlete, take a seat beside her.

"Wonderful night," he said, putting his head back and looking for the first star.

"Yes, isn't it." Not boldly, not forbiddingly, but casually she spoke, her eyes straight ahead on the moving highway.

"I noticed you on the road today," Arthur said. "It's a long haul to Florida if you drive by yourself."

Her eyes met his for the first time and he felt a stab of excitement. "How do you know I'm going to Florida?"

"Isn't everybody?" he said, waving his hand lightly through the air. "When you've made the trip several times, you can tell who's on a long distance trip and who's on his way to the mother-in-law's."

She laughed, a soft, stomach-tightening sound. She was taking a big chance, an attractive girl like her, traveling alone. "As a matter of fact, I'm just starting my vacation," she said. "At the end of a year, a bank can get awfully boring."

"Oh, I imagine so," he agreed.

"Are you on vacation, too?"

"Yes, you might say so. I travel for a hardware concern, but I enjoy it so much that I consider it a vacation whenever I'm out on the road."

"How nice! I wish I liked my job that well."

"As I see it, you have two alternatives," he said, grinning. "You can either change your job or get married."

She laughed again and his ears began to feel warm. "Neither one practical at the moment, I'm afraid." She got to her feet, drawing the towel around her. "It's getting a little too chilly for me."

He was on his feet in an instant. "Please don't think I'm forward, but it's early yet. Can I buy you a drink somewhere?"

"I don't believe so," she replied, her voice showing just a trace of withdrawal. "Good night."

He watched her walk away and wondered whether he had moved too quickly. It was so much easier when they trusted and liked him. Of course, if he had to, he could always do it the other way, but it really was distasteful to him.

Returning to his room, he showered and dressed, then went outside again. There was a family in the pool now, and if the little brother didn't drown his little sister before the night was out, it wouldn't be from lack of trying. A pool was probably as good a place as any for working out your frustrations. The mother wore a bathing cap which was so tight it wrinkled her forehead, and she clung spread-eagled to the concrete side of the pool. Dad, his hometown's contribution to the Olympics, surged back and forth across the pool, spouting like a whale at each turn.

Arthur was walking toward his car when he spotted the redhead coming from the ice machine with a pitcher. They were within smiling distance of each other. She was a study in nature in a dark green dress, her autumn hair the color of dying leaves. "Good evening again," he said.

"And it's still a wonderful night," she replied.

"Much too nice to spend alone. Will you change your mind and let me buy you a drink?"

She hesitated and he watched her debate with herself. Finally she said, "All right. I'll get my jacket."

It was ten miles to the next town, but he knew of a secluded place there with dimly lit booths and throbbing music.

"I love your car," she said, lifting her face to the evening breeze.

"Traveling as I do, I can't have a home of my own, so the next best thing is a good car. I bought it new last year and I treat it like a baby. The least little thing goes wrong and I fix it right away."

"You men are so lucky," said the redhead. "It must be so reassuring to know that if something goes wrong under the hood while you're on the road, all you have to do is get out and fix it. I've always thought I should take a course in mechanics, but I never seemed to get around to it."

He reached for her hand and held it up toward the windshield. He turned it over, then back, and ran his finger over the smoothly lacquered nails. Then he shook his head. "I'm afraid you don't have the hands for a mechanic," he said. "Might as well forget about it."

She reclaimed her hand delicately. "Maybe you're right. By the way, you haven't told me your name, or do we skip that formality?"

"Oh, how stupid of me! Arthur Trimble, ma'am, at your service. And you are Miss—?"

"Phyllis Redmond."

"Miss?" he repeated.

"Miss," she said, smiling.

"How did you ever find such a romantic little place?" She murmured as soon as the waiter had taken their order.

Arthur shrugged. "When you're on the road as much as I am, you get to know your way around. There are lots of interesting places once you get to recognize them."

"You must lead a fascinating life," she said, sipping her drink. "It's so much different from being tied down nine to five."

"I couldn't live like that," he said. "It would be just like prison. With pay, though."

"It makes you feel almost—well, reckless—when you get out on your own. As if you were set free for the rest of your life instead of only the next two weeks."

The little candle on the table played tricks with her eyes, illuminating them briefly, then flickering, leaving them large, dark and mysterious. He had difficulty breathing. He wondered whether the air conditioner was working properly. "Dance?" he asked.

"Love to."

She was like a cloud in his arms, soft, fragrant, weightless. She moved with the grace of a willow in the wind. He sighed softly. Like a symphony, he added.

"I admire you," she was saying. "It's easy to see you like the finer things in life."

"How can you tell?"

"Most men think they have to strangle a girl when they dance with her. You hold me lightly and I can sense your appreciation of the music and the rhythm."

Perceptive! Unusual in an attractive woman. Most of them think only of themselves. For the first time, he began to feel the stirrings of doubt. Maybe their paths had crossed for a different reason. Maybe there was something wonderful in store for them. Maybe he would have to change his plans.

But when he finally pulled to a stop at the motel, he came out of his dream. He had slid his arm along the back of the seat and instead of a kiss, received a smart slap across the face. Eyes flashing, she marched inside without a word.

"I sure can't figure this one," he said as he got ready for bed. "First she goes out with me and seems full of cooperation, and next thing you know she's off in a huff." He took up his seat by the window and waited for her light to go out. She was too fickle to waste time on. He would go ahead with his original plan. An hour after her light switched off, he stepped quietly outside and approached her car.

He set his alarm clock for two-thirty. No telling how much of a fanatic this girl was about getting an early start. He knew lots of travelers who started out at three and four o'clock. A quick glance out the window showed her car still parked in front of her door. If she didn't leave till dawn, he'd have a long wait, but those were the breaks of the game. It was the chance he'd have to take.

He took a quick, cold shower and settled down to wait.

He was dressed and in his chair by the window when she came out at six. He watched her load her suitcase into the car and start out the driveway, waiting until she reached the highway to put her lights on. He looked at his watch. He would give her a few minutes head start.

At six ten he set out at a leisurely pace, noting with satisfaction that there were only a few cars on the road. It would soon be light, but until then he had to watch carefully for her. It was a poorly surfaced stretch of road from the motel on, and before long he saw her red car at the side of the road. She was inside, and as he drew near, he could see she was trying to start it. He came to a stop behind her, got out and walked to her door.

"Good morning, Miss Redmond," he said pleasantly. "What seems to be the trouble?"

"Oh, I'm so glad to see you, Mr. Trimble. I can't imagine what has happened to my car. I was just riding along when it started to sputter, and I managed to get it off on the shoulder of the road before it stopped completely."

"Well, I'll have a look and see if there's anything I can do." He raised the hood.

"I guess I should have taken that mechanic's course after all," she called.

"I'm sure a lovely girl like you would never have any trouble getting assistance," he said, smiling. "Oh, here's something." He quickly attached the loose wire to the distributor. "This rough road jarred a wire off your distributor," he said.

"Is that serious?"

"Oh, no. But I guess it's serious enough if you're stuck and don't know what to look for." He wiped his hands on his handkerchief. "That ought to fix you right up."

"I don't know how to thank you, Mr. Trimble."

"By calling me Arthur, in the first place, Phyllis. I'd like that."

She smiled. "All right, Arthur. I'm very grateful."

"Always willing to help a lady in distress."

"You must let me buy you a drink or something to show my appreciation."

The "or something" intrigued Arthur, but he kept his voice steady. "It was nothing, really."

And as she sat there looking up at him, he suddenly remembered what the whole idea was. All he had to do was climb in her car and, holding the tiny gun on her, relieve her of her money, tap her gently on the side of the head to allow him time to make his escape, and then make it. He cleared his throat. He had never felt this way before. But then, none of his former victims had been as attractive as Phyllis Redmond.

She was still smiling up at him expectantly. "I insist," she said, her voice firm in a breathless way. "You follow me until we come to a town that has a package liquor store. We'll stop and buy a bottle and—take it somewhere with us?"

For dawn, the sun was sure hot. He could feel the perspiration trickling down the back of his neck. "You don't owe me a thing," he heard himself saying. And then a voice inside him whispered, *You set it all up, now get on with it!*

"Please!" she said.

"Lead the way, Princess!" He took off behind her and closed his ears to the voice. "I'll do it when I'm good and ready," he told it. "No harm in a little drink first. After all, this ride north and south and south and north can get pretty boring. I think I deserve a little diversion."

It was close to noon before they found a town with a liquor store. She drove up to the window, made her purchase, then eased out onto the highway. They were several miles out of town before they came to the first crossroad. She swung right and the two cars bounced along a winding dirt road. The soft silence was a relief after the slap of the tires on the concrete.

She stopped under a huge tree that covered the entire road with its leafy arms. A cow resting behind a fence watched them incuriously. He stopped and got into the front seat of her car. She was already opening the bottle.

"There are paper cups in the glove compartment," she told him.

Leaving the door of the glove compartment down to form a shelf, he set the two cups side by side and watched her fill them. They would have two or three drinks and he would feel more confident. It would be easier if she were a little high. Maybe he could even get her drunk enough so that she wouldn't remember him. *What dif-*

*ference does it make if she remembers you or not?* asked the voice. *She's just another woman, isn't she? There's nothing special about her. You don't think she's going to be so lovey-dovey after she wakes up and finds all her money gone, do you?*

She slid close to him as she reached for her cup. He smelled the fragrance of soap and cologne and her clean red hair. Oh, what a pity! Why couldn't she be another maiden schoolteacher or a mouthy salesgirl like that one last month?

She put the cup to her lips, but she didn't move away. She sipped slowly, her eyes holding his over the rim. He drank quickly and put his cup on the shelf. He slid his left arm across the top of the seat and rested his hand lightly on her back. She smiled at him. "Another one?" she whispered. He nodded dumbly and as she leaned toward him he could hear the liquid gurgling into the cup. Her face was close to his. It seemed a long time before she finally handed him the drink, but he didn't mind. The view was wonderful.

He didn't remember drinking it, but he must have because he suddenly noticed the cup was empty and he could feel the effects of it. He hadn't noticed the label on the bottle, but she certainly had bought some potent stuff. The voice was coming from a great way off now as it told him to get her money and scram. He tried to argue, but it came out fuzzily and didn't seem to make much sense. But he knew exactly what he had in mind. He was going to let this one go. He couldn't victimize her. She was lovely. She was friendly. She was cooperative. She was driving alone, taking a chance. "All kinds on the road," he told her. "Gotta be careful."

"Yes, I know, Arthur," she crooned. "All kinds on the road."

He leaned forward an inch to kiss her and the lights went out.

When Arthur opened his eyes, it was to stare at dusty grass and dry, dead pine needles. Lifting his face off the ground, he pushed himself slowly to a sitting position. Except for the cow, contentedly chewing her cud, he was alone on the dirt road with his car parked a few feet away where he had left it. Numbly he got to his feet and stumbled toward it. The cushions were pulled out, the contents of his glove compartment scattered over the floor and the seats. The car had been thoroughly checked.

Opening his thermos bottle, he poured the cold water over his head and rubbed his face with it. Pulling out a comb, he smoothed his short, blond hair. There, that felt better.

And then he began to laugh. He knew before he felt in his pocket that his wallet wouldn't be there. Boy, she was a slick one, all right! What was it she had said before the knockout drops got him? "All kinds on the road."

As he set his car back in order, he thought about her. Ordinarily she would have taken just his money and left his wallet. She must have had a rude surprise when she found there was no cash at all in there, not even a traveler's check. And it made her mad, so she took his wallet just as a way of getting even with him. "The car must have fooled her," he said to the cow. "Probably thought I was loaded." The cow munched on.

Leaning forward, Arthur pulled the cushion off the brake pedal, removed the fifty dollar bill and pressed the cushion back on. "Looks like I came out on the thin side of this deal," he said. "But, conversely, so did she."

Turning the car around, he headed back to the highway, laughing again. "Someday our paths are going to cross again on this golden road," he said to no one, "and when they do, well, who knows what we might work out?"

# The Truth That Kills

## by Donald Olson

Let's practice it once more," she said. "This time I'll be the cop."
Robert pretended to open the front door, faked a look of surprise. "Good morning, officer. Come in."

Sylvia hooted. "No, *no*. You're not supposed to sound as if you're expecting him. Just innocent surprise."

He tried again. She giggled. "Darling, you're hopeless. You'd make a lousy actor. Here, I'll be you. You be the cop."

This time she pretended to answer the door, stepped back with a blank look, then whirled and smiled at her husband. "See? You don't say anything until he does. He'll ask you if you're Robert Deraney." She turned and nodded as if to the imaginary policeman. "Yes, I'm Robert Deraney. What is it, officer? Did I park on the wrong side again? My wife? Why do you ask? Miss Kriegher said *what*? Good night, the woman's lost her mind. Yes, of course my wife is here—and very much alive." She looked toward the stairs. "Sylvia? Someone to see you."

Then she ran up the stairs, posed at the top like Joan Fontaine in *Rebecca*. "Good evening, officer. You wanted to see me?"

Dropping the act, she ran down and flung herself, laughing, into Robert's arms.

"Oh, darling, I can't wait!"

"You missed your calling. What an actress."

"I only hope it doesn't rain tomorrow. I'd rather not be dragged through the mud."

"Realism, my love. That's what we're striving for."

"As long as Old Snoopy's watching."

The next morning was bright and clear. Shortly before noon they were at the back door, as charged with mischief as a pair of teenagers, nervous as actors poised in the wings; the stage in this case being a broad stretch of lawn between the patio and garage. Sylvia's car was already backed into the driveway in full view of the neighboring Cape Cod bungalow where, it was hoped, the performance's sole audience had already assumed her accustomed seat by her kitchen window, opera glasses at the ready. It was Libby Kriegher's hour for "bird watching."

Just to make sure, they'd decided to stage a curtain raiser.

Sylvia winked at Robert. "Ready, darling?"

"Go to it."

She walked swiftly toward her car.

He called after her, "Sylvia!"

Halfway across the lawn she paused.

"Sylvia! Get back here, damn you!"

"No! I'm through. I've had it. I'm leaving you, Robert. I've taken all I can."

"I'm warning you, Sylvia. Get back here before I—"

"Before you what, you beast?" She went on from there, improvising a domestic quarrel at the top of her lungs. If Libby Kriegher weren't at her window by this time, she was either deaf or dead.

Robert gave it a few more seconds, then ran out and grabbed Sylvia's arm. She pretended to resist. A brief scuffle ensued and she appeared to give in and let herself be forced back toward the house. They yelled at each other a few more times; then, grinning at Robert, she let out a piercing scream. A moment later Libby Kriegher—assuming she was watching—might have seen Robert dragging an apparently unconscious Sylvia across the lawn; but as they were almost to the car she pretended to regain her senses, struggled out of his arms and crawled on hands and knees back toward the house.

Robert dashed into the garage, came out with a croquet mallet, grabbed her by the hair and made as if he were striking her severely upon the head with repeated blows of the mallet. She crumpled onto the grass. He stooped over her, pretended to listen for a heartbeat, then ran to the car, pulled the keys from the ignition and opened the trunk. With a quick look around—he was sweating as if it were all real—he picked up his supposedly dead wife and proceeded to stuff her into the trunk. He flung the mallet in after her and slammed the lid shut. He wondered if Libby had already called the police.

Seconds later he was out of the drive, and with a screech of tires was shooting down Meadow Lane toward the expressway.

The childish glee with which he'd performed his part faded quickly once he was out of the neighborhood. It began to seem like what it was, a pointlessly distasteful trick. He should never have listened to Sylvia. This was all so typical of her overexcitable imagination.

Instead of dealing with the problem like responsible adults, they had contrived this stupid charade.

The problem was really a minor one, scarcely worthy of such an elaborate solution. When they'd moved to this city they had neither friends nor relatives and had in consequence gratefully welcomed the help offered by their only neighbor, Libby Kriegher, a spinster in her early forties. She looked a bit like a rabbit, having rabbit teeth and eyes that were big and very shiny, but she was the soul of goodness and a mine of information. She had them in for meals until they were settled, ran countless errands for them, and even helped Sylvia pick out furniture for the house.

When they no longer needed her, however, she was still there. Her almost constant presence became a bore and a nuisance, and her vigilance made them feel as if they were living naked in a giant fish bowl.

"Someone sick last night?" Libby would phone, before either of them was out of bed. "Saw your bathroom light on at four-fifteen."

"Was that you two lovebirds talking so loud?" she would inquire with a tactless, ingratiating leer. "Hope you kissed and made up before bedtime."

Each time Sylvia prepared a summer meal on the patio the tempting aroma would draw Libby like a magnet. "Mmmmm. Something smells mighty good, chickies. Oh, what a scrumptious-looking salad. Tell me to go away before I drool all over your hollandaise."

What could they do? She'd been such a godsend in the beginning, could they tell her there wasn't enough for three, or to go drool over her own hollandaise?

They tried hints: Robert's were subtle, Sylvia's more direct; neither was effective. More than once, seeing her approach, they would lock the door and pretend not to be home; a flimsy stratagem, as she could see both their cars in the garage. After growing tired of ringing the bell she would go away sadly, humming a little tune, and when they ventured to open the door they'd be dismayed to find she'd left a really delicious-looking stew or casserole or perhaps a bunch of flowers from her garden. This would fill Robert with remorse. He would insist they invite Libby to dinner, Sylvia would refuse, and they would argue.

At last they knew something must be done. "Do you realize, darling," declared Sylvia, "that dear, sweet woman is ruining our peace of mind, and wrecking our privacy."

"But she's so good-hearted."

"That's the trouble. If she weren't, we could just tell her to flake off."

"I wonder, are we really that likable?"

"I think it's because she's that lonely."

"You know what she's done, don't you? She's adopted us."

Sylvia gave it some thought. "Suppose we make her *dis*like us."

He liked the idea. "We'll start by throwing our garbage on her lawn."

"Are you kidding? She'd pick it up, wrap it, put it into her own trash can, and thank us for thinking of her. No, it's got to be something very special. A woman like Libby is very sensitive of the impression she makes. That's why she tries too hard and turns people off. What we've got to do somehow is to make her look like an absolute fool—humiliate her—but in such a way that she brings it on herself."

Which was the germ of this repulsive idea. How could he have imagined it sounded either plausible or even decent? Libby would witness an apparent murder, she would call the police, they would arrive; Robert would act confused. Then Sylvia would make an entrance, and Libby would be left with such a mess of egg on her face she wouldn't ever dare face them again—or want to.

"And then I'll put up a fence," he'd said. "That will be that."

Now, driving down the expressway toward the side road where he could safely stop and let Sylvia out of the trunk, unseen, he wondered why he hadn't simply put up a fence in the first place. Why had they let the relationship thicken and sicken until a crazy damn stunt like this would actually appeal to him?

Busy with these thoughts, he nearly missed the turnoff and slammed on his brakes without seeing the panel truck behind him. It struck him in the rear left fender with a terrific jolt, sending his car into the ditch.

Dazed, he lifted his head and moved his limbs. Aside from shock, he seemed unhurt. He saw the truck driver's broad face at the window and at the same instant thought of Sylvia, crouched in the trunk.

"You okay, chum?" The man was helping him out of the car.

"Yes." There was no sound from the trunk. He didn't know what to do.

"You coulda been killed, pal. Both of us."

Helplessness and anxiety made him shiver.

"You don't look so hot, buddy. You better get to a hospital, just in case."

Robert stammeringly assured him he was all right. "Is your truck damaged?"

"This crate? A Sherman tank couldn't dent it."

He was one of those placid, bovine, inoffensive giants; the hardest to get rid of. Sweat was soaking through Robert's shirt. He couldn't keep his eyes off the trunk, yet he didn't dare go near it while the man was there. He thrust his card out, gave him his license number and insurance agent's name and managed finally to get the same information from him.

"You look kind of ropy, pal. Listen, you better sit tight and I'll go—"

"No! I mean, thanks a lot, but I don't need a doctor. I'm in sort of a hurry."

Still, the driver insisted on helping him get the car out of the ditch and only then, reluctantly, would he take his leave.

As soon as the truck disappeared, Robert swerved into the side road which wound among solemn dark pines past occasional black, rusting, oil storage tanks. Deep in the woods he backed off the road and parked behind one of the huge black cylinders. He prayed no one would drive by.

When he tried to unlock the trunk the key dropped from his shaking fingers. An oily residue from the tank oozed up around his shoes. Rusted beer cans and old bottles poked jaggedly out of the gummy soil. It was a dank, forbidding spot.

He got the key in and opened the trunk.

Her face was hidden from him, turned down, and yet he knew—from the settled unnaturalness of her body—that she was dead. He touched her, probed for some flicker of life. He turned her head. A thread of blood ran down her chin and onto the blanket.

The urgency of grief paralyzed every other emotion. He could see neither backward nor ahead, only the icy timelessness of now. The pines, the roily sky, her body, all seemed uncannily still, frozen; only his heart kept pounding, fighting to maintain its stubborn rhythm against an overwhelming desire to die. He looked at the exhaust pipe and thought how easily it could be done. What may have stopped him was the ugliness of the place itself: the litter of cans, the oily soil, the somber pines.

He scarcely dared consider the slim possibility that Libby might not have been watching them. By now she would have called the police, told them what she'd witnessed. They would be waiting for him at home, just as they were no doubt looking for him now.

Still, there *was* that one slim chance.

Blood had dripped on the blanket but not on the trunk itself. He wrapped her in the blanket and buried her in the soft oily muck behind the tank. He tossed the mallet into the woods, then lit a cigarette, got back in the car and drove slowly home.

A wave of fatalism engulfed him as he drove; he was prepared to submit to anything, to resist nothing. If the police awaited him at the house it would all be over; it would be pointless and craven even to try to make them understand.

So artfully had he woven himself into this web of despair, it was an actual letdown when he got to the house and found it deserted. He went inside and made himself a drink. He waited. The house was funereally silent, as if only a moment earlier a horde of mourners had driven away. The oppressive silence frightened him with its atmosphere of eternal bereavement. He took the revolver from his desk and loaded it, but his emotional state was too passive and too disorganized to act on the impulse. He would do nothing, neither call the police nor contact Libby.

At seven-thirty, after sitting first with a drink, then a cigarette, then another drink, in the empurpled twilight of the empty house, he began to shiver and roused himself to light a lamp. Its red shade created a sense of mild warmth.

The doorbell rang. Robert didn't move at first, unequal to the effort required to get up and open the door. When the bell kept ringing he finally got up and went to see who it was.

There stood Libby, that same familiar, ingratiating smile on her face, a covered pot steaming in her hands. "It's my own fault if it's a flop. The recipe didn't specifically say so but I think you're supposed to use yak meat. It'll probably taste like plain old beef stew with curry powder."

Her words made no sense. Though only mildly drunk, he felt as if he were seeing and hearing her through a frosted pane of glass.

"Robert? Are you all right?"

Her naturalness sounded obscene, yet he wasn't angry with her, and he was too emotionally drained to lie to her.

"No. I'm not all right."

"You haven't eaten, have you?"

"No."

"Time you did, then. Well, may I come in?"

She was soon rattling about the kitchen, humming to herself, giving little whoops of dismay at her own clumsiness. This homely stir and bustle dulled his anguish, but not until she called out, "Soup's on!" did he consciously wonder why she had not asked about Sylvia.

She had set one place for him and watched expectantly as he sat down. He looked up at her. "Libby—"

"Go ahead. Try it."

He took a spoonful and swallowed.

"Too much curry?"

He put the spoon down. "Libby, why are you doing this?"

"Well, someone's got to look after you."

"Sylvia's gone," he said dully.

"I know."

Their eyes met. He felt their thoughts were traveling on separate though parallel tracks.

She said, "You don't like it, do you? There *is* too much curry."

The absurdity of it all made him laugh. "No. It's good. It's just that I'm not hungry."

"No wonder. But you've got to eat."

Her obtuseness irritated him. He slammed down the spoon again. "Don't you understand? She's *gone*."

"I know that, Robert. I saw her leave." He looked at her. She ducked her head. "All right, you may as well know. I saw you take her away in the car after the fight."

What was she up to? He looked at the stew as if it might be poisoned. "Then you saw everything."

"Everything."

He hadn't meant to explain to anyone, or even to try to, but now those spoonfuls of stew seemed to have stimulated some anti-despair mechanism.

"Libby, I know how it looked. But, honest, I didn't murder Sylvia. That fight you heard and saw, all that business with the croquet mallet, was make-believe. I didn't really hit her. It was all a charade, a crazy stunt. If you'd been there you would have heard her giggle when I put her into the trunk. But something went wrong, Libby. It was awful. I had an accident—a truck ran into me before I could stop and let her out. When I got the trunk open she was dead."

She was actually blushing with discomfort.

"Libby, I *swear* to you—"

"Please don't, Robert. We've got to decide what to do. Is Sylvia still in the car?"

"No."

"No?"

"Of course not. Do you think I'd drive around all day with her body in the car?"

"But, Robert, it was an accident. You didn't mean to kill her, did you?"

"Then you do believe me?" He could almost see a sort of radiant aura, a saintly nimbus illuminating her figure; but she was shaking her head.

"I mean, when you hit her with the mallet. Of course I don't believe you *pretended* to hit her. I saw it all, remember? You were angry and you meant to scare her, but you just got carried away and didn't realize how hard you were hitting her. But what I meant, Robert, is that maybe it could be made to look like an accident."

"No. The police are too clever. They're scientists, too, you know. They have laboratories and they'd know how long she'd been dead. Besides, it's too late. I've already buried her."

"Oh, Robert, why did you do that?"

"Because I thought there was a slim chance you might not have seen us and called the police. I certainly didn't expect you to witness a murder and *not* call the police."

Her big, shiny eyes were moist with reproof. "You really don't know me at all, do you, Robert? Why, you and Sylvia were my only friends—my whole life. You came to mean everything to me. You were always so kind and sweet. You can't imagine how I felt when I heard her screaming at you, telling you she was leaving you. Oh, Robert, what an idiot she was. Didn't she realize how lucky she was to be loved by a man like you? You didn't mean to kill her, I know that. You just couldn't bear to have her leave you. It was so thrilling, Robert, I just sat there at the window and *shivered*. It was all so terrible and thrilling. It was like . . . Shakespeare! Like *Othello* . . . like *Romeo and Juliet*. Oh, it was marvelous!"

He was astounded. She was absolutely sincere; her eyes burned with the fire of romance. He didn't know what to think of her. It was touching, and at the same time ludicrous.

"And so you didn't call the police."

"The police! They would never have understood. I'll never tell on you, Robert. It was so tragic and so beautiful. I'll never forget it."

He felt suddenly hungry again and picked up his spoon and finished the stew.

She beamed at him. "Robert, where did you bury her?"

"Near an abandoned oil storage tank half a mile inside the old Cortwright Road."

"But what if they find her?"

"They won't."

"Even if they do, I'll say you were with me. I'll tell them I'd seen her entertaining other men. We'll think of something."

He gave her a long, affectionate smile. "Libby, you're the most remarkable woman I've ever met."

She blushed and lowered her eyes, looking almost pretty. "Oh, Robert."

It occurred to him, not out of vanity but because he did indeed think it extraordinary she could assume such an attitude about what she had witnessed, that she might be in love with him. He felt a pang of guilt for his many sins of omission where Libby Kriegher was concerned. He knew nothing about her, nothing about her past, her experiences, her lost or still-cherished ambitions. Had she ever been in love? No, he thought not. She was too wildly romantic to get involved in a commonplace love affair. Her nature was too poetic.

"I'll just wash up these dishes," she said. "Why don't you go in the den and watch television. It'll take your mind off things."

Yes, she was still going to be a nuisance, he decided. More so than ever. At the moment, however, this was no more than a rather pleasant bother. Eventually he would sell the house and move away.

Too bad he couldn't claim Sylvia's insurance.

That he could even think such a thought appalled him. The psychology of human behavior fascinated him precisely because he had only a fuzzy knowledge of it. It was no more to him than a constantly beguiling mystery. Which was probably a good thing, he decided, for if we ever truly understood our motives would we ever be able to live with ourselves?

This naturally led him to reflect upon the accident and the degree to which the collision with that truck had been purely accidental. Had he seen the truck behind him but not permitted his mind to register the image? Had some evil, dark, hidden design caused the accident to happen? *Had he for some as yet consciously inadmissible reason wanted Sylvia to die?* Or did he deliberately encourage these thoughts because he wanted to feel guilty and wanted to punish himself?

He sighed. The enigma was too perplexing. He lay back and shut his eyes.

He was half asleep when Libby woke him. "I thought you'd gone home," he said.

"I was just on my way when I got to thinking about the mallet."

He smiled. "What about it?"

"What did you do with it?"

"Tossed it into the woods."

"Oh, Robert, you should have buried it, or burned it. Maybe we ought to go back and get it tomorrow. Yes—it must be burned."

"Forget it, Libby. No one would connect it with Sylvia, even if it were found."

"Did you wipe off your fingerprints?"

"No. Why should I?"

"But you said yourself, Robert, they're scientists. They could find blood on it, and tissue."

He sat up and looked at her earnestly. "Libby, I want you to listen to me. It doesn't matter about the mallet. No scientist in the world would ever find Sylvia's blood or tissue on it, because there isn't any on it. That mallet never touched Sylvia's head. It appeared to, I know. It was supposed to look that way to you. That's the way we planned it."

She looked confused. "Planned it? I don't understand."

"Libby, as I said before, you're a most remarkable woman. But just in case you think you're making yourself an accessory to murder, let me relieve your mind. I was telling the truth when I said I didn't kill Sylvia. It was supposed to look that way to fool you."

She still looked bewildered. "Fool me? Robert, why should you want to fool me?"

He told her. There was no point in sparing her. If she were prepared to accept complicity in murder this would hardly even startle her. Besides, it might just put her on notice that she *had* been a nuisance and that he didn't like nuisances.

He wasn't sure how she reacted to his confession because he didn't quite dare meet her eyes; but when he was finished she said, "You've had a very busy day, Robert. Why don't you go to bed now? I'll be back in a little while to make sure you go to sleep. Would you like some warm milk?"

"No, thanks." He looked at her. She gave him a melting smile.

When she was gone he went to sleep right there on the sofa in the den. He hadn't the energy to get undressed and go to bed.

The light woke him. He squinted and made a little grunt of protest, then he came fully awake. Libby stood a few feet away, smiling and pointing a gun at his head.

"Libby? What is it?"

"Get up, Robert. There's pen and paper on the desk there. Hurry. Go over there and sit down and write what I tell you."

"Libby, have you gone crazy?"

"Do as I say!"

He stumbled to his feet and sat down at the desk. She moved closer. "Just say that you killed your wife because she threatened to leave you. And tell where you buried her. That's all, Robert."

"Libby, why—"

"Write!"

He did as she ordered.

"Now give it here." She read it quickly, smiled again. "Very good, Robert. I'm now going to shoot you with your own gun. The police will call it murder-suicide."

"Why, Libby? Why didn't you just call the police?"

"Because you spoiled it, Robert. I would have helped you—I would always have helped you. You shouldn't have made a fool out of me. It was all so real. When I watched you struggling with her; when I saw you run into the garage and get the mallet and kill her. Oh, Robert, it was the most exciting thing that ever happened to me. The only *real* thing." Excitement rose in a pink flush to her homely face, then faded to a bleak, dismal blankness. "And now I know it wasn't real at all. It was just an act. An act to make a fool out of me."

She stepped forward, raised the revolver. "Oh, Robert, why did you have to spoil it?"

She pulled the trigger.

# Where Is Thy Sting?

## by John F. Suter

**D**octor Arturo Gutierrez, seated in one of the loops of an S-shaped concrete bench, looked up at the sound of a footfall. He waved his cigarillo in polite invitation to his friend, Teniente Cervera. The police lieutenant, with a nod, seated himself in the other loop of the S, where he could talk tete-a-tete if he wished.

It was quiet in the plaza at early evening, although there was abundant activity to be seen. A group of musicians were busy setting up chairs on the concrete dais which had supplanted the traditional bandstand. Along one side of the square a *pulpito,* a horse-drawn carriage, went by with a subdued clop, clop. White-garbed Indians passed silently by without a glance at either man.

The doctor sighed. "It is a good city." He offered his friend a smoke.

The lieutenant put the cigarillo between thin lips. The match's flare lit his narrow, aquiline face. "Crime almost does not exist here. We have less than any other city in Central America," he said, waving out the match. "The *policia* are almost a decoration here. If I did not have an income from the money I put into my brother Juan's woven sisal products business, I should nearly starve."

Doctor Gutierrez smiled, a charming smile which showed very white teeth under his finely drawn moustache. He pointed with his chin to a small Indian boy busily shining the shoes of a tourist from the United States.

"More and more *Norteamericanos* are coming here these days. Perhaps they will bring some of their ways, as well. Perhaps you will yet earn your pay."

Teniente Cervera said unemotionally, "I shall be ready."

Both men smoked in silence.

Finally, the lieutenant said, "I am told that two *Norteamericano* friends of yours have just died. Yellow fever, was it not?"

Doctor Gutierrez nodded, his expression grave. "I should not call them friends. They insisted on going on the jungle trip to the ruins, in spite of all warnings. I, myself, did my best to talk them out of it."

Teniente Cervera said emphatically, "The government should

either send money to eliminate the mosquitoes in that region, or force Fernandez Tours to drop that trip. There was no yellow fever there, once, but the accursed mosquitoes have been coming with the planes—"

"The material for yellow fever shots would help greatly. Not a doctor in the city has it, my friend. However, it has been promised."

The lieutenant studied his friend's face intently. "You are certain that you warned these two? You did not *urge* them, instead? Or scoff at the danger? For I have heard—"

"I can guess what you have heard," said the doctor quietly. "So that you will not be misled by false rumors, I had better tell you all about it.

"You know that I spent three years in the United States, studying at an Eastern hospital? It was then that I met the woman who was Señora Estelle Martin, who just died. She was the Señorita Estelle Wright, then. You have seen her—while she lived, of course? That red hair, that flawless skin, those green eyes? A woman to turn the head of any man. She turned mine, I must confess.

"I am an honest man, and when I tell you that I was not unattractive, myself, it is not because I lack modesty. I caught her fancy, you see, and for a while she led me to believe that I, alone, mattered in her life. I was willing to stay in the United States to practice medicine, just to have her.

"There were others enamored of her, of course, but I did not know that. An old story, is it not? This Samuel Martin had more money than the rest, that is all. She married him, a simple business arrangement. I was told nothing in advance, not even a polite goodbye. So I salvaged what fragments of my heart remained, and returned. I lived here for four years, in forgetfulness."

"Then," murmured Teniente Cervera, "the Martins came, and you saw them accidentally."

"Not so accidentally. My younger brother, Rudolfo, is the manager of the Hotel Cervantes, as you know. One day, a month ago, he confessed to me a great passion for a guest, a tourist, a divine woman married to a clod of a husband. Clod of a husband, yes. Divine woman, bah!

"The next day, he introduced me to these Martins in the hotel lobby. Oh, Rudolfo can be very careful; they were presented as guests. I as a very good local doctor. She acknowledged previous acquaintance, to be sure, and very charmingly. Her husband, Martin, a boorish sort, did not realize who I was. To him, I was just another native to be patronized.

"I could see that this woman was reading my thoughts: that I cared not at all what her game would do to her husband, but that I did care what might happen to Rudolfo. You know how handsome Rudolfo is? But such an innocent. She knew that I feared she would devour my brother. But she would not turn aside. I could see the challenge, the deviltry in her eyes."

"The husband was not a good man, either," said the lieutenant thoughtfully. "There were rumors that he had bribed one of our customs officials to look the other way while he smuggled valuable primitive art objects out of the country."

"That is not my concern," said Doctor Gutierrez. "I spoke to Rudolfo about the woman, told him all I knew, pleaded with him. He laughed at me. In desperation, I went to the cathedral and placed it all in the hands of God.

"Two days later, my prayers were answered, although I did not know it then. Señor and Señora Martin decided to take the one-day jungle trip to the ruins in Fernandez's jeep. They surprised me: they came to me for yellow fever shots. They had tried other doctors, without success. Someone said that I might help. I could not, of course, for I had nothing to give them. All I could do was warn them not to go."

"I am surprised that you warned them," said Teniente Cervera. "You could have kept silent, for your brother's sake."

"I am a physician," said the doctor simply. "In fact, I have another surprise. I suggested that, since they could not get shots, they use insect repellent, if they were determined to go. In fact, I compounded this product for them."

"Compounded it? They could have purchased it at a *farmacia*."

"Yes, my friend," said the doctor, "as they would have said in their own country, they could have bought it at any drugstore. But you must remember that the Señor Martins of this world, the boorish, cloddish Señor Martins, do not buy 'at any drugstore' in countries such as ours. When I suggested that, he would have none of it. In his ignorance, he thought that they would sell him citronella or some other scent he considered sickening. He was unaware that most modern repellents have little odor. I recall his words when he asked me to make it: *have it smell sexy for Stell, and make it he-mannish for me. Comprez?* You note," mused the doctor wryly, "the sort of Spanish he had?"

"Such a one," said the lieutenant, "*would* prefer something made especially for him. Something custom-made, they would say? It is hard for an honest man to keep from taking advantage of fools like this one."

"Almost my very thought," agreed the doctor. "When he made the request—more of a demand, it was—Rudolfo's predicament was recalled to me. By compounding this material, I told myself, I could charge more and make some money. One of the realities of life."

"Our country is so poor," sighed the lieutenant.

"It is as you say," said Doctor Gutierrez. "We are indeed poor, yet our country needs to spend money to fight the mosquitoes. Otherwise, those who do have money will not come here. As a medical man, I want to see the mosquito go, even though Heaven sent one of them to save my brother."

They were silent again, smoking. A small, big-eyed Indian tot came toward them, eating a *nieve*, the flavored ice of the tropics, in a cone. The ice was not secure in the cone, and it slipped out, splashing on the ground. The child stared in sorrow for a moment, then walked on, munching the cone.

Doctor Gutierrez stared at the melting ice. The water would soak into the earth, he knew, and in the morning the insects would have disposed of every atom of flavoring. It reminded him, for the second time in recent weeks, that many more compounds, many more scents, attract insects than repel them.

A few notes of music floated from the dais in the center of the plaza. A mild breeze ruffled the bougainvillea on the walls of some of the ancient buildings surrounding the square.

"It is a good city," said Doctor Gutierrez.

Teniente Cervera nodded contentedly. "Crime almost does not exist here."

# Anatomy of an Anatomy

## by Donald E. Westlake

It was on a Thursday, just at four in the afternoon, when Mrs. Aileen Kelly saw the arm in the incinerator. As she told the detective who came in answer to her frantic phone call, "I opened the ramp, to put my bag of rubbish in, and *plop* it fell on the ramp."

"An arm," said the detective, who had introduced himself as Sean Ryan.

Mrs. Kelly nodded emphatically. "I saw the fingers," she said. "Curved, like they was beckoning to me."

"I see." Detective Ryan made a mark or two in his notebook. "And then what?" he asked.

"Well, I jumped with fright. Anybody would, seeing a thing like that. And the ramp door shut, and when I opened it to look in again, the arm had fallen on down to the incinerator."

"I see," said Ryan again. He heaved himself to his feet, a short and stocky man with a lined face and thinning gray hair. "Maybe we ought to take a look at this incinerator," he said.

"It's just out in the hall."

Mrs. Kelly led the way. She was a short and slightly stout lady of fifty-six, five years a widow. Her late Bertram's tavern, half a block away at the corner of 46th Street and 9th Avenue, now belonged to her. After Bertram's passing, she had hired a bartender-manager, and for the last five years had continued to live on in this four-room apartment on 46th Street, where she had spent most of her married life with Bertram.

The incinerator door was across the hall from Mrs. Kelly's apartment. She opened this door and pointed to the foot-square inner ramp door. "That's it," she told the detective.

Ryan opened the ramp door and peered inside. "Pretty dark in there," he commented.

"Yes, it is."

"How tall's this building, Mrs. Kelly?"

"Ten stories."

"And we're on the sixth," he said. "Four stories up to the roof, and the chimney up there is your only source of light."

296

"Well," she said, a trifle defensively, "there's the hall light, too."

"Not when you're in front of it like this." He stooped to peer inside the ramp door again. "Don't see any stains on the bricks," he said.

"Well, it was only stuck for just a second."

Ryan frowned and closed the ramp door. "You only saw this arm for a second," he said, and it was plain he was doubting Mrs. Kelly's story.

"That was enough, believe you me," she told him.

"Mmmm. May I ask, do you wear glasses?"

"Just for reading."

"So you didn't have them on when you saw this arm."

"I *did* see it, Mister Detective Ryan," she snapped, "and it *was* an arm."

"Yes, ma'am." He opened the ramp door again, stuck his arm in. "Incinerator's on," he said. "I can feel the heat."

"It's always on in the afternoon, three till six."

Ryan dragged an old turnip watch from his change pocket. "Quarter after five," he said.

"Took you an hour or more to come here," she reminded him. She didn't like this Detective Ryan, who so obviously didn't believe a word she was saying. For one thing, his hat needed blocking. For another, the sleeves of his gray topcoat were frayed. And for a third thing, he was wearing the most horrible orange necktie Mrs. Kelly had ever seen.

"Arm'd be all burned up by now," he said, musingly, "if it was an arm."

"It was an arm," she said dangerously.

"Mmmm." He had the most infuriating habit of neither agreeing nor disagreeing, just saying, "Mmmmm." To which he added, "Shall we go on back to your living room?"

Furious, Mrs. Kelly marched back into her apartment and sat on the flower-pattern sofa, while Detective Ryan settled himself in Bertram's old chair, across the room.

"Now, Mrs. Kelly," he said, once he was seated, "I'm not doubting your sincerity for a minute, believe me. I'm sure you saw what you thought was an arm."

"It *was* an arm."

"All right," he said. "It was an arm. Now, that would mean somebody upstairs had murdered somebody else, chopped the body up, and was getting rid of the pieces into the incinerator. Right?"

"Well, of course. That's obviously what's happening. And instead of doing something about it, you're sitting here—"

"Now," he said interrupting her smoothly, "you told me you were so startled by the arm you dropped your bag of rubbish, and had to pick it all up again. So you stayed at the incinerator door a couple minutes after you saw the arm. And you opened the door twice more. Once to see if the arm was still there, and once to throw your own bag of rubbish away."

"And so?" she demanded.

"Did you see or hear any more pieces going by?"

She frowned. "No. Just the arm." At the expression on his face, she added, "Well, isn't that enough?"

"I'm afraid not, ma'am. What's our murderer planning to do with the rest of the body?"

"Well, I'm sure *I* don't know. Could—could be that that arm was the last part to go down. He'd thrown down all the rest of it earlier."

"Could be, Mrs. Kelly," Ryan said. "But frankly, I think you made an honest mistake. What you thought was an arm was really something else. Maybe a rolled-up newspaper."

"I tell you, I saw the fingers!"

Ryan sighed, and got to his feet. "I tell you what, Mrs. Kelly," he said. "What you got here isn't enough for us to go on. But if a report comes in on somebody being missing in this building, that would kind of corroborate your story. If somebody's been murdered, he or she will be reported missing before long, and—"

"It was a woman," said Mrs. Kelly. "I saw the long fingernails."

Ryan frowned again. "You saw long fingernails," he asked, "in just a couple of seconds, in that dim incinerator shaft and without your glasses on?"

"I saw what I saw," she insisted, "and I only need my glasses for *reading*."

"Well," said Ryan. He stood there, fidgeting with that awful crushed hat, obviously wanting to be done and away. "If we get word on anybody missing," he said again.

Mrs. Kelly glared at him as he left. He didn't believe her; he thought she was nothing but a foolish old woman with bad eyes. She could hear him now, once he got back to his precinct house: "Nothing to it, just an old crank not wearing her glasses."

And then he was gone, and she was alone. And her irritated anger gradually gave way to something very close to fear. She looked up at the ceiling. Somewhere on the four floors above, someone had murdered a woman, and chopped her up, and thrown her forearm down the incinerator shaft. Mrs. Kelly looked up, realizing how close that terrible murderer was, and that there was to be no help from the police, and she shivered.

The next afternoon, that was a Friday, at just around four o'clock, Mrs. Kelly once more brought her rubbish bag to the incinerator. This wasn't a coincidence. Having lived alone for five years, Mrs. Kelly had developed routines and habits of living that carried her smoothly through her solitary days. And at four o'clock each afternoon, she threw the rubbish away.

On this Friday afternoon, very much aware of the murderer lurking somewhere in the building, she peeked out into the hall before hurrying across to the incinerator door. Then she quickly dumped the rubbish, but someone had thrown something greasy away recently, and a piece of paper stuck to the ramp. Wrinkling her nose in distaste, she reached in and freed it.

That's when it happened again. This time, it was an upper arm, elbow to shoulder, and it didn't pause at the sixth floor. It sailed right on by, elbow foremost, and left Mrs. Kelly staring at the blank brick walls of the shaft.

She was back in her own living room, the door locked and the chain attached, before she had time to think. And when she recovered sufficiently, she decided at once to call that smarty Detective Sean Ryan, because now she knew why there had only been the forearm disposed of yesterday.

Of course. The murderer was afraid to drop all of the body at once. It would take him half an hour or more, and someone on a lower floor would be bound to see something in that time. Besides, he might be afraid the whole body wouldn't burn in just one day.

That's why he dropped just one piece, each afternoon at four. The incinerator had been burning for an hour by that time, and so would be nice and hot. And it would have two more hours to burn before it was turned off.

Ah-hah, Detective Ryan, she thought, and reached for the phone. But then she stopped, her hand an inch from the phone, suddenly knowing exactly what Detective Ryan would have to say. "More arms, Mrs. Kelly? And this one didn't even stop, just whizzed right by? Do you know how fast a falling arm would go, Mrs. Kelly?"

No. Mrs. Kelly wasn't going to go through another humiliating interview like the one yesterday.

But what could she do? A murder had been committed, and what could she do if she couldn't even call the police?

She fretted and fumed, half-afraid and half-annoyed, and then she remembered something Detective Ryan had said yesterday. Corroboration, that's what he had said. Proof of murder, proof someone was missing from this building.

Very well, corroboration he would get. And then he'd have to swallow those smart-alecky remarks of his. How fast does a falling arm go indeed!

All she had to do was find proof.

Almost a full week went by, and no proof. Every afternoon at four, Mrs. Kelly stood by the incinerator door and in growing frustration watched another part sail by. Saturday, the left forearm. Sunday, the left upper arm. Monday, right foot, knee to toes. Tuesday, right leg, hip to knee. Lower half of the torso on Wednesday. Left foot, knee to toes on Thursday.

And Mrs. Kelly knew she had only three days left. The upper half of the torso, the left leg, and the head.

For the first time in her life, Mrs. Kelly disliked the automatic privacy that was a part of living in a New York City apartment. Twenty-seven years she had lived in this building, and she didn't know a soul here, except for the superintendent on the first floor. But the people in the sixteen apartments on the four floors above her were total strangers. She could watch the front door forever, and never know who was missing.

On Tuesday (right leg), it occurred to her to watch the mailboxes. It seemed to her that this murderer, whoever he was, would be staying in his apartment as much as possible until the body had been completely eliminated. There was a possibility he wouldn't even leave to pick up his mail. If there were a stuffed mailbox, it might be the clue she needed.

There wasn't a stuffed mailbox.

On Wednesday (lower half of the torso), she thought to go back to the mailboxes again, this time to get the names of the occupants of the sixteen apartments up above. That afternoon, clutching her list, she watched the piece go by, and repaired furiously to her apartment.

It was all that Detective Sean Ryan's fault, that rumpled man. He must be a widower, or a bachelor. No woman would let her man out of the house as rumpled as all that. Nor wearing a necktie as horrible as that wide orange thing Detective Ryan had had around his neck.

Not that it made any difference. Mrs. Kelly had had trouble enough for one lifetime with Bertram, rest his soul. Housebreaking a man was a life's work, and a woman would be a fool to try to do the job on two men, one right after the other. And Mrs. Aileen Kelly was certainly no fool.

Though she was beginning to feel very much like a fool, as day after day the pieces of that poor murdered woman fell down the incinerator shaft, and Mrs. Kelly still without a shred of proof.

Thursday, she considered the possibility of hiding in a hallway, where she could watch the incinerator door. According to the way the pieces were falling, there were four parts left. If Mrs. Kelly were to spend each of the four days hidden in the hallway on each of the four floors above, sooner or later she would catch the murderer red-handed.

But, how to hide in the hallways? They were all bare and empty, without a single hiding place.

Except, perhaps, the elevator.

Of course, of course, the elevator. She rushed out of her apartment, got into the elevator, and peered through the round porthole in the elevator door. By pressing her nose against the metal of the door and peeking far to the left, she could just barely catch a glimpse of the incinerator door. It would work.

Accordingly, she was in the elevator at five of four, and pushing the button marked 7. The elevator rose one flight and stopped. Mrs. Kelly took up her position, peering out at the incinerator door, and so she stood for three minutes.

Then the elevator started with a jerk, cracking Mrs. Kelly smartly across the nose, and purred down its shaft, stopping at the fourth floor. Someone else had called it.

Furious, Mrs. Kelly glared at the overcoat-bundled man who stepped aboard at the fourth floor and pushed the button marked 1.

On the first floor, the overcoated man left the building, while Mrs. Kelly dashed to the incinerator door, opened it, opened the ramp, and watched the left foot go falling by, to land in the midst of the flames below.

That did it for fair. There were only three days left now, and four floors to check. And if she didn't find out who the murderer was before Sunday, he would have disposed of the body completely, and there wouldn't be a shred of proof. Mrs. Kelly stormed back to the elevator, thinking, "Three days and four floors. Three days and four floors."

And the roof.

She stopped in her tracks. The roof. The top of the incinerator shaft was up there, covered only by a wire grating. It wouldn't be hard to bend that grating back, and drop something down the shaft.

Which meant it didn't have to be somebody in this building at all. It could be someone from almost anywhere on the block, coming across the roofs to drop the evidence as far from home as possible.

Well, there was a way to find out about that. It had snowed all day yesterday and last night, but it hadn't snowed today. The flat roof would have a nice thick layer of snow on it. If anyone had come across it to the incinerator shaft, he would have had to leave tracks.

Getting into the elevator, she pushed the button for the tenth floor, and waited impatiently as the elevator rose to the top of the building. Then she mounted the flight of stairs to the roof door, unbent the wire twisted around the catch, and stepped out.

She had been in too much of a hurry to stop and dress properly for the outdoors. It was cold and windy up on the roof, and the snow was ankle-deep. Mrs. Kelly turned the collar of her housecoat up and held the lapels closed against her throat. Her old scuffy slippers were no protection against the snow.

She hurried off to the right, to the incinerator chimney, circled it, and found no footprints beyond her own.

So, she'd wasted her time, frozen half to death and ruined her slippers, and all for nothing.

No, not for nothing after all. Now she knew for sure the murderer was somewhere in this building.

Friday morning, Mrs. Kelly awoke with a snuffly head cold and a steadily increasing irritation. She was furious at Detective Ryan for making her do his work for him. She was enraged at the terrible creature upstairs, who'd started this whole thing in the first place. And she was exasperated with herself, for being such a complete failure.

She spent the day sipping tea liberally laced with lemon juice, and at four hobbled out to the incinerator to watch the upper half of the torso bump by. Then, snuffly and miserable, she went back to bed.

On Saturday, the cold was just as bad, and her irritation was worse. She sat and looked at her list of sixteen names, and searched desperately for a way to find out which one of them was a murderer.

Of course, she could simply call Detective Ryan and have him come over at four o'clock, to watch the piece of body fall down the incinerator shaft. She *could* do that, but she wouldn't. When she called Detective Ryan, it would be because *she* had found the murderer.

Besides, he probably wouldn't even come.

So she glared at the list of names. A silly thought occurred to her. She could look up the phone numbers of all these people, and say, "Excuse me, have you been dropping a body down the incinerator?"

Well, come to think of it, why not? It was a woman's body, which probably meant it was somebody's wife. With her husband the murderer. Most of the people in this building were middle-aged or better, couples whose children had grown up and gone their separate ways years ago. So far as she knew, there were no large families in the building at all.

It would have to be an apartment in which there were only two people. The murderer wouldn't be able to hide the dead body from someone living in the same apartment.

So maybe the telephone would be useful after all. She could call each apartment. If a woman answered she would say she had a wrong number. If a man answered, she would ask for his wife. The apartment without a woman would be the logical suspect.

With a definite plan at last, she ignored her stuffed nose and sat down beside the telephone to look up the phone numbers of her sixteen suspects, and start her calls.

Two of the sixteen had no phone numbers listed. Well, if the other fourteen produced nothing certain, she would have to think of something else for those two. And she was suddenly convinced that she would be able to think of something when the time came, with no trouble at all. She was suddenly oozing with confidence.

She started phoning shortly after five. Eight of the fourteen answered, five times a woman's voice and three times a man's voice. Mrs. Kelly apologized to the women for calling a wrong number, and asked each man who answered. "Is the Missus at home, please?" Twice, the men answered, "Just a second," and Mrs. Kelly had to apologize to the women who came on the line. The third time, the man said, "She's out shopping right now. Could I take a message for her?"

"I'll call back later," said Mrs. Kelly quickly. "Do you know when she'll be back?"

"Fifteen, twenty minutes, probably," said the man.

She waited an hour before calling that number again, and she was so nervous she actually did dial a wrong number to begin with. Because this might be the end of the search. If the wife still wasn't home—

She was. Mrs. Kelly, disappointed, made the eighth wrong-number apology, and crossed the eighth name off her list.

She tried the remaining six numbers later in the evening, and only once found someone at home. A woman. Mrs. Kelly crossed the ninth name off the list.

She tried the five remaining numbers shortly after ten that night, but none of them answered. Deciding to try again in the morning, she set the alarm for eight o'clock and went to bed, where she slept uneasily, dreaming of bodies falling from endless blackness.

The upper half of the torso had fallen on Friday.

Mrs. Kelly's cold was worse again on Saturday. She forced herself to the telephone around noon, managed to lower the number of suspects from five to three, then gave up and went back to bed, rousing only to watch the left leg plummet by at four o'clock.

Only the head remained.

Sunday morning, the cold was gone. Not even a sniffle remained. Mrs. Kelly got up early, went to eight o'clock Mass, and hurried back home through the January cold and the slippery streets to have breakfast and make more phone calls.

There were three numbers left. One of them was answered, by a disgruntled man who said his wife was asleep, but the other two still didn't respond. She tried again at eleven, and this time the disgruntled man turned her over to his wife. Two numbers left.

Her second call was answered by a man, and Mrs. Kelly said, "Hello. Is the Missus at home?"

"Who's this?" snapped the man. His voice was suspicious and hoarse, and Mrs. Kelly felt the leaping of hope within her breast.

"This is Annie Tyrrell," she said, giving the first name to come to her mind, which happened to have been her mother's maiden name.

"The wife ain't here," said the man. There was a pause, and he added, "She's gone out of town. Visiting her mother. Gone to Nebraska."

"Oh, dear me," said Mrs. Kelly, hoping she was doing a creditable job of acting. "How long ago did she leave?"

"Wednesday before last," said the man. "Won't be back for a month or two."

"Could you give me her address in Nebraska?" Mrs. Kelly asked. "I could drop her a note," she explained.

The man hesitated. "Don't have it right handy," he said, finally. Then, all at once, he said, "Who'd you say this was?"

For a frantic second, Mrs. Kelly couldn't remember what name she had given, and then it came back to her. "Annie Tyrrell," she said.

"I don't think I know you," said the man suspiciously. "Where you know my wife from?"

"Oh, we—uh—we met in the supermarket."

"Is that right?" he sounded more suspicious than ever. "I tell you what," he said. "You give me your number. I don't have the wife's address right handy, but I can look it up and call you back."

"Well, uh—" Mrs. Kelly thought frantically. She didn't know what to do. If she gave him her own number, he might be able to check it and find out who she really was. But if she gave him some other number, he might call back and find out there wasn't any Annie Tyrrell, and then he'd know for sure that someone suspected him.

He broke into her thoughts, saying "Say, who is this, anyway? What's my wife's first name?"

"What?"

"I asked you what's my wife's first name," he repeated.

"Well," she said, forcing a little laugh that sounded patently false even to her, "whatever on earth for? Don't you even know your own wife's first name?"

"*I* do," he said. "But do you?"

Suddenly terrified, Mrs. Kelly hung up without another word, and sat staring at the telephone. It had been him! The sound of his voice, the suspicious way he had acted. It had been him! She looked at his name on her list. Andrew Shaw, apartment 8B, two floors up, directly over her apartment.

Andrew Shaw. He was the killer, and now he knew that someone suspected him. It wouldn't take him long to realize the call had come from someone in this building, someone who must have seen the evidence in the incinerator shaft.

He would be searching for her now, and she didn't know how long it would take him to find her. He might be much more resourceful than she; it might not take him as long as a week to find and silence the person who was threatening him.

Pride was pride, but foolishness was something else again. It was time to call Detective Ryan. She had the murderer's name for him now, and the head of the murdered woman hadn't yet been disposed of. It was time for Detective Sean Ryan to take over.

Thoroughly frightened, Mrs. Kelly fumbled through the phone book until she found the police station number, and had it half-dialed when she remembered it was Sunday. Of course, some policemen were at work on Sundays, but not necessarily Sean Ryan. Well, if he wasn't working today, some other policeman would have to do. Though she did hope it would be Sean Ryan. Simply to see the expression on his face when he saw she'd been right all along, of course.

When the bored voice said, "Sixteenth Precinct," Mrs. Kelly said, "I'd like to speak to Detective Ryan, please. Detective Sean Ryan."

"Just one moment, please," said the voice. Mrs. Kelly waited for a moment that seemed to go on forever, and then the same voice came back and said, "He's off to eleven o'clock Mass now, ma'am. Be back in about an hour. Want to leave a message?"

She knew she should settle for another policeman, that this was no time for delays, but she found herself saying, "Would you ask him to call Mrs. Aileen Kelly, please? The number is CIrcle 5-9970."

She had to spell her first name for him, and added, "Would you tell him it's important, and to call right away, the minute he gets there?"

"Yes, ma'am."

"Thank you very much."

And then she had nothing to do but wait. And wait. And look at the ceiling.

He didn't call till two-thirty, and by then Mrs. Kelly was frantic. In the first place, she was afraid her phone call to Mister Andrew Shaw might have him worried about maintaining his four o'clock schedule. He might decide to get rid of the head at three o'clock, when the incinerator first went on, and then there wouldn't be any more evidence. And in the second place she was terrified that he would find her right away, that any moment he would be knocking on the front door.

Half a dozen times, she almost called the police again, but every time she told herself that he must call in a minute or two. And when he finally did call, at two-thirty, he stepped directly into a tongue-lashing.

"You were supposed to call me directly after you got back to the precinct house," she told him. "Directly after Mass."

"Mrs. Kelly, I'm a busy man," he said defensively. "I've just this minute got back to the station. I had some other calls to make."

"Well, you hotfoot it over here this instant, Mister Detective Ryan," she snapped. "I've got your murderer for you, but with all your shilly-shallying around, he's liable to get off scot-free yet. They turn the incinerator on at three o'clock, you know."

"It's this business about the arm again, is it?"

"It's about the whole body this time," she informed him. "And there's nothing left of it but the head. Now, you get over here before even that is gone."

She heard him sigh, and then he said, "Right, Mrs. Kelly. I'll be right over."

It was then twenty to three. In twenty minutes, the incinerator would go on. She was positive by now that he would change his pattern, that he would get rid of the head just as soon as ever he could. And that would be in twenty minutes.

And then it was fifteen minutes, and ten minutes, and five minutes, and still Ryan didn't come, though the precinct house was only a block and a half away, up on 47th Street.

At two minutes to three, she couldn't stand it any longer. She peered out the peekhole at the hall, and saw that it was empty. Carefully and silently, she unlocked the door and crept down the hall to the incinerator. She opened it and stood staring in at the gray brick walls of the shaft, expecting any second to see the head go sailing by.

And still Ryan didn't come.

At three o'clock on the dot, she heard a thump from above, and knew it was the head. Without stopping to think, she thrust her arm into the shaft in a frantic attempt to grab it and save it for evidence. With her arm stretched out like that, she couldn't see into the shaft, but she felt the head when it landed on her wrist a second later. It was freezing cold, so he'd been keeping it in a home freezer all this time, and it was held by her wrist and a wall of the incinerator.

It was also sticky, and Mrs. Kelly's imagination suddenly gave her a vivid image of exactly what she was touching. She gave a shriek, pulled her arm back, and the head went bumping down the shaft to the fire far below.

At that moment, the elevator door slid open and Detective Ryan appeared.

She glared at him for a speechless second, then shook her fist in fury. *"Now* you come, do you? Now, when it's too late and the poor woman's head is burned to a crisp and that Andrew Shaw is free as a bird, *now* you come!"

He stared at her in amazement, and she shook her fist at him. "The last of the evidence," she cried, "Gone, burned to a crisp, be-cause of—"

For the first time, she noticed the fist she was shaking. It was red, ribboned red, and as she looked, the cold ribbon spread down her arm, and she knew it was the poor woman's blood.

"There's your evidence!" she cried, raising her hand to him, and fell over in a faint.

When she awoke, on the sofa in her living room, Detective Ryan was sitting awkwardly on a kitchen chair beside her. "Are you all right now?" he asked her.

"Did you get him?" she asked right back.

He nodded. A woman whom Mrs. Kelly recognized as her across-the-hall neighbor, though she didn't know her name, came from the direction of the kitchen and handed Mrs. Kelly a steaming cup of tea.

She sat up, still shaky, and realized thankfully that someone had washed her hand while she'd been in her faint.

"We got him," said Detective Ryan. "The incinerator had just gone on, and we got it turned off in time, so the evidence wasn't destroyed after all. And we got him stepping out of the elevator, his suitcase all packed. And he talked enough."

"Well, good," said Mrs. Kelly, and she sipped triumphantly at the tea.

"Now," said Ryan, his tone changing, "I believe I have a bone to pick with you, Mrs. Kelly."

She frowned, "Do you, now?"

"All week long," he said, "you've been watching pieces of body being disposed of, and not once did you call the police."

"I did call the police," she reminded him. "A smarty-pants detec-tive named Ryan came and refused to believe me. Called me a foolish old woman."

"I never did!" he said, shocked and outraged.

"You as much as did, and that's the same thing."

"You should have called again," he insisted, "once you'd figured out his schedule."

"Why should I?" she demanded. "I called you once, and you laughed at me. And when I finally did call you again, you lollygaggled around and showed up late anyway."

He shook his head. "You're a very foolhardy woman, Mrs. Kelly," he said. "You have too much pride."

"I solved the case for you," she told him.

"You took totally unnecessary chances," he said sternly.

"If you're going to give me a sermon," she told him, "you'd better get a more comfortable chair."

"You don't seem to realize," he began, then shook his head. "You need someone to look out for you." And he launched into his sermon.

Mrs. Kelly sat, not really listening, nodding from time to time. She noticed he was wearing that horrible orange tie again. In a bit, when the sermon was over and she felt less shaky, she'd go on out to the bedroom. She still had most of Bertram's clothes, his neckties included. There had to be one there to go with that brown suit of Ryan's.

That orange thing was going down the incinerator, it was.

# Murder Me Twice

## by Lawrence Treat

**B**urke, the assistant D.A., had a homicide recorded on tape, from beginning to end, and he had three eyewitnesses. They'd watched Lucy Prior reach for the drawer of the table, take out the gun and shoot her husband through the heart. Twice. And straighten up with a horrified expression, and say shakily, "I fear me, he is dead."

Perfect? Maybe on the face of it, and yet Burke had nothing. There wasn't even a crime, until he could prove felonious intent.

He was a nice guy, young but stubborn, and he lived with the fixed idea that somehow, the tape had the answer. In the privacy of his office he switched on the recordings and listened to them over and over again, in the hope that he'd pick up something new. Something besides the series of questions and their answers in Lucy's slow, languid voice, varied only by the buzz that was probably a plane flying over the city, by Will Prior's occasional cough, and the blur.

The Thompsons, who had been present when the recordings were made, gave a clear and succinct account of the background.

"Dr. Farham and the Priors were at our house one evening a few months ago," they said. "We were talking about Bridey Murphy, and Dr. Farham—he's a dentist, you know—told us he often used post-hypnotic suggestion on his patients, to avoid pain. He said it was effective, and that he'd had considerable experience. When we wanted a demonstration, he put Lucy under. He was amazed at how suggestible she was and he regressed her—I think that's the right word—to her childhood and infancy, and eventually to a former existence.

"It's fascinating how some people can remember the events of their previous incarnation, and Lucy Prior was one of them. She'd lived in Philadelphia in the 1850's, and her name had been Dora Evans. We met once a week at the Priors'. Dr. Farham would put Lucy in a trance and she'd talk about her life as Dora Evans, but she always stopped with that particular June morning. We wondered why she'd never go any farther, and we simply had to find out."

"Ever check up on what she said?" Burke asked.

"No, but we kept complete recordings; you have them all."

But Burke didn't believe in reincarnation. "Bunk," he told everybody. "Hogwash. This was cold-blooded murder, with the hypnosis for a cover-up."

He could visualize every detail of those gatherings in the living room that belonged to Will and Lucy Prior. It was a luxurious room. Will Prior could afford it, and he sat bulkily, filling a huge, tapestried chair that was drawn up alongside the massive library table. He sipped quantities of scotch and he chain-smoked, and a blue haze must have surrounded the plump bulb of his face.

The recording machine stood on an antique stand, conveniently near Lucy. She reclined on the blue couch while Dr. Farham, a couple of feet behind her, kept prodding her with questions.

Burke supposed she had that far-off look in her eyes, and her soft, slack mouth must have drooped at the corners as if she was pleading with them not to, to let her be, stop forcing her. Maybe that was why Dr. Farham always placed himself behind her, where he was immune from the lovely spectacle of her distress.

The recordings always started with Lucy Prior, under deep hypnosis, being led back until her mind made the big jump to the 1850's. Then, as Dora Evans, she talked ramblingly about President Pierce and slavery, the trip she'd made to New York by packet boat, and the dresses she'd brought home. But whenever Burke switched on that final tape, he tensed and felt a special, prickling excitement once Lucy—or Dora Evans—reached the events of that June morning.

"You told us last time," came Dr. Farham's smooth, persuasive tones, "that you were sitting in the rose arbor of your garden, in the summer of 1853. What happened then?"

"He was inebriated," Lucy said. At this point, her voice lost its languor and took on a tortured quality.

"Who was inebriated?"

"Hans, the gardener. We called him the tulip man. He was Dutch, and he grew the most beautiful tulips. Holland is famous for them."

"Hans was working in the garden?"

"No, he didn't work that day, and Charles had high words with him."

"Charles, your husband?"

"Certainly."

Burke wondered how Will Prior had reacted when he heard his

wife speak of another man as her legal spouse. But Will's time to react was growing short. Two minutes, one minute . . .

"Why do you keep telling us about the gardener?"

"Please, please! I don't want to go through it again. I've suffered too much."

"Suffered?"

"For what I did. But I don't have to talk about it, and I will not."

There was a short pause before Dr. Farham spoke again, intoning the fatal words. He uttered them blandly, almost casually. "If you don't want to talk about it," he said, "show us."

The tape hummed, and clicked off the few seconds left of Will Prior's life. Burke knew that Lucy had slid from the couch, climbed to her feet and walked slowly toward her husband. She bent down as if to kiss him. He said something to her, a blur that always made Burke lean forward and listen intently. But the words were a muttered indistinctness. Just that blur, followed by the sound of the drawer opening; and then a rough spot on the tape, and then the two shots. Mrs. Thompson screamed, there was a scuffling noise, and in the confusion somebody's foot caught the electric cord.

Finis.

So Lucy Prior was in custody, and it was up to Burke to prepare the people's case and prove she'd intended to kill her husband.

To Burke, struggling with his problem, the big jolt came when the police checked records and newspaper files and found out that a Dora Evans had actually been living in Philadelphia in 1853. And that one morning in June she'd shot and killed her husband.

Moreover, she'd fired two bullets into his heart, and she'd been tried for murder and convicted. She had died in prison about a year later.

Burke, however, had a theory, and he clung to it obstinately, with the desperation of a man who had no other alternative. "Dr. Farham was Lucy's lover," he reasoned, "and they deliberately conspired to murder her husband because they wanted to get married and needed his money. It's as simple as that."

In his interrogation of Lucy Prior, Burke got nowhere. Her eyes, blue and dark, were loaded with agony, and her ripe, sensitive lips quivered.

"I never heard of Dora Evans," she said. "I didn't read about her; I couldn't possibly have because I hardly ever read books."

"All right," said Burke. "Tell me when you first started going with Dr. Farham."

"With Dr. Farham?" she said, recoiling. "How can you think such a thing? I was married, I loved my husband."

"Is that why you killed him?"

"Please," she said softly. "Please don't say that again."

"What did he tell you, when you leaned over his chair just before shooting him?"

"I don't know," she cried out. "Oh, if only I hadn't been asleep! It's like a horrible nightmare. All I know is, I woke up and he'd been shot. By me!" And she burst into tears.

Burke, along with Lieutenant Drobney, in charge of the detective precinct handling the case, attended a high-level police conference. Briefly, the commissioner summed up the aims of the investigation.

"We got to show motive and intent," he said, "which means breaking down that reincarnation story. Because, if just one juror thinks reincarnation is possible, a verdict of guilty is out."

Burke listened to the discussion that followed, and then to a series of tapes which the laboratory had copied from the section with the blur. The copies were amplified and the frequencies were changed, modified, distorted, shaded, compressed. But to the group in the commissioner's office, the result was always the same: Prior's voice, blurred.

After the conference, Burke and Drobney got together over a cup of coffee in a nearby restaurant.

"All that brass," Drobney said, "and what do they come up with? Nothing."

"The heart of it," said Burke, "is the affair between Mrs. Prior and Farham."

"We been working on the pair of them, in relays," said Drobney. "And so far, it's no soap. If they were sweet on each other, they were pretty cagey about it."

"Sure they were," said Burke. "They pulled off the slickest homicide I ever heard of, so don't expect them to slip up by giving away their motive."

Drobney let out his breath in a swirl of air that lifted a couple of paper napkins six feet away and sent them sailing to the floor. "I got a feeling you and me are the fall guys," he said. "The big boys are sidestepping it; they dumped it right in our laps." Reluctantly, as if parting with a fortune, he dropped a quarter alongside his plate. "I'll be seeing you," he said and left.

Doggedly, Burke went to work on the hypnosis angle. A succession of experts sat across his desk and agreed unanimously that a hypnotic trance could be faked, and that there was no way in the world of proving it, one way or the other.

Burke's reaction was to send for Dr. Miles Farham, and try again. Farham, tall, personable, self-possessed, was as cool and smooth as a martini.

"You asked her a lot of questions based on a belief in reincarnation, didn't you?" said Burke.

"My own views are irrelevant," Farham said. "And in any case, you have the record."

"What made you keep pushing her? Why tell her to act out what she refused to talk about?"

Dr. Farham seemed to examine the question from a distance. "Intellectual curiosity," he answered thoughtfully. "A compulsion to delve into the mysteries of the human mind."

"How often did you see her as a patient?" said Burke.

"Maybe three or four times. I'd have to consult my files."

"How often did you see her on a personal basis?"

"Never." Dr. Farham smiled patiently. "I can see what you're driving at. Let me say that I'm not in love with her, but the tragedy has brought us close. I feel pity for her. A deep, abiding compassion, and a desire to make up for the suffering I unwittingly caused her."

A tricky answer, thought Burke, and a calculated one. And it left Burke high and dry.

In his spare time, Burke boned up on law and studied his notes. Gradually a suspicion formed in his mind, and he phoned Drobney. "Did Mrs. Prior tell you she hadn't read about Dora Evans?"

"Sure. Several times."

"What made her say that? Did you ask her anything about a book?"

"Me?" said Drobney. "What for?"

Burke grinned. "Thanks," he said, and hung up. He was still grinning as he switched on the intercom and asked for a detective assigned to the homicide bureau.

Burke's instructions were explicit. "There's a book about Dora Evans," he said. "I don't know the title, but try the library and the second-hand shops. You'll turn it up. Okay?"

Early the next afternoon, when Burke returned from court, he found the book waiting for him, with a note informing him that it came from a Fourth Avenue book store.

It was a dog-eared, vellum-bound volume. It had been printed in 1855 and the title read, "Famous Crimes of Lust and Passion." Forty

pages were devoted to the Dora Evans trial. Burke read them with
excitement and a growing absorption. When he had finished, he
went uptown to Drobney's precinct and entered the lieutenant's office.

Drobney was sweating over a stack of forms. "They ought to teach
these boys of mine to write English," he said irritably. "Or else stop
'em from making out reports." He shoved the papers to the side of
his desk. "Stuff about Farham," he said, "but we haven't even got
to first base on this affair between him and Mrs. Prior. If there was
one."

"Got any other explanation?" Burke demanded.

Drobney answered in a hoarse voice. "Burke, the Thompsons go
for this reincarnation, they're educated people, nobody can fool 'em.
Suppose there's something to it, huh?"

"What?" said Burke. "Don't tell me *you're* falling for that line.

The lieutenant wiped his forehead. "I was just kidding," he said
sheepishly. "Still, you can't help wondering. Where, for instance,
did she get all the dope on Dora Evans? The Philadelphia papers
carried the high spots, but Mrs. Prior knows Dora Evans like she
knows her own self. How come, Burke? How come?"

"From this," said Burke, handing Drobney the book. "Everything
Mrs. Prior ever said about Dora Evans is right here, in print. Mrs.
Prior even used the same words."

"Wow!" said Drobney. "Makes a dent, doesn't it?"

"It'll make a real dent only if we can prove she read it."

Drobney fingered the volume doubtfully. "She isn't the kind of
dame who'll leave any incriminating evidence lying around. But
we'll look, and we'll check second-hand stores and see if anybody
remembers selling her a copy. We might turn up something."

"You'll be interested in the account of the Dora Evans trial," said
Burke. "The state proved that she had a lover and they needed her
husband's money, and that she knew the gun was kept in a drawer
of the library table."

"Sounds familiar," said Drobney. "What was her defense?"

"Dora Evans? She claimed she was in the garden when she heard
shots, and so she rushed inside. She said she found her husband
sitting next to the table, with the gun on the floor, and she picked
it up and was holding it in her hand when the servants came in.
And—" Burke smiled as if he'd hit the jackpot—"her first words
were, 'I fear me, my husband is dead.' "

"What about this gardener?" Drobney asked.

"Dora Evans blamed the shooting on him. But he'd been drinking that morning and, according to the testimony at the trial, he was sleeping it off in a back room and was so blotto he couldn't even stand up straight."

"So that's why Mrs. Prior kept saying the gardener was stewed."

"Inebriated," Burke remarked. "But—was he?"

"Too bad they didn't have a drunkometer in those days. Man, what a modern lab could have done with the Evans case!"

"The question is what a modern mind can do with it, now. I'm going down to Philadelphia tonight and try to find out."

"What for?" said the lieutenant, puzzled. "A homicide over a hundred years old—what can you find out about it? And if you did, how would it help?"

"I don't know," said Burke. "Except that it's riding me, and I want to get to the bottom of it."

"I'd say you were nuts," said Drobney. "But I'll go to work on Mrs. Prior this afternoon, on the book angle. Maybe I'll have something before you leave."

Burke got the call just before rushing for his train. "Burke?" said Drobney. "I just got finished with Mrs. Prior. Know what she says?"

"She probably cried and said the subject was too painful to discuss."

"She did better than that. She says that if she used the same words that are in the book, it proves she *was* Dora Evans. She says I'm a real friend."

Burke groaned.

Two days later, Burke returned from Philadelphia. His briefcase looked as thin as it had when he'd gone away, but he hugged it under his arm and brought it with him to a lengthy conference with his boss. From there, Burke went to his own office, and slumped down in a chair.

Grimly, he picked up the phone and sent for Lieutenant Drobney, and for Dr. Farham and Lucy Prior. Then Burke stared at the ceiling and waited.

In about twenty minutes, Drobney rumbled in like a tank and said, "Well? How's the Evans case?"

"All right. And you? How about the Prior case?"

"Nothing," Drobney said flatly. "Nothing on the book angle. Nothing on the love-nest angle. Nothing but headaches. Lucy Prior's a smart cookie, Burke. She knows we can't touch her as long as she sticks to the reincarnation theory."

"Funny," said Burke. "In the beginning, she wouldn't commit herself. Claimed she was in a deep sleep and had no idea of what she'd done. Remember?"

"Yeah, but after the stuff in the papers and on the radio, most of it supporting the possibility of reincarnation, she's all for it."

"You're half-sold on it yourself, aren't you?"

"Me?" said Drobney, rubbing his jaw. "It's the Mrs., she goes for it. Sometimes I come out with what she said and don't even realize it."

The intercom buzzed.

Burke switched it on and a voice said, "Dr. Farham is outside."

"Send him in," said Burke.

Dr. Farham entered with quiet assurance. "You said it was urgent," he said, "so I canceled my afternoon appointments."

"Thanks," said Burke. "Sit down and let me ask you something about this book on the Evans trial. Did it occur to you that Mrs. Prior could have read the account and memorized it, and used the information while she was supposedly under hypnosis?"

"Supposedly?" said Farham. He caught the important word and sensed the danger in it. He sat up a little straighter, and his hand tightened on the arm of his chair.

Burke nodded. "That's right. How sure are you that Mrs. Prior was in a deep sleep during your sessions with her? Is it or is it not possible that she was pretending?"

Dr. Farham didn't answer at once. He turned slightly in Drobney's direction and noted Drobney's deep, perplexed attention. Then the dentist regarded Burke, a young man leaning back in a chair trying to look relaxed and casual.

"Pretending?" said Farham. "That would constitute a gigantic hoax."

"Wouldn't it?" Burke said pleasantly. "Can you swear that such a hoax was utterly impossible?"

Farham shrugged. "The words *utterly impossible* don't exist, in my vocabulary."

"Nor in mine," said Burke. "Suppose, for instance, it could be proved that Dora Evans didn't kill her husband. Then what?"

Farham's nostrils twitched. "You're joking!"

Burke opened his briefcase and took out an ancient, yellowed newspaper. "Here," he said. "Read it."

Farham's eyes fixed themselves on Burke. "What?" said Farham sharply. "What is it?"

"Philadelphia paper, dated 1859," said Burke. "With the news that Dora Evans was innocent."

"How can it—" Farham stopped in mid-sentence, with his jaws open and his head tilted, as if a sudden, paralyzing force had struck him.

"Better read it," Burke said. "Second column on the left."

Farham took the paper. He spoke between short, quick breaths. " 'Miscarriage of justice,' " he read. " 'Hans Hoven, former gardener to the late Charles Evans, of King Street, was fatally wounded in a street brawl last night. Before expiring, Mr. Hoven admitted slaying his employer six years ago and then feigning intoxication, with the result that the late Mrs. Dora Evans was accused of the crime and later convicted.' "

"You see the dilemma?" said Burke. "If Mrs. Prior was really the reincarnation of Dora Evans, Mrs. Prior would have known the truth. So how could she repeat a crime she never committed?"

Farham licked his lips. His fingers touched the paper gingerly, and a dry, shredded tatter fell loose. He studied the rest of the paper intently, to assure himself it was authentic. When he placed it carefully on the desk, he had regained his usual aplomb.

"Quite a problem, isn't it?" he drawled. "But you see, I'm only a dentist."

Burke gave Drobney a slight, barely perceptible nod. The lieutenant was poker-faced, and Burke reached out and touched a button on his desk. A moment later the door opened and Lucy Prior came in.

At sight of Farham, her face lit up and she stopped short. For a long, cryptic moment, she and Farham stared at each other without speaking. Then, very slowly, Farham stood up and smiled. As if she had caught a signal, her whole expression changed and she stepped forward.

"Dr. Farham," she said, in her softest, gentlest tones, "don't take it so hard. I'm sorry my poor psyche made so much trouble for you. If only we hadn't gone on with those awful experiments."

"Yes," he said. "I'm afraid I was playing with things I knew nothing about."

She smiled understandingly. "How could you guess that a tragedy of a hundred years ago would still contain its poison?"

"The poison," Burke observed coldly, "has been somewhat diluted."

She gave Burke a quick, darting glance of suspicion. He indicated the newspaper lying on the desk. "Better read that," he added. "For an antidote."

She approached the desk warily, picked up the newspaper and read. Suddenly she clapped her hand to her mouth. "Miles!" she gasped. "You fool! I told you we'd never—"

She froze, breathless, with her mouth open and her eyes blank with the horror of the words she'd just uttered.

Hours later, Burke returned to his office. Drobney, wiping the sweat from his forehead, followed him and closed the door.

"That was quite a session," he said. "They were a tough pair to crack."

Burke sat down wearily and stretched out his legs. "I'd sure like to see the commissioner when he finds out how she explained that blur we were so worried about." Burke chuckled. "Not a blur, but a burp."

"Yeah," said Drobney. "All that scotch Prior drank, why wouldn't he get the hiccups?" He closed his eyes dreamily. "Too bad, in a way, she's going to fry. Pretty, nice build. She was doing all right until you got your big break, in Philadelphia."

"I make my own breaks," said Burke. "I had that paper printed up. Special type fonts, paper treated chemically to make it look old. They did a nice job on it, too."

"It was faked?" Drobney said in surprise. "You faked it?" He let out a roar of laughter. "No wonder you looked so scared when Farham examined the newspaper. Scared he'd notice it was a phoney, huh?"

Burke shook his head. "Oh, no, I wasn't worried about that. What I was scared of is that Farham would say, So what?—the only thing Hans' confession proved was Dora Evans had waited a hundred years for the chance to kill her husband. How would I have answered that one?"

"But Farham didn't say it, so why worry?" Drobney stared at Burke, and added, "Well? Something else bothering you?"

Burke nodded. "Yes," he said. "Dora Evans. Do you think she really killed her husband? She never confessed, so maybe I *was* right, maybe the gardener committed the murder. But—" Burke sighed deeply. "But did he? *Did* he?"

# Not a Laughing Matter

## by Evan Hunter

**H**e hated the manager most.

Last night he had come to that realization. This morning, as he entered the department store with the Luger tucked into the waistband of his trousers, he allowed his hatred for the manager to swell up blackly until it smothered all the other hatreds he felt. The manager knew; of that he was certain. And it was his knowledge, this smirking, sneering, patronizing knowledge which fed the hatred, nurtured it, caused it to rise like dark yeast, bubbling, boiling.

The Luger was a firm metal assurance against his belly.

The gun had been given to him in the good days, in Vienna, by an admirer. In the good days, there had been many admirers, and many gifts. He could remember the good days. The good days would sometimes come back to him with fiercely sweet nostalgia, engulfing him in waves and waves of painful memories. He could remember the lights, and the applause, and . . .

"Good morning, Nick."

The voice, the hated voice.

He stopped abruptly. "Good morning, Mr. Atkins," he said.

Atkins was smiling. The smile was a thin curl on his narrow face, a thin bloodless curl beneath the ridiculously tenuous mustache on the cleaving edge of the hatchet face. The manager's hair was black, artfully combed to conceal a balding patch. He wore a gray pin stripe suit. Like a caricature of all store managers everywhere, he wore a carnation in his buttonhole. He continued smilling. The smile was infuriating.

"Ready for the last act?" he asked.

"Yes, Mr. Atkins."

"It is the last act, isn't it, Nick?" Atkins asked smiling. "Final curtain comes down today, doesn't it? All over after today. Everything reverts back to normal after today."

"Yes, Mr. Atkins," he said. "Today is the last act."

"But no curtains calls, eh, Nick?"

His name was not Nick. His name was Randolph Blair, a name

320

that had blazed across the theatre marquees of four continents. Atkins knew this, and had probably known it the day he'd hired him.
He knew it, and so the "Nick" was an additional barb, a reminder
of his current status, a sledgehammer subtlety that shouted, "Lo,
how the mighty have fallen!"

"My name is not Nick," he said flatly.

Atkins snapped his fingers. "That's right, isn't it? I keep forgetting. What is it again? Randolph Something? Clair? Flair? Shmair?
What is your name, Nick?"

"My name is Randolph Blair," he said. He fancied he said it with
great dignity. He fancied he said it the way Hamlet would have
announced that he was Prince of Denmark. He could remember the
good days when the name Randolph Blair was the magic key to a
thousand cities. He could remember hotel clerks with fluttering
hands, maitre d's hovering, young girls pulling at his clothing, even
telephone operators suddenly growing respectful when they heard
the name. Randolph Blair. In his mind, the name was spelled in
lights. Randolph Blair. The lights suddenly flickered, and then
dimmed. He felt the steel outline of the Luger against his belly. He
smiled thinly.

"You know my name, don't you, Mr. Atkins?"

"Yes," Atkins said. "I know your name. I hear it sometimes."

His interest was suddenly piqued. "Do you?" he asked.

"Yes, I hear people ask, every now and then, 'Say, whatever happened to Randolph Blair?' I know your name."

He felt Atkins' dart pierce his throat, felt the poison spread into
his bloodstream. *Whatever happened to Randolph Blair?* A comedian
had used the line on television not two weeks before, bringing down
the house. Randolph Blair, the ever-popular Randolph Blair. A nothing now, a nobody, a joke for a television comic. A forgotten name,
a forgotten face. But Atkins would remember. For eternity he would
remember Randolph Blair's name and the face and terrible power.

"Don't . . ." he started, and then stopped abruptly.

"Don't what?"

"Don't . . . don't push me too far, Mr. Atkins."

"*Push you*, Nick?" Atkins asked innocently.

"Stop that 'Nick' business!"

"Excuse me, Mr. Blair," Atkins said. "Excuse me. I forgot who I
was talking to. I thought I was talking to an old drunk who'd managed to land himself a temporary job . . ."

"Stop it!"

" . . . for a few weeks, I forgot I was talking to Randolph Blair, *the* Randolph Blair, *the* biggest lush in . . . "

"I'm not a drunk!" he shouted.

"You're a drunk, all right," Atkins said. "Don't tell me about drunks. My father was one. A falling-down drunk. A screaming, hysterical drunk. I grew up with it, Nick. I watched the old man fight his imaginary monsters, killing my mother inch by inch. So don't tell me about drunks. Even if the newspapers hadn't announced your drunkenness to the world, I'd have spotted you as being a lush."

"Why'd you hire me?" he asked.

"There was a job to be filled, and I thought you could fill it."

"You hired me so you could needle me."

"Don't be ridiculous," Atkins said.

"You made a mistake. You're needling the wrong person."

"Am I?" Atkins asked blindly. "Are you one of these tough drunks? Aggressive? My father was a tough drunk in the beginning. He could lick any man in the house. The only thing he couldn't lick was the bottle. When things began crawling out of the walls, he wasn't so tough. He was a screaming, crying baby then, running to my mother's arms. Are you a tough drunk, Nick? Are you?"

"I'm not a drunk!" he said. "I haven't touched a drop since I got this job. You know that!"

"Why? Afraid it would hurt your performance?" Atkins laughed harshly. "That never seemed to bother you in the old days."

"Things are different," he said. "I want . . . I want to make a comeback. I . . . I took this job because . . . I wanted the feel again, the feel of working. You shouldn't needle me. You don't know what you're doing."

"Me? Needle you? Now, Nick, Nick, don't be silly. I gave you the job, didn't I? Out of all the other applicants, I chose you. So, why should I needle you? That's silly, Nick."

"I've done a good job," he said, hoping Atkins would say the right thing, the right words that would crush the hatred. "You know I've done a good job."

"Have you?" Atkins asked. "I think you've done a lousy job, Nick. As a matter of fact, I think you *always* did a lousy job. I think you were one of the worst actors who ever crossed a stage."

And in that moment, Atkins signed his own death warrant.

All that day, as he listened to stupid requests and questions, as he sat in his chair and the countless faces pressed toward him, he thought of killing Atkins. He did his job automatically, presenting his smiling face to the public, but his mind was concerned only with the mechanics of killing Atkins.

It was something like learning a part.

Over and over again, he rehearsed each step in his mind. The store would close at five tonight. The employees would be anxious to get home to their families. This had been a trying, harrowing few weeks, and tonight it would be over, and the employees would rush into the streets and into the subways and home to waiting loved ones. A desperate wave of rushing self-pity flooded over him. *Who are my loved ones?* he asked silently. *Who is waiting for me tonight?*

Someone was talking to him. He looked down, nodding.

"Yes, yes," he said mechanically. "And what else?"

The person kept talking. He half-listened, nodding all the while, smiling, smiling.

There had been many loved ones in the good days. Women, more women than he could count. Rich women, and young women, and jaded women, and fresh young girls. Where had he been ten years ago at this time? California? Yes, of course, the picture deal. How strange it had seemed to be in a land of sunshine at that time of the year. And he had blown the picture. He had not wanted to, he had not wanted to at all. But he'd been hopelessly drunk for . . . how many days? And you can't shoot a picture when the star doesn't come to the set.

The star.

Randolph Blair.

Tonight, he would be a star again. Tonight, he would accomplish the murder of Atkins with style and grace. When they closed the doors of the store, when the shoppers left, when the endless questions, the endless repeats stopped, he would go to Atkins' office. He would not even change his clothes. He would go straight to Atkins' office and he would collect his pay envelope and he would shoot him. He would run into the streets then. In the streets, he would be safe. In the streets, Randolph Blair—the man whose face was once known to millions—would be anonymously safe. The concept was ironical. It appealed to a vestige of humor somewhere deep within him. Randolph Blair would tonight play the most important role of his career, and he would play it anonymously.

Smiling, chuckling, he listened to the requests.

The crowd began thinning out at about four-thirty. He was exhausted by that time. The only thing that kept him going was the knowledge that he would soon kill Mr. Atkins.

At four forty-five, he answered his last request. Sitting alone then, a corpulent unsmiling man, he watched the clock on the wall. Four fifty. Four fifty-two. Four fifty-seven. Four fifty-nine.

He got off the chair and waddled to the elevator banks. The other employees were tallying the cash register receipts, anxious to get out of the store. He buzzed for the elevator and waited.

The doors slid open. The elevator operator smiled automatically.

"All over, huh?" he asked.

"Yes, it's all over," Blair said.

"Going to pick up your envelope? Cashier's office?"

"Mr. Atkins pays me personally," he said.

"Yeah? How come?"

"He wanted it that way," he answered.

"Maybe he's hoping you'll be good to him, huh?" the operator said, and he burst out laughing.

He did not laugh with the operator. He knew very well why Atkins paid him personally. He did it so that he would have the pleasure each week of handing Randolph Blair—a man who had once earned $3,000 in a single week—a pay envelope containing forty-nine dollars and thirty-two cents.

"Ground floor then?" the operator asked.

"Yes. Ground floor."

When the elevator stopped, he got out of it quickly. He walked directly to Atkins' office. The secretary-receptionist was already gone. He smiled grimly, went to Atkins' door, and knocked on it.

"Who is it?" Atkins asked.

"Me," he said. "Blair."

"Oh, Nick. Come in, come in," Atkins said.

He opened the door and entered the office.

"Come for your pay?" Atkins asked.

"Yes."

He wanted to pull the Luger now and begin firing. He waited. Tensely, he waited.

"Little drink, first, Nick?" Atkins asked.

"No," he said.

"Come on, come on. Little drink never hurt anybody."

"I don't drink," he said.

"My father used to say that."

"I'm not your father."

"I know," Atkins said. "Come on, have a drink. It won't hurt you. Your job's over now. Your *performance* is over." He underlined the word smirkingly. "You can have a drink. Everyone'll be taking a little drink tonight."

"No."

"Why not? I'm trying to be friendly. I'm trying to . . . "

Atkins stopped. His eyes widened slightly. The Luger had come out from beneath Blair's coat with considerable ease. He stared at the gun.

"Wh . . . what's that?" he said.

"It's a gun," Blair answered coldly. "Give me my pay."

Atkins opened the drawer quickly. "Certainly. Certainly. You didn't think I was . . . was going to cheat you, did you? You . . . "

"Give me my pay."

Atkins put the envelope on the desk. Blair picked it up.

"And here's yours," he said, and he fired three times, watching. Atkins collapsed on the desk.

The enormity of the act rattled him. The door. The door. He had to get to it. The wastepaper basket tripped him up, sent him lunging forward, but his flailing arms got him a measure of balance and kept him from going down.

He checked his flight before he had gone very far into the store. Poise, he told himself. Control. Remember you're Randolph Blair.

The counters were already protectively concealed by dust-sheets. They reminded him of a body, covered, dead. Atkins.

Though he bolted again, he had enough presence of mind this time to duck into a rest room.

He was unaware of how long he had remained there, but when he emerged it was evident he had completely collected himself. His walk suggested the regal, or the confident calm of an actor sure of his part. And as he walked, he upbraided himself for having behaved like a juvenile suddenly overwhelmed by stage fright.

Randolph Blair pushed through the revolving doors. There was a sharp bite to the air, the promise of snow. He took a deep breath, calmly surveyed the people hurrying along, their arms loaded with packages.

And suddenly he heard laughter, a child's thin, piercing laugh. It cut into him like a knife. He turned and saw the laughing boy, tethered by one hand to the woman beside him, the boy's pale face, his arm and forefinger pointing upwards, pointing derisively.

More laughter arose. The laughter of men, of women. A festive carousel, in the show window to one side of him, started up. Its music blared. It joined in the laughter, underscoring, counterpointing the laughter.

Blair felt caught in a punishing whirlpool. There seemed no way he could stop the souound, movement, everything that conspired to batter him.

Then the sight of policemen coming out of the store was completely unnerving. They appeared to be advancing toward him. And as he pulled the Luger on them, and even as he was overpowered and disarmed, a part of his mind felt that this was all unreal, all part of a dramatic role which he was playing.

But it was not a proper part for one wearing the red coat and trousers, the black belt and boots of a department store Santa Claus, the same clothes three thousand other men in the city were wearing. To blend into their anonymity, he lacked only a white beard, and he had lost his in the frantic exit he had made from Atkins' office.

And of course to a child—and even to some adults—a Santa Claus minus a beard might be a laughing matter.

# The Graft Is Green

## by Harold Q. Masur

When a judge, a federal judge yet, calls on the phone, sounding urgent, and says please come to his home that evening, you go. You do not make excuses, especially if you are a lawyer practicing in the same district.

His Honor, Judge Edwin Marcus Bolt, U.S. District Judge, a lifetime appointment, fifteen years with a Wall Street firm, twenty years on the bench, was tall, spare, iron-haired, and physically fit. Twice married, his present spouse was a cool, slender beauty of thirty, exactly half his age.

Judge Bolt was currently presiding over a case that commanded daily headlines: The United States versus Ira Madden and Amalgamated Mechanics, for misappropriation of union funds to the tune of one million American dollars; misappropriation—a euphemism for stealing, embezzling, the larcenous juggling of books—with Ira Madden, union president, as chief malefactor and prime beneficiary. The authorities had not yet been able to locate the proceeds, although they had certain suspicions. In the past year Madden had made several trips to Switzerland, probably visiting his money.

So that evening, obeying the judge's summons, I took a cab to his East Side town house. I saw that he had a number of visitors ahead of me, leaving their cars parked alongside the curb in direct violation of parking regulations. None of the vehicles, of course, would be ticketed. No meter maid in her right mind would tag a police car.

I should have forgotten the whole deal and walked away, but curiosity needled me. The man in blue guarding the front door put a hand against my chest. I told him why I was there and he convoyed me to an upstairs corridor.

Sergeant Louis Wienick, swarthy, heavyset, bald, lifted a spiky eyebrow and shook his head. "Well, well! Scott Jordan. Wherever there's trouble. What cooks, counselor?"

"I was invited."

"By whom?"

"Judge Edwin Marcus Bolt."

"When?"

"This afternoon."

"What for?"

"I don't know. He called and said he wanted to see me. Urgent. So here I am. Where is His Honor?"

"In his study." Wienick gestured theatrically. "This door. Be my guest."

I should have known—but it always comes as a surprise. Judge Bolt was sitting behind his desk, smiling. The smile was purely technical, lips pulled back in rigor over porcelain dentures. His face was tissue-gray, eyes blank and sightless, staring into the far distance of eternity. A single bullet had pierced his right temple, plowing through the jellied matter of his brain and emerging over his left ear. I should have known because Wienick, after all, was Homicide. Why else would he be here if someone's exit had not been accelerated through violent means?

My stomach convulsed like a fist and I got the hell out of there. Wienick's grin was more or less genuine.

"Well, what do you make of it?" he asked.

"Contact wound," I said. "Somebody didn't trust his marksmanship. He walked right up close and pulled the thing. I believe I saw powder burns at the point of entry."

"You said, 'He walked up close.' How do you know it's a he? Maybe it was a she."

"Maybe. Manner of speaking, that's all."

"You know the judge's wife?"

"Met her once."

"The rumor is they were feuding. Seems she occasionally strayed from the fireside for a little extracurricular activity."

"I don't listen to rumors, sergeant."

"Yeah. Anyway, this one knocks the props out from under the U.S. against Ira Madden."

"Not likely," I said. "They'll declare a mistrial, naturally, and then start all over again."

"So the taxpayer gets clobbered again. All that time and money down the drain."

"A drop in the bucket, sergeant. Look how much we waste on wars, on hardware lobbed into space. Look how much we pay farmers not to grow things."

"You a Communist or something?"

"Hardly. What cooks with this shooting? Are there any clues?"

"Not yet. We only caught the squeal about an hour ago. The M.E. hasn't even arrived yet."

"Who notified you?"

"The widow."

"She contribute anything?"

"Only a couple of sentences. Said she'd been to a late movie and found him like this when she came home. Then she began to get hysterical, running around like a chicken, accusing union goons. A truly magnificent performance. Then her doctor rushed in. He got a hammerlock on her and used his needle. Must have been one hell of a blast. In two minutes she was horizontal. She's in her bedroom now, sleeping it off."

"Any servants?"

"One. Housekeeper. This is her day off."

"So the judge was all alone when it happened."

"Alone except for one other person—his executioner."

"You're really clicking today, sergeant. Any sign of the weapon?"

"Who'd be stupid enough to leave a piece that can be traced?"

"Have you searched the house?"

It got me a long-suffering look. "Up, down and sideways. Nothing." But his eyes seemed evasive.

"Come on, sergeant," I said. "Lift the lid."

"You clairvoyant or something?"

"I can tell when you're sitting on something."

"Keep your nose clean, counselor. This is police business. The lieutenant would skin me alive."

"Where is the lieutenant?"

"Convention. Philadelphia."

"We always pool our information. You know that. So, please, sergeant, lay it out for me."

Wienick lapsed into a small private huddle. He worked his lips for a moment, but finally he sighed, shrugged, and said, "On the other side of the judge's study is a bedroom. Adjoining door. Cigarette smoke in there, a lot of it. Not stale. And many butts in the ashtray. The assassin was sitting in there, waiting for him to come home."

"Not the judge's butts?"

"The judge smoked only cigars." Wienick looked piously down his nose. "Genuine Havanas. I hear he bought them from a Swedish diplomat."

"The wife's butts maybe?"

"She quit smoking when the Surgeon General made his announcement, she says. The doctor verifies it. But hell, that's not conclusive. Somebody gets uptight—back to the old habits."

"You're too eager, sergeant, straining to tag the wife for this."

"We don't have anybody else."

"What about Ira Madden and his union muscle? Or outside talent for hire? Would it be the first time those clowns tried to break up a trial?"

"It's a possibility, sure, and we'll check it out. We'll have help, too. With a U.S. judge involved, maybe the FBI will stick its nose in." Wienick showed me his teeth, like the yellowed keyboard of an old piano. "Those boys will not take kindly to the meddling of a local mouthpiece."

"I am not a mouthpiece, sergeant. I am a high-class attorney and counselor-at-law."

"I beg your pardon."

"Granted. I am not meddling. The judge initiated this visit. He was worried about something and he wanted to see me."

"He had reason to be worried. So what are your plans now?"

"Maybe I'll just go home and forget about it."

"That would be a very wise decision. Still, the lieutenant may want to see you when he gets back."

"The lieutenant knows my number. I'm in town for the duration." I paused at the door and waved. "Happy hunting, sergeant."

The sudden and violent demise of Judge Edwin Marcus Bolt was too late for the evening paper—not plural; singular. A city like New York—eight million people—and only one evening newspaper; all the others had folded. Bad management? Excessive union demands? Who knows? But the morning papers—and only two of those—bannered it big, with editorials. Nobody had the answers.

Then, early in the afternoon, I had another call—from the widow this time. Could I please come over for a family conference? The judge's daughter from his first marriage and her husband would be there. But please come a little early. The widow would like a few moments alone with me.

Laura Bolt, nee Pederson, a tall blonde Scandinavian type, at nineteen a cover girl in great demand by leading fashion photographers, at twenty-eight the bride of a highly respected jurist, at thirty a widow, had large blue eyes set at a wide tilt, gaunted cheekbones, flawless fine-grained translucent skin, perfect teeth nervously working on her fingernails. Impatiently she brushed aside the amenities and expression of condolence.

"I need your help, Mr. Jordan."

"To do what?"

"The police have made it quite clear that they consider me a prime suspect. I don't like it and I'm frightened. I need legal advice. I need a lawyer. I know that my husband thought very highly of you. In the twenty-four hours before he died he mentioned your name several times. I am asking you to represent me."

"Did you kill your husband?"

"No," she said emphatically.

"All right." So I was back in the case whether the enforcement people liked it or not. I said, "They haven't accused you openly yet, have they?"

"Mr. Jordan, they went through everything in this house, with special attention to my bedroom and my possessions. I know they were looking for a weapon. I reiterate, I am innocent. I admit that Edwin and I were not getting along, but we still had our good moments. I liked being married to him; I liked the distinction. A judge and his lady perch high up on the social scale. A judge's position is—how shall I phrase it . . . ?"

"Sacrosanct?"

"To outsiders, yes. There is something awesome in those black robes, sitting on the bench, sentencing people. However," she made a fluttering gesture, "I hate to say this, but sometimes it's all hypocrisy and sham."

"How do you mean?"

"I have a suspicion that Edwin just may have tainted his honor."

"In what way?"

"He was in trouble. Very deep trouble. I believe that is why he wanted to see you."

"Please. What kind of trouble?"

"Bribery." It soured her mouth. "They say he took money. He was being investigated."

"By whom?"

"The Justice Department."

"Whose money?"

"Ira Madden's. The union man who is under prosecution in Edwin's courtroom."

"How do you know?"

"Edwin told me. He was upset, brooding, agitated. We were having one of our good moments together and he confided in me. He desperately needed to confide in someone. I was shocked. I do not know what evidence they have or where they got it, but if Edwin were innocent, if the charges had no substance, I cannot believe that he would have been so troubled. My husband, Mr. Jordan, was a terribly tortured man—and there was nothing I could do about it."

I pondered the revelation. Could it possibly be true? A man of Judge Bolt's position, his stature, accepting a bribe? What would be the *quid pro quo*? Well, a judge presiding over a trial carries considerable clout. The payoff could be a very handsome quid for the quo. In myriad ways he can influence the proceedings—by his attitude, facial expressions, biased rulings, and ultimately a prejudiced charge. But Judge Edwin Marcus Bolt involved in such paltry shenanigans? One never knows. Money is a powerful persuader. They say that every man has his price—just make it big enough. The union coffers were bulging, and Ira Madden certainly didn't want to be shipped over. Maybe they had threatened the good judge, frightened him into compliance.

"Question," I said. "Did you personally ever see the judge in the company of anyone from Amalgamated Mechanics?"

"Edwin was not an idiot, Mr. Jordan. Whatever else, not an idiot. He would never have openly consorted with anyone even remotely connected with a defendant on trial in his courtroom."

"You want me to help you, Mrs. Bolt?"

"Of course."

"Then please lay it out for me, everything you know. Was the judge secretly in contact with those people?"

Strain lines deepened around her mouth. She put a thumb knuckle between her teeth. She walked away and peered out the window. She came back. Her voice was low. "Edwin is dead. I have to protect his reputation."

"Be concerned about your own. Nothing will bother him now. To get you off the hook, we may have to elect another suspect."

She thought about it and then nodded slowly. "Last Sunday, in the afternoon, Edwin was here in the house, working with Andy—"

"Just a moment. Andy who?"

"Andrew Stock, his law clerk."

"All right. Continue."

"They had brought some legal reports from the library and they did not want to be disturbed. So they disconnected the phone in the study. Any calls came in, I took them in my bedroom."

"You and the judge had separate bedrooms?"

"Yes. Edwin was a long-standing insomniac; a nighttime reader, a floor pacer. As it happens, I'm a very light sleeper, awake and up at the slightest sound. Well, you know how it is, a lady needs her beauty sleep. Edwin knew that and was sympathetic, so separate bedrooms was his suggestion."

"All right," I said. "On the Sunday in question, you were available to answer the telephone."

"Yes. Only one call. Male. He wanted to talk to the judge. I tried to fob him off, told him the judge was busy, but he was adamant. He kept insisting, finally gave me a name and demanded I pass it on."

"What name?"

"Oster—Floyd Oster. Does it ring a bell?"

"It rings. Floyd Oster is one of Ira Madden's lieutenants at Amalgamated Mechanics. Did you pass it along to your husband?"

"Yes."

"In Andrew Stock's hearing?"

"Well, Andy wears a hearing aid which he keeps turned off unless he's directly involved in a conversation. I do not know whether or not he heard."

"What did your husband do?"

"He went into the adjoining bedroom and took the call in private."

Not good, I decided; stupid, in fact. The judge should have flatly refused any contact, avoiding even the faintest taint of impropriety—at best, an indiscretion; at worst, a serious breach. Folly or greed had adulterated his judgment.

The bell rang and she went to the door. She came back with her stepdaughter and husband.

One did not have to be an astute observer to read Carol Denby. She was a demanding, frivolous type, with thin lips, dissatisfied eyes and fussy, constantly moving hands. Dressed in black, her eyes were red-rimmed from a night of mourning. Her father had been a very handsome man. Some aberrant chromosome must have produced this highly unappetizing creature. She did nothing to conceal her attitude toward Laura Bolt, and one could sense that her dislike was monumentally reciprocated.

Her husband, Clive Denby, insurance agent, was a plump, smug, humorless man, scented and pomaded and nattily dressed in a shaped suit of knitted acrylic.

He was curt with Mrs. Bolt, but solicitous of his wife, and he immediately took the floor as spokesman for the team.

"I understand, Mr. Jordan, you came to see my father-in-law last night."

"That's right."

"Would you tell me why?"

"Because he asked me."

"Do you know what he wanted?"

"I didn't then. I do now."

He put his hands on his hips. "Well?"

This kind of imperious behavior always gets my back up and turns me stubborn. "Sorry, Denby. It was a confidential matter. If the judge had wanted you to know, he would have confided in you."

"The judge is dead. That wipes the slate clean on privileged communications between lawyer-client, doctor-patient, everybody."

"Dead wrong. You don't know what you're talking about. Besides, the rule doesn't apply here, since the judge never retained me, formally or otherwise."

He curled a lip. "Ha! You never spoke to the judge. How would you know what he wanted to see you about?"

"Mrs. Bolt told me."

Carol Denby wheeled toward her stepmother and demanded in a shrill voice, "Why did Daddy want to see a lawyer?"

"Let me handle this, dear," her husband said. "All right, Laura, we have every right to know. What's this all about?"

"I can't tell you without my lawyer's permission."

"Lawyer? Who's your lawyer?"

"Scott Jordan."

He threw his arms up. "Why do you need a lawyer?"

"Because I'm under suspicion and you damn well know it because you made it perfectly clear to the police last night that Edwin and I were having difficulties."

"Well, it's the truth, isn't it?"

"The situation was not that bad. You put the worst possible face on it. As a matter of fact, Clive, the way you act I believe you think I'm guilty."

"Does the shoe fit, Laura?"

"Drop dead!" She spat it out and stormed furiously out of the room.

Denby was pleased with himself. He looked at me and said, "Are you going to defend her if she's charged?"

"It hasn't come to that yet. Maybe enough evidence for an indictment won't be found."

"My father-in-law's gun is missing. Who else but Laura would know where he kept it?"

*A new wrinkle.* "The judge owned a gun?"

"Yes. A Colt .32 automatic."

"The police know about that?"

"Of course. I told them." He folded his arms across his chest. "You haven't answered my question. Will you defend her?"

"Defending people accused of a crime is my business."

"That's a scrubby kind of business, wouldn't you say?"

A less civilized man might have loosened a few of the man's teeth but I just shook my head pityingly. It bothered him and he switched the baleful glance to his wife. "We're wasting time on this character. Let's get out of here, Carol."

"Why should *we* leave?" she said, her tone surly. "I have as much right in this house as anyone."

"That depends on the judge's will," I told her sweetly. "For all you know, he may have left the house to his wife."

The very notion changed her expression to one of alarm and confusion. "Oh, no! I was brought up here. That can't be possible. Clive, what is the man saying?"

He gave me a nasty look. "I suppose you expect to probate the will, too."

"That's up to the executor," I said. "Whoever is named in the will."

"We may have to contest it."

"On what grounds? Undue influence? That he was *non compos mentis*?"

Carol Denby snapped, "He certainly could not have been in full possession of all his wits when he married that creature."

"You'd be wasting your time and your money. Too many people knew the judge as a shrewd, levelheaded jurist."

"He was obsessed by that woman. Mesmerized. She had a ring in his nose"

There is a limit to my endurance, and I'd had enough. Without a word, I turned on my heel and headed for the door, knowing they would follow shortly after. Neither that house, nor any other, regardless of size, was large enough to hold Laura Bolt and the Denbys.

Outside, I glanced at my watch. The afternoon was still young. Much as I dislike the subway, it is the only means of rapid transit that Manhattan has to offer.

The U.S. Courthouse on Foley Square is a tall, antiseptic building, more functional than distinctive. I consulted the hall directory and then rode an elevator up to the chambers of Judge Edwin Marcus Bolt. His law clerk, Andrew Stock, was in the anteroom. Stocky, somewhere in his middle thirties, he had a Pekingese face, colorless hair, and bifocals that magnified his eyes.

He looked apathetic, forlorn and cheerless; and why not? Any new appointment to the bench would certainly insist upon a law assistant of his own choice. Mr. Andrew Stock's job was in serious jeopardy.

He saw me coming through the door and turned up his hearing aid.

I knew him as a fairly competent researcher who found it easier to concentrate on legal complexities with all auditory distractions eliminated, which gave him a chance to put his hearing defect to good advantage. Having tried a case before Judge Bolt only seven months ago, my identity was familiar to Stock.

I commiserated on the death of his sponsor and divulged my connection with the case. He nodded morosely.

"Yes, I knew the judge had called you. As a matter of fact, it was I who dialed your number. We had discussed various alternatives when the trouble arose."

"The bribery investigation?"

He blinked through his bifocals. His tongue rimmed his lips. "You know about that? I thought he was already dead when you reached his home."

"His wife informed me. Was there any substance to the charge?"

He started a denial, then swallowed it and shrugged. "I don't know. I just don't know. It's hard to believe, but I'm afraid I have to admit it's possible."

"Ira Madden of Amalgamated Mechanics?"

"One of his men, yes. Acting on Madden's behalf."

"Floyd Oster?"

Stock nodded. "He's the one."

"So you think it's possible the judge succumbed."

He slowly nodded. "Yes, I do."

"Why?"

"Because the investigation had him on edge. I never saw him so nervous. If they had the goods on him, you know what it meant. Disgrace. Drummed off the bench. Perhaps imprisoned. Loss of income. Everything gone. All the years wasted."

"Was he delivering?"

"I don't know. I do not attend court sessions."

"And if he failed to deliver?"

"Would he take their money and then double-cross them? Do you play games with those boys?"

"Have you heard rumors about the trial?"

"Yes. He and the prosecutor were feuding."

"Then the judge may have been fulfilling his contract. Nevertheless, the judge is dead. How do you like Mrs. Bolt as a candidate?"

"That was not a good marriage. You see, the judge used to work at home a lot. We did our research here, but most of the jury charges and decisions were written at the house. I was often there to help him. He had a small desk installed in the bedroom for me, so that he could have seclusion in the study. Sometimes Mrs. Bolt would join him there for an argument, and I could catch it if my hearing aid was on," Stock said.

"What did they argue about?"

"Money, mostly. Or sometimes the late hours she kept. She was a compulsive spender, that woman. When the bills came in at the end of the month, he'd hit the ceiling. She spent the stuff like it was going out of style."

*So the judge needed money,* I thought, *and maybe Ira Madden's offer looked attractive.* "I understand he had a gun."

"That's right, permit and all."

"Why a gun? After all, the man was a respected citizen. He didn't travel around with jewelry samples. He didn't use it for hunting, not a hand piece."

"It was a hobby. Target practice; he had a range in the basement. He knew how to handle the thing, a first-rate marksman. It had a practical aspect, too. Several of the convicts he'd shipped over had made threats on his life, promised to ventilate him when they were released. That's how he got the permit."

I wondered if the police knew about that and were checking the federal penitentiaries. "What are your own plans now, Mr. Stock?"

He looked dejected. "I don't know. It's too late for me to start a private practice. Besides, I don't have any clients, prospective or otherwise." He eyed me hopefully. "Do you need a good research man?"

"I'll keep you in mind. And I'll ask around."

It seemed to cheer him a little. He gave me a weak smile and raised his hand as I went through the door.

Outside, I patronized a telephone booth and got through to Sergeant Wienick at Homicide. He was not overjoyed to hear my voice. I asked about the autopsy.

"All finished, counselor. Instantaneous death from a bullet wound in the head. Second shot not necessary. A little bonus for the corpse. You want the whole pathology?"

"No sir. What's all this about a second shot?"

"Through the heart. You just didn't look closely enough. Or maybe the lack of blood threw you off."

"Please," I said, "elaborate."

"Hardly any blood at all on the judge's shirt. Figure it out yourself."

"Did you find any bullets?"

"Yep. One on the judge's desk and one lodged against his spine."

"What caliber?"

"Thirty-two automatic."

"Why an automatic?"

"Because an automatic ejects the shells and we found those too, counselor."

"I understand the judge owned a gun, also a .32 automatic."

"Correct. and we found it."

"Where?"

"Taped under the left rear fender of your client's car. We put the arm on her half an hour ago and she's been screaming for you ever since. Said she retained you this afternoon. Now why in hell would an innocent woman want a lawyer before she's even charged? Tell me that, hey? So we're doing a ballistics check and five will get you twenty the lady's gun shelved her husband."

"Motive," I said, "where's the motive?"

"Money, counselor, money. I don't know how the judge was fixed, but he took out an insurance policy only one month ago, five hundred thousand buckeroos, half a million. How does that grab you for motive?"

"Who's the beneficiary?"

"I haven't seen the policy, but who do you think?"

"It complicates matters," I said.

"No, sir, it simplifies them. Okay, counselor, I'm talking too much. The lieutenant says I suffer from a loose lip. So no more conversation. *Fini.* You're on the other side now. You want more conversation, talk to the district attorney. It's his baby now. So please get your educated carcass over here on the double. The judge's widow is hollering bloody murder. She wants her lawyer."

The receiver clicked and the line went dead.

Laura Bolt had not yet been processed and was still at the precinct house. She had been politely and judiciously handled, advised that she was entitled to counsel from the inception of custody, and she had refused all dialogue. She knew enough to keep her tongue disconnected, but in those surroundings she was out of her element, pale and strained. They allowed me a brief private session. My eyes encompassed the room in a broad sweep, searching for bugs, but of course nothing was obvious.

"Keep your voice low," I said. "What do you know about the gun?"

"I don't know anything about the gun."

"You knew the judge had one."

"Yes."

"Where did he keep it?"

"In the drawer of his bedside table." She shook her head, whispering fiercely. "But I didn't take it, I didn't use it, and I didn't hide it."

"Did your husband mention a new insurance policy?"

"Yes. He had borrowed heavily on his old one and there wasn't much equity in it. He wanted a new policy and he wanted to give Clive Denby the business."

"You know the amount?"

"Half a million dollars. He thought Clive could use the commission."

"Who is the beneficiary?"

"My husband's estate."

"Does he have a will?"

"Of course. He drafted it himself and Andy Stock typed it."

"Is it in his safe-deposit box?"

"I don't think so. I remember he told me that he kept most of his important papers locked in a file in his chambers at the courthouse. Just as safe as a bank, he said, and more easily accessible."

In a way, he was right. It was unlikely anyone would break into a federal courthouse to ransack a judge's chambers. Too, if he needed an important document at night, it would be available.

"If your husband named you as executrix in his will, would you want me to handle the probate?"

"Yes."

I took out a piece of paper and a pen, wrote out a brief retainer and had her sign it. She returned the pen and plucked at my sleeve.

"Are they going to lock me up for the night?"

"I'm afraid you'll have to remain in custody until the preliminary hearing."

"Then what happens to me?"

"You'll be bound over for action by the grand jury."

"Will they grant bail?"

"Not on a murder charge, I'm afraid."

Her eyes swam in quick moisture. "Oh, what are they trying to do to me?"

"Whatever it is," I said, "I'll try to stop it. But I have to get out in the field to help you. Now, you know the script. No statements. Button up and stay buttoned. Am I clear?"

She nodded, gulped, and smiled like a woman suffering from an attack of mumps.

A phone call to Judge Bolt's chambers caught Andrew Stock just as he was leaving for the day. I asked him if he remembered who had been appointed executor in the judge's will. He remembered. The judge's wife. I told him that she had retained me to handle probate. He had not yet heard about the arrest.

"Can you open the judge's confidential file?" I asked.

"Yes. I have a key."

"Good. I'd like to see the will and perhaps file it with the surrogate tomorrow morning. Please bring the will home with you and I'll pick it up later."

He said he would and he gave me his address. He seemed pitifully eager to cooperate with me.

Ira Madden, I knew, was out on bail. Naturally; only money was involved. Money can be replaced, but the big crime, murder, could never be undone. I realized that an attempt to see Madden, insulated by union retainers and isolated in a special apartment atop union headquarters, would be futile. The judge's demise, I suspected, had probably initiated festivities. They would be celebrating the declaration of a mistrial. Union lawyers knew that the longer a trial can be delayed, the harder it gets to convict.

So I decided on an alternative. A telephone directory gave me the address of Floyd Oster, Madden's hireling. I found it to be a renovated brownstone near Lincoln Center. By osmosis, perhaps, Floyd Oster might absorb a faint trace of culture. As I climbed to his apartment on the second floor, I realized that I had devised no approach, no campaign. I would have to play it by ear.

He answered the bell, a carp-faced, sulphurous and savage little man in a white T-shirt, holding an empty whisky bottle like a club.

"Mr. Oster?" I said.

"Who wants to know?"

"You probably never heard of me. The name is Jordan, Scott Jordan. I'm a lawyer, you see."

"I heard of you." From the sound it seemed as if someone had permanently ruined his larynx.

"Could we talk in private?"

"About what?"

"Ira Madden and Judge Edwin Marcus Bolt."

The carp face suddenly closed up completely; it went utterly blank. "The judge is dead."

"True. But Ira is still alive."

"And just where do you fit in?"

"The judge's widow has retained me."

"To do what?"

"Defend her in court. They think she killed her husband."

He smiled, if the mechanical distortion of that blade-thin mouth could be called a smile. "How about that?"

"I thought you might help."

"Yeah? How?"

"The judge's widow will have to get up a decent fee. I'd like to know where the money is."

"What money?"

"The money you paid Judge Bolt to throw Madden's trial."

He lowered his voice to a harsh whisper. "You lost your marbles, counselor? You off your rocker, making an accusation like that? You know what the penalty is for bribing a federal judge?"

"Not as heavy as the penalty for killing one."

"That's no skin off my nose, buster. Go defend your client."

"She's innocent."

"So prove it in court."

"I intend to, by showing who really did it."

It got through to him and a muscle started throbbing in his temple. "Get lost. If we bought the judge, why would we knock him off? You can't have it both ways. You can't—"

He clamped down on the rest of it because we suddenly had a pair of visitors mounting the stairs behind me. Two clean-cut, brush-cut, muscular all-American types joined us and politely inquired, "Floyd Oster?"

I pointed. "Him."

"And you, sir, who are you?"

"Just a visitor trying to get some information."

"Afraid you'll have to get in line, sir. We have a warrant for Floyd Oster's arrest." He flashed his wallet. "Federal Bureau of Investigation. The charge is bribery and corruption of a government official."

I edged sideways along the wall, anxious to avoid a crossfire if Oster were foolhardy enough to resist. But the boys were trained and highly efficient and in the single blink of an eye they had Floyd Oster by each arm and were hustling him toward the street so that his toes barely touched the stairs.

I followed them down and watched as they bundled him into a car and hauled him off. For all his bravado, I had a feeling that Oster would quickly melt under heat. Ira Madden's celebration was probably premature.

Suddenly it hit me that I was hungry. I had been cruising around the city all day, working, talking, ignoring the inner man, so I blew myself to a steak, with a large stein of beer.

Renewed, I sallied forth to take possession of Judge Bolt's last will and testament from his clerk, Andy Stock.

It was an old prewar building on Lex. A palsied self-service elevator took me to the fifth floor. The radio was playing some heavy classical music. I rang the bell and waited. I rang again and waited some more. I tried the knob and it turned and the door opened.

The music was appropriate—a volcano of sound from Richard Wagner. It fitted the scene. Somebody had taken a carving knife to Andrew Stock and opened his throat from ear to ear.

I almost lost my expensive steak.

No more problems for Mr. Stock, no worry about a new job; his life and his career and his dream were over. He had joined his late employer. I did not bother calling a doctor. There would be no point in wasting a doctor's time. What Andrew Stock needed was a mortician.

I saw his briefcase resting on the dresser. I anchored it with my elbow and maneuvered the zipper, leaving no prints. I had no reservations about lifting the document. A quick look informed me that, following a few specific bequests, the judge had divided his residual estate equally between wife and daughter. I refolded the will and tucked it away in my inside breast pocket.

Then I used Andrew Stock's telephone and called Sergeant Wienick. On hearing the latest bulletin, he had a few choice Anglo-Saxon words for me.

They had done what had to be done, all the technicians, the photographers, the fingerprint men, then the assistant medical examiner, and finally the basket boys for hauling the remains to the morgue.

Now Sergeant Wienick and I were on our way in a police car to see Carol and Clive Denby. I needed some information about the judge's insurance policy. Neither of the Denbys, I knew, would give me the right time, but with the sergeant to back me up they would probably cooperate.

Apparently the lid was off and Wienick had instructions. "Well, counselor," he said, "I spoke to the lieutenant, long-distance, and he told me to work with you in concord. So here it is. Ballistics finished their check. It locks it up for Mrs. Bolt. The bullets that killed her husband match the gun we took from her car, the grooves, the rate of pitch, the whole bit, micrometer accurate."

"I had no doubt they would."

"It doesn't worry you?"

"A little."

"And you know what else we found?"

"What?"

"A shoe box stuffed with money, large bills, fifty grand. The FBI thinks it's union money, they think the judge got it from Ira Madden."

"What clued them in?"

"They've had Madden under surveillance for over a year. They bugged his phone, heard incriminating talk. It led them to Floyd Oster and they picked him up."

"I know."

He lifted an eyebrow. "Who told you?"

"I was there."

He took it in stride. "Cash," he said. "Crazy. They must have been spreading it all over the lot. Even that Andrew Stock. Thirty-five hundred in brand-new fifties stuffed into a shoe in his closet. What's with the shoes these days? Don't these people trust banks?"

I had nothing to say to him. But my mind was racing. All the little jigsaw pieces were falling into a discernible pattern.

The Denbys greeted us without enthusiasm  In her nasal voice,

Carol Denby opened fire at once. "I heard on the radio that you arrested my stepmother. Is that true, Sergeant? Did you really?"

"It's true," he said.

"Good," she snapped with grim satisfaction. "I'm not surprised. I never trusted that woman from the first moment I met her. A vain, greedy piece of baggage after my father's money. I'm sorry only about one thing, that they've abolished capital punishment in this state. I hope you put her away for life at hard labor. A little sweat and humility would do her good."

Clive Denby said, "If Laura's guilty, we want to see her punished. Is there anything we can do to help, sergeant?"

"Jordan, here, has a few questions."

I got a look of poorly veiled disapproval. "Isn't this a little irregular, sergeant? Jordan represents the accused. He wants to exonerate her and you two most certainly would be working at cross-purposes."

"We just want to nail down all the facts, Mr. Denby."

He shrugged in a gesture of long-suffering forbearance. His eyes focused on me.

I said, "I understand you recently wrote a new life insurance policy for your father-in-law."

"Eight, nine months ago."

"For half a million dollars?"

"That is not an unusual amount for a man in his position."

"And you knew, of course, that his estate was named as the beneficiary?"

"Of course I knew."

"Were you also aware that under the terms of his will both his wife and his daughter would share equally in the proceeds of that policy?"

"He had so informed me."

"I take it that the policy was in force at the time of the judge's death?"

"Oh, yes. My father-in-law was meticulous about paying premiums. There were no arrears."

"Does the policy also contain that lovely clause providing double indemnity in the case of death by accident or violence?"

"It does."

Wienick's pursed lips emitted an awed whistle. "You mean the five hundred grand becomes one million because somebody put a bullet through the judge's skull?"

Accurate, but indelicate, especially in front of heirs, but par for the course with Wienick.

"That is true, sergeant." I turned back to Denby. "Is the policy nullified by suicide?"

"Yes. It is a standard provision in such contracts. Self-destruction cancels the policy."

"So if the judge knocked himself off, your wife gets nothing. Zero. She's out in the cold."

Carol Denby gasped. "That's a terrible thing to say. Only a deranged man would take his own life."

"So." I cocked an eye at her. "You yourself told me that your father must have been unbalanced when he married Laura."

"Now, wait a minute," Wienick broke in. "Hold on here, counselor. Let me get this straight. Are you intimating that nobody killed Judge Bolt, that we're whistling up a tree, that the man was a suicide?"

"I am not intimating," I said. "I am proclaiming it outright. The judge was not a homicide victim. He took his own gun, pointed it, pulled the trigger, and blew out his own brains."

Carol Denby gave a stricken cry, her hands a bowknot of distress at her throat.

Her husband said, his face simulating a look of lofty contempt, "This man is demented, sergeant. He has rocks in his head. He is utterly irresponsible."

Wienick's narrowed eyes searched mine. "How do you figure it, counselor?"

"Judge Bolt," I said, "was frightened unto death, scared spitless. He knew that he was under investigation for accepting a bribe. He knew too that he was guilty and that—"

"My father?" Carol Denby shrilled. "A bribe? What are you saying?"

"We found fifty thousand dollars cash in a shoe box," Wienick snapped. "Where the hell do you think he got it?"

Her hands were fluttering, her mouth spluttering. She subsided when her husband put a protective arm around her.

"When the boys began to move in on the judge," I said, "he knew the game was up. He was afraid the contact man, Floyd Oster, would make a deal and turn state's evidence. He did not need a crystal ball. He could see the future—disgrace and a prison sentence—staring at him. The pressure was too great. He could not face it. He was terrified and distraught, half out of his mind with despair. There was no way out—except one—and he took it. A bullet in his head."

"Come off it," Denby said. "You can't know that for a fact. If the judge killed himself, what happened to the gun?"

"You took it," I said.

*"What!"*

"You took it, Denby. You arrived at the house shortly after it happened. You went up to the study and you saw him sitting there, dead, and you knew what it meant. You could see that half a million dollars go down the drain. A terrible loss. So you acted. He had dropped the gun on the floor and you picked it up. You had to get out of there, but first, for insurance, to bolster the murder angle, you pumped another shot at him. Death by violence. Double indemnity, and double the ante. One million bucks."

A spasmodic twitch pulled at the juncture of Denby's jaw. "Slander," he said hoarsely. "In front of witnesses."

I laughed. "You've got a lot more to worry about than slander. And if you're talking about witnesses, hell yes, there was a witness."

Wienick's hand clamped over my arm. "A witness? Who?"

"Andrew Stock," I said. "The judge's law clerk. Stock saw it."

"How do you know?"

"Remember the cigarette butts? And the smoke? They were his. He was there, as usual, in the next room, the bedroom, working. He did not hear the first shot because his hearing aid was disconnected. Routine for him. But then, probably because he had found some rule of law or precedent he wanted to show the judge, he turned it on and headed for the study. That's when he heard the second shot. He peeked through the door and saw Denby, standing there with the gun. He never said a word. He was in shock. He backed away, thinking only of saving his own life. Maybe he even hid in a closet."

Clive Denby smiled, a hideous grimace. "Guesswork," he said. "All guesswork."

"It's a lot more than that, Denby. There was almost no blood from the second shot. Meaning the judge was already dead. That was thoughtless, Denby. Careless. You weren't thinking clearly. You were nervous, under pressure."

"You could never prove anything like that. Stock is dead."

Sergeant Wienick gave a start.

"Exactly," I said. "But how would you know? It hasn't been broadcast yet. You know because you yourself put him on the shelf. Poor, ugly, ineffective Andrew Stock. When he thought it over, he realized he'd be out of a job. No work, no income. And then he had the glimmer of an idea. He had information. He knew something that was worth money. Why not make it pay off? So, Denby, he shook you down for a slice of the insurance money. You were on a spot and you had no choice. But all you could raise at the moment was thirty-five hundred dollars. We found it in Stock's apartment. You searched for it, didn't you? But couldn't find it, because you were in a hurry and didn't look in the right place. You could have found it in one of his shoes."

"More guesswork," he whispered.

"Is it? Suppose we check your bank account for recent withdrawals. What will it show? Have you pulled thirty-five hundred dollars in the last twenty-four hours?"

What it would show was etched on his face. He crouched back, his breathing ragged. watching me with a kind of reptilian venom. His wife edged away from him, staring in vacillating faith bordering on shocked incredulity.

"Andrew Stock," I said, "that poor sad little clown, did not know what he was getting into. He did not know that there is only one solution for handling a blackmailer. Unless you want to keep on paying until he milks you dry, you have to stop his clock for good, once and for all. You have to end the demands by ending the blackmailer—and that's what you did. You finished him off with a carving knife from his own kitchen."

Wienick had moved closer, watchful and alert. He said to me, not taking his eyes from Denby, "And are you telling us this man framed the judge's widow by planting the gun in her car?"

"I am telling you exactly that. Oh, he's a shrewd one, all right. It threw up a smoke screen to mislead the police. If it worked, if she were implicated and convicted, Denby's wife would rake in all the chips, the whole million, because under the law a murderer is not permitted to inherit from his victim through the commission of homicide. Cold-blooded? Letting an innocent woman take the rap? You bet your life! But he felt no compunction at all because he hated the woman. So he began to spin his little web of duplicity to mask the truth and line his pockets."

Clive Denby's eyes were feverish, abnormally bright, and his breathing had a harsh catarrhal quality. He kept shaking his head.

"Whatever you may think of Laura Bolt," I said, "she is no cretin, no imbecile. She would never hide a murder weapon in her own car.

She's at least smart enough to maybe drop it off the Staten Island ferry where it would be lost forever."

Moisture bathed Denby's face from hairline to chin. His whispered voice sounded hollow and forced. "No proof. You have no proof. Not one iota of proof."

"Wrong," I said. "Dead wrong. Haven't you ever heard of the nitrate test? Whenever a man fires a gun, some of the unburned powder grains are blown back and buried in the skin of his hand. Powder tattooing, it's called, and it can be picked out with a forceps to show whether or not you've handled a gun. It doesn't come off with soap and water, Denby. They're going to test you, sure as hell. You can't stop them. Is there any nitrate residue on your hand now, Denby?"

He clenched his fists and held them near his chest for a moment. Then he opened his right hand and looked at it—and then he left the rails completely. In a sudden obliterating fog of mindless rage, bellowing obscenities, he lunged at me. I sidestepped and as he went past, Wienick rabbit-punched him at the base of the neck. Wienick's hand is like a cleaver. Denby went down on his knees, gulping for air. His wife cut loose with a long despairing cry and then bent over, covering her face.

I didn't feel particularly sorry for either of them.